# HOW TO SURVIVE A FAIRY BARGAIN

**By Laura J. Mayo**

FAIRIES AND FAMILIARS

*How to Summon a Fairy Godmother*
*How to Survive a Fairy Bargain*

# HOW TO SURVIVE A FAIRY BARGAIN

FAIRIES AND FAMILIARS: BOOK 2

LAURA J. MAYO

orbitbooks.net

orbitworks.net

Cover design by Alexia E. Pereira
Cover illustration by Zoë van Dijk

Author photograph by Anna Solo Photography



Orbit
Hachette Book Group
1290 Avenue of the Americas
New York, NY 10104
orbitbooks.net
orbitworks.net

First Edition: October 2025

Orbit is an imprint of Hachette Book Group.
The Orbit name and logo are registered trademarks of Little, Brown Book Group Limited.



Library of Congress Cataloging-in-Publication Data
Names: Mayo, Laura J. author
Title: How to survive a fairy bargain / Laura J. Mayo.
Description: First edition. | New York, NY : Orbit, 2025. | Series: Fairies and familiars ; book 2
Identifiers: LCCN 2025024969 | ISBN 9780316581165 trade paperback | ISBN 9780316580731 ebook
Subjects: LCGFT: Novels | Fantasy fiction | Fiction
Classification: LCC PS3613.A96298 .H694 2025
LC record available at https://lccn.loc.gov/2025024969

ISBNs: 9780316580731 (ebook), 9780316581165 (print on demand)

*To Will, Isla, and Malcolm*

*I love you.*

# Chapter 1

# Where Theodosia Balfour Is Doing Fine. Absolutely Fine. Better Than Fine, Actually.

No-longer-a-lady Theodosia Balfour was at her harp in the drawing room of a fairy's expansive manor, playing music with her friends in their loose interpretation of a band while watching the party around her. From her vantage point through the wide doorways, she had prime viewing of most of the downstairs.

In the back of the drawing room, three fairies were unwittingly playing tug-of-war with a goat, attempting to retrieve a length of silk the ruminant had latched on to and apparently found quite tasty. Surprisingly, the fairies were losing. No one knew why the goat was here, where he came from, or who brought him. The creature himself did not seem at all bothered by his attendance, presumably finding the accommodations of a fairy's abode a few steps up from a barnyard and, to a potentially lesser extent, due to simply being a goat. The cavernous main foyer was hosting a large game of blindfolded tag crossed with hot cockles, where the wearer of a blindfold wandered around having to guess which fairy had just slapped him in the face. The blindfolded fairy had yet to guess correctly, so it had been his turn for the past half hour. By this point his cheeks were such an angry, glowing red it looked as though he had put blush over a severe sunburn. Luckily, he was so drunk anyway that the odds of him feeling any of it were about as likely as the successful retrieval of fabric from a goat who had a penchant for jaunty cravats. And of course, in front of the band danced a copious number of drunken fairies, humans, and other delightfully inebriated creatures of the magical realm.

In another corner, some fairy's human familiar was stooped behind some furniture, throwing up into a vase while being patted on the back by another familiar with a mix of care and mild revulsion. Theo had no idea as to either of their names but had seen both these women around before. The first woman retched again and the other woman took a step back, grimacing. Theo knew Cecily would easily clean this up later with a snap of her fingers, but given the familiar's reaction, Theo was going to request Cecily just throw the whole thing out—magically clean or not.

Shortly after becoming a familiar herself, Theo discovered that there were limits as to who could transport a fairy's familiar, and those boiled down to whether the familiar was willing or unwilling to be transported. If the familiar was willing, anyone with the capability could transport the familiar, regardless of who their fairy was. However, if the familiar was unwilling, the only ones able to do so were the familiar themselves, the familiar's fairy they were bonded to, or another familiar bonded to that same fairy—something about having the same magic.

So having a familiar be as out of sorts as the one behind the furniture presented quite the predicament. The cookie-tossing familiar could barely stand up, so the act of transporting herself out of here was not a viable option—not to mention the gamble it would be to have her try to conjure a swirl of wind with the hopes that said cookies stayed contained. And unfortunately, the familiar who was now best friends with a vase had no desire to go anywhere. Which meant the back-patting familiar was left with only one option if she wanted to remove herself from the situation, and that was to find a particular fairy.

Theo very much hoped they would find that fairy quickly—for everyone's sakes.

She wasn't exceedingly concerned about the sick familiar getting back safely, more annoyed that it hadn't happened already.

All in all, a standard party at Cecily of the Ash Fairies' manor.

Cecily was wafting about, dressed in her usual finery, offering greetings to her friends and guests as any good host would do. When not mingling, she was on the dance floor spinning, twirling, and cheering the loudest at the end of each song.

It had been less than a year since Theo had fulfilled the bargain with Cecily, taking her stepsister Beatrice's place as one of the fairy's familiars. The time didn't go by in the blink of an eye, but nor did it crawl. In fact, it almost seemed silly for Theo to track the time at all, seeing as how she was practically immortal now, her life tied to Cecily's. So, marking the days and months was relatively pointless. And that was pretty much how she spent her time—without any point whatsoever. She slept in when she felt like it, ate where and when she felt like it, and was a regular fixture at Cecily's parties. Tonight's party was no exception.

The band had shrunk from its original incarnation and now consisted of Theo playing jauntily on the harp; Beric, a fairy strumming complementary notes on his handheld harp; Torian, the lute player; and Lowen, the fiddle player. Occasionally other fairies would join in, but only when they felt like conjuring their instruments, which wasn't very often.

They were set up in their usual spot. Normally the room had multiple seating areas scattered around, but on the nights when the band played, the couches, chairs, and tables were pushed to the walls so that the revelers could have enough space to dance. This evening, someone had even rolled up the rug, exposing the intricately patterned tile floor underneath. Theo loved when that happened. The sound of feet moving to the rhythm of the song sounded like a drumbeat echoing throughout the room, the joy of it intertwining with the music.

However, there was one fairy who wasn't doing much of anything except watching the band from where he stood in the corner, alone. As he had been for over an hour now, Theo noted. He paid no mind to the fairies around him who were laughing, dancing, or simply talking to one another, and was not searching the crowd for anyone who might let him join in. The lack of drink in hand—plain fruit punch or something stronger—suggested he either was fully hydrated already or didn't want to partake. Likewise with the food. Individually, none of these would suggest he wasn't in a celebratory mood. But stacked one on top of the other, it seemed unlikely he was here for the festivities.

Like his manner, his dress was severe and very plain. Theo had found it hard to come by lackluster clothes living with a fairy who delighted in the beautiful and unusual, not to mention one who supplied her entire wardrobe. She had thought, and was led to believe by example, that every other fairy felt the same. But this man was wearing the antithesis of adornment in a white tunic with plain brown pants the exact color of boredom. Even buttons were too flashy. The lines of the outfit were so simple it was as though he based it on a child's drawing, the sleeves stopping precisely at his wrists, the collar sitting straight across his neck. His shoulder-length copper hair was basic and unfussed, doing nothing other than staying neatly tucked behind his pointed ears. Apparently, he'd created his look as an homage to utility, with the guiding mantra of *I am thoroughly against fun in all its forms and need an ensemble to reflect that.*

This wouldn't have otherwise been anything to note since, normally, being the fairy equivalent of a blank sheet of paper would have made someone unexceptional. But here among an entire manor full of fairies dressed to impress; it did the exact opposite. He was a mule standing in a herd of zebras. If he wanted to blend in, he'd have been better served by painting himself in glue and rolling around in gemstones. This wasn't the first time she had noticed him at one of Cecily's events, either. For the past few months, he'd appear at a party, watch the band play with a dour yet intense expression plastered on his face, and then disappear again. She hadn't given him much thought the first few times, but the repetition was getting bizarre, to the point that even the other band members started to notice. And most disconcerting of all was how he was paying most of his attention to *her.*

Mid-song, Theo leaned over toward her friends. "What do you say we take an intermission after this?" Usually, she preferred playing her harp over mingling at a party. But right now, she needed this stranger to stop gawking at her. The sooner she could get away from the staring fairy, the better.

Thankfully, the band agreed, Beric with a flick of his wavy burgundy hair, Lowen with an enthusiastic nod, and Torian with relief manifesting in a droop of her posture.

When their song ended, Beric snapped his fingers, vanishing both his and Theo's harps, as her minute amount of magic from being a familiar didn't extend to conjuring or unconjuring anything.

She turned around so her back was to the room, letting her friends in on the real reason she stopped playing. "Beric, that fairy is here again."

"I saw. Do you think he wants to join in?"

"I don't know. He just stands there. It's making me uneasy.

But anytime I am close enough to ask who he is or why he's here, he leaves."

She shrugged but turned to face the room again. By then, Torian and Lowen were also ready. As the four of them made their way out of the drawing room, their path took them straight past the dull fairy. Right on cue, when he saw that they were all watching him and coming toward where he was standing, he launched into movement in the opposite direction. Theo was glad to be rid of him.

Her friends continued on to the game room, receiving compliments and accolades on their superb playing as they went. She had almost made it there, too, before she was stopped by a group of fairies who had followed her out of the drawing room: three friends, each now having conjured a drink for themselves after their whirlwind dancing. By the way they were dressed, it seemed to Theo they had come to do just that. Their coordinated dresses were short, only hitting below the knee so as not to interfere with dancing feet. Each dress was a different shade of blue and looked as if it had been dipped in water, the colors swirling like ink.

And unfortunately for Theo, the three fairies were smiling earnestly at her.

It wasn't long into her bargain that she found working for a fairy different than living with and being fully indebted to a fairy. And Theo hadn't formed any imaginary ideas as to what it might be like long-term, either, seeing as the decision to be here was rather sudden. And yet, she was still surprised by the quantity of unglamorous, non-magical moments it involved. What she found was that in most circles of fairy society, as a familiar, she might as well have been on the same level as a pet parakeet. Less, even. Fairies took as much notice of other fairies' familiars as they did the upholstered settees that dotted the manor. Their eyes would drift over them, only to bounce off like humans were made of springs. Human familiars were almost ever-present, but similar to a nose in one's peripheral vision, eventually the brain just pretended they didn't exist in any meaningful way. Humans were, above all, less than.

Except in Theo's case. She was noticed for her musical ability, fairies seeking her out to hear a particular favorite tune or another. The first time she'd ever played for fairies had been a highlight—and with that, a sense of belonging. But during the months at Cecily's manor, her harp playing had turned her into a novelty, her talent reduced to a party trick. And when the music stopped, so did her equal social standing among most of the fairies. Worse still, the fairies thought it was adorable. That human who believed herself to be one of them. How cute! How quaint!

Theo knew a backhanded compliment when it hit her across the face. The problem was the fairies didn't even realize they were doing it. To them, they were being nothing if not flattering, as though Theo's only wish in life was to bathe in their praise, and they were more than happy to oblige.

So Theo knew what the fairy leading her cheerful gaggle of ladies was going to say before she even said it. And unfortunately for these fairies, Theo had been growing rather tired of it as of late.

Sure enough: "You are just so talented. Honestly, it is remarkable you can play a fairy harp as well as you do, for a human!" The leader of the gaggle said this slowly, with a radiating smile as though Theo were a dog who had just done some sort of neat trick. All that was missing was a pat on the head. Theo's talents were always qualified with her humanness, like she'd overcome some sort of hardship by being what she was.

Theo stifled the scoff and eye roll and instead matched the fairy's overcooked smile. "If my harp playing impressed you, you should see how well I balance treats on my nose."

The fairy, not expecting anything other than a groveling *thank you, thank you, thank you*, gave her a polite yet confused chuckle, looking to her friends to see if they understood this perplexing creature. Their stunned faces said they did not.

Theo held her expression, if only to see how long these fairies could stand in the awkwardness—a politeness *pistols at dawn* to see who would fall first. She knew she had won when their smiles deflated to grimaces.

But Theo wasn't about to let them walk away just yet. "Well, you are welcome to join us anytime. I'll lend you my harp and you can show me how it's really done."

The woman laughed at what she thought was Theo's joke, her face muscles happy to have a purpose again. "Oh, I don't play the harp."

"My mistake," Theo said with a slow blink and a smile melting with condescension. "I thought since you are a fairy, you must be so much better at it than I am." Then, with a shake of her head and a high-pitched laugh of disbelief, she said, "I must say, if I were you, the fact that a human was better than me at *anything* would inspire so much infuriation I don't think I could find a wall high enough for it to drive me up. I could only dream of having your poise and graciousness."

The fairy finally caught on to Theo's real joke and huffed. "I don't know why you're being so impolite. Do you not know how to accept a compliment?"

"I do, actually. You just weren't paying me one. Or maybe I'm just too much of a meager human to understand it. Feel free to give it a go and I'll really pay attention this time to see if I can find the compliment." She nodded encouragingly for the fairy to try again.

The fairy scowled and then opened her mouth to speak. But before she said anything, her eyes caught something behind Theo. Or someone. Cecily stepped up next to her familiar, swirling a glass of red wine in her hand. The fairy gave Theo one more pinched smile as if to say, *Now you're in trouble.*

"Cecily, your familiar is being quite rude. I was telling her what a fantastic harp player she was, and she said…" The indignation that kept her going sputtered, her anger having forgotten to add coal to the firebox. "She said I must be better than her at it." Her steam engine of self-righteousness stalled on the tracks.

"Don't forget my envy of your composure," Theo added.

Cecily nodded and turned to Theo. "My commendatory Theo, if I've said it once I've said it a thousand times: Refrain from being complimentary to my guests." Her casual smirk made an appearance as she readdressed the fairy. "I promise my delightfully talented Theo will never say a nice word about you again. Will you, Theo?"

Theo smiled. "No, never."

"There. Problem solved."

The fairy's wineglass must have been made of diamonds to withstand how tightly she was clutching it. Clearly wanting to take the parting shot, she narrowed her eyes. "You should get your little pet under control."

It did nothing to dim Cecily's smirk. She cocked her hip. "What you should know about my dear Theo is that you can't poke the, by your admission, fantastically talented human and expect her not to return the favor"—she took a swig of her wine—"fantastically."

The fairy stomped off, her confused friends following.

Cecily's devilish grin remained firmly in place as she and Theo watched them leave the manor. "Well then," Cecily said with lightness as though she didn't just send guests scampering. "I believe I saw Beric shuffling some cards. Let's go and he can deal me in as well."

Theo walked to the game room, head held high. But the months of this situation playing out before tonight made it increasingly harder to do. The more these "compliments" started piling up, the more she felt like a pet, and the more joy was being sucked out of performing.

Or most things, for that matter.

Once in the game room, Theo took up a seat at the table next to Torian, Cecily also pulling up a chair. Theo wished it was only the musicians and Cecily at the table, but there was one extra fairy dealt in. A handsome fairy, the ends of his dark hair tinged an emerald green the exact color of his eyes.

*Locklan.*

It wasn't unusual to see Lock at Cecily's parties, him being the fairy's younger brother and all. When Theo first arrived, he'd stayed away from the manor at her behest, as Theo was upset about being kept in the dark regarding his secretive inclusion in her plans. And if she was being honest, she was embarrassed when she found out the truth—that everyone around her had known something she didn't. Because of him, her pride in herself and her accomplishments had been tainted. He didn't need to flirt and compliment her—that was never part of Cecily's plan. Back then, he had explained that it was because he really did like her. But now, all it did was put their friendship on shaky ground because she didn't know where they stood. Even if he had been truthful, Theo wasn't sure she was ready to let bygones be bygones. But after a few months, Cecily insisted Lock be invited again. Lock had tried a few more times to have a meaningful conversation with Theo, but whenever he did, Theo would excuse herself and spend the rest of his visit in hiding. Up to that point, Cecily had voiced both relief and excitement that Theo was no longer holing up in her room, burying herself in blankets like a depressed hibernating hedgehog with that level of personal hygiene. So when Theo started avoiding parties again, Cecily made it clear to Lock that his continued enjoyment of said parties was contingent on leaving Theo alone.

However, Theo and Lock shared friends in Beric, Torian, and Lowen, which made him sadly unavoidable, especially when the cards came out. She'd never had friends before this fairy group and, aside from Cecily's former familiar, Kaz, never had anyone who was genuinely interested in her. And she tended not to think about him too much, lest she fall to pieces in front of everyone. On occasion, she did talk with other human familiars, but being set apart by fairies hurt her here, too, as the familiars didn't quite know what to do with her. They didn't hate her, nor were they mean in any way, but were standoffish enough that it was difficult to make friends with them.

So, even though she no longer carried the torch for a romantic relationship with Lock, she found herself missing their friendship. Unfortunately, she did nothing to foster communication with him, and instead their conversational highlights ranged from *I do believe it is your turn* to *Pardon me, I need to use the restroom.*

Not this evening, though. Like the last few weeks, the chatter tonight centered on the latest gossip. And it was no wonder no one could stop talking about it—it was a doozy.

According to the rumors, the missing fairy princess had been found.

Theo had picked up bits and pieces of information about the former royal family in the last few months of living among fairies. Tace of the Oak Fairies was the current regent, who was uncle of the late King Redren of the Oak Fairies. Up until roughly a thousand years ago, King Redren ruled the fairy realm with his wife, Queen Lilliana. And by all accounts, they were well-loved and oversaw a peaceful kingdom. They had two children, Princess Amabel and Princess Iara.

But the king's reign came to a sudden and shocking end one random night.

While Redren and Lilliana were getting ready for dinner at court, the children playing together in the nursery, a maid came around to light the fires for the evening, as she usually did. Everything had apparently been normal: The wood had been stacked neatly into each clean fireplace, according to the only staff member who managed to escape. All the maid needed to do that evening was simply snap her fingers and conjure a fire in the already-made piles of wood. With ease and efficiency, she lit the fires, room by room, starting with the nursery and ending in King Redren's suites.

What no one realized until too late was that the wood—oak logs, typically—in the fireplace had been replaced with yew. And yew was incredibly toxic to fairies. Even the faintest whiff of smoke was enough to make a fairy quite sick. Unfortunately, the chopped-up yew was indistinguishable from the normal wood, likely causing the maid to light the fires without doing a thorough log identification. What she also failed to notice, for much the same reason, was that the flues had been closed.

Since the maid was good at her job, she had the fires blazing within seconds.

The family was the first to succumb to the smoke. Next, guards who had been positioned outside the family suites quite literally dropped dead. Another guard, seeing his colleagues lying down, knew enough to realize they weren't both taking simultaneous naps and ran to get help. Another guard rushed toward the suites but was also overtaken by the effects only minutes later.

By the time anyone figured out what was happening, it was well beyond too late.

Everyone died. Supposedly.

Tace, the only person in the direct line of succession, suddenly found himself in charge of the kingdom and the current crisis. He evacuated the palace and called upon elves, dwarves, trolls, and any other creature not affected by yew to come and help. Anyone who could enter the family suites was sent to put out the fires and open every window. No fairy could even go near that entire wing until the smoke was well and truly cleared.

When fairies were finally able to enter the nursery, knowing the horror of what they would find, they discovered only the little body of Amabel lying on the rug, toys strewn around her, and the nanny in the rocking chair nearby as though she had just fallen asleep.

But Iara was nowhere to be found.

Word of the missing princess spread throughout the kingdom as fast as the yew smoke in the palace. Search parties were organized, everyone galvanized by the thought of being able to do something in defiance of their complete helplessness at the situation. Hands needed to be useful, words needed to be filled with soft, delicate hope that maybe all was not lost. But by that point, it had been almost a full day and any hints as to her whereabouts were gone.

Iara had not been located in the subsequent thousand years, but many believed that the true successor to the throne was still out there. Since enough fairies held on to this hope, Tace was never able to claim the throne as true king. Instead, he was made regent, keeping the seat warm for whenever Iara might decide to grace the fairy kingdom with her presence.

Of course, foul play was initially suspected, but blame was

difficult to distribute, seeing as every potentially responsible party also died in the incident. The maid who had lit all the fires died shortly after leaving King Redren's room and was found slumped against the wall, the lingering smoke she had inhaled in each room finally doing her in. No one could trace who may have put yew in the fireplace, and no one could find anyone who would want to. Naturally, Tace was first on the list of suspects, but even when his path to the throne was clear, he did not accept the position, content to be regent.

The most shocking suspect was Endlin of the Birch Fairies. Before Lilliana, King Redren had been romantically entangled with Endlin, and many thought she would be the next queen. Her mother, Ursula, was known to have been very excited about the prospect, some saying she had been secretly planning their wedding. However, before they were even engaged, their relationship ended—amicably, by all accounts. But in the entirely fruitless murder investigation, people were grasping for any shred of blame they could find, and Endlin was the best they could do. Some said it must have been a jealous rage, or that her intended target was everyone but Redren so she could get him back and cement her status as queen. Even Ursula made statements saying that until Endlin would answer questions under iron, she would be unwelcome at the palace or anywhere near Tace and her brother, Aimon, Tace's longtime consort. Endlin agreed immediately, proving her innocence to many, though she still went into hiding for five hundred years or so, until the scandal largely blew over.

Without motive or murderer, it was proclaimed a horrible accident.

"I've heard the princess is plotting her spectacular comeback and will be taking the throne any day now," Beric said, while dealing a round of cards.

"What, just stroll into the palace and shout 'I'm the missing princess! Where's my throne and crown?'" Theo said, organizing the cards in her hand. Though this wouldn't be unheard of, her stepsister being a prime example of someone who walked straight through the front doors of a castle and became a princess beloved by the masses.

"Something like that," Beric said with a laugh.

"What I want to know," Theo said, "is where she's been all this time."

"Excellent question, Theo." Cecily saluted with her glass.

"Have you heard anything?" Beric asked Lock and Cecily.

Lock shook his head.

"No, not a thing," Cecily added. "Though, I can't imagine why we would."

This was unsurprising. Though Aimon was Lock and Cecily's cousin, and they may have been close as children, they certainly weren't close now.

After a bit more conjecture about the hypothetical princess, conversation moved on to more recent topics.

And once those topics petered out, Beric drummed his hands on the small bit of table still visible, the glasses jingling with the impact. "Well, I think I'm ready to start playing music again instead of cards. What about you all?"

"I'm all for it," Torian said. "But where is Lowen?"

The group all looked toward his empty chair, staring at it like they could make him appear if they tried hard enough.

Theo hadn't even noticed he'd left, and it seemed like the rest of them hadn't, either.

Theo stood a bit too quickly, her legs threatening to seat her right back down again. "I'll find him!" she said with fake cheeriness, eager to have a valid reason to excuse herself from the table where Lock still sat. With the resolve for facing her problems as sturdy as an underbaked cheesecake, Theo chose *flee* as her best option. As was, at this point, tradition. However, Lock annihilated her best-laid plans with a simple "I'll look with you, Theo."

Fortunately, she did not have to figure out a new method of ditching him. Before she could say anything, two fairies began calling out to him and were fast approaching their group. Theo's first reaction was to use this distraction to make a hasty retreat, but surprise halted her steps. Her mouth dropped open. These two fairies never came to Cecily's parties, but Theo knew exactly who they were: Lock's Aunt Ursula of the Birch Fairies and his cousin Endlin.

# Chapter 2

# Where Theo Searches for a Friend

Ursula was a diminutive woman, standing a full head shorter than Theo. If shrunk down further, she could pass for a doll with her wide, glossy eyes and button nose. But unlike the soothing, pretty cloth dolls Theo had slept with as a child, Ursula was more like the creepy porcelain dolls she used to shove to the back of her closet. This was possibly due to Ursula's habit of not blinking with any sustained frequency and seemingly turning her head only when people weren't looking. She stood so stiffly upright that, if tripped, she would go down like a felled tree. But she would never trip, her steps too measured and controlled to allow it, as well as the dearth of people who would dare attempt it anyway.

What she lacked in stature and warmth, she made up for in condescension and pretension; she spent her days, nights, and fashion statements making sure no one forgot that she still had a starring role in the royal family. The dress she wore looked as though she had gilded a wedding dress, complete with a train that rippled out behind her. She would only command more attention if she had bespelled the dress to shout *All eyes on me!* Her flaxen hair was pulled up and away from her face, the bulk of it piled in braids on top of her head. The gemstones and gold-dipped flowers tucked throughout created the illusion of a crown, which added to both her height and her aura of self-importance.

Lock's shoulders drooped and he sighed. "Please, Theo, just wait a moment. I really need to speak with you." And with that, he turned toward his aunt and cousin, who were closing in fast.

Annoyance at Ursula's presence seemed to be a family trait, as their aunt certainly wasn't in Cecily's circle of favorite people, either. Before Theo was Cecily's familiar, she had been tasked with stealing a necklace from Endlin. Ursula had owned the necklace that made fairy magic immune to iron, which was a necessary tool in getting through Beatrice's fortifications. But even knowing what had transpired between Cecily and Beatrice and that Cecily's missing magic was making her sick, Ursula would not hand over the necklace to help her niece. That a human had pulled one over on a fairy was seen as a great family embarrassment to Ursula. Thus, she had viewed helping Cecily as enabling such problematic behavior and said she would have no part in "digging Cecily out of the mess of her own making."

And Endlin wouldn't step out of line and let her cousin borrow it behind her mother's back. Hence Theo's need for theft. Theo punching Endlin in the face to do it was just fortuitous serendipity to Cecily.

Theo begrudgingly waited, though her eyes kept moving from the door she wished she could run through to Ursula and Endlin's hushed conversation with Lock. She tried to listen in but couldn't make out what Ursula was saying over the din of the party. If Theo tried to move any closer from behind them, she might as well put her chin on Ursula's shoulder. But just when she thought she could maneuver herself into a better position, Ursula spun on her heel, her skirts flaring, nose pointed to the sky. Given its raised position, she must have been concerned her nose would slide right off her face if she tipped it below sea level. Theo was not sure how Ursula could even see the people around her. If anything, she was only giving herself a prime view of the ceiling. As her sense of sight was otherwise occupied, it was only her sense of superiority that prevented her from walking into anyone. But it also acted as a superior deterrent, and most people moved out of her way regardless.

Only Endlin followed. While her mother's face was raised to show off her nostrils, Endlin's face was made of lead, hanging down and avoiding eye contact with anyone. Since Theo was still so close, once the duo turned toward her to make their exit, she could finally hear quite clearly what Ursula was saying, this time her condescension pointed like a pistol straight at her daughter.

"Honestly, Endlin. Everyone is staring at you and it is not because you're pretty. Do you think any men are going to approach you if you look miserable? Fix your face and stand up straight." Then, more of a mumble to herself, she added,

"At least one of my children knew how to keep a royal partner and solve their own problems."

Ursula apparently couldn't figure out why her daughter would be anything less than enthusiastic about being here, but Theo knew all too well, her own mother's "helpful" comments still ringing in her ears almost a year since she'd last seen her. But if Theo were to compare cutthroat behavior directed at daughters, Martha Balfour had been using a verbal feather compared to Ursula's broadsword. And one of the barbs of memories from her own past that stung the most was that Ursula was correct about her daughter's posture and temperament, but for all the wrong reasons.

When Ursula wasn't around, Endlin was bright, bubbly, and to the untrained eye, self-assured. But standing next to her mother, Endlin looked less like a flower in springtime and more like a houseplant someone had put in a dark corner—muted, hunched, and stretching little by little to get back to where there was light.

Her pummeling of Endlin's self-esteem complete, Ursula went back to judgmentally gliding out of the room, passing directly by Theo. Normally, Ursula took no notice of familiars. But tonight when Ursula saw Theo, she paused. She glared at Theo for only a second, but that second was filled with so much vitriolic recognition Theo wasn't sure if Ursula actually knew who she was after all. Theo stood still anyway, taking the arctic hare approach to self-defense and hoping she'd simply fade into the surrounding landscape. It seemed to do the trick, as Ursula strode out of the room without any further interaction. Cecily assured Theo after the theft that

Endlin most likely did not share the full extent of the evening with her mother, as it involved her being so drunk she couldn't make a positive identification of her own assailant. Plus, Ursula was the type of mother to be less concerned about her daughter's assault than how the behavior leading up to it reflected upon her.

Unlike her mother, Endlin did interact. Theo tried to look away, pretending the pattern of a nearby tablecloth to be of particular interest, but it didn't work. When she looked back up to see if Endlin had followed her mother, she instead found the fairy staring straight at her.

If looks could kill, Theo would be gravely injured, potentially missing a limb, Endlin's decorum not allowing for her face to go full feral. Theo felt again that she was in that standoff moment between a hunter and its prey, where the prey knows full well it is being watched, the hunter knows the prey knows, and neither makes a move.

Theo thought about offering a smile, but that seemed inefficient; Endlin was never going to like Theo. So what Theo ultimately tried to express to Endlin was empathy. If there was something Theo knew about this situation, it was how it felt. But she didn't get any acknowledgment before Endlin stomped her exit.

---

Lock had also left, she noted with a sigh of relief. Theo wasn't going to bother looking for him; if he wanted to talk to her so badly, he could come and find her.

She wandered through the game room scanning for Lowen. She thought it would have been easy to pick him out of a crowd given that he had a propensity for wearing bold ensembles. Tonight, he was wearing a vest of pink peonies, the color made all the more striking against his sepia skin and long, curly black hair. And that was toning it down for Lowen. Once, after taking inspiration from tropical birds, his shirt squawked so loudly at the high notes that the band had made him change his outfit two songs into their set.

And yet, the walking bush that was their fiddle player was nowhere to be seen.

Outside the game room was the same story. And so was everywhere else she searched. No matter where she looked, she couldn't find him, and Theo was starting to reach the limits of her patience for the night.

Just as she was about to give him up for lost and form a larger search party, she spotted him walking out onto the veranda. Like a salmon swimming upstream, she fought against the current of drunk party guests who were inadvertently pushing her every which way except the way she wanted to go. And with every second, Lowen was getting farther afield. She tried shouting to him, but her voice wasn't loud enough to carry itself over the wall of laughter and conversations that was between her and outside.

She finally squeezed herself to the edge of the party and popped out the veranda doors like a champagne cork, nearly crashing into the people outside. There were plenty of partygoers here, too, but thankfully, a much calmer sort. And because there was enough space between each person, she could see all the way to the yard, where she spotted Lowen walking away.

"Lowen!" she called out. He didn't turn and was continuing to make his way to the gardens.

Throughout her vast back lawn, Cecily set up tucked-away locations for anyone at the party seeking a bit more privacy. Benches were hidden near statues, under willow trees, or behind hedges with minimal lantern light. And tonight, they were certainly being used as intended. Theo took a lantern from a post and went after the flighty fiddle player. While she found plenty of huffs of indignation and quick adjustments of clothing as she shined her light on benches and behind trees, she didn't find Lowen.

The farther she got away from the manor, the larger her concern for her friend. He wasn't known for wandering. Her lantern light was losing the battle against the darkness that surrounded her, now unable to cast anything other than a small glow around her, but she wasn't about to leave Lowen out here alone.

With the meager light, she was just barely able to see Lowen in the distance, standing at the very edge of the tree line leading into the forest. This time, he was facing her.

"Lowen!" she shouted to him. "There you are. What are you doing? Beric sent me to find you because we're going to play again."

He didn't respond. Instead, he turned around and stepped into the forest.

"Wait!" she called after him. He hadn't before, but she was still surprised when he didn't listen to her directive now and carried on into the forest.

Theo turned to look behind her. The light from the party hugged the manor, making it glow like a planet in the absolute darkness that surrounded it, and she suddenly felt very far from home. A debate raged in her head over whether she should follow her friend into the woods and get him before he hurt himself, or turn around and gather more of her friends to help but lose sight of him. Unfortunately for her critical-thinking skills, his extremely out-of-character behavior was wiping the slate clean every time she thought she came to a decision.

She could now just barely make out Lowen's form in the distance.

Not wanting to lose him, she went into the woods.

Lowen wasn't waiting to see if she was behind him. The light from the party all but disappeared when she entered the forest, and she was glad she'd had the foresight to bring her lantern. The biggest threat to her own safety right now was an errant root.

She couldn't tell exactly, but she also knew that as far as she had walked into the woods, she was past Cecily's property. Out here beyond the confines of safety, she felt like she was in true wilderness, where she was the interloper entering into a world she didn't quite belong to. Not in her present form, at least. And while she knew where the manor was, she was just far enough in the forest where she could no longer see it.

Now she could just barely make out Lowen. He was leading her down a scantly visible deer trail that wound between the trees cutting through the undergrowth. She picked up her pace as best she could.

"Lowen?" she called.

A small clearing came into view, though just barely. The canopy above her was so compact it was as though a lid was put over the treetops, making the open forest floor look like an abyss even with the few fallen logs that dotted the ground. Thankfully, the clearing was small. She held up her lantern higher, casting its meager light to the other side, which was only about twenty paces in front of her. What the lantern didn't shed light on was Lowen, who was suddenly nowhere to be found.

She called his name again, deciding she should go no farther than this clearing, lest she become lost herself. The dense vegetation around her muted the sound of her voice as though she'd been calling his name into a pillow, offering no echo or reverberation.

She stepped to the middle of the clearing and held her lantern high. There was not a trace of Lowen, not even a footprint to show he'd been through here. Her instincts and intuition had finally decided to join her on this walk and were now screaming at her that something was not right.

Theo turned to leave back the way she came to get the rest of her friends. Instead, she slammed face-first into a solid wall of nothing and then fell backward, landing hard. Her lantern dropped from her hands and crashed with her to the ground, the light immediately snuffing itself out.

# Chapter 3

# Where Mushrooms Prove to Be Formidable Foes

Without her lantern light, Theo was in almost complete darkness, hardly able to even see her own feet. No matter. If she couldn't get back via the trail she'd used to get here, she'd just find another way.

But at the far side of the clearing, she ran into the same exact wall of nothing as on the other side. Putting up her hands and tamping down her growing panic, she pressed on this invisible force holding her in. It was cool to the touch and flat, like she had her palms against a smooth exterior wall. Walking slowly clockwise she tested the barrier, finding it to be intact everywhere she could reach. She patted it at eye level, waist level, and as high as she could before kneeling on the ground. When she reached the grass and leaf litter, she felt something else. Little mushrooms dotted the ground, curving around in an exact copy of the barrier.

*Oh no.*

A perfect circle of mushrooms ensnaring a human.

She'd unwittingly entered a fairy ring.

Rare, but not unheard of. In fact, that's all the familiarity she'd had with fairy rings, only merely hearing about them and never encountering one—a flippant remark from Cecily along the lines of *Oh, and if you ever see a ring of mushrooms, don't go in it. You'll be stuck until a fairy comes and gets you. And half the time they forgot they set them in the first place, so don't count on that, either.*

In broad daylight, they'd also be a bit easier to spot, a perfect circle of mushrooms seemingly popping up in the middle of nowhere being a dead giveaway. Or maybe Theo only thought that way because she had been around fairies for a while now. Humans were notorious for being trapped within them, wandering across the low line of mushrooms and apparently leaving their minds on the other side. Stories said that, stuck within the magical confines, humans would dance until they died, lose track of time, go mad, or all of the above. From what Theo learned, though, and from her admittedly anecdotal proof that she still had her bearings and faculties, all the fairy rings did was keep the human in place. But that wasn't much of a comfort to her right now.

The first solution for escape that came to mind was to simply break the mushrooms. No mushrooms should have meant no ring. But as she clear-cut them, her hand acting like a miniature scythe, they sprouted back up immediately. Frequency and speed didn't seem to make any sort of difference. Though that didn't stop her from trying that, either. Her hand was oscillating with enough fervor to make shoe shiners worried about their job security.

Maybe those faculties were slowly going after all.

She was well and truly trapped.

Exertion turned her panic into a brief moment of anger and indignation, though panic tried to wrest control once again quite quickly. She was alone in the dark—and far, far away from anyone who could hear her. The only way of getting out of one was to have a fairy either break the ring or take out the human...

But wait. Though true that she was a human, she was also imbued with bits of fairy magic thanks to being a familiar. Theo exhaled softly—she'd never been more relieved to remember that she was magically bound to a fairy.

She ran through her magic repertoire: First, she could transport herself from one place to another in a swirl of wind. She had pretty much mastered wind transportation within the first few months of being a familiar. It wasn't even that hard. Mostly it just involved thinking—thinking of a breeze blowing around her and of where she wanted to go. And then, *voilà*, she was in a new location of her choosing. Phineas had gone with her the first few times, just to make sure that she could get herself to a destination and then return safe and sound without leaving any necessary body parts behind. Though he had also been impressed at the speed by which the skill was acquired.

She called forth a breeze now, picturing the veranda. Wind

whipped around her, gathering up the leaves at her feet until the clearing was obscured from view. Determination grew as the wind died down, but just as the wind settled, she realized she hadn't moved an inch.

So she tried again. And again. Nothing. All she was doing was making a giant mess of the leaf litter on the ground around her like a windmill throwing a temper tantrum.

Fine. This was fine. She had other things she could try. So, humans couldn't get out of a fairy ring with wind.

What about hedgehogs?

The ability to change herself into a woodland creature was the second bit of magic she could utilize. All familiars had an animal form, supposedly to make performing sneaky tasks for their fairies easier, though why the magic paired each animal and human still seemed to be a mystery. Phineas could sail through the skies with ease as a mockingbird, which did match his penchant for preening and quick gossip; her former familiar friend, Kaz, stunned as a quiet fox, matching his brooding personality.

It was a surprise to everyone when Theo first changed from a person into a tiny, spiky woodland mammal. Cecily squealed with delight and quickly conjured a mirror so Theo could look at herself. The creature staring back at Theo looked like a spiky loaf of bread, with four little feet propping it up only slightly off the ground. Her face was covered in dark brown fur and tapered down to a slightly upturned nose.

Even better, Cecily could hear Theo speak when she was in this hedgehog form, which proved incredibly helpful in completing tasks. The fairy couldn't hear thoughts—only what

Theo "said" to her, which at the particular moment of her first transformation was primarily screaming.

Not surprisingly, "hedgehog form" wasn't a skill set she used on many occasions, as she couldn't very well play the harp, drink, or talk with her friends while presenting as a teeny tiny creature. She did find sleeping was sometimes enjoyable as a hedgehog, but only when she was in the comfort of her own bed. The one time she accidentally fell asleep as a hedgehog in the woods resulted in her waking up to a very aggravated squirrel whose home she'd apparently invaded. If his chattering was any indication, he was very put out by Theo's lapse in squirrely decency.

Now, with hope renewing and spikes sprouting out of her butt, Theo changed into a tiny, adorable hedgehog ready to take on the fairy ring.

First, she called out to Cecily with her mind, using all the power she could muster. But she knew, even when she was doing it, that Cecily was just too far away, the party simply too loud. She would have shouted for Phineas, but unfortunately, they could only speak to each other this way when *both* of them were in their animal forms. Theo highly doubted Phineas was at the party as a mockingbird; it'd be very difficult to pick up men that way.

No matter. She had another hedgehog trick up her proverbial sleeve. Maybe the fairy ring couldn't differentiate between a full-time and a part-time hedgehog. Maybe she could simply jump over the fungi boundary.

Nose twitching, paws gripping the forest floor, she released a high-pitched battle cry and launched herself at the now-eye-level mushrooms. She was moving with such haste it was as though she sprouted wings made from pure, unadulterated fury. In a show of roly-poly agility and athleticism, she tucked her front legs tightly to her chest as her little back legs kicked off the ground. She made to soar over the mushrooms, her claws only a wisp above the caps. And as she was about to extend her front legs for the landing, she once again smacked her face against the barrier. The impact of her escape attempt sent her sprawling backward, crashing down on the mushrooms that she had tried to leap over. She rolled farther into the ring, coming to rest on her back, stunned and looking at the night sky.

Adding to the indignity, when she managed to roll over, mushroom caps were skewered on her back like kebabs. As her nearly absent neck allowed for only so much movement, she didn't waste any energy trying to unimpale the mushrooms in her present form. Instead, she transformed back into a human, the caps falling off her and landing with a little pitter-patter around her feet.

But the broken mushroom caps had her dropping to her knees again, hoping that maybe somehow spearing them with hedgehog quills was what finally undid the magic. She knew the logic of this was as twisted and folded in on itself as taffy, but fairy logic tended to do that, too.

Alas, no. The ring was once again whole.

With a yell of frustration, she plopped to the ground in the center of the ring, covering her face with her hands in a futile effort to prevent her tears from falling.

A moment later, a scuff of bark and a rustle of leaves came

from somewhere close—somewhere within the fairy ring. She went quiet.

Then, a new noise. The sound of sniffling.

"Who's there?" she asked the dark, rising to her feet and wiping her eyes.

The sniffling ceased.

"I know you're there. Show yourself," Theo tried again, with as much bravado as she could muster, hoping whoever she was talking to didn't realize her only defense mechanism was turning into a forest critter and running in a circle as fast as those toothpick legs could carry her.

"Sorry," came a small, almost childlike voice. "I thought, since you were upset, I could be, too. I didn't mean to interrupt. I honestly didn't think you'd be able to hear me at all, since your shout was so loud, but I apologize if I disrupted you."

Even though her eyes had adjusted to the incredibly low light, Theo still had a hard time seeing. She took a cautious step forward. "Well, I thought I was alone. I didn't realize anyone was here." She couldn't decide if she should be annoyed or embarrassed that someone was commenting on the volume of her misery.

"I was hiding. I didn't want anyone to see me—I'm very sneaky when I want to be. I wasn't sure what you were doing out here."

"Oh, well, I was searching for my friend. Actually, did you happen to see a fairy walk through here a moment ago? Wearing a bright floral vest. Very distinctive."

"No. Just you."

She wanted to ask a few more questions about whether this currently bodyless voice saw Lowen go by, but first said, "Would you mind coming a bit closer so I can see you? I feel a bit silly talking to nothing."

"I'm not nothing," the voice said with a hint of indignity.

"No, that's not what I meant. I'd just like to speak with you face-to-face, if you don't mind. Right now, it feels as though I'm talking to the darkness."

Theo heard the scraping of bark as whoever it was climbed off the log, followed by a sound like marbles clacking together in time with short, light footsteps. The noise continued until the mystery person was close enough for Theo to see. And even then, she almost missed him, as she had been looking around at her own eye level, not at the knee height of the goblin who was now in front of her.

He was little, about the size of a human toddler, but this was average stature for a goblin. With his short, stumpy legs holding up a rotund torso, he reminded Theo of a teddy bear come to life. But he was not what anyone would call cute. He looked more like a stuffed animal that had been left out in the rain—time and weather taking a bit of shine off and giving him a droopy quality. His big, black, watery eyes took up a disproportionate amount of facial real estate above his feline nose. His ears stuck out like bat wings off the sides of his head, and there was a tuft of hair sticking out the top of his otherwise bald crown. She'd seen goblins before and knew that while she couldn't see him quite clearly, his skin was a green shade almost exactly the color of lichen, with the insides of his ears being a soft pink.

Theo knew almost instantly why she hadn't noticed him. Over a dark shirt and leather breeches, he was wearing a long leather jacket, its wrinkles and color giving it the appearance of tree bark. If he wandered off and decided to lie down on the forest floor, Theo was not convinced she'd be able to find him again. His camouflage was all the more remarkable when he bowed to her, the back of his jacket blending in with the scenery so well all she could make out was his head that now looked disembodied.

The clacking sound was also easily discernible. The goblin decorated himself in shiny rocks, his necklaces, bracelets, rings, and earrings rattling when he moved. Theo hoped he stayed far away from any bodies of water, including bathtubs and buckets, as he was liable to sink right to the bottom with the weight of them all.

When he stood back up, he wiped his nose with the back of his hand, sniffling again. And while he looked so terribly sad, he also was peering at her hopefully and expectantly. So she curtsied in return.

"My name is Theodosia, but you may call me Theo."

He nodded, his ears flapping. "I'm Alby. You can call me that, too. Not Theo, I mean. That is not my name. Call me Alby. Because that is my name."

"Hello then, Alby. While I wish we were meeting under better circumstances, it is still nice to make your acquaintance." Not knowing what to do with herself now, she sat cross-legged on the ground, adjusting her skirt around her. Alby plopped down next to her.

He was still watching her, and she wasn't sure what else

to do, so she decided to continue conversing. "Are you stuck here, too?"

Alby nodded again, his ears making a *flap-flap* noise.

"Have you been stuck for long?"

"I've been here since yesterday."

"Yesterday?! Have you had anything to eat?"

"There's a log over there, and plenty of bugs underneath. I know I found it, so by rights they're all mine, but I'm willing to share if you're hungry."

"Thank you. I'm . . . not hungry at the moment."

He sighed. "I was hoping that maybe you would have a way out, but then you started crying and I figured that you were also now trapped. Which made me cry because that meant that *I* was still going to be here and you can't help me get out. I did try, you know. Just in case you thought I did nothing. I tried playing my triangle, since that's the only thing I have, but that didn't break the ring."

"Wait, does music break a fairy ring?" Theo asked, hope rising slightly.

"Bells, sometimes. Not the triangle. I learned that recently."

"Oh."

"I was just trying to come up with ideas," Alby said as an explanation.

"It was a good idea," Theo concurred. "You play the triangle?"

"Yes."

"Well, I play the harp in a band. When we get out of here, you should join us."

"You'd let me play with you?"

"Sure! We don't have a triangle player, so you'd be a great addition."

Alby's face lit up, but after only a moment it shrank. "Well, that is a lovely thought. But we're not getting out of here. The bugs can last us for a little while, but we'll most likely die from starvation or exposure. Possibly from dehydration. If it gets down to it, we'll have to have some serious talks on who will die first. I'm small and easier to kill, so it would make sense to end me. If I were to offer you the same mercy, it might not work. My arms are very weak. Then you'd just be in pain." He sighed. "Have a think on it and let me know what you decide."

"Oh . . . um . . . that is a kind offer, but I'm hoping my friends will find out I'm missing and come get me before then."

"Well, unfortunately for us both, only a fairy can get us out. If your friends can find one, then maybe you'd stand a chance."

"My friends are fairies. Except for one, who is another human familiar, but if he were to find me, he'd just get Cecily, who is a fairy, and she'd get me out of here."

Alby tilted his head and scrunched his brow. "That's unusual."

"So I've been told."

"Fairies don't really want anything to do with goblins."

Theo shrugged. "They don't usually want anything to do with humans, either."

"You look human, but I saw you turn into a hedgehog. What are you?"

"You're right, I am a human. But I am also a familiar to the fairy Cecily of the Ash Fairies."

"What do you do?"

"Uh, well..." She realized she didn't have anything to say. What did she do as a familiar? A whole lot of nothing. She didn't help Cecily with tasks, like Phineas. She mostly hung around the manor and played music. Theo supposed she could say that, but music wasn't really in the job description of a familiar, it was just how she occupied herself. But before she could think of something worthwhile to say, they both turned toward a short crackle of leaves and then the smallest snap of a twig, like someone was moving closer to them from deeper in the forest.

They weren't alone in the woods. Again.

And whoever was out there was coming their way. The mystery feet continued their approach. The woods were still so dark she couldn't see the edges of the ring, much less beyond it. And with the vast nothingness surrounding them, she could hardly figure out exactly where the noise was coming from.

Alby and Theo looked at each other, and she could see her own fear reflected in his big black eyes. Together they stood up and backed away from whatever was making its way closer to the edge of the fairy ring. Just when it was about to reach them, a large crashing noise came from the direction of the trail.

She turned to see lantern lights bobbing through the darkness like giant fireflies. And shortly after, she heard the familiar sound of her name being called.

Whatever had been slinking toward them stopped.

She took her chance. "Over here! I'm over here!"

Preceded by the sound of twigs cracking, leaves crunching, and people pushing into one another, Beric, Torian, and a very surprised Lowen spilled into the clearing.

"Theo! Oh, we're so glad we found you!" Beric put his hands on his knees as though he'd sprinted the whole way. Torian immediately put down her lantern and hugged Theo. While she did that, Lowen approached the fairy ring, investigating for only a brief moment before he dragged his foot through the mushrooms, breaking their caps. When he did it, the mushrooms all shriveled up and sank back into the earth, as though time and decay had sped up one thousandfold. The clearing was back to its original state, with craggy edges and no discernible outline whatsoever. Which made the fairy ring that much more insulting to Theo, as it now felt like she'd been bested by fungi simply for being a human.

Lowen looked back up at Theo, glad to see her. But while the whole point of being out here was to find him, now that she had, or rather he found her, she was in no mood for a happy reunion.

"Why did you lead me into the woods and then leave? I was calling for you—did you not hear me?"

Lowen, Beric, and Torian tilted their heads at her as though she had spoken gibberish.

"What are you talking about?" Lowen asked. "I've never been here."

"Yes, you were," Theo said. "I followed you all the way from the veranda to this fairy ring."

"Couldn't have," Beric cut in. "Right after you left the game room, Lowen came back. We thought you must have found him, but then after a minute we realized you were now missing. So we searched for you in the manor, but someone said they spotted you going outside. We then followed the trail of annoyed paramours who told us you went this way. Lowen was with us the whole time."

"But..." Theo started, unable to figure out just how he managed to be in two places at once.

"Are you sure you thought it was me? Maybe it was another fairy?" Lowen asked.

Theo had been so sure it was Lowen. But...it was dark. Could it have been someone who looked like him? She supposed it was possible, though it seemed highly unlikely.

"Why are we still standing around?" Torian asked. "We can have this conversation inside."

"Excellent point," Beric said. "Let's go."

"Wait. We need to get Alby." Theo pointed to the ring.

"Who?"

Theo walked back into the clearing. "Alby, come on!"

Alby had retreated to the far side but slowly, cautiously made his way out of the darkness.

"He was trapped with me. And lucky for us, he plays the triangle. He's going to play with us. Right, Alby?"

She couldn't quite read the goblin's expression. He looked at the three fairies and Theo, lingering the longest on her, then nodded.

"Great!" Beric said.

But as they all turned to go, Theo still had a lingering question. "Who even made this?" And a question she didn't voice: *Why would someone go to the trouble?*

"Good question," Torian said. "Are we still in Cecily's woods?"

"I don't think so," Theo said, knowing that while she did come out to these woods, she'd never gone this far into them before.

"Then it could have been any fairy, really," Beric said. "It could also be very old."

"Lowen, you really weren't out here?" Theo asked, still not quite understanding how she'd made it this far into the woods. "You'd tell me if you were, right?" Plenty of tricks had been played on her in her past life. But never here, and never with her friends. She was desperately hoping they didn't start.

"Theo, I swear," he said, shaking his head vehemently. "Trapping my friend in a fairy ring would not be my idea of fun. I don't know who you saw, but it wasn't me."

"You were right, Theo," Alby cut in from the darkness a bit behind her, a hint of awe in his voice. "These fairies really seem to like you! I thought maybe you were making it up. But they came for you, just like you said they would!" Alby finished as though he had just seen proof of something wild and impossible.

She stopped walking and turned to the goblin. "Come on, Alby, follow me. Are you hungry? I can get you something to eat before we play. If you still want to play with us, that is."

"You're serious?" He didn't ask as though he was in disbelief, rather, with what Theo was finding to be his tone of awe and wonder at the overall situation.

"About the food? Of course."

"About all of it. You really just want me to play with you?"

"Theo!" came Beric's voice from farther down the trail. "Seriously, if you get lost again you'll never be allowed out of my sight. Let's go!"

She began walking, making sure Alby was with her. "If you'd like to join us, Beric mentioned earlier he has some new sheet music he'd like to try out, so it should be a fun time."

In the glow of the lantern light, Alby's big, cue ball eyes glistened. He nodded, his ears gently waving, and then followed along as they made their way down the trail back to the party.

---

Upon reentering the manor, she and her friends once again made for the drawing room and resumed their places at their instruments. Beric counted off and they fell into an easy, spirited tune. At the very first notes, a crowd began to form and dancing started up again. Alby took out his triangle from one of the many hidden pockets of his jacket and began to play along.

Even though Alby had not made any promises as to the quality of his playing, he still had oversold his musical abilities. The goblin was bouncing around the stage, banging his little metal instrument to whatever beat he felt like, regardless of the time kept by anybody else. But that was fine with Theo and the rest of the group. Alby seemed to be having the time of his life, and given his earlier experiences, Theo was not about to quash his joy.

She did manage to introduce Alby to Cecily and Phineas

somewhere in there, too, both of whom he found to be exceptionally charming, marveling over their relaxed relationship.

Shortly thereafter, the party began to wind down. Fairies were making their way home and Cecily's manor was clearing out little by little, until eventually the only ones left were the band members. Theo said good night to her friends and went to bed, the lingering question of the fairy ring still at the forefront of her mind.

# Chapter 4

# Where Theo Takes a Self-Flagellating Trip Down Memory Lane

She didn't have to look at the clock or the sun outside to know it was late afternoon when she woke up. The drool on her pillow and her own handprint on the side of her face were clues enough to know she had slept for a very long time. One small benefit of being a fairy's familiar was the ability to heal quickly, which meant things that would have otherwise hampered her the morning after parties were pretty much nonexistent. That didn't necessarily mean she felt great after a night of partying, though; she found herself to be so exceptionally parched and with such little moisture in her mouth a cracker could prove to be a colossal challenge.

So after slugging four glasses of water, she plodded to the bathroom to clean herself up. The mass of hair on her head was looking more like a brown thicket than thick brown locks. Detangling the knots would have to come before anything else, lest she leave it to become an even more suitable dwelling for wayward spiders that were there to catch the other things that found her hair attractive. Then, while she waited for her giant slipper tub to fill, she opened the windows to let in the afternoon air. As she looked outside at the manicured lawn sloping down to the woods that surrounded it, she wondered if the goat from the party had wandered home or if she would see it later eating the flowers outside.

What no one else—friends included—knew was that, in addition to playing music, Theo had cultivated another habit while she was in the fairy realm. And today, she was going to partake. It did involve a bit of travel, but that was now very easy to do since she could transport herself wherever she wanted.

In the time since she had become a fairy's familiar, she took a few trips to Avenshire, just to check in on her mother and her sister, Flo. She never let them see her, usually turning into a hedgehog to spy on the goings-on of the estate. Theo didn't know what Beatrice had told them about her disappearance, but it didn't seem like her sister and mother were missing her too much. Flo was living out every fantasy she'd ever had. Granted, her fantasies weren't larger than *be married to a royal* and *have babies*, but she succeeded just the same. She and her husband, Ambrose, seemed to have a very nice life, all things considered. And her mother resided in the manor with them, living out her days with no responsibilities. Theo spotted her once having tea with other noble ladies and she seemed to be enjoying herself immensely if her dainty laughs were any indication. Though Theo still bore the scars of everything her mother put her through, she was happy for her. And just as happy to close the door on that part of her life.

She had returned to Merrifall only once, just to see how it felt. For better or worse, it didn't feel like anything. The estate and manor she grew up in had been turned into a boarding school for orphans—one of Princess Beatrice's many pet projects. Theo knew this when she visited but wasn't prepared to see the estate returned to its former glory, the fields and gardens restored with children running all around. Like her sister and mother, Merrifall itself seemed to benefit from her absence, moving on as though she'd never been there at all.

And out of sheer curiosity about how her stepsister's life was going, she decided to see Princess Beatrice. Her stepsister wasn't aware she visited, either—Theo hadn't even gone inside. She watched from the hillside, catching a glimpse of the princess and her prince as they made one of their now-frequent public appearances. If Theo was a stagnant puddle in time, her stepsister was a raging river. Beatrice, now able to leave the palace without fear of being abducted by a fairy, made plenty of use of her new freedom by touring the kingdom, continuing to win hearts and minds by showing up places and smiling a lot.

The iron that had been placed around the castle was still there, but instead of keeping fairies out, it was a promotional tool for the abundance of the kingdom, encouraging foreign countries to purchase from them. Her garden project had expanded, too, her adoring public eager to copy what she was doing. What once was simply Beatrice's attempt at a florally toxic barrier to fairies was now a kingdom-wide movement. Because of what they thought was her affinity for Saint-John's-wort (and really was her affinity for not being taken as a fairy's familiar), having fields and fields of the medicinal plant became somewhat of a status symbol. Theo even went to see a few, but she stopped after visiting too many farms left her in danger of pulling a facial muscle with all her eye rolling, frowning, and general harumphing. Beatrice encouraged all of this for *the health and wellness of the people.*

Her people loved her for it.

Theo tried not to be bitter and resentful. She really did. But suppressing those feelings was next to impossible when watching Beatrice get everything she ever wanted, thanks to Theo's sacrifice. She knew she made that sacrifice willingly, but that didn't mean she had no opinions on the matter.

Like with Merrifall, Theo had made a visit to the castle only once.

On the other hand, where she was going today she'd been plenty of times.

However easy it was to transport herself now that she wasn't locked in a fairy ring, she couldn't do it from anywhere within Cecily's manor. First, the protection wards prevented her from transporting herself in or out of the manor's interior. Only Cecily was capable of that. Second, as Theo was keeping this hobby close to the vest, she didn't want to do it in the middle of the lawn where anyone could see her. So, if Theo wanted to leave the property without questions or interference, she had to do it in the woods.

Theo stuck her head out of her suite door, listening carefully for any movement. Hearing no one, she tiptoed out of her room, down the stairs, and out to the veranda at the back of the manor. Once outside, it was a quick walk to the tree line. She did a cursory glance down once or twice to check that there were no more fairy rings around—something that she now assumed she'd have to do frequently—but found none.

She walked just far enough into the woods on the edge of the property so she could no longer see the house, reasoning that anyone in the house then couldn't see her. Conjuring a breeze around her, she made for a city in the human realm.

When the wind cleared, she was standing in a copse of trees on the edge of a park, a newly constructed area for the common people. After peering around the trees to make sure there were no witnesses, she changed into her woodland form. Then she scurried out of her hiding place and toward her favorite spot by a tree closer to the street in order to do her spying.

She'd never bothered to stay human during her trips to the city, as she wouldn't have blended in the way she'd intended to. Her only clothing options were whatever Cecily supplied her with and weren't exactly the fashion du jour of the human cities. Spying was much easier to do in the comfort of a hole in a tree in her hedgehog form.

The newness of the park she was now in extended to the entire neighborhood. The paving stones on the sidewalks were perfectly level without a single corner sticking up above the rest. Even the clumsiest person would have to try hard to find something to trip over. The rows of town houses stood neat, orderly, and nearly identical, wearing their brick exteriors, flowered window boxes, and gates the way soldiers donned uniforms, the windows like gleaming medals. Each was three stories tall with a door on the left and a large bay window on the right, and every town house had a small front yard, something that was apparently a status symbol.

The house directly in front of Theo's hiding spot had the windows open to the warm air and she could hear the man inside preparing to go for his late-afternoon walk through the park. After a moment, the man walked out the door, shutting and locking it behind him.

He was a smartly dressed man in a gray suit and crisp white shirt, every gleaming button fastened as though he spent some time in front of a mirror to make sure he faced the day fashionably. His hair was cut shorter than Theo had ever seen it. All the better to style it—a slightly off-center part, black hair brushed straight back. The man must have been buying hair cream by the gallon given the hard work it was doing to keep his hair pressed to his scalp. A commendation letter to the owner of the hair cream company extolling its superb work in plastering was certainly in order.

This put-together man was a far cry from the person Theo had once known. In fact, if she hadn't been watching him for the past few months, she wouldn't even recognize Kaz now.

It was unusual for a human familiar to leave the service of a fairy. Most familiars were simply killed off when either the fairy or the human had had enough. If they were ever dropped back into the mortal realm, it was with their memories wiped so they couldn't pass on the knowledge of anything they had seen or heard while in a fairy's employ. Cecily had been rather forthcoming about where she had deposited Kaz after he left her service, probably expecting Theo would use the information as closure instead of to spy on him. He was given a good bit of money to get started, renting a room at a boardinghouse and finding a job in a furniture factory as a manager. Success in employment followed, and he soon was able to purchase a new house on the edge of a park. Theo had only watched him, never interfering, never making herself known since it wouldn't have mattered much anyway.

He wouldn't have remembered her.

Sometimes, like today, she would sit in her hidey-hole and imagine what it would be like if she lived there, too. Kaz would come home to her after his work was done. He'd stop at the flower shop on the corner and buy her a bouquet. She would greet him at the door, graciously accepting the flowers, offering him a kiss on the cheek, then arranging them in a vase they had received as a wedding gift. After dinner, she'd pour him a glass of his favorite honey wine and they'd play cards in the parlor. She'd win more often than not and claim he was letting her, but he would swear up and down that she'd bested him fair and square.

Theo never thought she'd picture herself living a simple life until she saw Kaz doing it. The life she was supposed to have. With him. Their life together, starting from scratch, where they answered to no one but each other.

A life that went somewhere.

Kaz strode across the street and into the park. It was

customary for him to look over the park. Looking for what, she didn't know, but he did it all the same, every time she was here. But he only looked briefly at the hole she was in, taking in the scene as he would anything else in the environment. But when he did, she caught a glimpse of those honey-molasses eyes. She also wished she could see them crinkle in the corners when he smiled, but she hadn't seen him do that in a very long time.

*There is no fairy-tale ending for you. The world owes you nothing*, Lady Martha Balfour's voice snarled into her mind. Usually, when Theo was at her lowest, her mother's derogatory voice would make itself heard. It was there to remind Theo of what she already knew: She could sit here and pretend all she wanted. This was not her happily ever after. Those were for other people.

She didn't hate or blame Kaz for moving on. Of course he would have. He'd been a familiar for three hundred years. He was ready to step back into the flow of time and live. How was he expected to do that if he was still pining for a woman who would stay the same forever? He deserved the simple, beautiful life he'd crafted for himself, even if it wasn't with Theo.

The house in front of her was empty, Kaz now far enough away so she couldn't see him anymore. There was no point in staying here watching nothing. Like any good pity party, this one was only worth staying at for the entertainment. So she dashed back to the dense area of trees on her hedgehog legs, transformed into a human, and transported herself to the woods of Cecily's manor. The woods were quiet and she was able to sneak inside without any witnesses. She made a quick detour to the kitchen, stocking up on food and a pot of tea for herself before returning to her room, uninterested in eating at the table with anyone yet. So instead, she changed into cozy sleeping clothes and tucked herself under a blanket on a couch in front of the fireplace.

---

She was still nursing that pot of tea when there was a knock at her door. Before she could say anything, Phineas popped his head in.

"Mind if I come in?" he asked, though he didn't wait for her to answer before strolling through the door and shutting it behind him. He had been doing this since she got here—checking up on her every once in a while. On days like today, she wasn't usually in the mood for talking but was appreciative of him just the same.

He dropped down onto the couch opposite her. He was wearing his usual royal-blue silk pajamas with white cording and a matching robe around him, tied up neatly with a bow like he'd been professionally gift wrapped. Not because he was cold—Cecily would rather eat glass than allow a draft in her manor—but because he knew it made him look dashing and debonair. Even in bedclothes, Phineas managed to be supremely fashionable.

He crossed his legs, put his elbow on the arm of the couch, and rested his head on his fist, watching Theo with a small smile, taking in her simple cotton smock and the steaming mug in her hands.

He sighed with a smile. "Having one of those days?"

"How could you tell?"

"I wasn't sure you'd left your room today, which usually means something is wrong."

She had to give him credit. He had no idea she was sneaking off to see Kaz, but he was a good enough friend to notice she was a bit more depressed on the days she did. "Yes, I'm having one of those days."

"Understandable."

"Is it?" A genuine question. Phineas rarely seemed to have bad days. The only one she could remember since being here was when he became slightly peeved that one of his conquests was still in his room hogging the blankets the morning after.

He shrugged.

Theo tucked her legs underneath her and stared into her mug, not ready to make eye contact, but at least a little ready to be honest. "I sometimes feel that I am doing nothing with myself. With my life. I am quite literally stationary in time. And on days like today, I can't figure out if it is a bad thing or not."

Phineas nodded. "I think, right now, you're doing what you need to get by. This life is not an easy adjustment. You've got time. Take as much of it as you need."

"I don't even know what I'm adjusting to. I got what I wanted. I didn't get married—my wild scheme worked. But...I never really planned past that. I thought it wouldn't matter, that I'd have every opportunity to figure it out. But it doesn't feel like I'm in a room with every door open for me. It feels like I'm out at sea on a dinghy surrounded by nothing and

I don't know which way to go to reach land. Instead of doing anything about it, I'm mostly just wishing for something that could have been." Theo frowned into her mug, watching the swirl of dark liquid instead of at Phineas. "And to be honest, I thought this life would be different. But besides my ability to turn into a hedgehog, it is almost exactly the same. I spent my early life beholden to my mother, to society, telling me what I can and cannot do, what is acceptable, what is not, and why everyone else should have the right to make decisions for me. Here, well, I feel like all I did was trade one gilded cage for a slightly larger, bit more magical gilded cage. No matter what, I am still not my own person."

Phineas watched her for a moment. "Did I ever tell you how I came to be a familiar?"

Theo shook her head.

"Well, since we've just established that you've got nothing better to do, it's story time. Settle in. I don't know if you can picture it, but five hundred years ago, I used to be a court jester. I was good at my job; the old king loved me. And I had a partner, with whom I was madly in love. His name was Dante and he worked in the castle as a servant. The kindest person I'd ever met. He was one of those people that you meet and it is just difficult to not like them, you know? And for some reason he thought I was pretty great, too. Oh, and he was ridiculously handsome. He looked like he had just walked out of a field under the summer sun. Tanned with hair that should have been black but was a sun-kissed brown. He had a few freckles on his nose that you could see only if you were up close, so they felt like they were there just for me."

His wistfulness at the memory died with his next words, his smile weighed down in the corners. "At one especially large banquet, I was doing my usual bit, telling my standard jokes. I made one at the expense of a viscount."

"And it was a bad joke?"

"Come on, Theo. Think of who you are talking to. It was a *great* joke. The king laughed nearly out of his chair; so did the rest of the banquet. The only one who didn't was the viscount. Well, and his wife. I didn't say the thing with the farm animals was true, mind you. Just that it was a possibility," Phineas added with annoyance. "He was so upset that, afterward, he made an official complaint with the king. But again, I was the king's favorite entertainer and he didn't think it was a big deal, so he denied the petition."

"So what happened?"

Phineas's smile disappeared completely. "I thought the whole thing was over, but the viscount was not happy with the king's decision. He wanted revenge. I didn't know it, but he had his lackeys follow me to find out what I cherished most, something he could destroy that would hit me the hardest. It wasn't hard to discover Dante.

"Suddenly, Dante went missing. No one knew where he went. I looked for him for a week. On the seventh day, I found him."

Phineas paused. "They'd dumped his body on the riverbank. Pinned to him was the joke and a letter telling me everything they had done to him before killing him. My Dante. The viscount brutalized him. All over an inane *joke*. I went to the king to see if anything could be done, but Dante was 'just a servant' and the viscount denied involvement, saying that anyone could have written the letter because nearly all of the kingdom's royalty had heard the joke and agreed with his feelings.

"I didn't think I could break further, but that refusal to do anything about it shattered me. It was all my fault. If I hadn't told that joke, or if I had just begrudgingly apologized, Dante would be alive. I fell into a deep depression, only able to think about Dante being taken from me. One night, in a drunken rage, I stole a silver knife from the kitchens and went down to the river to be done with it, this wretched life without him. I found a nice spot on the bank, surrounded by these little flowers that Dante would have liked. I didn't realize what I had done, but when my blood reached the water, Cecily showed up. She was certainly confused by the state of things.

"She asked why I had summoned her and then figured out pretty quickly that I hadn't actually meant to. So she asked me what happened. I told her everything in my blubbering, drunken state. Then she offered to help me."

"To get Dante back?"

Phineas sighed. "No. Not even fairy magic can bring someone back from the dead. She asked if I wanted revenge. I said yes, but I had nothing to barter with. So I told her she could have me. That she could take me and do whatever she wanted with me if I could get one night of revenge with the viscount."

"And she gave you that night?"

Phineas looked straight at Theo. "She gave me seven. An even exchange for how long Dante had been taken away from me. For the first time in my life, I had power—not just magical, but control over a situation. And during those seven days,

I didn't need to sleep. I didn't need to eat. And neither did the viscount. And I repaid him for every misdeed cast on my love. On the seventh day, Cecily reappeared with a knife for me to finally end it. I did. What I didn't know until later is that, during those seven days, she had visited the king. I'm not sure what she did to him, but he was never the same after that. His son had to take the throne pretty soon after.

"Once it was done, she took me by the hand and brought me back here. She asked nothing of me. Not a thing. She let me take all the time I needed to grieve. I pretty much stayed in my room for seventy-five years."

"Seventy-five years? What were you doing all that time?"

"Crying, mostly. And wishing for something I knew I could never, ever have—a life with Dante. But slowly, I got better. Sometimes I faltered, felt like I had slid all the way to the bottom again, but climbing out of that hopeless pit of despair got easier and easier over time. Cecily gave me a purpose again. Something to look forward to, even just something to do with myself. I owe her everything. Everything. I am hers for as long as she wants me."

He slapped his knees and got up. "All that to say, I know what longing feels like, and I know how hollowed out it can make you feel to hope for something you can't have. I'm here if you need to talk."

---

Theo sat for a while after Phineas left, long after her mug was empty and the fire turned to embers.

She'd been stuck in time, the world turning without her. But what if she didn't have to be? She was lamenting a future she couldn't have and it was time to stop. Kaz was moving on. Maybe she should, too.

Now she just had to figure out exactly what that meant for her and how to do it.

# Chapter 5

# Where the Regent Unveils a Clock Tower

The next day, after her bath, Theo selected a simple scoop neck silk dress the color of buttermilk printed with a pattern of blue and pale pink flowers. If she had been dressing for a fairy party, the flowers would have been blooming in front of her eyes, but as her big event today was her hunt for food, the fabric pattern was stationary. She tied her hair back in a matching ribbon and didn't bother with jewelry. Looking in the mirror and declaring herself good enough, she went downstairs to eat a late breakfast, or early lunch, depending on how one viewed eating as it related to time of day.

Cecily was already seated at the large claw-foot table, sipping tea and opening her mail, filled with various letters and invitations. They spread out in front of her in a haphazard pile, as though someone delivered them by dropping them from the ceiling.

"Good morning, my somnolent Theo," Cecily said as she sorted papers. Theo returned the greeting and then said her good mornings to Phineas as well. When she sat, Cecily conjured a simple breakfast of eggs and toast for Theo in her usual spot.

Cecily combed through her pile and picked up another letter, this one closed with a green wax seal of an oak leaf surrounded by small birch leaves—the royal seal of the regent and his partner. She tore into it with gusto and scanned the first page. "Tace is throwing a garden party."

It seemed to Theo that the regent and his partner, Aimon, would find any opportunity to throw a gala. From the fifty-seventh anniversary of the installation of the small water feature in the west garden to the party themed around Aimon's new favorite cocktail, they celebrated them all. They even held celebrations for the sad events. Theo would have been thoroughly unsurprised if they were organizing a ball in lieu of a memorial service for the four-month anniversary of the death of Aimon's second-favorite houseplant.

"It seems we've been invited to his weeklong celebration for his new clock tower installation," Cecily said, still scanning the paper. Once she'd gleaned enough details from that page, she moved on to the second one. As her eyes moved farther down the page, a smile grew. "Well, isn't this interesting." She looked up at Theo. "Seems your harp playing has caught the attention of some very important fairies. You have been invited by name to perform at the party. Followed by tea in the regent's private drawing room."

"The band has been invited to play?" Theo asked, not bothering to mask the shock.

"No," Cecily said, rescanning the page. "Just you. A showcase of your talent." If Cecily's eyes glowed any more she'd be able to see in the dark.

"May I see it?" Theo asked.

Cecily obliged and passed the invitation to Theo. The first page was indeed for the garden party, stating all the standard invitation items. But the second piece of paper was, while addressed to Cecily, written for Theo. Simplistic in style, but elegant just the same. The writing was neat and concise: *summoning the human familiar of Cecily of the Ash Fairies, Theodosia Balfour, to play harp in the lilac garden.* Followed by the time, as well as the invitation for a post-performance tea.

Overall, a very strange invitation indeed. Her name on any sort of fairy invitation would have been odd. A human familiar having an official invite to the Palace of the Fae was unheard of. And yet, here it was.

She set down the invitation to find Cecily watching her, head slightly tipped to the side. "I can't help but notice you're not jumping for joy."

"And I can't help but wonder if this is to showcase my talent as an accomplished musician, or if it is to parade me through the Palace of the Fae like a show pony."

"Well, my darling, we wouldn't want to pass up this invitation. So, if they want a show, let's give them one. Show them a neat trick and then kick them in the teeth. The party is in a few days. I'll RSVP for us immediately. In the meantime, I have some preparation to do. No matter what, I'm going to make sure you look great doing it." With that, Cecily swept out of the room, leaving her familiar to the rest of her breakfast.

---

For the regent's clock tower party extravaganza, Cecily stayed true to her word and spared no effort to dress Theo to impress, maintaining her positively giddy attitude at the prospect of showing her off in front of the entire party. She wanted Theo to shine, and so Theo did, both literally and figuratively, in a dress made to look like stained glass. While a glass dress would have been impressive on its own, Theo's was a shattered cathedral window reassembled with no design, the result a maelstrom of jagged, multicolored shards cascading around her. It was illuminated from within, the light flickering and dancing as though a fire burned behind it. The black lead intersected the fragments with a ferocious brutality. The fabric felt smooth against her skin, but to the casual onlooker, the glass looked sharp enough to cut.

There was an entire protocol to arriving at parties that Theo learned only after being a guest and not being snuck in. To avoid fairies magically appearing directly on top of one another, fairy manners dictated that invited attendees arrived in the grand foyer before making their way to the party. Since Cecily had an invitation, she was able to transport herself and her two familiars directly into the Palace of the Fae. Anyone who wanted to come in without an invitation would have to go to the front doors and hope that they were allowed in after careful consideration by security.

After arriving, the group followed the crowd through the massive glass-ceilinged atrium to the garden outside. As far as Theo could tell, there was no rhyme or reason behind its layout: It hugged the entire back of the palace, extending outward for what must have been hundreds of acres until it touched a forest so far in the distance the trees looked like an oil painting. Unlike the gardens of Theo's youth—tilled, paved, and pounded into submission until tame and willing to do as it was bid—the palace's garden was unplanned, wild, and free. Stone paths were arranged in such a way as to look like they had chosen the layout themselves, winding haphazardly like dropped balls of yarn. Following them felt like following a child's treasure map to secret alcoves and hidden-away sections.

The main garden was open, consisting mostly of fountains and statues dotting the landscape. The very first time Theo ever saw the garden happened to be at nighttime, and the statues looked terrifying. But in the light of day, they weren't scary at all. The statue garden was a mix of all sorts of figures, including the minotaur she'd seen the first night. But at a party shortly after she'd come to stay with Cecily, she returned to the garden and realized that the statue of the hulking figure was carrying stone flowers. The rest of the statues were just as random in subject and location as the minotaur, as though the person who was placing them got tired midway through and decided wherever they put each one down wasn't such a bad spot for a statue after all.

Regent Tace, adorned with his customary gold tunic and matching gold oak leaf crown, and his paramour, Aimon, who wore an effortlessly suave smile, were already on their thrones upon a stone dais at the base of the very large, newly installed clock tower. Built as an ode to the Oak Fairy line, it was made of dark gray cobblestone but carved with intricate knots and bark to look like a huge oak tree. At the very top was a large clock, its face and hands gold and glittering in the sun.

The big reveal was to be at noon, when the clock would sound for the very first time. Now the hands said only two minutes left. People were beginning to crowd around the base, waiting for the hands to line up at their topmost position. Theo expected the regent to make a grand speech, seeing as how he loved to be the center of attention, but he instead held Aimon's hand and watched the party with enthusiastic anticipation.

The two hands moved to twelve and the clock tower bloomed. Stone limbs and branches that had been bare a second prior burst to life, sprouting thousands and thousands of emerald oak leaves. A compartment directly above the clockface opened up and a song began to play. This wasn't a giant bell, nor was it lots of little bells. It was hundreds of chimes instead, all working together to create a beautiful burst of sound for each strike of the clock.

The applause immediately after was loud and genuine; Tace beamed from his chair. He stood and, with all the humility he could muster, put his hand on his heart and tilted his head only the slightest amount.

Now that the reason for the entire party had occurred, fairies and their familiars began to disperse to other parts of the garden to commence the celebration portion of the event. Most of the entertainment happened in the other areas of the garden, including the dancing and music, thus the area in front of the regent and his partner was full of the more reserved revelers, who preferred gossip and verbal barbs over physical displays.

Since Theo's invitation specified she was to play in the lilac garden, she, Cecily, and Phineas went there. As soon as they arrived, Theo stepped off the stone path and onto the dark green moss that covered the ground. It was customary to not wear shoes in the garden, likely to not trample the delicate plants. But Theo enjoyed it for the freedom of earth underfoot, the moss springy and soft like cotton on her toes. Somehow enchanted, the lilac trees grew bigger than their non-magical counterparts, their fragrant purple and white flowers growing more like wisteria, providing a shady retreat from the afternoon sun. A river of not water, but bluebells, wound through the garden. Footbridges that looked as though they had been hewn from single blocks of wood crossed over the flowers.

Standing in the far corner of the garden under a lilac tree was the copper-haired fairy. And he was once again staring right at her with curiosity, as though she were a zoo animal and he was waiting for her to do something interesting, though she couldn't guess as to what that might be.

She turned to Cecily, who was standing next to her. "Cecily, don't make it obvious, but standing at the far side of the garden is a copper-haired fairy. Do you see him?"

Cecily made a show of slowly sweeping her eyes across the entire party, not lingering on any one spot in particular. When she was finished she took a big gulp of her wine. "I do. Honestly, if I looked any longer I would have fallen asleep. Who is he?"

"I was hoping you would know. He's been coming to your parties and doing very much the same thing he's doing now. Just standing in the corner watching."

"Odd."

"Very."

But unfortunately, she could ponder no more. It was time for her to perform.

The tables sprinkled throughout were all full of fairies, and those who hadn't found seats were mingling in between. It appeared that it would be as full of a house as the garden would allow for her performance. A harp was sitting on a small, raised dais between two of the towering lilac trees, the seat tucked snugly next to it. At present, no one was paying it much mind. But they would, Theo was sure. She had spent the days between the invitation and today practicing, taking Cecily's words to heart. If they summoned her here to show them a party trick, she'd give them the best one they've ever seen.

With the well-wishes of *Break a nail—and if it goes poorly, tell them you never met me* from Cecily, Theo went to the harp. By the time she had finished a quick tuning and warm-up, most of the garden had turned to face her, conversations shushed by the music hovering in the air. As soon as her instrument was ready, she began to play.

This was no time for fun, light, upbeat, danceable music. She had something to prove. Her first piece was a whirlwind of sound—complex and dizzying, where one misstep meant the entire melody would crumble. But her confidence in her fingers, in the feel of the harp strings on her flesh, was the one constant in her life, and she knew she wouldn't falter. Her fingers moved across the strings with the precision of a surgeon, life hanging in the balance.

The song ended with a wistful note. She knew she had them when she wasn't met with raucous applause, but with wide eyes, slack faces, and drinks ready to slip out of hands. Cecily, meanwhile, was grinning with a look of triumph. Lock had also appeared, taking up a spot under a lilac tree, watching her with rapt attention.

But there would be no rest. She launched into her next song. And then the next, each different in tone, each trying to best the preceding in difficulty.

Finally, she came to her pièce de résistance: She had them on their backs and was taking no prisoners—now it was time for the kill. The song was torment in D minor. A cavalcade both haunting and brutal as it charged through the audience. Theo wasn't a harpist, she was a general. Notes rang out like a battle cry, the harp seeming to know it was a weapon of war. She poured everything she had into it. If they thought they could minimize her, she would show them what an impossibility that was.

And when the song ended, she felt a lightness in her heart she hadn't felt in a long, long time.

Theo stood, finally acknowledging the crowd. And they, in turn, regained their faculties, erupting in applause. She curtsied just the right amount. Not too low, lest they think she was kowtowing to them, and not too high for them to think what she did didn't matter. It was only after she stood that she noticed Regent Tace at the very back, eyes wet. But before the clapping ended, he had turned back to the palace.

Theo left the stage and made her way to Cecily. The fairy handed her a glass of wine as soon as she reached her.

Cecily smirked. "Murdering the audience via music. I must say, that is a neat party trick."

"They wanted a show." Theo shrugged with a grin.

"You certainly gave them one. Make sure to drop my name when giving your thank-you speeches."

The crowd was slowly returning to its pre-music mingling state, and Theo saw Lock still under the tree. With her newfound lightness and in the spirit of moving forward, Theo went to finally talk with Lock.

---

Lock watched her approach, his smile growing with every step she took. He was in his usual black pants with a thundercloud gray tunic embroidered with silver ash leaves on the sleeves and collar. His hair was slicked back, exposing the sheared sides of his head and pointed ears.

"Theo, that was incredible," he said. "I've never seen anything like that."

She grinned, knowing it was a genuine compliment. "Thank you."

The conversation halted there, both of them looking at each other, neither saying anything.

"Can we talk for a moment?" Lock ventured. To a casual onlooker, he may have appeared relaxed. But even though he wore a casual smile, from his slightly shuffling feet to his hands that he stuffed in his pockets, Theo could see that he was anxious. "Good. I've been trying to talk to you for a while now." He gave her a nervous laugh. "It seems every time I try, I am somehow prevented from speaking with you. Most recently when my aunt, of all people, showed up."

"That was odd," Theo said. "I can't recall her ever being at Cecily's parties. What was she doing there?"

Lock rolled his eyes. "I don't even know. She said she had something to discuss with me about the vineyard, but she could have just put it in a letter."

The conversation petered out, both of their mouths twitching like they were trying to think of something to say. Theo wasn't sure how she was supposed to spur him on. Instead, they continued to stare at each other.

Before either of them could die of awkwardness, Lock took a deep breath. "In the interest of not keeping you, I'll just come out and say it. Theo, I miss you, and I miss your friendship. I was hoping we could try that again."

"We are friends."

"Are we? I think most of the time we pretend to be friends for the band's sake, but this is the longest conversation we've had since you got here. Listen, I know you probably still hold a torch for Kaz, and I understand. I'm not looking for anything romantic—I just want to be counted among your friends. Can I?"

Hearing someone else say Kaz's name felt like a jolt of lightning to her chest. And Lock wasn't saying it in any sort of cruel or facetious way. He knew how she felt about him and was making no effort to change her mind. A far cry from when he told her to be careful of Cecily's former familiar.

Maybe Lock really did mean what he was saying.

Kaz wasn't coming back. And maybe for Theo, it was time to accept that and start moving forward.

"I'd really like that, Lock. I'll be honest, though, I don't know how we start over. But I'm open to trying."

He grinned. "I think it would mostly begin with you actually having a conversation with me that revolves around something other than you needing to use a bathroom."

She laughed. "I didn't think you noticed. However, it appears you are the one to bring up bathrooms in this conversation."

Just as Lock was about to make a rebuttal, a figure walked up next to them.

Nearly incognito in his blandness was the copper-haired fairy, eyes trained on Theo.

"Theodosia Balfour," he said, more statement than question.

Her patience with him, having been draining from her like a slow leak, had finally dripped its last drop. Not bothering to cap her frustration, she rounded on him. "Now is not a good time. And this—you following me and staring at me—has sailed past odd and is now floating in creepy and bizarre. Had you approached and asked directly, I probably would have said yes. But since you have now escalated to following me in a new location, I'm going to have to say no. No, you cannot play in our band. And before you make any appeals, I must tell you, the band agrees with me." Theo hoped she sounded stern enough to have him turn tail and slink off in embarrassment.

Alas, no.

"Excuse me?" he said, reeling back as though she'd swung at him. "I have no interest in playing in your little band."

"Then scamper off," she said, frustrated that her attempt to be brave and speak with Lock was foiled by the staring fairy, as though he waited for the perfect moment to sabotage her. That frustration led her to shake her hands at him like she was shooing away a pesky animal.

He remained where he was and instead responded with "Theodosia Balfour, familiar of Cecily of the Ash Fairies, you're to come with us immediately."

# Chapter 6
# Where Theo Learns About Her Past

Theo learned very quickly what "us" meant in this situation as two guards appeared next to the copper-haired fairy, identifiable by their identical forest-green uniforms, gold oak leaf detailing on the sleeves, cuffs, and pants. And for some reason, they seemed to defer to the copper-haired bore as though he was the one in charge.

Lock put his arm out in front of Theo, creating a physical barrier between her and the approaching guards. "And what exactly is this about?"

"This doesn't have anything to do with you," Copper Hair said to Lock, and then turning back to Theo, he added, "Now, come on." He extended his arm, gesturing down the path that would lead them to the palace. His outright dismissal of Lock, and his lapse in manners in not introducing himself, set Theo on edge.

"Seeing as I have no idea who you are or where you're expecting me to thoughtlessly follow you to, I'm sure you'll understand when I say *no, thank you*. If you have any further questions, I suggest you take them up with Cecily," Theo said, doing her best to sound at once polite yet pertinacious.

The fairy looked at her with narrowed eyes. "I am Arlys of the Maple Fairies."

"You see how that answers no questions, though, right?" Theo snapped.

Arlys seemed to believe he'd talked enough about his identity and instead said, "We are here to take you to the tea with the regent."

Theo's eyebrows twisted in confused annoyance. "Why didn't you lead with that?"

Arlys, apparently allowed only a small number of answers per day, ignored that, too. "If you don't come with me, they'll drag you." He pointed to the guards. She wasn't sure his threat was real. By all accounts, those two seemed just as confused by the whole thing as Theo. Plastered on their faces was the same expression she had, silently saying this was all a bit much for tea. For the life of her, Theo could not understand the hostility. This party was their idea and Cecily already told them Theo would be there. Why was she being treated like she had no say in the matter and must be forcibly brought there?

But before any dragging occurred, Cecily sauntered up, followed closely by Phineas.

Cecily put her hands on her hips as she calmly gave Arlys a once-over. "Why does it look like you're about to arrest my familiar?"

"He says he's here to take me to the tea party," Theo said.

"Under duress?"

"Apparently."

Arlys huffed. "Let's get going, then."

"I'll go to tea," Theo acquiesced, her hands up in surrender before Arlys made good on his guard threats. "But they're coming, too." She gestured to Lock, Cecily, and Phineas. Theo was well aware that inviting extra guests to an event when she was a guest herself was abhorrently rude. But so was aggressively enforcing attendance to a tea party, so by all accounts, they were equal in their lapse in manners.

"Excellent." Cecily smiled. "I love a bit of mandated fun. Having your guests try to decide whether they're at a party or a hostage situation is an underrated parlor game, in my opinion."

Playing into Theo's assumption of Arlys avoiding answers, he merely rolled his eyes and gestured to the path that would lead them back to the palace.

---

For as many times as Theo had been in the palace, she hadn't ever gone down these hallways. The parties there mainly took place in the atrium and its surrounding rooms and balconies, or the garden. The long corridor they were currently walking down was, besides them, empty. Theo didn't know the architectural layout of the palace so had no idea where they were headed, only that it seemed with each carpeted step, she was moving farther and farther away from the parts of the palace she knew. The group said nothing as they followed Arlys. They passed door after door, all nearly identical, with oak leaf motifs carved into the wood, which Theo was assuming was also oak due to their rich, golden honey tones. She was almost impressed when Arlys came to a stop in front of one of the many identical doors and wondered how he had known which one he was even looking for.

He ushered them into what must have been the drawing room. Four green upholstered sofas sat in a square formation around a low table. Arlys motioned for them to sit down. He, however, did not take a seat, and instead stood between the sofas and the door, his gaze never leaving Theo. The two guards were flanking the exit, not paying attention to her as much as they were to the possibility that someone new might come in.

They sat in silence for a while, dull Arlys watching her like he was afraid she'd try to sprint out after he went to all that trouble of catching her. Maybe it was due to her prey-like posture, her back strained from perching on the edge of the sofa like she would need to leap from it at any moment. He said nothing and gave nothing away, but she still couldn't shake the feeling that she was being called to the headmistress's office for a stern admonishment instead of accepting an invite for tea.

Speaking of, if she knew anything about tea parties—and she did—it was that no matter the time, location, or theme, they all found common ground in serving tea. Which was suspiciously absent from the room now. And nary a finger sandwich to be seen. With the addition of guards, which she had never before seen in all her tea partying, Theo was beginning to suspect the regent forgot about this little shindig entirely.

In fact, he did not. She had only just finished judging the host for his ill manners when in strode both Regent Tace and his royal consort, Aimon. Good news for her former manners tutor: Even thoroughly annoyed at the situation, Theo hadn't forgotten her decorum and stood when they entered, curtsying to noble authority in the way she'd been relentlessly trained. Aimon looked a little wary, but Tace was beaming as he took in Theo. She hoped the confusion wasn't shining through too brightly as she curtsied.

Lock and Phineas had also stood. Cecily, meanwhile, remained draped over the couch. Instead of a curtsy, she only gave Tace the barest of waves for her greeting, and an even smaller one for Aimon. Her cousin glared, but Tace merely spared a quick look at her before turning his attention fully to Theo.

As the regent approached, Theo couldn't help but notice the crown atop his head. She was surprised by its simplicity, given his propensity for extravagance in every other facet of his life. It was made of gold but styled to look like tree branches filled with oak leaves. And it was otherwise unadorned—no jewels to be seen, the gleaming from the precious metal alone. His short brown hair was styled neatly around it, adding to the effect of looking like it had grown out of his head.

He had his arms outstretched like he was about to embrace Theo, to which she responded by taking the smallest step backward, her legs bumping into the couch. He tracked the movement and put his arms down, but his face was still radiant. Indeed, Theo had seen less enthusiastic and wide smiles on a small child showing off a missing tooth. His green-hazel eyes were shining, the skin around them crinkling like parchment.

"Oh, oh dear, I'm just so delighted to meet you. I can't even begin to say..." He trailed off, tears glistening in his eyes. He reached for her hands and squeezed them in his, holding on as though they were about to be taken away. Thankfully for her circulation, he released her and motioned for them to sit back down again.

If he was trying to be complimentary, Theo wasn't having it. Even if it was genuine, crying at guests before introductions was an odd way to start a party, no matter how she was brought to it. Her desire to be respectful in front of the noblest of the fairy nobility was waning, taking her patience along with it. Without that, perplexed irritation was filling in the gap. "Where to begin, where to begin," Tace muttered to himself, still watching Theo.

"Tea?" Theo suggested.

"Interesting recommendation," Cecily said to Theo with a smirk. "What ever made you think of that?"

"What?" Tace asked to both of them.

Theo's eyebrows were very close to going rogue, only contained because neither they nor Theo could figure out whether they should be going up in confusion or down in annoyance. "Where to begin. I was invited for tea—well, *invited* seems to be the wrong term; I was forcefully brought here for tea. Maybe we should start with that." Theo might not have brought her facial expressions into this and, even though she had a touch more respect for royals than Cecily, still hoped she sounded at least somewhat accusatory.

"I guess we should just jump right in," Tace said, plowing on as though Theo had said nothing at all. "All right, well, I am the regent because the king, my nephew, was killed. Do you know any of this?"

Theo nodded, puzzled at the statement.

"Right, good. So you know the story about how the royal family was killed?"

She nodded again while Tace held a pause.

"And the rumor of a survivor?"

More nodding. More pausing.

Cecily sighed. "Tace, being coy doesn't suit your complexion or fashion sense. Leave that to the professionals"—she pointed to herself—"and come out with it already."

There was a slight joy watching Cecily try to set off Tace like a firework.

But the regent closed his eyes for a brief moment, dousing the fuse, and then smiled once more at Theo. "And here you are! Returned to us once more!"

Theo looked around the room at the faces of everyone there. Lock's, Cecily's, and Phineas's mirrored her own incredulity, but dull Arlys was looking as stern as ever. Aimon was watching Theo with resignation, and Tace was still looking at her with hope.

"Me?" she finally managed to choke out. "What are you talking about? I'm... That's not... That can't be. I'm afraid there has been some sort of mix-up. I was invited here to play harp at the party and then come for tea."

"My dear, that was a ruse to get you to the palace. Success!" Tace said, bright with joy.

Not that it had been loud before, but now the room was dead silent.

*Alert the kingdom's squirrels: The regent has gone nuts.*

"Shouldn't someone call a doctor?" Theo knew better than to look at Cecily for a serious answer, but no one else in the room except for Lock and Phineas seemed to agree with Theo's observation.

"Let's not," Cecily said, the corners of her mouth twitching upward, proving Theo right. "He may have fallen off his rocker, but I, for one, would like to behold the landing."

"It may sound preposterous," Tace said, glaring at Cecily before returning his attention to Theo. "But it is true. After the royal family was discovered dead and you missing, we decided to keep you a secret. We knew someone was out to get you, too. You had inhaled some of the smoke. Not enough to kill you and your nanny, but enough to make you incredibly ill. For a little while there, we weren't even sure you'd make it.

"The only way forward was to put you into slumber, hiding both you and your magic. In that state, you are well and truly immortal and cannot be killed. We kept you hidden and safe, locked away in a place known only by the secret keeper"—he gestured to Arlys—"who guarded you. The killer had done their best to make it look like an accident—and that is the official story told to the public—but putting that much yew in that many fireplaces could be no mistake. And if there had been a bargain made, no fairy was showing any signs of it not being carried out."

Theo tilted her head, unwittingly becoming invested in his outlandish tale. "What do you mean, no signs of a bargain?"

"The investigators assumed that even if they interviewed someone who had an alibi, that doesn't mean they didn't make a deal to get the job done and keep their hands clean. However, since you were not killed—but were a target—it can be safely assumed that whatever bargain someone made for the murder of your family was never fulfilled. Magic involved in bargains can only be released when the bargain is paid back."

"Yes, I know all this. Better than you'd think. But wouldn't that take a while?"

"Of course, which is why, after one thousand years, we decided we could safely take you out of the enchantment. Any fairy involved in the bargain would be long dead by now. Your magic was safely sealed away, leaving you, for all intents and purposes, human. Then we found a lovely family who had a newborn baby named Theodosia who was sickly. When she died, we swapped you out, the parents none the wiser they were raising a fairy changeling."

The bits of information were hitting her sharply, quickly, as though he was whipping pebbles straight at her face, but with that last line, he had hurled a boulder.

"Wait," she said, holding up her hand. "You just . . . replaced a baby?" Never in a million years would Theo be described as motherly, but even that seemed beyond the pale.

"Yes. With you."

"So you're saying my parents aren't actually my parents?"

"Of course your parents are still your parents!" Tace said with a smile reserved for four-year-olds. "Redren and Lilliana will always be your parents, no matter what form you're in."

"No. No, I'm talking about my *parents*. Martha and Thomas."

"Oh, right. No. They're a human couple who had a child

who was about to die. We saved them the pain and suffering of losing a child, and they got to raise fairy royalty! Everyone benefits!"

Theo's stunned silence left him an opening to continue his story. "What we weren't planning on was—Thomas, did you say his name was?—dying and your mother taking you to live elsewhere. No matter, really. We tracked you down, sure enough, and then watched you from there. We planned on coming to get you on your twenty-first birthday. Imagine my absolute shock when Arlys told me you were missing!"

Theo peeked at Arlys, who was giving Tace a look cold enough to turn his tea—if he had any—into a solid block of ice. Tace hadn't looked over and was therefore none the wiser as he plowed on.

"As I recall, they finally found you only to discover you were back in the fairy realm! And now I get to sit here with you! My long-lost grandniece and heir to the throne!"

Everyone was watching Theo, waiting for her to do something, but she didn't know what. Finally, she managed to let out a garbled "You're saying you believe me to be the missing princess, Iara?"

It was one of the only times Tace's smile faltered. "Oh, um, no. You are Princess Amabel. Are you well, my dear?"

No, Theo was not. She was frozen to her seat and seriously doubted she'd be able to do anything other than stare. The walls were warping like a tarp in a breeze, the whole room seeming to go in and out of focus. She might as well have been underwater for all the air she was able to inhale. *He thinks he's being serious.*

She was finally thrown a life jacket in the form of Cecily, who tipped her head back and burst out laughing. "Tace, I was simply enraptured by your storytelling. Have you been taking lessons?" She stood up from the couch. "Since my companions and I have not been offered tea or anything to drink, I think we'll take our leave. Thank you for the entertainment." Cecily then motioned for Theo, Lock, and Phineas to join her.

But Tace held up his hand, prompting the guards to take a collective step forward.

"While I understand this is a lot to learn at once," Tace said, hand still raised, "we still have business that will need to be conducted tonight. Most pressing being the fact that our princess is currently your familiar. Before I continue, please know we've already looked into your bargain with her and chalked it up to an extremely unfortunate coincidence, and we have ultimately chosen not to prosecute you for engaging in bad bargaining." He returned his attention to Theo. "But we will need to remedy this immediately if we are to unseal your magic and return you to your true fairy state."

There were only two ways for fairies to rid themselves of a familiar. The first was to kill the familiar, thus ending the bond. The second was to find a replacement—the scenario that put Theo into her bargain in the first place.

As though thinking the same thing, Tace continued. "Since we obviously want you alive, the only option for Cecily is to find another familiar to take your place. Then your life will no longer be tied to hers and you can become the fairy you were destined to be."

"I still maintain I am not a fairy and you have me confused with someone else," Theo said, not liking where this conversation was headed. Nor did she appreciate that Tace appeared to have the whole plan already figured out, with absolutely no input from Theo, who, arguably, should have the most say.

"Interesting perspective, Theo," Cecily said, tapping her finger to her chin in contemplation. "Meanwhile, I can't help but think this is a ploy of some kind to steal my vexed Theo away from me."

Tace jerked back. "What reason could I possibly have for that?"

Cecily shrugged. "Needing a royal harpist? I wronged Aimon, forgot about it, and this is revenge? I don't know. You're the one with the ploy."

"Not a ploy!"

"Not convinced. But let's say I believe you. It is not as easy as you might think to find someone to make a bargain in exchange for eternal servitude. Have anyone in mind?" Cecily drawled.

Tace put up his hand and opened his mouth to make a rebuttal, but Aimon's hand on his shoulder shut him down. "Now, let's just all hold on a moment," the regent's partner said, his voice quiet and calm as though reading a bedtime story. "I think Cecily is correct. It has been a long day for all of us. There is a lot of information for the princess to digest, and we seem to have come to her limit, which is entirely understandable. How about this." He turned to face Theo directly. "Why don't we all end here for the day, and then first thing tomorrow morning we can reconvene and discuss in more detail Cecily finding a new familiar." Aimon raised his eyebrows expectantly and nodded, first at Theo and then at the rest of the assembled party.

Aimon's nanny-esque tone seemed to be working on Tace, but Theo was not too fond of him acting like she was an irrational child who was told she would have no dessert before bed.

Tace's face softened and he looked at Aimon. "My love, I do believe you're right, as usual."

Theo stood. "Now that you have all decided what to do with me, I would like to go home now." Even though she had plenty of other thoughts that she wanted to say, that was all the fight she could muster at the moment.

"Why, Princess Amabel, you are home," Tace said with a glowing smile.

"Oh, stop that," Cecily snapped. "You know full well what she meant."

Tace glared at Cecily. "*You* may return to your residence. The princess will be staying here where we can keep a close watch on her." He put his smile back on and turned to Theo. "And, Amabel, welcome back."

With that, he stood, nodded to Arlys, and marched out of the room. Aimon gave Theo one last apologetic smile and bid his goodbyes before following his partner out the door.

# Chapter 7

# Where Theo Spends an Uncomfortable Night in the Palace

With every step away from the drawing room, Theo was getting that much angrier. She had just decided she was ready to move on and have a fresh start. And yet, once again, nobility was being foisted upon her. She was used to this treatment in her past and she *hated* it. She entered into an eternal fairy bargain to try to get out of life as a royal in a world where none of her choices were her own. Everyone else had been telling her what she should or shouldn't be doing, who she was and wasn't.

Theo never dreamed that would be an inescapable part of her life now.

*No, no, no. For a myriad of reasons, no.*

Arlys then escorted Theo out of the room and down a hall. They passed a row of windows and she could see out into the garden. Fairies continued to mingle, eating and drinking. It felt odd to see the party still going, everyone else carrying on as though nothing at all had happened. To them, nothing had.

When she and Arlys rounded the corner at the end of the hall, the atmosphere of the palace changed. She wasn't quite sure if it was the softer glow of the sconces, the slightly more plush runner, or the portraits of fairies on the wall, but all of it gave this section of the palace a much cozier feel. She knew who the subjects of the paintings were immediately, even though she'd never seen their likenesses before, and pieced it together that she must be in the palace's family wing.

Arlys stopped in front of one of them, hands clasped behind his back as he gazed into the face of the king. Redren was portrayed standing in the garden, a wide forest swelling out behind him like a green wave. Theo regarded this painting the way she would any other painting of people she didn't know. Interesting to look at, demonstrative of the artist's talents, but unable to evoke any personal emotions.

Meanwhile, Arlys was on the verge of a religious experience. Theo knew the king had been well-liked, but the fairy next to her was admiring the image of Redren like he had decreed every one of his subjects would be given absolution of all sins and a puppy. If Arlys's eyes got any mistier, the windows would start fogging. Theo wasn't sure if he was praying.

When he looked to her, she offered him a shallow nod as a polite acknowledgment. However, his sneer suggested this was not the appropriate response. But if he was hoping she'd also get into the spirit and weep tears of joy upon viewing the image, he was going to continue to be disappointed.

He huffed. "He was a great man, your father."

Without waiting for a reply, Arlys moved to the next painting. This one was a family portrait.

King Redren was standing behind the woman who must have been Queen Lilliana. Her caramel hair was pulled into a loose braid that she had tucked over her shoulder. While still regal, both the king and queen were smiling, Redren with pride, and Lilliana with joy.

Sitting in front of them were two little girls, both wearing white dresses, both with miniature versions of Tace's crown on their heads, holding each other's hands. The smaller of the two looked to be about a year old, still with her round baby cheeks and pudgy legs sticking out in front of her like tiny loaves of bread, her smile showing off only her two front teeth. The other girl was only slightly older. Her hair was the exact color of her mother's. It was left loose to fall down her back in waves. Her eyes were green hazel, just like her father's, except with black freckles, like the opposite of stars, sprinkled in. Theo had grown up not looking like anyone in her family. Her eyes were always different, her hair was always unusual. And yet, looking at this portrait, she saw familiarity.

Arlys again watched Theo. And again, it didn't seem like Theo had made the correct emotional display, as his now all-too-familiar expression of annoyance returned.

After that, he gave up trying to elicit a worthy response from her and continued down the hall. At the end, she was led into a well-appointed suite. Whoever the interior decorator was took "ode to Oak Fairies" to heart. The main room was a deep green the color of late-summer oak leaves, just before the color retreats for autumn. Oak leaves and branches were carved into the woodwork that was made out of (what else?) light oak. At first, Theo thought the area rugs were spared from the oak onslaught, but when she looked a bit closer, she saw that the intricate gold pattern around the cream-colored rug was comprised of little oak leaves. And the same was true for the throw pillows and drapes. If she looked any further, images of oak leaves would be imprinted on her eyelids.

Aside from the arboreally monotonous design theme, the main room was otherwise comfortable. Candles provided a warm glow, and paintings of people and places hung in various spots along the wall. On the other side of the room, she noticed a seating area in front of a stone fireplace. The fireplace was empty and sparkling clean, not a speck of soot to be found. Theo wondered if that was done to make her feel better given the obvious history she was facing, or if the family suites no longer used the fireplaces at all anymore.

"Through there is your bedroom, princess," Arlys said, pointing to a door farther into the room. "You'll also find your closet and bathing room as well." It was unnerving hearing Arlys call her *princess*. She would have expected him to say it with disdain or, at the very least, muted sarcasm. But he said it with earnestness and Theo didn't know what to do about it.

Just as it seemed like Arlys was about to conclude his rudimentary tour, a guard came to the door and stood in the entrance to the suite. He was holding a small wooden trinket box.

In the verbal equivalent of slamming a door in the guard's face, Arlys said, "The guards are to be stationed farther down the hall." The guard nodded but proceeded to enter anyway, setting the box down on a small side table and opening it.

"What do you think you're doing?" Arlys tried again.

The guard pulled from the box what looked to be two thin metal bracelets and turned to Theo. Arlys halted him with a hand, preventing him from getting any closer to her.

"Who authorized this?" Arlys snapped, which Theo found to be a very odd reaction to jewelry.

"The order came from the top, sir," the guard said. "You're welcome to take it up with him. Another safety measure."

Arlys was not placated. "This is ludicrous and unnecessary. The room has already been warded. No one can transport themselves directly inside or get anywhere near her. Even if they did, she's still a familiar, and therefore can't be taken anyway."

"It was thought best to add some further security measures," the guard said, unperturbed by Arlys's increasingly frustrated tone.

The lengths of chains were bracelets, all right, but it was what they were made of that was the problem. As the guard walked toward her, she could both see and feel that they were solid iron.

Besides being fifty years out of style, thin strands of iron jewelry wouldn't have otherwise bothered her. However, iron was a known fairy repellent, since simply being in proximity to it lessened fairy magic. Princess Beatrice had used it to great effect when she was hiding from Cecily. So seeing and feeling it now was wildly unusual, as no fairy would want it anywhere near them. Because Theo's magic was fairy magic, too, iron had the same effect on her. Even just being near the bracelets gave her the sensation of shoving cotton in her ears, except this feeling was muffling her magic.

But before Theo could do anything other than shudder, the guard had a bracelet on each of Theo's wrists, snapping them in place with a locking mechanism that closed so seamlessly the bracelets looked like thick, solid rings of black fitting snugly right at her wrist bones.

With the bracelets on, her magic was all but gone.

The guard snapped the trinket box closed and walked out without a backward glance. Arlys immediately went after him, leaving Theo alone in the room.

Even though she knew she wasn't leaving the palace tonight, with these on she felt well and truly trapped. There was no way for her to transport herself, and no way to use her animal form to try to find rodent holes in the wall that she might leave through.

There was little hope of removing these bracelets by herself. She did give the room a cursory once-over, just in case some fairy with a propensity for chaos or minor home repairs stashed any hand tools in her vanity or next to the fireplace. No such luck.

She took a few deep breaths, steadying herself, then went to the door, closing it and clicking the lock into place. A pointless gesture, really, seeing as how they could just bust down the door with magic should they want to. Or use the key they probably had. But she needed a morale boost and the machinations gave her the tiniest inkling that she was in charge of something.

Though it was only the tail end of late afternoon, Theo was

absolutely exhausted. Yet with the hurricane of information swirling around her head, she knew sleep would be impossible. When she tried to pick out something tangible from the vortex, she ended up with bits and pieces of usable information combined with the informational equivalent of partial barn doors and uprooted trees. But an existential crisis could only last so long before the quiet of the room and ennui of pondering big ideas overtook it.

For lack of anything better to do, though, she decided to get ready for bed anyway. She was still in her stained glass dress, which, while shockingly comfortable, was wholly inappropriate for bed. Luckily, in the closet was a selection of nightgowns. She put on the first one she found, not caring in the slightest that it was flimsy, floor length, and about four inches too long at the bottom. But since she was only planning to wear this to sleep, she didn't see the point in searching further for something better suited to her stature.

And yet, even after going through the bedtime motions, then flopping face-first onto the bed, sleep still wouldn't come. The sounds of the room were few and far between and fleeting when they did happen—the windowpanes rattling with the wind, the distant sound of water in the pipes. But all that lack of sound did was make her want to fill it with the noise of people who were not here. More than anything, she wanted her friends. She would tell them everything that happened and they would tell her it was going to be fine.

Evening arrived before she finally felt sleepy. But just as her eyes fluttered closed, the sound of clacking woke her back up again.

When she sat up, there, on the end of her bed like a granted wish, was a friend.

"Alby!" She smiled broadly at the goblin. "What are you doing here? How did you find me? How did you even get into the palace?"

Alby shrugged. "It wasn't hard."

"Not hard? This place might well be the most guarded area in the realm. I know you said you were sneaky, but I had no idea. I'm glad you are."

"Me too! I was wondering where everyone went. Then Cecily and Phineas came back without you, so I thought you might be in danger! I poofed my way here, though I did get lost once and had to try again. I saw you walk down the hall and came as soon as the guards weren't looking. I am very good at not being seen when I don't want to be." His chest puffed out ever so slightly with his admission. "So why *are* you here?"

Not one to waste an opportunity, she launched into the full story, Alby listening with rapt attention. She held up her wrists to show him the bracelets when she got to that part. He ran his fingers over the metal.

"Does iron not affect you? Can you magic me out of here?" Theo asked, hope blossoming at the prospect of an escape plan.

The goblin shook his head, ears flopping. "I'm not strong enough to transport anyone but myself out of here—even without the iron." He looked at her for an awkward minute. "Well, I came to see why you are here and found out. I'll be on my way."

"Do you want to stay for a bit?" she asked, not liking the idea of being trapped alone in here.

Alby smiled, eyes wide. "That sounds nice."

Theo did not hide how glad she was to have company as they shared the food that was left in her room and talked until evening finally gave way to night. Not long after, she and Alby both fell asleep.

# Chapter 8

# Where Theo Puts Up a Fight

She opened her eyes to complete darkness and little slaps on her face. But when she went to ask Alby what he was doing, he put one hand over her mouth and a finger to his lips. Once he was sure she wasn't about to say anything, he pointed to his ears and then the door. And that's when Theo heard it, too. Something was scratching at the lock on the door to her suite. There was the smallest sliver of light shining underneath the door bisected by moving shadows cutting across the floor in jagged shapes. It took her sleepy brain only a few seconds to realize someone was kneeling in front of her door and trying to pick the lock.

Theo sat up, her bed thankfully not squeaking with the movement. She turned to Alby, his big goblin eyes watching her with fear.

"*What do we do?*" Alby whispered.

Her voice barely above audibility, she answered, "*Can you sneak back out of here?*"

Alby nodded but then said, "*What about you?*"

*"I need you to go get help. I'm stuck here. But can you find Cecily and tell her I'm in trouble?"*

At first it looked like he was going to stay, but then he hopped off the bed. Before she could really see where he went, he was gone.

Now that she was alone with no means of escape, she had to hide. But while she looked for hiding spots, she knew that the most obvious places to hide would also be the most obvious places to look for whomever was trying to break in. As quietly as she could, she scooted to the edge of the bed and stood. She did her best to pad across the floor with as little noise as possible. The rest of her suite was so silent, the only sound masking her getaway attempt was the noise of the lock picking from the very people she was trying to run from.

But wait. The wards. Arlys said there were wards in place. And plus, with these iron bracelets on, no fairy would be willing to get too close anyway—or do much about it magically if they did. So, while she didn't love the fact that someone was trying to break in, at least she'd be safe until Cecily could come and help her. Unfortunately, just as she reached this conclusion, she heard the horrid noise of the lock clicking free.

She bolted into the closet, heading straight for the ball gowns, to one in particular with a skirt the size of a small tent. She shimmied underneath and waited, ears straining to hear as the tulle muffled everything but the pounding of her own heart.

The skirt was hanging just high enough off the ground that when she put her head down to look, she could see the room through the small gap. At first, all she saw was the empty bedroom.

There was a slow thudding noise, clopping, like a bull was meandering into the room.

Two gigantic ogres lumbered into view, stopping just in front of Theo's bed. While they almost looked human, it was as if an artist, having never before seen a person, was told secondhand about what one looked like and then had to draw it from memory. They both had human-esque features, but every single aspect was somehow out of proportion to the rest. Their eyes were like little buttons on a gray hot air balloon, made all the more insubstantial compared to their droopy, warty noses, the skin covering them looking like a craggy sourdough starter. Tubby yet tiny chins were the only thing supporting thin, wide mouths, making sure they didn't slide all the way down their necks. Their legs were too short, their arms too long, their torsos too large. One ogre had some hair on the top of his head, but it had grown in like unruly grass, his hack job of a haircut continuing the sentiment, as it appeared that his hairdresser must have gone after it blindfolded and using a scythe. The other ogre was completely bald, his head like a wrinkly, overripe peach left in the sun too long.

Their shirts were probably white at some point in the past but hadn't been washed since then and now looked dirty and moist enough to grow mushrooms on. Theo didn't even want to guess what color their brown, threadbare pants had been.

They were both standing in front of her bed, studying it as though they simply couldn't believe someone wasn't in it.

"Where is she?" the first one asked, his voice so deep it rumbled in Theo's chest.

The other, using the one brain cell he owned, started to turn around, as though Theo was just simply standing behind them. When that didn't produce a body, at first he started to look at the ceiling, then underneath the nightstand, the gap so small that even if she was a hedgehog she'd have a tight fit.

"Only find, right? No kill. Just take," he said, lifting up a completely see-through glass end table that had already demonstrated no one was underneath it.

So, they were coming to take her. But first they had to find her. And as the ogres continued to search in the fireplace and behind the sheer curtains, the tiniest shred of relief began to grow. She just had to stay hidden until Cecily got here, which wouldn't take long. The feeling sat comfortingly in her chest until the big ogre said, "Check the closet."

There was nowhere to go, and no place to run, as an ogre grabbed her by the arm and yanked her out from under the dress. The moment his meaty hand wrapped around her forearm, she belted out a scream that would have shattered him had he been made of crystal, the pitch so high and out of tune she was surprised neither her ears nor his were bleeding.

While her vocal cords did most of the heavy lifting in her attempt to not be kidnapped, her limbs were no slouches, either. She was a water droplet on a hot pan, sizzling with adrenaline and fear, arms and legs having no discernible direction other than *not this spot*. The ogre holding on to her was also so surprised at her level of rabidness he nearly let her go before his other hand came up and pressed over her face, his palm so large it covered not only her mouth but her eyes as well.

His efforts did stop her screaming, but not her flailing. She reached out for anything that she could hold on to, but instead of grabbing something substantial like the doorframe as he moved out of the bedroom and into the main room, or a large piece of furniture, she managed to grip on to the ogre's pants, her fingers finding purchase on the loose fabric around his pocket. Her grip plus the force exerted on her from the ogre trying to wrest control over what was now the human equivalent of a windmill meant that his pant seams were first to give up the fight. The contents of his now-pointless pocket scattered on the floor. The ogre released one hand to check that his pants were still on his body, and she used the opportunity to go with a new tactic.

With her free hand not holding the remnants of an ogre's pants, she swung with purpose, hitting the ogre square on the nose with her iron bracelet. While it looked as though it would have been quite squishy, it had the solidity of wet sand, and the bracelet smashed into her wrist instead. The burst of pain made her cry out, though it was still muffled by the ogre's palm, and it was all she could do to cradle it to her chest as she continued her involuntary upward trajectory onto his shoulder.

This was it. She was well and truly captured now. He was going to walk right out of the room with her and she could do nothing to stop it.

But he didn't take more than a half step before he dropped her.

The floor was an unforgiving landing spot for her tailbone, the pain of that so shocking she almost didn't see the ogre falling directly over her. He had gone completely stiff, eyes glazed, tipping slowly at first, like a tree cut at the base. Theo did her best to scoot backward out of the way but was hindered by the nerves shooting through her body from her bottom and only made it a few inches. Had she remained where she was, she would have been smooshed so flat they could have rolled her up like a carpet. Just a hair's breadth separated her from the ogre crashing face-first into the floor hard enough to rattle her bones.

Standing where the ogre had been was Lock. Had she not known about fairy magic, she would have thought he took down her assailant solely with his expression. His brows looked like they were about to crush the bridge of his nose, his mouth twisted into a silent snarl.

But while his face said *murder*, the rest of him said *chamomile tea and a snuggly blanket*. He was wearing merino long johns with fluffy woolen socks. He must have been sleeping hard when he was woken up because his customary slicked-back hair was rising up and over the side of his head like a cresting wave.

She didn't linger too long staring at Lock, though, considering that there was another ogre who had tried to kidnap her, but when she looked to him, she found he hadn't fared much better. He was also in a heap on the floor, Cecily poised over the body. Like her brother, Cecily was in her pajamas, her usually coiffed hair simply braided and very askew. Unlike Lock, she was in a flowy, satin nightgown.

A hand gripped Theo's elbow. She turned to see Phineas holding on to her, looking her over as he helped her to her feet. "Are you hurt?"

"No. No, I'm fine." Theo wasn't sure that was true, but for the sake of not returning to her screaming state, she went with it.

"Are they dead?" Theo asked while Cecily prodded an ogre with her foot.

"No, just incapacitated," Cecily replied.

Subdued to unconsciousness, but at least alive. Good. Then at least someone could question them about who sent them and why.

Next to the ogre that had held on to her, she could now clearly see what had spilled out of his pocket. Theo moved closer and picked up a folded piece of paper and a small cloth drawstring bag, heavy and jangling with the movement. When she opened it, she found a mix of coins inside.

"What is that?" Lock asked.

"I'm not sure," she said.

Just as she went to unfold the paper, frantic footsteps resounded down the hall.

With nowhere to hide it on her own person, she tossed the bag to Phineas.

"Hide this," she hissed. He quickly shoved the bag into his pocket. Theo stuffed the paper down the front of her nightgown, removing her hand just as the footsteps reached the room and the palace guards came pouring in, Arlys in the lead. A very unimpressed Cecily, now done with her inspection of the ogres, came to stand next to Theo, crossing her arms.

"What are you doing here?" Arlys shouted. "Step away from the princess!"

Cecily did no such thing as the rest of the guards took in the scene in front of them. "As to your question," Cecily said, "we rushed here as soon as we heard our currently defenseless Theo was in danger and managed to subdue her attackers." She pointed to the ogres. "And well done asking the correct question, Arlys: What *are* we doing here? Why did we need to rescue Theo? Where were you while this was going on?"

"We were only just alerted to interlopers being present in the room," Arlys said.

There was a flurry of activity at the door as even more guards, twenty at least, now piled into the room. Behind them, Tace, Aimon, and Ursula took in the scene like a fractured tableau, their eyes darting every which way to try to comprehend what had happened.

"What is the meaning of this? What is going on here?" Tace shouted, not having come up with any answers by himself.

Arlys turned to the regent. "There's been an attack, Your Highness."

"I'd define it more as a kidnapping attempt," Cecily said.

Arlys continued as though Cecily had not interrupted. "Two ogres. We managed to subdue them."

"*Excuse me?*" Lock sputtered, unable or unwilling to match Cecily's level of composure. "My sister and I managed to knock them unconscious before they left with Theo and *then* you showed up."

"Arlys, is this true?" Tace asked.

While Arlys didn't speak, his normally pallid complexion now looking like it was on fire from the inside said enough.

Tace didn't press the issue, but he looked back at Lock, who had now moved to stand next to Theo and Cecily.

"How did you two get here anyway?" Tace asked the siblings.

Theo spoke up instead. "I heard the ogres trying to pick the lock. My friend was with me and he left to alert Cecily at my behest." At the mention of Alby, the goblin appeared behind Cecily and gave a little wave. He must have returned only moments ago, apparently not content to be left behind at the manor.

Theo thought Tace was about to blow, but instead, he ran his hands through his already messy hair as a cracked, strangled noise came out of him. Theo realized it was a sob.

"This was a terrible idea," Tace said, mostly to himself as he struggled for composure. "She's not safe here. We are not ready." And then, even quieter, "I can't lose her. She's all I have left of my family. I can't lose her."

Aimon, who had up until this point looked unsure at the goings-on, went to his partner's side. "Tace, my love," he said, gently taking the regent's hands. "We won't let that happen."

Ursula, seizing her moment to take charge, turned to the guards standing by the wall. "Take these ogres to the dungeons." With every word out of her mouth, she seemed to grow in stature, bolstered by the rapt attention. The guards, finally having something to do other than stand silently and watch the effects of their failures, split into two even groups and went to the ogres.

Arlys, though, was not bothering to even pretend to be listening to the regent's partner's mother, who ostensibly had no authority whatsoever. Instead, he was conferring with another guard, the conversation too quiet for Theo to make out from where she was. Ursula spoke again, ignoring the fact that she herself was being ignored. "Now, you," she said, snapping her fingers at Arlys.

Even Theo raised her eyebrows at that.

He stopped talking and turned to her as she continued, Ursula either unaware or unconcerned that she was not being dutifully obeyed. "From you, Arlys, I want a full report on how this even happened. On how two lumbering ogres the size of carriages managed to sneak into this palace and into this room all without being noticed by you."

If his employment as a bodyguard didn't pan out—and it was looking more and more like that would be the case—Arlys could certainly find work in a bathhouse with the steam now erupting from his ears. But, with what must have been hundreds of years of control, Arlys managed a calm "With all due respect"—which Theo guessed was none at all—"I do not answer to you."

"But you do answer to me," Tace interjected. "And you will do as Ursula instructed and spell out for me how your ineptitude nearly cost us the princess!"

Arlys's nod was nigh imperceptible as he acquiesced.

Ursula, even more bolstered by the backup from Tace, continued. "Given this astounding security lapse, I think it pertinent to conduct an independent investigation. With your blessing, I shall contact my associate, Perran of the Hornbeam Fairies, as I do believe he will be impartial."

"Absolutely not," Arlys said. "I will be conducting the

investigation, and I do not need any assistance besides my own people who I trust."

Theo couldn't help but notice Aimon during their standoff. He was watching them, eyes darting from one to the other with a look of concern like they were tossing the wedding china to one another instead of words. Just as Ursula unclenched her jaw to add more, her son spoke up with his signature soothing tone.

"Now, Mother, we all agree you have a great plan, but Arlys will also need to conduct an investigation. How about this, everyone? We will bring the ogres to the dungeons for Arlys to question." He held up his hands when his mother looked like she was about to protest. "But we will allow Perran access to them as well when he arrives."

It struck Theo then that she had actually never heard Aimon talk in a voice that wasn't calming and filled with ways to mollify the situation. And it was the slight fear in his eyes that had her wondering if maybe he'd had to do this his whole life. Especially with his mother.

Regardless, his method worked. Tace considered Aimon's suggestions. Then, turning to the guards, he reiterated them. The guards gave quick, jerky nods in response to the regent's orders, then proceeded to carry the unconscious ogres out the door.

"A wise decision, Your Highness," Ursula said as though it was Tace's idea all along, while Arlys ground his teeth together.

"Excellent," Cecily said. "While that gets done, I will be taking Theo home." Theo could think of nothing better than to be in her own bed again.

"I'm afraid that won't be possible," Tace said with a solemn expression. "She is not safe there."

"His Highness is correct," Ursula said. "Cecily, Locklan, you are dismissed."

Cecily merely smiled at her aunt. Unlike her cousin, she was not in the habit of pacifying anyone, ever. And it seemed she wasn't about to pick up the hobby now. Meanwhile, Theo was surprised she couldn't hear ringing coming from Lock as he vibrated like a tuning fork with the strength of his anger. "She's certainly not safe here!" he shouted.

Tace held up his hands. "I agree with you on that. Which is why she won't be staying here, either. We have made a mistake bringing her back. Clearly the murderer is still at large."

Aimon, a hand on Tace's back, said, "If someone can get to her here, they can get to her anywhere, Cecily. Bringing her back to your house would just make you unsafe as well."

Cecily clicked her tongue. "I know that works on everyone else in your life, dear cousin, but don't get your hopes up that your tone will stop me from rocking boats."

"Honestly," Ursula cut in, exasperation tainting her poise. "Enough of this nonsense. You have thwarted His Highness at every turn, refusing to remove yourself from this situation."

"Thwarted? Goodness. Vapid ne'er-do-well to calculating schemer." She smirked at her aunt. "You flatter me."

"No one has actually asked me what I want to do yet," Theo interjected, finally sick of simmering in silence while everyone continued to talk about her instead of with her.

"Oh, Theo, always bringing up the important questions. You are absolutely correct, my darling," Cecily said. "What do you want?"

"I want to go home."

"See? There you have it. By royal decree, the princess would like to leave. To *our* home, Tace."

Tace shook his head again. "No. No, Aimon is correct. You are not only putting the princess in danger, Cecily, but yourself. The killer could just as easily go after you to kill Amabel."

Even Ursula startled at that, and for the briefest of moments, she gawked at Cecily, as though the thought of her niece being in danger never crossed her mind. But it sure did now. "He's right," she gasped. "How could you be so careless?"

Having a familiar's life tied to and contingent on their fairy was a sort of built-in fail-safe for fairies so their underlings couldn't just kill the fairy to get out of the deal. But it also made familiars dangerous when they wanted to leave, hence why killing off familiars was a very popular method for their removal. Though it had never occurred to Theo that someone else would want to use that method to get to her. Nor had it dawned on anyone else in the room, either, given everyone's faces now morphing from confusion to horror to outright hostility. Except for Lock, who had decided to stick with shock as he took in his sister and Theo.

Though Theo was getting there, too. Because anyone using Cecily to get to her would also be killing Phineas.

"For that reason," Tace said to Theo, "we will be putting you back into slumber."

Theo jerked back. "Slumber?! Like I supposedly was for a thousand years before I took the place of a child who died?"

"Precisely."

"And then what? Wait another thousand years to bring me back again?"

"Yes."

"Will I keep my memories?"

"Probably not."

"Well then, here is my own simplistic and unhelpful answer: no. I'll have no part in your princess slumber flight of fancy, thank you."

"An answer both concise and clarifying," Cecily said with an approving nod.

Tace balled his fists. Aimon held up his hands and moved them toward Tace like he could physically put back the anger roiling off him. "Now, now, my love. Let's all take a moment and talk this through. After all, it is still the middle of the night. Why don't we all have a lie-down, a nice breakfast tomorrow morning, and then we can discuss this?"

"And who is going to keep her safe until then?" Tace cried. "Him?" He pointed an accusatory finger at Arlys, who looked ready to bite it off. "No, that will not be happening. I know you mean well, Aimon, but she is the last family I have left. My last and only heir. I can't let anything happen to her."

Aimon's eyes flashed in the smallest bit of hurt, but before he could carry on, his mother stepped in. "Your Highness," Ursula said, "I think we should move her to another section of the palace and she can be kept under lock and key until we decide the best course of action."

It did not get past Theo that Ursula's idea was just her son's, uncredited and rehashed in a harsher way.

"I did not ask your opinion on this," Tace shouted at her, his earlier deference vanishing with his rationality. Tace, Aimon, and Ursula—with the occasional gruff response from

Arlys—carried on, each trying to figure out what to do with the princess now. But the more this went on, the more people disagreed with him, the more Tace dug in his heels.

But by this point, Theo could think of only one thing: *Enough.*

Theo knew that unless she did something to save herself, this was not going to go well for her. Thankfully, during Tace's tantrum and Aimon's coddling, no one noticed Theo stepping closer to Cecily.

"*We need to get out of here,*" she whispered to the fairy.

Instead of answering, Cecily discreetly flicked a nail on Theo's bracelets. Theo understood what she meant—there would be no transporting.

But that wasn't Theo's plan. The fairies were used to magically solving their problems, including escape attempts. What they wouldn't expect was the very human solution of making a run for it.

*"I need a distraction."*

Cecily responded to that with a raised eyebrow and a smirk. She said something Theo couldn't quite make out to Lock and then took a few almost imperceptible steps away from the group, Phineas in tow.

"Ready?" Cecily said to her, not bothering to whisper.

Theo nodded.

"Then here we go. See you soon, darling."

She had only just finished saying it when Lock pulled Theo into a tight embrace as the suite exploded.

# Chapter 9

# Where Nightgown Hems Are Not to Be Underestimated in Preventing Slumber

A boom like a firework thundered and sizzled while she was tucked in tight to Lock. For all Theo knew, it very well could have been a firework that was launched at the guards and regent, since acrid black smoke accompanied the noise. Theo realized after the explosion why Cecily had moved away from Theo. There was no way the fairy would have been able to create magic that large standing next to the iron Theo was wearing on her wrists. Theo didn't even want to think about what the explosion would have been had no iron been present—the palace would have been missing a wing.

But what a distraction it was. The guards around them were

mostly on the floor, coughing and moaning. Someone in the corner was simply repeating, "*Ouch, ouch, ouch.*"

Time to go. She grabbed Alby's hand as Lock took her other. Lock seemed to have caught on to the plan quickly as Theo pulled both of them through the disarray to the door. She didn't know who was blocking their way, the smoke too thick to see much farther than her own nose. But when Lock pulled her to a stop, she heard the distinct sound of flesh meeting flesh, and then someone next to them hitting the ground.

The trio burst through the door and began sprinting down the hall, Lock still with a vise grip on her while Alby dangled off the ground like a flailing suitcase.

But the unfortunate sounds of a singular pursuit followed them.

"Stop!" shouted a voice behind them that they did not listen to. Theo turned her head to see Arlys nearly flying down the hall after them. He had been in the front row of the explosion, his face and shirt covered in soot as though he took a nap in a doused fireplace.

Lock, the fastest of the trio, ran in front, yanking her and Alby along. "Faster, Theo!"

They were coming up on a sharp turn, and unless they were planning on barreling straight through the wall in front of them, they would need to slow down.

Arlys, an apparently accomplished runner, was right on her heels, his arms outstretched, hands poised to grab her. Theo wasn't known for her sprinting abilities, and certainly not in a long nightgown. When needing to move quickly in any sort of lengthy dress, it was wise to use at least one hand to grab the extra fabric at the bottom and hold it out of the way of running legs. As Lock was holding one hand and Alby the other, Theo's were otherwise occupied. At almost the exact moment Arlys's fingers brushed her upper arm, her foot hooked the hem of her nightgown. How fast she was running, coupled with the force now exerted on her, meant she went straight down, hitting the hallway floor like she was belly flopping into a swimming pool. Her lungs revolted at the sudden impact and all her breath was knocked out of her. And because she was holding their hands so tightly, she took her friends down with her.

Now they weren't a target so much as an obstacle that Arlys had no time to react to. Instead of clasping her arm, he tripped over her like he had been launched from a catapult. Theo looked up in time to see him soaring overhead, arms flapping like a copper-haired duck trying to take flight, only to smack into the stone wall face-first at the speed at which he'd been running. His nose made a cracking sound like the snap of a branch. He tumbled down, landing in a jumble, dazed and groaning.

She scrambled to her feet, Lock and Alby doing the same. "We have to go!" Lock said through labored breaths. Far down the hall, other fairies were starting to leave the still-smoking suite.

"Wait! We can't leave Cecily and Phineas! They'll be taken to the dungeons!" Theo said.

"Not likely," Lock said. "She's probably already transported herself and Phineas out of here. We'll catch up with them soon. Now, come on!"

Lock took hold of Alby, leaving Theo's hands free to hold her dress up and out of the way as they ran.

In fairness to Theo, she hadn't had time to figure out the best strategy for escape before implementing this one. But it was only when she was sprinting through the corridors of the palace that she realized a major flaw in her plan. She had no idea where she was running to after she got out of the palace. Because she'd always been brought by Cecily to the palace, Theo had never thought about just how far away her home was from here. And with that infernal iron on her wrists, her only means of escape was just how fast her feet could carry her.

Goblin dangling from one hand, Lock began trying door handles, finding most of them to be locked. But finally one turned and they ducked inside. He shut the door behind them as quietly as he could.

Theo was already to the window, throwing open the sash. Thankfully, they were still at ground level, so the risk of harm while defenestrating herself was minimal. Still, she landed hard, sinking to her knees before standing to help Alby out of the window. He jumped into her arms and she set him gently down. Lock followed after, having the distinction of being the only one landing with any poise whatsoever.

Once again, she found herself in the garden. The party was still going strong and would be for another six days, so the revelers were too busy with their champagne and food to notice a fairy, a human, and a goblin jumping out the window. Lock pulled them along, walking just fast enough to get to some of the lesser-used paths, but not fast enough to arouse suspicion. When they got to the quieter parts of the garden, they were able to pick up the pace; the only people who could have been witnesses were either drunk or sleeping.

Over the bluebell river and through the woods the trio kept running until they were past the far reaches of the garden and into the forest. By this point, Theo's lungs were crackling like kindling and her legs felt like putty.

"Lock," she wheezed. "I have to stop. Will we be safe here for a moment?"

Lock thankfully slowed, slightly out of breath himself. Alby was the only one not winded, since he had the benefit of being carried the entire way.

While she tried to slow down her breathing and heart rate, Lock kept watch of the direction from whence they came. The forest was silent, the bugs and birds of the night not appreciating the intrusion. All the better, though, since now any twig snap or rustled branch would be heard without any interference.

"I need to get these bracelets off," Theo said, holding up her wrists. Lock stepped up to her, grabbing a wrist but keeping his hands well away from the iron. Even still, he shuddered. He was looking for what Theo already knew he wouldn't find—any way to free her from them.

"And clothes on," she said, looking down at her nightgown that was doing the bare minimum against the cold night.

"I can do neither with that iron." Lock let her arm drop and rubbed his face. "I don't know how to get those off. My magic won't work on them."

"Well, can you get a saw?" Theo asked.

"What?"

"We can saw off the bracelets."

Lock shook his head. "Any one I conjure with magic wouldn't work."

"So go actually get one."

Lock's eyebrows raised in surprise and then tilted back down in annoyance over not thinking of such a simple solution. "Fine. You two stay here and remain quiet. I'll be back."

With that, he moved farther away from her and thus the iron. His figure disappeared before the sound of his footsteps on the forest floor, and quickly thereafter, those vanished as well. Theo watched the spot where she last saw Lock, hoping he would return instantaneously. Because now that she was alone with Alby in the woods, she was regretting having him stay by her side—presently in more danger than if he had hunted down tools. He came to stand next to her and grabbed her hand, giving it a light squeeze. Then, with enough earnestness and honesty to shrink Pinocchio's nose back into his face, he looked up at her and said, "Theo, I will do everything I can to keep you safe until Lock comes back."

Footsteps sounded in the forest and they both froze, until Lock bounded back to her side, saw in hand. Being away from the iron on Theo also meant he could change out of his pajamas finally, and he was now wearing actual clothes.

He also wasn't alone. Walking with him were Cecily and Phineas.

Cecily had changed and was no longer in her nightgown. She was in her customary sultry dress, this time a snug-fitting burgundy lace number that ended just above her ankles. The sight of it brought an odd comfort to Theo. Things might be literally and figuratively exploding around her, but this small glimpse of normality was a flickering candle flame in the dark. "Well," Cecily said. "After my fiery demonstration, I don't think we'll be invited to the palace anytime soon."

"Ah, but what a show," Phineas said, stepping up to give Theo a hug. He, too, had changed out of his pajamas and into breeches and a smart jacket.

"How did you find us?" Theo asked.

Cecily waved a casual hand. "Easy. Lock and I have a meetup spot. Not frequently used as such, but I don't often explode royal suites and take a princess on the run. And good thing, too! I'd love to go straight back to the manor and sleep in my own bed, but seeing as how everyone in said incendiary suite knows where I live, I've decided we should find another place to hide out. Lock came by after grabbing this tool and explained you were still stuck in the woods behind the palace."

Her mentioning the tool had Lock holding up a hacksaw the length of his arm.

"This ought to do it," he said.

However, instead of the moonlight glinting off shining teeth ready to cut through iron, the blade was speckled with rust, as though the tool had come down with a very bad case of the pox. It was questionable whether the saw would come out the victor in the matchup against the iron bracelets or if the teeth would snap off on contact.

"Did you find that at the bottom of a pond?" Theo asked as Lock motioned for her to put her arms out. Theo would just have to hope that if he nicked her skin with the blade, he'd get the bracelets off fast enough to save her from lockjaw.

"It was the best I could do on short notice. And unfortunately, this one also has a bit of iron in it. I think I might be sick," he groaned.

Cecily and Phineas moved in to help, one holding Theo's arm steady, the other holding the bracelets in place. The three of them crowded over Theo's wrists to the point she couldn't even see what they were doing, knowing only that Lock was sawing. He was doing it in short bursts, presumably to keep the noise to a minimum. Alby was pacing around them, his eyes on the woods, keeping watch.

"What happened after we left? How did you two get out of the palace?" Theo asked Cecily.

"We took advantage of the pandemonium in your room and took off in the other direction."

Lock cut through the first bracelet. Theo not only felt it physically come off of her wrist, she felt the release of the iron's hold on her magic, too. It was like one's sinus clearing after a cold—she could almost breathe again, but the other half was still stuffed up. Cecily was holding the bracelet out in front of her like it was a dirty diaper she needed to keep far away from her. She took two steps backward and threw the iron as far into the woods as she possibly could. Then the group got to work on the second one.

What Theo wanted to do after that was convince everyone that she was not the princess. But how could she convince them of something she's not? She could say she's not a teapot and they would still say *prove it*. And the more pressing matter was that those who wanted to put her into slumber, as well as the mystery murderer, believed that she was.

What she needed was a plan. Step one being getting these bracelets off. Step two being finding somewhere safe where she could formulate a plan of how to keep herself alive. A few short seconds after, the second bracelet was cut and summarily thrown into the woods. The saw followed soon after. Step one complete.

"Great," Theo said, massaging her wrists and relishing all her magic returning. "Let's go."

But a voice rumbled from behind them, "You are not going anywhere."

# Chapter 10

# Where Theo Makes a Bargain No One Is Happy With

Arlys, still coated in soot, his hair a tangle of knots and singed ends, and now with blood spattered on his face and all down the front of his bland ensemble, had somehow managed to sneak up dangerously close to them. Theo had seen his emotions range from mildly annoyed to intensely angry, but he was reaching new depths here in these woods. If she didn't know better, Theo would have been safe to assume his burnt self was the result of anger-induced spontaneous combustion.

But before she had any time to move away from him, he lunged, grabbing her by the arm and yanking her backward. "Princess Amabel, you're coming with me back to the palace," he growled.

Having been taken wholly by surprise, Theo let out an

involuntary shriek. Lock, meanwhile, grabbed Theo's other arm, trying to pull her back toward the group. Since only her legs were free, Theo attempted to help by kicking out at Arlys.

Suddenly, from the direction of the palace came the sounds of pursuit—crunching leaves underfoot, branches being pushed out of the way, and the shouts of guards telling one another exactly where their target was, Theo having announced it for them.

Arlys turned his head just a bit toward the oncoming noise. Theo expected he would call out and let them know his exact location, but not only did he stay quiet, he tried to tug her in a new direction away from the guards.

Why would he not alert them?

No matter what, Theo had no desire to be dragged back to the palace. Thankfully, Cecily agreed. Right before the guards spilled out around them, the group vanished.

---

In a blink, they went from one forest to another, this one even darker than the woods outside the palace. Unfortunately, Arlys had managed to hold on to Theo and was thus transported with the group.

At first he was still trying to pull her away from her friends, not bothered by Theo continuing to kick him in the shins.

"You don't even know where we are and you can't magic me out of here. Let go!" Theo shouted as Cecily, Phineas, Lock, and Alby surrounded him.

After taking stock of the scene, surprisingly, he halted and released her.

He held up his hands in surrender. "Fine. I just want to talk."

"That's a bald-faced lie, but do go on," Cecily said. He glared at her before turning his attention back to Theo.

"Listen to me," he said, speaking slowly, directly to Theo, hands still up in front of him. "You are in danger. I am trying to protect you. I have spent my life protecting you. I have been one of your secret keepers for a thousand years. Keeping watch while you were in the human realm. You must go back into slumber. For the sake of not only yourself, but Cecily and…" He stole a glance at Phineas, clearly not knowing what his name was. "Him."

Theo shook her head. "Finding my would-be assassin would accomplish the same goal, you realize. You'll have to do better than that if you want to convince me to throw away my memories on your whim."

She had every intention of ending the conversation right there, but Theo latched on to something else he said. "Wait, what did you mean when you said 'keeping watch' when I was human?"

He nodded solemnly. "You wouldn't have noticed me, but yes. In disguise, I would come to your estate to check in to see how you were."

"You were spying on me? My whole life?"

"Yes."

Memories prickled the back of her mind. Little snippets of odd encounters with strange people over the years, who often behaved quite similarly to Arlys at the parties, now that she thought about it. Acting like a person who thought they knew how someone should behave, but couldn't quite get it right. "Were you that questionable delivery driver who pulled up to the front of the house instead of the back and then didn't know what or where the scullery was?"

Arlys stared at her.

"And the excruciatingly daft tailor's assistant who kept pricking Flo with pins because you kept looking over at me but not in a complimentary way?"

He frowned.

"What about the footman who only lasted one day because my mother found him wandering the halls after dinner?"

"No, not that one."

"Oh. Just a poor hiring choice, then."

Arlys shook his head, his frustration creasing his brow. "Not the point. But I have your best interests at heart. Come with me back to the palace and we can be done with all of this. They can come, too." He gestured to Cecily, Lock, Alby, and Phineas. "You can have a chance to say your goodbyes."

Lock scoffed. "Your offer is that you'll allow us to, for all intents and purposes, watch her die?"

Theo crossed her arms. "No, thank you. I wonder what you're like when you think you aren't being magnanimous."

Arlys took a deep breath that Theo assumed was meant to steady him, but she could see the tendons in his neck twitching. He took a step closer to the group, to which Theo took a step back. With the same speed he'd used to grab her earlier, he lunged. But instead of reaching for Theo, he grabbed Alby.

The little goblin screamed as he was pulled from the ground

by the scruff of his collar, Arlys holding him out like a shield in battle. "I didn't want to have to do this, but you've left me no choice," he growled. "If you want this goblin to remain unharmed, you will come to the palace with me and be put into slumber."

Theo was surprised her hair hadn't lit on fire with the lava-temperature anger roiling through her now. But she managed to keep her voice even. "Then it seems we are at an impasse. You won't let my friend go until I come with you, and I will not be coming with you because you are holding my friend hostage. You said you are trying to get me to come with you because you want to help me. Then help me. Let me escape."

"Absolutely not," Arlys gritted out through clenched teeth.

She could see that Cecily, Lock, and Phineas were also trying to figure out a way to end the standoff, each shifting from foot to foot, seeing if they could find any opportunity to help Alby. Sadly, they were limited in scope as well since no one wanted to use magic to solve this. If anyone hit Arlys with a magical offensive maneuver, Alby would also be on the receiving end. Almost a moot point anyway. Theo had learned from witnessing many drunken fights that fairies knew how to block one another's magic because, should they not know how, fairies would be blasted to bits on a nightly basis.

Also, as much as she loved her friends, none of them were on their way to a second career as a prizefighter. So the physical fighting was off the table, too.

Alby was crying now, and Theo was close to that outcome as well. She was trying to be reasonable. She was trying to save the situation, her friend, and herself.

What she needed was her own bargaining chip. Unfortunately, Arlys did not have any small friends with him whom she could hold hostage in return.

But... bargaining.

*Oh.*

She did have one.

Like a corpse flower blooming, its rotting stench permeating everything around it, so, too, did a terrible idea. No matter what, Arlys, Tace's guards, and the assassin were going to keep coming for her. Her options were already extremely limited, regardless of whatever she did now.

Her new idea would add complications to her basic plan of *run for it*, but it would also solve at least a few of her current problems. She just had to convince Arlys to go for it.

"You will come with me—" Arlys tried again.

"I will make a bargain with you!" Theo blurted out, a chorus of *What?* ringing out from the rest of the group.

But she had Arlys's attention. "You can't take me back to the palace unless I want you to. I think I have been quite clear that your demand has been denied; you can't force me. So let's make a deal. You will give me two weeks to find whoever is trying to kill me. When the two weeks are up, if I have not named the killer, I will go with you willingly. Then you can take me anywhere you want."

"No," came the replies from most of the group—Arlys with anger, Lock and Phineas with abject panic. Cecily just tilted her head.

"Come with me if you want," Theo tried. "Follow me the whole time."

"You won't survive two weeks from whomever is trying to kill you," Arlys said. "I'll give you five more minutes, maximum, before I end this."

"A week and a half, then."

Arlys's arm faltered, just a fraction. Theo went for the throat. "I want you to consider my offer very carefully, because it is a very good deal for you. You have already erred by holding my friend hostage in an effort to control me. This next part is vital—you will regret crossing me. That is a promise. I will make your life so difficult you'll wish the assassin had done their job. You'll think a plague of locusts is a relaxing break from me. Don't for a moment think that I don't know how to strike you where it hurts. Make the deal."

Cecily chuckled. "Believe you me, Arlys. She means it."

Lock shouted from behind her. "Theo, no! You can't!" She waved him off, focusing on Arlys and Alby.

Arlys still held the goblin but lowered his arm. "Two days."

"Two? A week," she countered.

"Three."

"Four."

Arlys was staring at her with a mix of confusion, incredulity, and, like seasoning in his soup of emotions, a hint of hostility. But just as she thought he would turn her down and she'd have to come up with another goblin-saving scheme, he said, "You will have four days to find the killer. Not just name them—find them. I will accompany you for the entire four days. At the end of those four days, at the stroke of midnight, if you do not find whoever is after you, you will return to the palace with me and be put into slumber." Then, as an afterthought, he added, "And I will release the goblin immediately if you agree to the bargain."

"Four days, then," Theo said, ignoring more protests from behind her. "If I don't find the assassin, I'm yours."

Arlys nodded.

"Also, you can't tell anyone we're here," she added. "You can't give my location to anyone. Or the location of anyone else with me. Or the location of... wherever we are right now. And you will not touch any other friend of mine. You will not use them to threaten me. You will not transport them anywhere."

It was a bit shallower this time, but he nodded again.

The terms she herself introduced were not only impossible—she only realized just how monumentally ridiculous they sounded when he said them back to her. How was she going to solve a thousand-year-old murder in the span of less than a week? She wasn't.

She knew she didn't have a chance at succeeding. Arlys could have bargained with twenty minutes and she would have taken the deal.

She needed to free Alby. Plus, when she didn't complete the bargain, she would owe Arlys her life, thus claiming her as his familiar to do whatever he wanted with. Which meant that Cecily would no longer need to find someone to replace her. Additionally, with Theo's familiar arrangement with Cecily concluded, Cecily, and by extension Phineas, would no longer be a target.

Theo knew how to make a fairy bargain.

So, much to everyone's dismay, excluding Cecily, she said, "Then it's a deal."

Satisfied, Arlys put Alby on the ground. The goblin sprinted to Theo and she knelt down to hug him close.

When she stood, she looked at Cecily.

Cecily was smirking, that very particular glint in her eye. "My, my, aren't you clever." Cecily then spoke to the group. "Cleverness runs in the Balfour household. Her stepsister excelled at it. Coming from me, that is high praise indeed. And, Arlys, Theo is better." With a chuckle to herself, she turned around and motioned for them to follow. "Consider that professional courtesy. I'm positive you'll earn what you get at the end of these four days. Now let's go inside and we can get something to eat. Blowing up royal suites really messes with my appetite."

# Chapter 11
# Where Theo Ponders Clues

Cecily turned on her heel and sauntered into the darkness, the rest of the group and Arlys following behind.

While the forest outside the palace was wild, it held on to a bit of the calm of the gardens, as though it wanted to be a part of the landscaped art. The forest she found herself in now made Theo feel as if this was the first time anyone had ever stepped foot in it. The trees were ancient, their gnarled limbs crooked and bent. Clawing ever upward, the branches looked as though they were holding up the sky, their leaves the only barrier protecting the forest from its weight. The forest floor was a carpet of moss and low-lying ferns, making the ground underfoot soft, like she was walking across a giant mattress.

"Here we are," Cecily said from ahead. And as she walked, luminaries at her feet began to light up, forming a path to a small cottage, which also began to glow from within.

The cottage sat squeezed between two trees, as though assembled elsewhere and shoved into this location like it was made of clay. Both stone and wood made up the facade, with windows sporadically placed throughout, giving no hints as to the layout of the interior. There must have been at least a few, though, as the topmost point was aligned with the treetops around it. The roof was made of slate tiles, its pitch not even close to being symmetrical, as though whoever designed it had frequent changes of heart when constructing but didn't want to undo the work already completed.

While the rest of the group was making their way up the stone path, Cecily was already at the door, throwing it open without bothering to knock. She took two steps inside but then halted and turned to face everyone.

"Right, then," Cecily said with a smirk. "Come in." She sauntered into the cottage. "Don't mind the furniture, it was built for much smaller people. Give me a moment and I'll fix it."

Theo walked in. Instead of being in some sort of entry hall or foyer, she was in one large room, not quite square, but shaped to accommodate the house's footprint. In one corner was a small table and two chairs that were made with twigs and branches, likely collected from right outside. In another corner was a seating area with a few sofas and a low table in the center. These, too, had the aura of being crafted with whatever materials could be found around the house, the cushions mostly made of moss and the table just a few planks of wood propped on top of some logs. And against the far corner, tucked in the back, was a staircase that disappeared into the floor above.

"Whose house is this?" Theo asked. "Won't they mind that we are all inside?"

"I guarantee you the owner does not mind, dear Theo, seeing as the owner is me," Cecily said. "Well, and Lock."

Yet this did not look like the home of a fairy. Cecily, noting Theo's examination, elaborated. "This is Lock's and my childhood hideout. We used to come here and play when we were little, hence the size of the furniture. Here." With a snap of her fingers, Cecily conjured a full-size table and two couches that were more appropriate for adult-size bodies, still with rustic charm, but looking like an adult crafted them this time.

Cecily pulled out a chair from the table and sat, leaning back and crossing her legs, the picture of relaxation among everyone else's tension. Theo, Lock, and Phineas took seats on the couch, and Alby sat in one of the child-size chairs, which was still a bit too roomy for him. Arlys, who wasn't about to surprise anyone with new behavior, stoically stood by the door with his arms crossed.

Cecily conjured everyone a glass of wine, including one at the empty seat across from her. "Arlys, stop looming and have a seat." At first it seemed like Arlys was going to continue doing his best impression of a disgruntled gargoyle, but he went to the table.

But before he sat, she held up a hand. "You may want to consider adjusting your ensemble. Not that I don't think this look is a much more interesting choice than your usual dreariness"—Cecily motioned to his charred outfit, blood splashed all down his front from his nosebleed—"it is just that you look like you slept in an abattoir and smell like a campfire. And given everything else that has happened already, snapping my fingers to remove the stains from my chair just wouldn't be worth the effort."

Arlys glared at her, which Cecily took no note of, but with a swish of his hand, his pants and shirt once again returned to having as much visible interest as a white wall.

"And, Theo, let's clean you up a bit while we're at it." With a snap of Cecily's fingers, Theo's nightgown was changed into a plain, cream-colored silk dress, quite comfortable for a warm summer night. "Perfect," she said, admiring her own handiwork. "Oh, and I did have an important question for you, dear Theo. Now that we know you're the missing princess, should we start calling you Amabel? Princess Amabel if you enjoy the title?"

*Absolutely not.*

"Theo is fine," Theo answered. Cecily looked ready to move on, but in part because of the fairy's nonchalance, Theo had an important question of her own. "Why do you not seem surprised about this?"

"That you're actually a fairy in disguise?" Cecily took a big gulp of wine and then shrugged. "It makes sense."

"How so?"

"First of all, you can play the fairy harp. That would normally mean you have fairy ancestry."

"She does," Lock said. "She could also play her mother's fairy harp. So, Theo, you were able to play it long before you had any part of the fairy realm."

"My *mother's* harp?" Theo asked. "Where did you get that

idea? My mother never touched that harp. She couldn't find a melody if you put it in front of her face and still gave her a map. That was Beatrice's mother's harp. Wait…that was a fairy harp?"

Lock looked at her. "You told me it was yours when I asked about it at my party."

"Oh. Right. I lied." For reasons she was not about to get into right now.

"But yes, Theo, it was a fairy harp," Cecily said. "And while I knew it wasn't your mother's harp, you could still play it. Even so, I highly doubted you had any fairy ancestor holding on to a branch on your family tree. In the human world, people with fairy ancestry are charismatic, charming, and increasingly likable. Don't worry, dear. We know that isn't you." She gave Theo a knowing look. "But it does sound like your stepsister, doesn't it?"

Theo scoffed. "How does that point to me being a changeling, though?"

"Unlike people with fairy ancestry, changelings in the human realm are not readily accepted. People tend to think they're strange, or unnerving, or uncanny, and don't generally like being around them. Though, I can't blame them. If a wolf wearing a sheep's very lovely dress told me it was simply a sheep, I'd be a bit suspicious, too." Cecily took another sip of wine. "I will confess, finding out you are the missing princess did throw me for quite a loop."

It might have been a loop for Cecily, but it was a barrel over a waterfall for Theo. Having no friends, having people not want to look into her eyes. All because she was a fairy in a disguise. One she didn't even know she was wearing. She didn't even want to think about Beatrice being loved for the exact opposite.

"Though I fully appreciate this must be very difficult to wrap your head around," Cecily said. It was. But since Cecily wasn't one to dwell, she went on as if she hadn't just taken the floor out from underneath Theo. "On to more pressing matters. Thanks to your new bargain, we only have four days to produce an assassin," Cecily said.

Arlys joined the conversation with a snort. "I'm not sure how you think you'll be able to solve a thousand-year-old murder unless you have some idea the investigators haven't tried."

Alby jumped up, waving his arms like he was in a classroom wanting the teacher to call on him. "We could go see the puca!" He looked around expectantly for everyone else to join him in celebrating his winning idea. But Cecily, Phineas, and Lock were waffling between doubt and awkwardness and Arlys was barely concealing a sneer. Theo was just confused, as she didn't even know what a puca was, and therefore didn't understand their reactions.

"Oh. Well, I thought it might be a good idea," Alby said, deflating like a sail that lost its wind.

"Why isn't it?" Theo asked the group, trying to mitigate her friend's sadness as well as relieve her ignorance.

Cecily started to explain. "Pucas tend to be—"

Arlys snorted again. "Ludicrous creatures who are real ass—"

"—unreliable," Cecily cut back in.

"But what are they?" Theo asked.

"Shape-shifters," Phineas said. "Spirits who take the form of animals and can provide prophecies, should they want to. However, they are also known for having a propensity for mischief. They'll ask for gifts and just as readily give you nonsense as predict the future."

Lock elaborated. "A puca can sometimes give information or prophecies, but many times it is one sentence wedged into complete twaddle, which turns it completely indecipherable until the thing you were asking about comes to pass, then you figure out what he meant. And if that is what happens, why bother finding out anyway? Or the puca will begin spouting information or bits of conversation that are coming to him, but most of the time they aren't for you."

Phineas held up a finger. "Or even worse, he starts getting trapped in whatever it is he is seeing and then conversation is pointless until he comes back to reality again. That could be in a few minutes, hours, or months, depending."

Alby's green complexion and the tips of his ears were flushed as he sat back down.

Lock watched him. "But, Alby, it is a good idea. We will keep it in our back pocket, all right?"

That seemed to bolster the goblin, and Theo gave Lock a grateful smile, glad he stuck up for her friend.

Looking at Theo, Arlys huffed, then added shaking his head to his repertoire of demonstrating disgruntlement. "If it was at all a viable solution, don't you think we would have tried it a thousand years ago, or any of the intervening time? For all I know, someone did, and it still hasn't produced results. There have been people working on this for a good long while. Not only is the murder a thousand years old, so are any clues. And you are no detective."

True, all Theo knew of investigative work she learned from seeing the headlines in her mother's morning paper. Which was usually all she could read of it before her mother *tsked* and found the social section. And those headlines were usually just a recap of the detectives solving the case. She knew nothing about finding clues, interviewing witnesses, or having good hunches. But Arlys was wrong about two things.

"I may not be a detective, but I did deduce this much: I'm not trying to solve a thousand-year-old murder. I'm trying to solve an hours-old kidnapping attempt. I'm going to go out on a very sturdy limb here and say the two are connected. And in regard to clues, I have some." Theo reached down her dress and pulled out the paper she had stashed there. She then motioned for Phineas to pass her the cloth bag he had hidden in his pocket.

"Where did you get that?" Arlys asked.

"The ogres," Theo said. "This came out of one of their pockets when he was trying to take me."

"Why didn't you say anything?"

Theo didn't bother with a vocal answer and let her face say what she thought about that question.

First, she upended the bag. About twenty coins, varying in size and material, rolled out onto the table. Some were as small as her fingernail, others almost as large as her palm. Some were made of gold or silver, but others appeared to be made of brass, copper, and in a few instances, seashells.

Everyone leaned in to get a closer look. It wasn't too often she came across money in the fairy realm. Fairies had no real use for it, their payments and trades made almost exclusively in bargains. Theo had seen Cecily's coins only a handful of times, but those had her embossed face on them and were mostly used symbolically as a visual representation of a bargain, should that be necessary, and it usually wasn't.

"Where are they from?" Theo asked, picking up random coins.

"All over," Cecily said. "These don't belong to anyone in particular. This, for example, is the currency of a tree nymph." She held up a brown disc made of resin.

"Why would ogres have a use for this many types of currency?" Theo asked.

"I have no idea," Cecily said.

Arlys huffed and threw the coin he was looking at back onto the table. "This only expands our list of suspects, not narrows them down. So much for a clue."

Theo didn't want to admit he was right, but the coins offered no answers. She moved on to the paper, picking it up to inspect it. While the paper was dirty, leaving Theo with the distinct feeling of wanting to wash her hands, the folds were still crisp, the edges not soft or worn. She unfolded it and spread it out on the table, revealing that it was no bigger than a postcard. Drawn on it was a very rudimentary map in black ink, made with either very little skill or very little time. But Theo recognized none of the landmarks—what looked to be a mountain range and a forest.

"Do you know where this is?" she asked the group.

"No, but we don't need to," Cecily said as she picked it up. She flipped it in her hand and then nodded. "It is bespelled to send us to this location, and then we follow the map when we get there."

"That's it? No protections on it or anything? If it is that easy, why would the ogres carry it with them? If they got caught, which they did, the location is now easily accessible."

"Maybe they didn't think they'd get caught," Lock said.

Phineas made a noise of agreement. "They weren't exactly criminal masterminds. I've seen spoons sharper than those two."

But this only raised more questions for Theo. "Why kidnap me at all? Why not just kill me? They had every opportunity."

"Excellent question, Theo," Cecily said. "But one I can't seem to answer. You were in heaps of danger, and yet they didn't finish the job."

"It seems like 'finishing the job' was to take me here," Theo said, pointing to the map. "So that's where I think we should go to find some answers."

# Chapter 12

# Where Theo Visits a Cave

True to the hand-drawn map, Theo, Cecily, Lock, Phineas, Alby, and Arlys, who insisted on coming along, were in the foothills of a great mountain range. These behemoths stood in tight formation, a phalanx of disciplined infantry, with pikes pointed to the sky, their cragged tops void of life, gray and unforgiving. Dawn was breaking, the sun peeking out from between the mountains, not yet defeating them for dominance over the horizon. Remnants of avalanches slashed down their sides like ancient battle scars.

The foothill they were on felt as if it had shrunk itself down in the face of these titans, bowing to its superiors. Theo and the others weren't on its peak, but were just above the tree line on a rugged outcrop of rocks and boulders sitting atop one another as though a giant created a precariously built cairn. The shrubs and undergrowth were short, stocky, and scarce, most deciding it wasn't worth the effort to grow in this harsh, sustained alpine weather with nothing to offer protection.

Theo was feeling the same way. The wind was biting at her skin, whipping her loose hair into a frenzy. It wasn't often Theo regretted wearing the dresses Cecily conjured for her, but wearing silk on the top of a mountain made Theo long for something warm and cotton. Though, if she was wearing any more fabric, she was likely to turn into a kite and fly right off. What she wouldn't give in that moment for sturdy pants. Theo didn't want to stand out here any longer but didn't have any idea of which way to go. The ridiculous map had marked a spot around here somewhere, but there was nothing besides rock for as far as she could see in any direction.

Cecily, still holding the map from when she used it to transport them, was walking ahead. The rest of the group followed, moving through the rocky ground, avoiding the big boulders and stepping over the small ones. Though Theo was behind Cecily, she saw it first, the others having walked right by it—the entrance to a cave. Among the slate boulders and the shadows between the rocks, the black mouth of the cave didn't stand out, even though it was a few feet taller than Theo, and wide enough to fit two people abreast.

She was about to peer in before Arlys grabbed her arm. He shook his head, then pointed at his chest, signaling he would go first. That was fine with her, as she was more than happy to pass the role of line leader to Arlys. If he wanted to play hero and walk into a hole in the side of a mountain not knowing what might be in there, she was willing to let him.

He vanished into the blackness like he'd been swallowed up. But only a moment later, he stuck his head back out and motioned them all to follow.

Arlys had conjured a lantern and was holding it up in front of him as the rest of the group went in behind him. The entrance was a switchback, changing directions abruptly, and then again once more, winding like the belly of a stone snake. But the design turned out to be quite useful. The wind outside was almost immediately silenced. And while it was still cold in the cave, the draft was gone as well.

The tunnel emptied out into a chamber. The space wasn't too large—about the size of her bedroom at home—and Arlys's singular lantern could light the space with ease. It was roughly rectangular, though its walls and ceiling were formed naturally, as opposed to hewn from the rock. But no one's head was in danger of bumping into the top, as everyone could stand comfortably in the room and still have a few feet above them to work with.

And it wasn't empty. On the far wall was a bed, the frame made from boards that were propped up on top of rocks, a layer of dried grass covered with a wool blanket making up the mattress. But the wool had been either eaten away by moths or turned threadbare by use, as enough of its stuffing was popping out of the holes to make it look like a miniature field.

A table was on the other side of the room, this also made from a combination of stone and wood slabs. Two thick logs acted as chairs. A small fireplace was built into the wall, a rudimentary fireplace crane built into the side. But while some pots were hanging near it, the crane held nothing, and looked as though it hadn't in some time, the fireplace itself void of ashes. A rustic bookshelf, made of a plank of wood balanced on some rocks, held both books and trinkets.

This was someone's home.

But whoever lived here hadn't been back for a while. There was a layer of dust on every surface, so thick it looked like freshly fallen snow. Cecily ran a finger on the table, making a track through it. "Let's have a look around, see if anything jumps out at us. Not literally, of course. Shout if that happens."

The group fanned out, searching the space. Theo went to the bookshelf, picked up a book, and flipped through its pages. It wasn't in any language she could understand and appeared to be a series of runes in patterns of squares and lines. She put it back and kept looking, examining some of the trinkets. They didn't seem to be anything other than acorn caps or dried leaves.

Theo walked slowly down the long row of books until she came to the end. Propped up against the wall was a portrait of two trolls, painted on a small slab of wood no bigger than her hand. It had the distinction of being the only item in this entire place that wasn't covered in dust. Trolls were not ones for socializing with fairies, so Theo hadn't met very many during her time with Cecily. But the few she had met were memorable enough to leave a lasting impression. Like other trolls, the two in this portrait were gray, dappled like the rocks that made up the cave and landscape. One was taller and bulkier, an arm wrapped around the slightly smaller of the two—a man and a woman. They both had gray eyes that appeared almost white, like snow on a cloudy day. Lengths of black hair cascaded down their backs. Theo turned the portrait over, hoping there might be some clue as to who they were, and found more of the same runes. She was about to put it back when Arlys came up behind her, looking at the portrait over her shoulder. "It is a dialect of troll," he said, pointing to the runes. "That says *Hodd and Skella.*"

"You can read troll?"

"Only a little. King Redren encouraged his staff to learn as many different languages as possible. We could have used magic to speak with visiting dignitaries, but the king believed it was a sign of respect that we, and thus him by extension, took the time to learn. You weren't quite at the age when you would have taken lessons, but he encouraged the fairies around you to speak in all manner of languages and dialects. He was a great man, your father."

Having no desire to encourage Arlys to wax poetic about a king she'd never met, she simply replaced the portrait.

He sneered at her lack of emotion but then added, "We'd best keep looking, then. See if we can find anything."

"And just when I thought you couldn't shock me with new behavior," Theo said.

"What is that supposed to mean?"

"Well, in the spirit of honesty, I'd have thought you'd want to sabotage all my efforts. That way, you'd get what you want."

Arlys rolled his eyes. "Why, yes. How astute. I'm actively working against trying to find the assassin. Why would I want to find the killer and thus keep the princess safe? Best make sure she can't succeed. That way, I can spend another thousand years watching over the ungrateful entity that is you."

"You're quite the enigma. Oh, I'm terribly sorry that I haven't shown you appreciation for your hard work and dedication to kidnapping attempts. And always with that sunny disposition that wins hearts and minds. As soon as we get back, I'll make sure my thank-you card and bouquet are in the mail so we can remedy your hurt feelings posthaste. And do not call me princess."

He huffed.

It was Theo's turn to roll her eyes. "I can only assume you get paid per surly mouth noise with the amount you seem to do it. Maybe next time you can delight us all by expressing your displeasure in song." Theo turned on her heel and marched the short distance to the others. But their individual investigations were finished, too, no one else finding anything of note—no drawers, no cracks or crevices, and no hidey-holes where something could be hidden. After a few minutes, the enthusiasm for the task petered out, and after a round of shrugs, they left the cave, disappointment the newest member of their cohort.

While they were investigating the cave, the weather outside took an even more dismal turn. Fog covered the mountain, obstructing the landscape enough to see only outlines and general shapes, leaving everything around them looking limewashed, colorless, and dull. The group continued working their way farther along the mountain toward the peak. But as they crested the top, the three fairies abruptly stopped, stiffening to horrified statues.

Fanned out below them was the forest from the map. It was a sea of gnarled evergreens, a rich, dark green of tangled branches speckled with small red berries, the crooked tops impenetrable for all except the tiniest of birds. The bases were thick, with bark that looked like cords of rope wound up the trunks.

"What's wrong?" Theo asked the frozen fairies.

Finally, Cecily spoke, her lips forming one single word: *you.*

"Me? What does that mean?"

Lock pointed to the trees. "No, Theo. The forest. They're yew trees."

# Chapter 13

# Where the Best Offense Is a Spiky-Butted, Sharp-Toothed Defense

A forest of toxic trees was, all at once, both a great and a terrible sign. Theo's stomach clenched as she looked down on the evergreen murder weapons. There was no forest fire raging, but even the smallest splinter could cause serious harm should any of the fairies accidentally sideswipe a tree.

But while she wasn't thrilled with the fact this coniferous battalion had their guns trained on the fairies, in this instance, being human made Theo bulletproof. That, and given how little they learned in the cave, it was currently their only lead.

"We need to leave," Arlys growled to both the group and the forest.

"On the contrary," Theo said. "I think I should go down there."

"Absolutely not," he snarled. "That is *yew.*"

Theo crossed her arms and looked at him. "Well aware, thank you. And that wasn't a question I was putting to a vote."

"It is too dangerous for you to go alone," Arlys still protested, fists clenched.

"I'm not asking you to go with me, but who says I'm going alone? Phineas and Alby can come with me. We can see if there are any clues in there and then come back out safe, sound, and unpoisoned."

Phineas frowned but agreed anyway, and Alby, thrilled to be included, ran up to stand at attention next to her.

"Superb," Cecily said. "If we're all in agreement—"

"We're not," Arlys grumbled.

"Then feel free to stay here and entertain yourself while we're gone. I saw some pretty rocks over there; you can start a collection. For the rest of us, let's get down. As long as we don't touch it or spy any forest fires, we'll be fine," Cecily said. With that, she transported everyone except Arlys down the mountain and to the mouth of the forest. Arlys came on his own a blink behind, his scowl signaling he was not appreciative of being left behind or the suggestion to take up amateur geology.

"As I have no desire to get sick and die—and I believe my fellow fairies agree—we'll wait right here for you intrepid explorers to return," Cecily said, conjuring a glass of wine and finding a large boulder to sit on. Lock joined her.

Theo, Alby, and Phineas started walking toward the forest, but they turned when they were followed by one extra set of footsteps. Arlys was behind them, prepared to join. Theo halted, but it was Cecily who spoke up again.

"You know, Arlys, the bargain disappears if you die via yew. No other fairy is going to follow her in there. So come sit. Relax. I'll get you another glass of wine. Any angrier and you're liable to start sparking. Wouldn't want to light a fire here." He swiveled his head between Theo and Cecily, but thankfully, when Theo entered the forest, he didn't follow.

The trees crested up and over them like the open maw of a great beast, the darkness inside ready to swallow them whole. The plants on the forest floor were few and far between, the evergreen leaves ensuring no light would ever reach any that tried to grow. But the ground underfoot was soft and squishy. The trio wove between the trees as they continued deeper in, and soon, the fairies they'd left behind were completely hidden from view. Theo didn't have any idea what she should be looking for and was finding nothing out of the ordinary anyway. It appeared to be a standard, if not monotonous, forest. The farther in they walked, though, the more convinced she was they weren't going to find anything. After almost an hour, she began preparing herself for this to be another dead end.

"We should probably turn around now," she said to Alby and Phineas. "I'm not seeing anything that would point to who actually cut down the yew."

Phineas nodded his agreement and the three started their walk back, a little less pep in their step.

On their return, Phineas was once again staring at her.

"Why do you keep looking at me like that?" Theo asked.

"I must say, Theo, you are quite calm about your impending slumber in four days' time. If it were me, I'd be a blubbering wreck that you'd have to scrape up off the floor. And here you are, leading a murder investigation."

"Maybe I'm confident I will complete the bargain," Theo said lightly.

He cut her a look that suggested he didn't quite believe her. "And when you do, will you become a princess?"

Theo sighed. "I have no desire to be a princess."

Phineas didn't respond, and Theo offered no further explanation—and why should she? She shouldn't have to justify not leaping at responsibility and a noble title when she just got through ridding herself of that life.

Instead, they continued on in silence.

But they had taken only a few more steps when Alby froze.

His ears were stiff and wide on his head, like a prey animal who suspects danger, eyes large as he stared at something in the distance. "There's someone in the forest."

As Theo and Phineas followed his sight line, they saw, walking from the direction they had come, a figure emerging from between the trees. It was a fairy, his telltale features becoming more and more distinguishable with every step closer.

But before the group could do anything, the fairy looked up, spotting them instantly. And it was the expression of shock that morphed into terrifying focus that had Theo shouting, "Hide!" at Phineas and Alby.

The fairy started to sprint for them.

Alby dove for a nearby tree, becoming invisible against the bark almost immediately. Phineas quickly changed into his mockingbird form and flew high into the treetops, while

Theo turned into a hedgehog and ran behind a few trees until she found a hole to dive into.

The fairy was coming closer. And when he reached the area where she was hiding, it was only her hedgehog senses that told her he had stopped running.

What was a fairy doing in this death trap of a forest?

"Princess Amabel," the fairy said from nearby, his voice light and slow. "Come out now. I am here to help you."

*Theo*, came Phineas's voice in her head. *I am giving you the benefit of the doubt and guessing you have no intention of revealing yourself.*

*Not a chance*, she replied. *Where are you?*

*Good. I'm in the tree next to you. Stay put and I'll keep an eye on him.*

*Did he see me?*

*I don't think so.*

She peered out of her hole as much as she could while still remaining hidden and was able to catch a glimpse of who was hunting for her.

If someone had told her this fairy had been chipped out of a block of ice, she'd believe it. He looked like Jack Frost—like icicles should be forming under his feet as he walked, plants shrinking and shriveling at his passing. His bone-white hair was cropped short, with spikes throughout like haphazardly grown gypsum crystals. His skin was pale and sallow, stretched tight over his skull like a drum. Glacial blue eyes were scanning the forest with an intensity that had Theo convinced he could see through the trees. There was a hollowness to him that wasn't just due to his sunken cheeks—he looked ghostly.

Only, he didn't have the fluid gait of a ghost, or a fairy, for that matter. He instead moved in choppy segments, the way a cat would sprint and halt, making sure whoever was watching couldn't guess at its next movements. And, like a cat, this fairy expertly moved through the forest, seeming to know where every rock, root, and tree was.

But what Theo couldn't reconcile, whether it was the darkened forest or her vantage point on the ground, was the strange feeling that something about him was wrong. Uncanny.

"I know you're here, Princess Amabel." His voice was as chilling as his appearance, the temperature dropping with each word. "Come with me and we'll get you back safe and sound to the palace."

He turned toward the tree Theo was hiding in and she quickly scooted backward. She could no longer see him, but he then wouldn't be able to see her, either. She could still hear his footsteps nearby, but they seemed to be moving away from her.

*Theo, RUN!* screeched Phineas's voice in her head.

Only, she didn't have time before a hand flew into the hole, grabbing her. She let out a high-pitched scream as he yanked her out of her hiding spot.

She debated turning back into a human, but that wouldn't have helped her anyway. And if anything, it would have made her a bigger target. Right now, size was on her side. Size, her quilled butt, and her very, very sharp teeth.

She curved her back, jamming her quills into his palm. And at the same time, her incisors sank into his finger like mini combat spears, followed by the metallic taste of blood bursting into her mouth. He shouted and shook his hand but continued to hold on tightly to her body.

Until the mockingbird went for his face.

Mimicking her hedgehog shriek as his battle cry, Phineas dove for the fairy, wings flapping, talons piercing any flesh he could grab. His attack had the desired effect. The fairy instinctually swatted at the bird with both hands. And as Phineas swiped across the fairy's eyes, he swung upward. Theo was flung from his hand like a shot put, only catching glimpses of the mockingbird fight as she hurtled through the air, and then rolled on the ground.

It was not the most graceful exit she'd ever made, but it was successful. Momentum had her tumbling over bumps and roots, but thankfully for every part of her body, not only was she fast to heal, but the forest floor was soft when she came to a stop.

This, however, did nothing for her sense of equilibrium. She managed to get her feet under her, but like a little drunk hedgehog on stormy seas, she completely lost the ability to run a straight line. Though this also turned out to be a benefit. The fairy had finally dislodged Phineas and was sprinting for her. But as his quarry was now not only extremely small, but also scampering in a myriad of directions, neither he nor the hedgehog had any idea which way she'd go next.

Phineas caught up again, and the fairy was once more forced to split his attention between two violent and unpredictable woodland critters. But right before the fairy could grab Phineas and gain the upper hand, he dropped to the ground, Alby having thrown a rock at the back of his knee. The fairy not only was slowed down but needed both his hands to push himself back up again. This was just the opening the three of them wanted. They wouldn't be able to overpower him, but they could make a getaway. Alby took off to the trees, again blending in seamlessly. Phineas flew skyward to the upper branches, and Theo ran as fast and far as she could into the forest.

Given how hard the fairy was trying, it was no surprise he remained persistent. He righted himself and ran right behind her. She wasn't sure how much longer she could keep going on these tiny legs that weren't used to physical exertion in either of her forms. In an effort to lose him, she wound behind and around a few more trees before finding another small hole. She leaped in. It wasn't as roomy as her first one, and he probably saw where she'd gone, but she had no choice.

And while he had already experienced and overcome her two natural defenses, she did have another idea. Using her claws, she began scraping at the inside of the tree until slivers of yew came off on the ground in front of her. She picked up the largest shard, still no bigger than a toothpick, and clutched it in her front paw. If he grabbed her again, she had a poison dagger at the ready.

She lay in wait, her little weapon shaking in her paw, her heartbeat reverberating in her ears.

The fairy's footsteps were slowing again. This was it.

But he came no closer.

She waited for what felt like ages until she risked peering out. The fairy was still slowly walking nearby, but unlike his previous look of intensity, he was searching the woods with a look of confusion—a soft expression, like he had entered a room and forgotten why.

Theo matched his confusion when he then turned around and walked back the way they had come. Soon, he was fully out of sight.

She might not be hunted in forests by mystery fairies on a daily basis, but she did know enough not to assume the chase was over and lay down arms. With her paw still gripping the sliver of yew, she seized the opportunity to leave the second hole. She had no firm idea of where she was going, only that she needed to put as much distance as possible between her and the odd ghost fairy. Since she had seen both Phineas and Alby make their escapes, her best bet was to keep going and catch up with them when she knew the coast was clear.

But a flap of wings overhead had her nearly crying with relief.

*Phineas! Are you all right?*

*No worse for wear! No one expects a face full of bird.*

*Did you see where he went?*

*He fled back the way we came. Apparently, he's given up.*

*Have you seen Alby?*

*He is running around here somewhere. I did see him get away. We'll find him.*

She didn't want to risk returning back into a human just yet, though. If by some chance he was still lingering, he'd definitely see her and she wouldn't be able to transport herself out fast enough. So she kept running.

Up ahead, a sliver of light pierced through the trees, illuminating a small section of forest in front of her. At first she had every intention of running straight past it, figuring a conspicuous bright spot was not as ideal as a dark and hidden spot for turning back into a human and transporting herself out of the forest. But when she saw what was in it, she halted.

It was the smallest fragment of a clearing, barely able to be called that at all, and instead looked as though the trees there simply forgot they could grow leaves in that direction and fanned out elsewhere, leaving only enough sunlight to illuminate that one small spot.

A fence, simply crafted with sticks and branches, reaching waist-high, formed a rectangle around the space. It seemed that whoever constructed it did so with the intent not to keep anything out—Theo could have pushed it over with her pinkie finger—but to signify what was inside. A grave.

The headstone on this singular grave site was not one that she would have found in any other cemetery she'd seen. Instead of chiseled into a shape not normally found in nature and then polished to a gleaming shine, this wasn't so much a headstone as it was just a large stone. There was no gleaming here. Unlike the rocks on the top of the mountain that were shiny from the fog and moisture, this was soft around the edges thanks to lichen that covered the surface like paint spatters. And moss had turned the back of the stone flocky and green. But it was placed too centered, too precise to be anything other than intentional.

Whether it was the strangeness of the location or simply morbid curiosity, Theo didn't know. But whatever motivated her had her scooting under the fence to get a closer look. It was only when she was right near the front that she could see runes like the ones on the back of the portrait carved into the stone.

She hadn't heard any footsteps for a good long while and the forest around her was silent and still. To get a better look, she decided to change back into her human form. Much easier to examine the inscription on the headstone without craning a neck that couldn't move in much of an upward direction. She was still clutching the toothpick of yew, and since it was currently the only weapon available to her, she tucked it into her pocket for safekeeping.

Phineas flew down to join her, changing back into his human self as well. And as he stepped up next to her, Alby stepped out from behind a tree.

"Alby! Glad you're safe!" Theo knelt down to him. "Thank you for that quick thinking with the stone. He quite literally didn't know what hit him."

"Anytime!" he said, standing just a little bit taller. Then he looked around, joining the other two in investigating the grave and headstone.

"I wonder what it means," Phineas said, pointing to the runes.

"It says *Skella*," Theo said, recognizing the shapes. "The same writing was in the cave. Arlys told me what it meant."

But unlike the portrait, there were not runes for Hodd on it. There was no need to look around the clearing for some alcove hiding another grave. This clearing was only big enough for one. So where was Hodd?

The three of them had a cursory look a bit farther around the clearing for the missing grave but found nothing.

Not knowing where the grabby fairy had ventured off to, they were hesitant to transport themselves directly back to where they started. But since Alby didn't need to conjure wind, he volunteered to see if Cecily, Lock, and Arlys were where they left them. He vanished in an instant and was back seconds later giving them the all clear.

Sure enough, when Theo, Phineas, and Alby came back, the fairies were exactly where they left them, the only difference being Arlys pacing and grumbling as opposed to standing and grumbling.

"There you are," Cecily said, gesturing with her wineglass. "I was about to give you up for lost and host a vigil. Any longer and we'd have to collect Arlys's head when it inevitably popped off his body like a pea out of a pod."

Arlys rolled his eyes but said nothing.

"Theo almost got kidnapped by a fairy," Alby supplied. To which Cecily responded with a quizzical look, Lock looked aghast, and Theo was beginning to believe that Cecily hadn't been wrong about the precarious state of Arlys's head as he fumed.

"You didn't see him run past here?" Theo asked.

"I would like to believe I would have noticed a fairy cavorting by, but just in case, what did this fairy look like?" Cecily took a sip of her wine.

Theo, Phineas, and Alby described the fairy.

Cecily nodded. "That's Perran. My vicariously vainglorious Aunt Ursula's right-hand man."

"The one she said was going to conduct an investigation into the ogres?" Theo asked.

"That very one, yes."

Lock spoke up. "But then what was he doing in the woods? How did he know you were there?"

Theo shook her head. "I don't think he did know at first. We seemed to take him by surprise, but when he saw me he knew who I was. He must have gotten the ogres to talk and they told him about the woods." She then relayed to them, to varying degrees of shock and anger, what happened. "And we found something," she said when they got to the graveyard portion of the story and the description of the strange, singular grave.

Once the recap was complete and there was nothing left to do in the woods, Cecily brought them back to the tree house.

# Chapter 14

# Where Secret Tree Houses Only Stay Secret If Everyone Keeps Them a Secret

Cecily transported the group directly into the tree house, where they all promptly found their seats again.

Theo sprawled out on the nearest sofa. Every part of her felt like it was coated in cold molasses, making it both difficult to peel her limbs off the upholstery and feel sluggish when she did. Even when Cecily conjured her a cup of tea, she was too worn out to reach it, watching the steam rise instead.

Theo's sense of time had been thoroughly battered—she could have been easily convinced a week had gone by instead of just one day. Apparently, she wasn't alone in the feeling. Cecily yawned. "I, for one, can't remember the last time I've had such a jam-packed day. If I ever complain about my social calendar again, feel free to remind me of this little adventure. So, unless anyone has another suggestion, I propose we all go to bed. And, Arlys, should you feel the strong desire to join our slumber party, I have a spare bedroom for you."

Though the sun was just barely touching the evening horizon, sleep sounded fantastic to Theo right now. The clock was ticking on her bargain, but she wouldn't be good for anything if she was asleep on her feet. Everyone else seemed to agree that bedtime should be the priority.

Leading the way, Cecily made for the stairs, with everyone, including Arlys, following along. Like the rest of the house, the stairs had a very childlike quality to them. The spindles were simplistic, made from slightly crooked branches, the railing just one long limb. As she climbed up to the first landing, Cecily pointed to a few rooms, assigning them to Phineas, Theo, and Alby, and vaguely waved a hand in the direction of another to Arlys. Theo bid everyone good night and shut her door.

The room in the tree house was nothing like her suite at home. There was a small bed tucked into the corner, covered with a simple quilt and a solitary pillow. The only other furniture was a bedside table, on which Cecily had conjured a plate with some bread and butter. Theo would save that for when she had the energy to move the knife.

As soon as she could, Theo fell into bed. For a little while, she was unsure that sleep would come for her. Her malfunctioning gramophone of a mind was spinning around and around with princesses, ogres, fairies, and magical maps leading to evergreen murder weapons. And just when she reached the end, it would start back up again with a jarring crackle. But before she realized, sleep came for her.

---

The sun was rising and thus another day was thrust upon her, pushing her ever closer to her self-imposed deadline. Cecily had stocked the small closet in her room with a few ensembles, and Theo had changed into a simple and practical lavender day dress. Who knew what nonsense she was going to find herself elbow deep in today, so she figured she might as well wear something with at least a fraction of practicality. In the same spirit, last night she had put the sliver of yew on the bedside table and made sure to hide it carefully down the front of her dress today.

She came downstairs to find Cecily, Phineas, and Alby eating breakfast at the table. Arlys was downstairs as well, but he had stationed himself near the far window and cradled a steaming mug of something, doing his best to pretend he was alone in the house. She wondered about him then, if he had a family, if he had a partner who he normally groused over a morning meal with. And yet her curiosity was not enough to outweigh her intense desire to not speak with him, so she sat down at the table to her own conjured breakfast.

Theo said her good mornings and picked at her plate. Lock came down shortly thereafter. It was the quietest meal she'd ever attended, no one bothering to make any small talk or discuss the weather.

"So," Cecily started over her mug of tea. "What is on the agenda today?"

The room stayed silent, everyone knowing full well that both clues Theo had presented yesterday had been exhausted.

"We haven't yet found Hodd," Theo said. "Do we have any way to track down a troll?"

Pulling up a bucket from his endless well of pessimism, Arlys supplied, "Who may not even be alive."

"While I'd like to think I have a more positive outlook than Arlys," Cecily said, "we unfortunately don't have that capability in our limited amount of time."

Everyone else might have looked disappointed, but Alby still seemed full of hope. He raised his hand like he was in the back row of a schoolhouse, wanting to be called on. "We could go see the—"

"Don't say *puca*," Arlys snapped.

Alby lowered his hand.

But Lock gave the goblin a small smile and a nod. "Back pocket," he said to Alby, which seemed to make him feel better.

Before Theo could lay into Arlys about his rude outburst at her friend, he said, "I need to go back to the palace. I want to ask those ogres a few questions, as well as see what Perran found out." He looked at Theo. "Princess Amabel, you are to stay here. Don't go outside while I'm gone."

"There seems to be some confusion," Theo said in return. "I do not take orders from you. And I think we've been over my thoughts on being called a princess." Having missed her window of opportunity for a sharp shot, Theo hoped her tone came off as authoritative. From the withering look he gave her in return, she felt more like a petulant child.

With no further goodbyes or instructions, Arlys strode out the door and vanished a bit beyond the walkway.

Only a moment later, Alby hopped off his chair and walked to the door, his large ears quirking toward something outside. He stood on the threshold, staring into the dark woods. Remembering this look from yesterday, Theo's stomach dropped into her shoes and she knew what he was going to say before he said it. "Someone is here."

Theo thought it would be none other than Perran, somehow having tracked them to this location, but someone else walked out of the dark toward the tree house. Make that three unfortunate someones: Ursula, flanked by two palace guards.

At the sight of her, Alby ducked back into the house, while everyone else moved out of the view of the door. Theo crept to the window, peering up slowly to get a better look.

Ursula marched toward the house like a one-woman army, her gown whipping out behind her, the delicate blue fabric now acting as her banner flag. The guards were barely more than decorative as she launched her ground advance. But their tromping was just as threatening, as it signaled they had no need for stealth.

Cecily turned to the group. "Lock and Phineas, you stay. If you're gone, she'll suspect something. And luckily, Ursula hasn't seen you yet, Theo. I'd suggest turning into a hedgehog at your earliest convenience."

Theo was about to make a run for it up the stairs. But just as Ursula reached the walkway, Cecily snapped her fingers, transporting Theo and Alby out of the house. She didn't send her familiar and goblin friend far, presumably because she didn't have very many places left to send them. Instead, they were hidden in the woods far enough away where Theo could still see the house, but the people inside couldn't see her. As instructed, she immediately took on her animal form.

But that also meant that Theo couldn't hear what was going on. Not content to be a sitting duck, she instead decided to be a moving hedgehog. Theo scampered back toward the house, climbing halfway up a tree that abutted one of the windows. Alby followed her, turning all but invisible against the tree bark.

Phineas had taken up a spot on the couch in the corner, doing his best not to be noticed. Lock and Cecily were seated on one side of the table, Lock bouncing his knee, Cecily reclined in her chair, her now-lit pipe dangling from her fingers. Ursula sat across from her niece and nephew, her eyes narrowed into slits, lips so firmly shut they lost their color. The guards, meanwhile, were clomping around upstairs, presumably searching for Theo.

Though Theo missed the first bits of conversation, she could easily tell it wasn't going the way Ursula had planned. With every syllable, Theo could hear the rumblings of anger and incredulousness trying to escape but being tamped down by Ursula's decorum. "You'll seriously have me believe your other familiar isn't here with you?"

Cecily made a show of looking around the room. "Do you see a princess here?"

"You are acting as though this is another silly game at one

of your ridiculous parties. Your life is in danger and I seem to be the only one working to fix it!"

"Not true, dear aunt," Cecily said after puffing on her pipe. "I'm here, aren't I? I had the good sense not to go back to my house."

Lock spoke up. "How did you find us here?"

Ursula leveled a look at her nephew so sour it could curdle milk into cheese. "Use your head, Locklan. This place could not be kept secret from me. You used to play here as children with Endlin and Aimon. Aimon wants nothing more than to save your life, Cecily. He gave me a list of places you could be. You're lucky he still cares a great deal for you. Otherwise, I might never have found you before the assassin." She pointed her nose that much farther to the ceiling. "Aimon understands his duty to put the needs of his family above all else."

"Ah yes, Aimon: the crème de la crème of bootlicking. Yours must be sparkling."

Ursula didn't dignify the dig with a response. "I know you see your familiars as something akin to family, but they are, at best, pets."

"Well, they certainly rank higher than goldfish in conversation."

Ursula attempted to pivot. "Then she will be far better protected at the palace than she is with you. Tell us where she is so we can protect her."

Cecily let out a surprised chirp of laughter. "I'd say the fact that you can't find her is proof positive I'm doing a far superior job than you, your son, his partner, his men, and all the king's horses as such could hope to do."

The more Cecily went on, the more Ursula's temper rose. "There is a killer out for your head, you foolish girl."

The smile Cecily gave her aunt was a lesson in condescending patience.

Not able to sway Cecily, Ursula switched targets.

"Locklan, if you know where the princess is, now is the time to tell me. You have always protected your sister, as any good brother would do. But now she is dragging you into illegal activities. It is time to say *enough*. You need to stand up to her and do what she won't: protect our family." Ursula crossed her arms and gave him a firm nod, as though she just wrapped a rousingly motivational speech.

Lock remained unmotivated. "I don't know where she is." When Lock didn't offer his cooperation, Ursula looked ready to scream. For a moment, Theo thought Ursula might actually put her whole body into it and flip the table, maybe find a tower of children's blocks to kick over. What prevented her from truly letting loose were the guards coming back down the stairs.

Ursula shuddered, as though her anger was merely a sneeze she had stifled, and took a deep breath. She turned to the guards, who shook their heads.

"Well, it seems your familiar is not here," Ursula said to Cecily, as calmly as if she had been talking about the house decor this whole time.

"As I said when we started this conversation," Cecily drawled. "Good luck finding her, though. I would offer you tea or a hefty puff on my pipe for your nerves, but I think it is best that you go. Give Endlin and Aimon my regards."

Cecily stood and sauntered over to the door, throwing it open and flicking her head to the exit.

But Ursula wasn't leaving. At least, not alone. It took Theo's brain a moment to catch up to what exactly was happening, as Ursula reached into a pocket while simultaneously grabbing on to Cecily's wrist. Before Cecily could pull her hand away, an iron bracelet was around it. At the same time, a guard seized Lock and did the same.

*No!* Theo wanted to scream. Damn that woman and her iron-nullifying necklace. She must have passed the second set of bracelets to the guards before they walked to the house.

Phineas actually did shout that, leaping up from the couch.

"I didn't want to do this, but you've left me no choice. By royal decree of Tace of the Oak Fairies," Ursula said, "Cecily and Locklan, you are both remanded to the palace for harboring the princess as well as for your own protection. You will only be released when you tell us where the princess is, or when she is caught."

"Aunt Ursula," Lock said. "You can't be serious!"

"I will not have my niece and nephew running around the kingdom with targets on their backs! You should be thanking me for saving your lives!"

Meanwhile, Cecily was standing next to her aunt with her hip cocked. "Phineas, my love, I'll get this sorted and see you soon."

Before she could say anything else, Ursula nodded to the guards. Without warning, Ursula, the two guards, Lock, and Cecily vanished.

# Chapter 15

# Where Theo Learns How Flammable Wooden Houses Can Be

The moment he was alone, Phineas ran outside. Theo saw him turn into a mockingbird and fly into a nearby tree.

*Theo, where are you?* he called.

*On the tree behind the house. I'll be right there.* She and Alby scurried down their tree and to the base of the one Phineas was in.

But before they said anything else, Ursula reappeared, walking once again to the front of the tree house.

*What is she doing back here?* Theo asked. But she didn't have to wait long for the answer.

An eerie calm had taken over Ursula as she looked at the tree house. "Princess! You have ten seconds until I burn down this house! Show yourself!"

*Wow. She hasn't so much lost her marbles as thrown them off a cliff,* Phineas said.

Theo was inclined to agree.

After Ursula's warning failed to produce a princess, she held up her hands toward the house, concentrating as mushrooms began sprouting from the ground in a circle around it. A fairy ring just wide enough for someone to leave a burning house but not leave the property entirely.

And a fairy ring just like the one Theo had been trapped in not too long ago.

Was Ursula the one who had set up the fairy ring in the woods outside Cecily's manor?

Why?

But Theo's thoughts were interrupted by flames. In fairness to Ursula, the fire did start at the top and work its way down, proof she really was trying to smoke Theo out of her perceived hiding spot like a rabbit in a den.

Even from where Theo was actually hiding now, Theo could see a manic energy dancing in Ursula's eyes, and would not have been surprised if, at any moment, Ursula began dancing for real, praying to some sort of ancient god responsible for sacrifice by fire.

But her vigil was broken when, out of the woods, a new fairy appeared. He hadn't announced himself, arriving farther back in the forest where Theo couldn't see, and she spotted him before Ursula did. Perran's unsettling aura had not dimmed in the slightest since yesterday, and he marched up behind the other fairy with his uneven walk, face blazing hotter than a childhood tree house as he watched the flames.

"What have you done?!" he bellowed without warning, making Ursula jump as her focus was ripped away from the house pyre.

While she might have been taken by surprise by his tone and presence, she did not back down from him, composing herself quickly. "My niece and nephew are not part of this," she said, her tone suggesting she knew exactly why he was here and what made him so riled up.

"You had *no right* to interfere!" Perran shouted.

"I had every right!"

"You hid them in the palace and then decided to burn down the house? Why? Do you not even want me to find her?"

"Of course I want you to find her. You're the one who let her slip through your fingers yesterday. Why do you think I'm here? I set a fairy circle to trap her. If she was in the house, she'd be forced to come out where you could get her."

Theo might not have been a detective, but it didn't take her too much analyzation to figure out they were talking about her.

"Then where is she?" Perran asked with the flat disdain of someone who already knew the answer.

"She's obviously not here."

"That's correct. In fact, thanks to you, she's probably long gone by now. All you've done with the house is guarantee she won't be coming back. Did you even bother to check the woods first? Or did you just come blazing straight into the house, letting everyone know you were here?"

"Why would I bother checking the woods?"

"Because she can turn into a hedgehog, you daft twit! And Cecily's other familiar can turn into a mockingbird. I would bet they were watching the whole time you were here." Theo scooted just a bit farther behind the tree. "Instead of giving them a place to come back to so we could actually catch her, you *burned their hideout to the ground.*"

By Ursula's dumbfounded look, both Theo and Perran could see she had not taken that into consideration whatsoever.

"She could be anywhere by now and it is *your fault,*" Perran hissed through clenched teeth. His anger was nearly tangible, and as he trembled with the force of it, Theo thought he almost looked blurry. "You remain in the terribly predictable habit of underestimating familiars, and that cost me the only lead I had. I will not be making the same mistake." Dropping his voice to an even more menacing growl, he added, "Do not get in my way again, or I will make you regret it." With that, he stomped off the way he came.

"Who do you think you are to threaten me?!" Ursula shouted after him.

"You know exactly who," Perran answered back from where Theo couldn't see him. Theo couldn't help but wonder, *And who might that be, then?*

The entire time Ursula and Perran were arguing, fire was still eating the house. Now the structure was fully engulfed. Ursula stared at it, changing her posture now that Perran was gone. Unfortunately, her arson did not result in any measurable successes, and so the regent's partner's mother was left standing with nothing but Perran's admonishment. Instead of continuing to watch it burn, Ursula snapped her fingers and the house crumbled. The fire was extinguished immediately like a match dunked in water, and all that was left was unrecognizable burnt remains, the pile of blackened beams sticking out like a giant sea urchin.

When it was done, Ursula collected herself, forcing her nose back up into its original position and squaring off her shoulders.

And then, for the second time, she was gone.

---

Theo, Phineas, and Alby remained in their hiding spots for a little bit longer, worried that Ursula was going to make a third appearance and find something else to take or destroy. But the woods stayed silent and still, so the two familiars changed back into their human forms.

Theo put her hands on her head as she and Phineas walked a bit closer to the wreckage.

Well, this was certainly a pebble in the shoe of her plan. Cecily and Lock were now imprisoned until Theo was caught. And her whole strategy for success relied on her not getting caught. Would Ursula really hold them until then?

What if Theo managed to stay on the run for a hundred years? Would they be languishing in the dungeons?

Unlike Theo, Beatrice didn't have to deal with any of this when she made her fairy bargain. Her plan of action was much more straightforward since she didn't have to worry about anyone but herself.

But Theo still had days left. For the sake of Cecily and Lock, she'd continue on.

She was just about to ask for suggestions on what they should do next when Alby, having been otherwise quiet, suddenly turned toward the same direction Ursula had come from, his ears once again on alert. Theo and Phineas watched him with nervous anticipation, Theo trying to figure out if they should run for it.

"Someone is—oh." He shook his head and sagged, deflating like a balloon. Before she could ask who it was, out of the woods came Arlys, running toward them.

If the fairy was upset by the lackluster welcome, he didn't show it. Instead, he looked at each of them in turn, then what remained of the house, hands out, scrunching his brow until it looked like a raisin. "What happened to the tree house?"

"Ursula came and took Cecily and Lock," Theo said. "Then Ursula burned the house down in an effort to force me out of it. Now, let's all take a moment to appreciate that I did not, in fact, listen to your directive to stay in the house or you would be currently speaking to a familiar en flambé, Arlys."

"I know Ursula took them," he said, not bothering to acknowledge Theo's jab with more than narrowed eyes. "I just saw them wearing iron bracelets and being led into the palace suites."

"You saw them and didn't do anything about it?"

He glared at her. "I have no authority to decide who is or isn't a prisoner. I was there looking for Perran."

"Why?" she asked in a tauntingly sweet tone. "Were the ogres not as forthcoming for you as they were for him?"

"The ogres are dead."

*"What?"*

"He was the last person on record as having seen them. I needed to know what the ogres had told him, but he wasn't there. I was searching the palace when I saw Lock and Cecily."

"That's because he was here," she said, and then launched into what had just transpired. But when she got to the part about Ursula setting the fairy ring, the memory of the last time she'd been trapped rammed through her head again. She turned to Alby, who had been watching her with rapt attention. "Do you think Ursula set the fairy ring?" Theo asked the goblin.

"We just saw her set it, Theo," Phineas said, pointing to the mushrooms that were still around what was left of the house.

"No, not that one," Theo said. "The one in the woods behind Cecily's manor."

"That's how Theo met me!" Alby said brightly.

But Arlys and Phineas were staring at her in shock.

"You were caught in a fairy ring at Cecily's house?" Phineas asked.

"The woods past her property, but yes. Strangely, Ursula was at the party that evening. And Lock did say it was for no good reason, even though she tried to convince him it was."

Phineas scratched his chin. "Was this before you found out who you were?"

"Yes." Theo turned to Arlys. "You must have known who I was if you were at the party, right? Could Ursula have known who I was then, too?"

"The only ones who knew were supposedly Tace, Aimon, and myself."

"Well, all evidence suggests Aimon can't keep his mouth

shut," Theo said, motioning to the former house, current ash pile. "But then, why would she have tried to get to me first? And it is very strange that a woman whose only hobby is hurling her children to the top of the social ladder would be aiding an investigation into the royal family's assassin." Theo sighed. "So, back to the task at hand. I suppose launching a rescue operation is out of the question."

Phineas nodded his agreement. "As much as it pains me to say it, I think you're right. We'd never manage to sneak inside without anyone noticing. Not to mention I don't know where the dungeons are, and I think two familiars asking for directions might make us a bit suspicious." He pointed to Arlys. "He's certainly not going to help us."

Arlys huffed. "Help you sneak into the Palace of the Fae and try to take two prisoners out? No, I will not help. If you really want this to end and get Cecily and Lock released, now would be the time to come with me back to the palace to slumber."

"You'd love that, wouldn't you?" Theo sneered.

"Yes, I would. I don't think I've been keeping that a secret."

Theo crossed her arms. "You'll have to do better than suggesting a convenient plan that gets you exactly what you want and yields me nothing."

"Nothing except *not dying*," Arlys growled.

Theo rolled her eyes. "I can very much promise you my intentions are neither death nor slumber."

A vein bulged in his forehead and a muscle in his jaw twitched. Theo could see the fraying of the mooring line holding his anger to the dock as he closed his eyes and took a breath. When he opened them again, he looked at her and said, "You are very unlikable, princess."

Theo laughed in surprise at his lackluster attempt at putting her in her place. "Is that the best you can do? *Unlikable?* Given what other people have said to my face for most of my life, that is not only extremely uninspired, but practically a compliment. Supposedly you've been watching me my whole life. This can't be a new revelation."

"You're right, it's not," Arlys said. If he kept up this level of teeth clenching, he could rent himself out as a nutcracker. "But I thought you were treated that way because you were a changeling. I was wrong. Turns out, people treated you that way because you are intrinsically detestable."

Theo narrowed her eyes, but since Cecily wasn't here to do it, she also kept a smirk firmly on her mouth. If Arlys wanted to step in the ring and go toe to toe with her, she was more than willing.

"What to do, what to do," Theo said, feigning contemplation and tapping a finger on her chin as she began pacing. "Let's see. I could take the high road and say nothing. That would be a good choice if I was looking to prove you wrong about me. But I don't care what you think of me, and your mind seems to be made up anyway." She added a thoughtful head tilt. "Maybe I could take a slight step down and try to deny it. But then I run into the issue of you finding me more contrarian than persuasive. Where is the line of a lady who doth protest just the right amount to be taken seriously? Hmm. Tricky! I could sink to your level and call you unlikable and detestable in return." Her smirk bloomed into a full smile as she shook her head, waving her hand like she was clearing that silly idea from her mind. "But that wouldn't do justice to how I really feel."

She snapped her fingers and stopped pacing, then turned to face him. "So how about I dig a pit and tell you that you have the fortitude and strength of character of a boiled carrot with the personality to match. You boast the leadership skills of an army drummer who lacks any sense of rhythm. I wouldn't follow you two steps to the left without wondering if it was a good idea. Though, on second thought, it might be better to never let you out of my sight. Not because I'm worried about what you might do, but because you are so boring my short-term memory of you is reduced to that of a goldfish whenever you leave; that's how quickly you vacate my mind. Honestly, the next person I speak to could just as easily convince me you don't exist and I'd probably believe them." She nodded. "Yes, I think I'll go with that option. Did you need me to repeat it or did you catch it all?"

Arlys glared and ground his teeth. "I *cannot wait* to put you into slumber."

"Ah yes, that's right," Theo said. "You like your princesses asleep. And *stop* calling me princess."

He opened his mouth to volley a rebuttal, but Phineas stepped in. "Why don't we table this disagreement for a little while until we figure out what we're going to do next? Arlys, you should know you will never win this. It is in your best interest to stop now. It isn't even a remotely fair fight. Save whatever self-esteem you have left before Theo burns it down faster than this tree house. You should also know I am doing you a huge favor here, and a massive disservice to myself, because there is nothing quite like the spectacle of Theo in her element.

"And, Theo, we really need to figure out what we're going to do. Preferably where we should go because we can't stay here for much longer. It would be rather demoralizing to have to explain to Cecily later that we were caught because you couldn't stop insulting Arlys, no matter how much he deserved it."

Like a lioness interrupted from the hunt, Theo grumpily let her prey get away. She knew she was being nasty. He deserved it, but she was playing right into what he thought of her. "Fine. We are still out of clues, though, and I don't know where we should go."

Alby, who had been watching the entire exchange like it was a stage play, piped up. "I know! We could go to the—"

Arlys growled at him. "Don't say the puca! I swear, goblin, if you say *puca* one more time, I will make sure you can't say another word for the rest of your life."

And in an instant, their fragile détente was shattered, and Theo got her claws back out. "At least he's trying. Your method of problem-solving involves snarling and growling when your one idea gets shut down repeatedly. So you know what? I think we should go with Alby's idea. Going to see the puca is a great plan! The puca might give us some next steps. I would love to go see the puca. And I'll keep saying puca. *Puca, puca, puca, puca.*"

Everyone was silent for a moment, the last *puca*s ringing in the air like the echoes of a bell. Arlys's eyes were burning with fury—an expression that Theo had no trouble mimicking. Phineas was looking very uncertain about Theo's outburst, and Alby was staring at her like she was a sunrise.

"Are you sure you want to do that?" Phineas asked, working hard to suppress a grimace.

"Yes!" Theo said with all the bravado she could muster. "Alby, how do we get to the puca?"

"Oh." His ears drooped. "I don't know."

"You don't know where he is?" she asked, her voice a bit higher than a fearless leader's should have been.

"No," Alby said. "I've never been. I just thought it might be a good idea."

The corners of Arlys's mouth quirked up into the beginnings of a smile, and not the nice kind. His smile was being propped up by the smugness of being proven right. "Don't bother asking me. Even if I did know where he was, I wouldn't want to tell you."

Theo feigned shock. "You're *not* going to help me with a simple problem that would affect you very little but could very well save my life?" She put the back of her hand on her forehead. "Quick! Someone get me a fainting couch before the sheer surprise of it knocks me down." She put her hand back down. She knew she was approaching going too far, but she couldn't seem to stop, her defense mechanism manifesting as over-the-top snark. "I guess that's why I didn't ask you."

Not one to try something new, he rolled his eyes at her.

"Phineas," she said, ignoring Arlys in favor of trying a new tactic. "You knew about the puca. You must have visited."

He shook his head. "No, I'd only heard about the puca secondhand after he came home from his task for Cecily."

"Who?"

"Kaz."

Theo couldn't hide her disappointment at the dead end she had walked down. They couldn't get into the palace to ask Cecily, and Kaz wouldn't know who they were if they showed up, much less what a puca was and where to find one. If only his memories hadn't been wiped. But that gave Theo an idea.

She spun to Arlys. "Can a familiar who left the service of a fairy have their memories restored, or are they gone forever?"

"Yes, they can be restored. But I'm assuming you're going to ask next if I can help you with that. And the answer is no."

"It is as though you want an encore of the fainting couch joke," Theo said.

"Doesn't matter anyway, Theo," Phineas said. "I don't even know where to find him." But his eyebrows raised in a silent question when Theo's shoulders didn't sag like his did.

She turned to him with a sheepish look. "I might know where to find him."

"How?"

"I might have been sneaking off to spy on Kaz in the human world."

"You have? When?"

"Since around the time I learned how to transport myself places. Cecily told me where he was, and I've been sitting in a tree near his house as a hedgehog. That being said, if Arlys is willing to put aside his pride and stop being difficult, we can get his memories back and go see the puca."

"Even if I wanted to—and I don't—I wouldn't do it for free."

"Fine, then. What do you want in exchange?" Theo asked.

He gave her a withering look that suggested she already knew the answer. She did; she just didn't like it.

"Look," she said. "You need to heed my words. For my sanity, and yours. I will not be going with you willingly before my bargain with you is concluded. That being said, I'm willing to take time off my bargain."

Phineas balked. "You're going to give away even more time?"

She waved him off. "Trust me, it really doesn't matter."

But Arlys was intrigued. "How much time?"

"If you restore Kaz's memories, our bargain will be concluded four hours before the stroke of midnight at the end of our original bargain."

Arlys considered this for a moment, then said, "I give whoever this Kaz person is his memories back so he can tell us where the puca is. In exchange, our bargain ends *a day* earlier than initially agreed to."

"It's a deal." Theo started a swirl of wind at her feet. "Now, let's go."

Selfish, she knew, but she didn't want to just see Kaz one more time. She wanted him to see her, too.

# Chapter 16

# Where Theo Is Worried Memory Lane Might Be a One-Way Street

Theo transported the group to where she always landed in the copse of trees. This time, however, she did not change into a hedgehog.

"All right. Everyone head to that bench over there and have a seat. I'll let you know when we see Kaz. And then—"

"Do you really think it's a good idea that he's here?" Arlys interrupted, pointing at Alby. "He has no idea how to interact with humans and is going to stick out like a sore thumb, bringing way more attention to us than is safe."

Theo rolled her eyes and continued as though Arlys hadn't spoken. "Yes. Right, so when we see him—"

"What do you think your friend is going to do when he sees a goblin? He doesn't have his memories, so the answer is *run screaming.*"

Theo huffed in annoyance and turned to Arlys. "First of all, this was mostly his idea, so of course Alby gets to come along. Second of all, he's known for being sneaky. And third, I have no doubts he could fit into the human world better than you ever could, and he's green." Then she turned to the goblin. "Alby, what is and where would you find a scullery?"

Alby cleared his throat. "The scullery is the room in the manor where you'd do the washing. It is found in the back of a manor near the kitchen."

"You told him that," Arlys scoffed.

"Maybe." Theo shrugged. "Or maybe he had the good sense to ask. Take a word of advice from our horrifying friend Perran. Just because you think you're better than us doesn't make it true." She turned back to Phineas and Alby, who were both smiling. "Where was I? Right. When we see Kaz, Phineas and I will approach him. When he's stopped, Arlys, you will do what you need to in order to bring back his memories. Wait, what do you need to do to bring back his memories?"

"He needs to be standing still for a moment, so if you don't want anyone asking questions, it would be best to bring him back here where we won't be seen."

"Fine. When we see Kaz, Phineas and I will figure out a way to lure him back here. Arlys, why don't you wait at the ready and we'll bring him to you. Let's go."

Unlike every other time Theo stepped out of the copse of trees, now she was doing it as a human and, surprisingly, felt more bare than she did in her nude hedgehog form. Phineas walked beside her as they went to the bench, and Alby walked on the grass. True to what he had said, Alby was a master of disguise. Whether it was his clothes or innate magic, Theo could easily lose track of him if she wasn't looking. And if she hadn't known he was there, she wouldn't have noticed him at all.

Phineas and Theo sat on the bench as Alby stood next to the tree, blending seamlessly.

Theo's heart suddenly picked up its pace. She'd only ever come here to watch Kaz, and now, waiting for him and knowing she was about to talk to him, she wasn't sure she'd made the right choice. She might be madly in love with him, but he had zero notion of her existence.

What if he saw her and immediately wanted nothing to do with her? With all his memories and therefore feelings about her wiped away, would he find anything about her compelling at all? Or would he sneer and walk off?

How would she even approach him? Should she start with *Hello, Kaz* and take him completely by surprise? Or should she go with a more refined *Excuse me, sir, do you have a moment to discuss a very important matter in that secluded copse of trees over there? Yes, where that strange man is leering in the shadows.*

"How long do you think we'll be waiting?" Phineas asked, breaking her spiral.

"He usually comes home for lunch, so probably pretty soon."

Almost like she had summoned him, Kaz came around the corner, heading for his house.

Phineas let out a low whistle. "He did all right for someone who didn't dress himself for three hundred years." Theo knew he was commenting on the fresh suit and slicked, short hair. Even his scruff was gone, highlighting his jawline that much further, though she missed that little hint of ruggedness on him.

Oh no. He was here, and now she was supposed to do what she came here for. This was a terrible idea.

"Phineas," she said quietly. "Maybe we should go."

She stood before she knew what she was doing, Phineas doing the same. But she couldn't move. She wouldn't call out to him, she'd just watch him go into his house and she would leave. They could find another way to get to the puca.

Kaz fished his keys out of his pocket, and like he always did right before he stepped through the gate, he looked at the park.

His eyes met hers and passed right over. It was one thing when he did it when she was a hedgehog. Him looking at her now with no recognition hurt more than she expected it to.

But before Theo's heart could shatter completely, he took one more step forward and froze, then spun to face her, staring in shock from across the street.

"Does that look like the face of a man who has no idea who we are?" Phineas said out of the corner of his mouth, while both he and Theo stared back at Kaz.

"I don't know. Maybe not. Maybe we just look very out of place?" Theo said.

"Theo? Phineas?" Kaz shouted from across the street. "Wait!"

"For what? We're not going anywhere!" Phineas shouted back, signaling that they were, and continued to be, stationary.

Kaz wasn't answering, though. He had his eyes so focused on them that Theo was worried he was going to get hit by a carriage or cart if he wasn't careful. Thankfully, he still had sense enough to look both ways and avoid an errant hackney or a horse that had something to prove before dashing to the park.

When he got to the park he looked at them again, a sense of relief evident on his face. "Oh, thank goodness, you waited."

"Of course we waited," Phineas said. "We're here to see you. Or did you think this is a coincidence and we just enjoy boring human parks with equally boring benches? Though, of all the parks that fit the description, this one is perfectly adequate."

Kaz smiled as Phineas closed the small distance between them to pull him into a hug with some hearty pats on the back.

"You look different, my friend," Phineas said, giving Kaz a once-over.

"You look exactly the same." Kaz grinned.

Phineas nodded. "I've spent quite a bit of time perfecting this look. Why change a good thing?"

Kaz turned to Theo. They both watched each other for a moment, Kaz's joy dimming to match Theo's stunted smile. Her arms became strangely problematic in terms of what they were supposed to be doing, so she clasped them in front of her like she was about to sing carols. Any more awkward and they might as well have been teenagers at their first parent-arranged courtship meeting.

She could have gone with a bunch of different openers, the most common and obvious among them being *hello*, but in the spirit of not making things too easy for herself, she said, "So you remember us, then?" at the same time he said, "You're looking well." They both regarded each other for a moment before he gave her a small smirk and said, "Seems that way," answering her question. Right when she said a meager thank-you.

"Ah," Phineas said, watching their awkward spectacle with a smile. "If I had a drink, I would be toasting to happy reunions."

But Theo barely registered he'd said anything at all as she stared at Kaz, the realization in his gaze startling her.

He had his memories. He remembered her. *He remembered her.*

Her heart soared like a bird. This was everything she had wanted. Every time she had been a hedgehog in a tree, she could have been Theo on a bench. With Kaz. Because he remembered her.

But that bird was an ostrich, she discovered, as her heart plummeted back down to earth with a clumsy thud. All this time she'd been pining over him, wishing he knew who she was, he did.

And he never came for her.

Because he didn't want to. He'd wanted to move on. He preferred to live his life without fairies, without familiars, without magic.

Without her.

She didn't know what to do with that, so she looked down, hoping he wouldn't catch too much of her embarrassed blushing.

She was right. This was a horrible mistake.

Kaz was still smiling at them. "How did you know where to find me? Did Cecily tell you?"

Even before anyone said anything, Theo's face was abandoning blushing in favor of going red all over.

"Theo's been coming here for a while now," Phineas said, his eyes glinting with his usual mischief.

"You have?" Kaz asked, looking straight at her. "I've never seen you."

Once again, Phineas answered for her. "She said she was hiding in a tree as a hedgehog."

Kaz watched her again, but Theo was looking anywhere else, knowing full well she could pass for a tomato.

Kaz, in his mercy, decided not to torture her by asking for more details, or didn't care to, and instead asked, "So what are you doing here now?"

Phineas held up a finger. "Now, that is a fun story. Have a seat, as it is also a long one."

Together, the three of them sat down on the bench.

"Turns out Theo here is a changeling," Phineas said with no shortage of amusement.

Kaz turned to look at Theo, appraising her as though he'd never seen her before. "Huh," he said with a contemplative frown. "You know, that does make sense."

"Oh, here we go," Theo mumbled.

"That's not even the best part," Phineas said, drawing the attention back to himself. "She's a very particular changeling. This missing princess."

On that, Kaz's eyes went wide, his mouth falling open.

"No," he breathed. "You've got to be joking." He tried a smile on them, as though attempting to signal he was in on their scheme and wouldn't be taken for a ride. But after a few moments of Theo and Phineas not breaking into any version of *You should have seen your face!* his morphed back into shocked confusion. "You're Iara?"

"No," Theo said, lighter than she had meant. "The princess who actually survived was Amabel." Theo sighed. "I'm Amabel. Or so I've been told, and everyone around me seems to believe it."

Kaz made another noise of contemplation. "Is that why you came?"

Phineas laughed. "If only it were! We are here to get some knowledge from that head of yours. Specifically, about the puca."

This really set Kaz off-balance. "Now, why would you ever want to go see him? You'd get more sensical advice from a random person off the street here than you would from that hatter."

"Too late now!" Theo said, not doing anything to tame the annoyance in her voice. "My bargain ends in approximately two days and the uncourteous assassin has been inconveniencing us with a tragic deficiency in clues. It was the only way forward we had."

"What is happening in *two days*?!" Kaz sputtered, his eyebrows and face in serious danger of tying in a knot.

"If Theo doesn't complete this wild bargain she made, she's going to be put into slumber," Phineas said. "Though, she's handling her impending mortality with unfathomable grace and serenity for someone who faces nothingness in a few days' time."

"We skipped over a huge chunk of the story," Theo said to a horrified Kaz.

"Isn't that right," Phineas said. "You'd think the excitement would stop at 'princess,' but that tidbit of information is the crudités platter of the party. There's much more filling news to be had."

Together, Phineas and Theo took the opportunity to fill in the gaps, including the ogres and Arlys.

Kaz spent the remainder of the story like he was a child in the front-row seat of a magic show, with his wide eyes and floppy jaw.

But to his credit, once they were done, Kaz stood and said, "Well then, let's go. Apparently time is a commodity you are lacking."

"You're coming with us?" Theo asked.

"I have to," Kaz said. "He lives in the middle of a labyrinthian fen. I could not even begin to draw you a map by memory. If you want to get to the puca, we have to go to the edge of the fen and I'll have to walk you the rest of the way."

"And also," Phineas interrupted. "I highly suspect Kaz is wholly unable to turn down the opportunity to work together again." He gestured between himself and Theo.

Kaz stood up from the bench. "And I would also say it is way more fun than sitting in my house having lunch, but that's not a fair comparison because most things already are."

His justification for participating stung. Nowhere in his reasoning did he mention any desire to be near her or help save her. For Theo, that was all the confirmation she needed. He truly didn't want her anymore.

Fine. She would have his help to find the puca, be in his company for just a bit longer, and then say goodbye for the last time. Maybe this would be the push she needed to finally move on.

Kaz was about to say something else before his eyes caught on the tree behind them. "Are you aware there is a goblin standing against that tree?"

Theo turned to look. "How rude of me. Sorry. Alby, why don't you come out and meet my friend Kaz. And, Kaz, this is my friend Alby."

Alby stepped away from the tree, so well camouflaged Theo almost forgot where he was.

Kaz was suitably impressed, too. "Clever. You were all but invisible. Well done." He knelt down and offered Alby his hand to shake, which Alby took a bit warily, but still with a slight swell of pride.

"How could you see me?" Alby asked.

"I was Cecily's familiar for roughly three hundred years. I've seen plenty in that time." This answer seemed to satisfy Alby.

"Now that that's settled, let's go see if Arlys hasn't imploded in the time we've been gone," Phineas said.

With that, the four of them walked to the copse of trees.

Unfortunately, Arlys was perfectly fine, still in his default state of annoyed at everything. They had given Kaz a quick but exact overview of Arlys. Kaz was, predictably, unimpressed.

"About time," Arlys said with a barely concealed sneer

when Theo, Phineas, and Alby led Kaz to the trees. Apparently, good first impressions were of no consequence to Arlys. "Hold him still."

Theo put up her hand. "Actually, that won't be necessary. As it turns out, Cecily did not take away his memories."

Arlys rolled his eyes. "Of course she didn't."

Kaz smiled. "Hello, I'm Kasra, but my friends call me Kaz. Feel free to call me Kasra." He made no effort to extend his hand the way he did for Alby. "You must be the fairy hell-bent on killing Theo."

"Oh, no, Kaz," Theo said with an overly polite laugh. "He doesn't want to *kill* me. He wants to take me from all I've ever known and put me into slumber for a thousand years or until he decides it's safe. I'm sure he's also hoping that when I wake I won't have any memories, and then he can mold me into someone much more compliant. It's very different, you see."

Arlys added a growl to his sneer this time.

"And don't take that personally, Kaz," Theo said. "This is what he does. Sneer and growl. It is like traveling with a disgruntled gopher."

Theo thoroughly enjoyed watching Arlys force his face to be expressionless, lest he prove her correct. She didn't look to see Kaz's expression, though. What happened a moment ago felt too familiar, too natural. And if she didn't stop herself, there'd be no getting over it when he left her again.

With that, the group wasted no more time in the park before departing to find the puca.

# Chapter 17
# Where Theo Meets the Puca

With Kaz's directions, Theo transported the group. She noticed that when she did, Kaz made sure to stand away from her, putting Phineas and Alby between them.

As soon as Theo saw the fen, she knew Kaz had not been exaggerating—it was the kind of pandemonium only nature could create. Rushes, reeds, and grasses dominated the flat landscape, with streams and small ponds carving intricately chaotic patterns throughout. The footpaths that intersected the water made the fen look like a giant shattered mirror.

If Theo had tried to find the puca on her own, it very well could have taken her weeks.

But Kaz seemed to remember the way through the maze just fine as he led them farther into the fen. They walked single file on a trail that stayed slightly above the waterline, Theo keeping her shoes dry, but only just barely. One wrong step and she would announce her arrival via splash. When they had reached almost the middle of the wetlands, Kaz stopped in front of a wall of cattails that blocked the rest of the trail from view. "We're here."

He pushed aside the plants that were bowing across the path, and Theo did the same, holding them for the others. When they were all through, they found themselves in a small clearing. In the center was a large boulder and, next to that, a stunted pine tree, tiny and crooked thanks to growing where it shouldn't.

But other than that, the clearing was vacant.

"Where is he?" Theo asked, aware that she really had no idea what he looked like. And as a shape-shifter, he could look like anything.

A small green frog came hopping out of the water. It stopped in front of her and turned to stare, straining its little fat neck to look up at her face. This must be the puca, then.

Wanting to make a good first impression, she did a small curtsy.

"Did you just curtsy to that frog?" asked a slightly braying voice from the boulder.

She and the rest of the group looked up from the curious amphibian to the top of the boulder in the direction of the source of the voice. And now that she saw the being to whom the voice belonged, it was quite obvious the frog was not the puca.

A goat, fur as black as coal, was watching them with expressionless yellow eyes. As far as goats go, description-wise, he was fairly typical and representative of the goats Theo had seen before. Until, that is, she factored in everything else about him. For starters, this goat was wearing pants—tan-colored and hemmed just above his hooves. He was also sitting up, those back hooves crossed, his front legs on his hips. His appearance almost reminded Theo of a satyr, except there wasn't a man's body on the upper half. No, it was still all goat, complete with a wine barrel belly, hooves on all four feet, and curved horns on his head.

"I, uh, yes, I did," Theo said. "I thought it was you, assuming you are, in fact, the puca."

"I am indeed the puca. You thought I was a frog? Why would you think something as ridiculous as that?"

Kaz scoffed. "As a general rule, we assume any animal staring at us for longer than two seconds could turn into a person, or in your case a puca, at any time."

"And it was staring at me," Theo added.

The puca crossed his front legs. "Maybe it thought your face looked like a bug."

Seeing as she needed this puca's help, she decided to take a page out of a childhood morality tale and say nothing, as she had nothing nice to say.

"So why have you tramped all the way out here to speak with the frogs?" asked the puca.

"I was hoping to ask you for some information."

"About frogs?"

"No."

He jumped down from the rock, landing on all fours, but then stood up so he was on his back legs pacing in front of the group. "You seem to be a frog enthusiast."

"I have no opinions on frogs one way or another," Theo said, but he ignored her.

He stopped suddenly, arms slackened by his sides and a dreamy look on his face. After a few moments, he shook his head with a little laugh and began pacing again, then said, as if he was speaking to someone else, "It is a good thing he's terrible at it. They could at least get away. But I don't think he'll be invited to any more gatherings anytime soon!"

Theo was just about to interrupt, but then the puca caught them out of the corner of his eye with an expression of surprise.

"What are you still doing here? Didn't you leave hours ago?"

Theo's eyebrows bunched. "No? We only arrived mere moments ago."

The puca nodded to himself as he proceeded to pace more. Then, to no one in particular, he blurted out, "Goodness, that is quite a lot of yellow flowers! And good thing there are door hinges! Tricky!"

He repeated this again, and Theo was hit with the thought that maybe this wasn't a good idea after all.

He finally stopped walking and looked at her. "Do you like my home?"

"It is quite lovely," Theo said, firmly believing it. She thought it would be rather enjoyable to live in this fen, with its myriad of animals. And the sunrises and sunsets must have been beautiful reflecting off the water. The others nodded their agreement.

"Nasty place. I hate it. I'd much rather go with you. Maybe I'll visit." He then started to hum a little tune to himself.

"I... what?"

Arlys snorted, a release valve to let out the pressure from trying to hold in his *I told you so* with such ferocity.

She knew her own revelation at the situation should have been obvious given what she was thinking, but she was disappointed just the same. The goat was talking nonsense.

The puca had picked up a stick and was poking the ground but creating nothing of note, much like a bored child at the market whose parents were taking too long haggling.

He spoke again. "You said you wanted more information?"

"Yes," Theo replied.

"About what? Being a princess?"

"Yes. You know that?" A genuine question given what he'd been spouting only moments ago.

"I know lots of things. And about who is trying to kill you?"

"Mostly that, yes."

"What will you do for me if I give you this information?"

Good. Now at least they were getting somewhere.

"What would you want?"

He put a hoof under his chin, which Theo assumed was his attempt at looking contemplative. Then he made a motion like he was snapping his fingers, though hooves not being able to snap, no sound was made. "I need something," he said slowly, with an air of suspense. "From the Dell Sprites. They took something from me. Something important." His eyes narrowed and he watched her, once again saying nothing.

"Well?" Theo asked after a moment of silence. "What was it?"

"I forgot."

"Forgot? Then how was it important?"

"I don't remember what they took. Only that it was important. And I want it back."

"Is it an object of some kind?"

"Don't know."

"Bigger than a loaf of bread?"

"No idea."

"So, to give me information, you want me to go see the Dell Sprites and ask about something you forgot. Anyone in particular? Any idea as to their location?" She was trying not to let the frustration come through in her voice, and her efforts might have worked if Arlys hadn't kept snorting.

"The queen! You will need to see the queen. Shouldn't be a problem seeing as how you're royalty yourself. And they live in the dell. Ah! This is very fortuitous!"

Kaz mumbled, "And yet he didn't see this coming."

The puca continued, either not hearing Kaz or choosing not to care. "I'll send you to the dell. You get what I need from her, bring it back, and then I'll give you the information you seek. Deal?"

Theo was still considering the pros and cons of making a deal with a puca when Arlys said, "Absolutely not. We're leaving, Princess Amabel."

Theo wasn't sure if it was his demanding tone or his use of "Princess Amabel," but whatever it was had Theo shouting, "It's a deal!" with an involuntary response akin to a sneeze.

The puca perked up his ears, widened his eyes, and pulled his lips back over his teeth in the closest interpretation of a smile that a goat face could make. "Wonderful. I can't wait to figure out what it was I forgot! I will take you just outside the dell, since any closer and they will probably try to take something else from me as well. Let's go!"

Before they could do or say anything further, he clapped his hooves together, and in a blink, they were all taken away from the fen.

# Chapter 18

# Where Theo Realizes Just How Little She Thinks About Bells on a Daily Basis

They stood in front of a small stone church. It was nearly square and only large enough to hold a few rows of pews at best. The steeple on top did not end in a point and, instead, reminded Theo more of a chimney, the spire either missing or never having been put there in the first place. The wood of the door was warped and chipped but fit in the doorframe still. The grass surrounding it was mostly dead, great beige swaths overtaking any remaining greenery. And the grass that was living was patchy and sickly. Yet it looked trimmed, as though someone had been trying to care for it.

But they were not going into the church. The puca pointed

to a small path leading to the back of it and said, "That way!" before vanishing.

The group started walking down the path.

"Have you ever spoken to sprite royalty before?" Phineas asked.

She had met sprites at parties but had never had any sort of long interaction. They would often dance when she was playing music but spent most of their party time out by the trees or flying near the ceiling. And often, if it was an outdoor party, she had trouble seeing them anyway, as they blended in with their surroundings rather seamlessly. "Can't say that I have."

"Well, the Dell Sprites are a fairly small court, both in numbers and stature. But the queen thinks highly of herself and of Dell Sprites in general. Bear that in mind, she will want you to fawn a bit."

She nodded, not sure how she was supposed to do that, but figured she'd cross that bridge when she got to it.

They had reached the back of the church, the path cutting straight through the cemetery. It was a fairly gloomy place, even without the gravestones. Like the yard in front, the vegetation here was also wasting away. The new growth on the trees and bushes was ropy, thin, and malformed, barely able to hold the weight of the leaves and buds. The grass back here was also dry and limp, as though it hadn't had water for weeks, even though the ground was wet. There was a gardener's shed in the far corner, but given how depressing this place was, she couldn't imagine it was being used with any regularity.

When they reached the very back of the graveyard, the

ground began to slope down, ending in a wooded valley. The dell, then.

Theo kept her eyes firmly on the ground where she was walking. The fallen leaves were damp, making the path as slick as waxed tile. With each footstep, Theo's shoes were making a soggy squishing noise instead of a satisfying crisp crunch. And they still had some color left to them, as if the trees collectively decided they weren't going to wait any longer for summer to end, the woods now a patchwork of greens shifting to browns and yellows, the forest floor like a sun-bleached blanket.

This left the trees woefully underdressed, displaying their bare, gangly, lanky bodies. Without their plumage, they reminded Theo of underfed ducks after butchering, their slim bodies only discovered when the feathers were mostly gone.

A maple tree sat in the center of the dell. Not having received the instructions that it was meant to look sickly, this one still had a full, puffy crown of leaves on a thick, perfectly straight trunk, like a giant green dandelion about to go to seed. And covering the trunk were windows, each no bigger than the palm of Theo's hand. At the very bottom was a wooden carved door inlaid with a deliberate swirling pattern of moss.

The dell was silent save for the light rustling of leaves and branches in the breeze far above them. Nothing else was moving. Where were all the sprites? Did the puca send them to the wrong dell? Had this one been abandoned?

Nothing to do but knock, she supposed.

Theo walked to the door, used the acorn knocker that

hung in the center to knock three times, then stepped back to wait. Just when she was about to try again, thinking maybe whoever was inside hadn't heard, a latch clicked, and the door swung open.

The sprite who opened the door was small, even more so than Alby, standing only up to Theo's midcalf. His wings were translucent and fragmented by white veins. His skin was the orange color of a newt, with the same blotches of brown. And just like a newt, Theo would have expected the color to clash against the other hues of the forest, and yet this sprite blended into the scenery quite well.

He was wearing a covering fashioned from maple leaves around his lower half, with a sash of braided, dried grass across his chest. Its purpose was rather obvious, as at the sprite's hip, tied to the sash, were flasks made of butterfly chrysalises and hollowed-out acorns acting as pouches.

The way this sprite was standing—his chin out, legs planted—Theo was expecting a heralded message of some sort decorated with *Her Majesty, the Queen* and posturing about seeking an audience.

But his face had twisted into a tiny scowl. Then, waving his hands at Theo the way one might chase off chickens that had gotten into the feed, he said, "What are humans doing here? Shoo! Shoo!"

Before Theo could say anything, Kaz spoke up. "Princess Amabel of the Oak Fairies to speak with your queen."

The sprite's eyes went wide and he ran back inside, slamming the door behind him.

Theo looked at Kaz in disbelief.

"Not you, too," she hissed.

Kaz shrugged. "We need to make a good first impression. Do you think the queen wants to speak to Princess Amabel or Theo the familiar?"

"You're right. Who would want to spend time with regular old Theo," she said, glaring at him.

Kaz's small grin dropped. "No, that's not what I meant."

She gave him her best indifferent shrug. "You don't have to explain yourself to me."

Kaz opened his mouth to say more but was interrupted by Phineas. "You two may want to quit it for a moment," he said out of the corner of his mouth.

The sprite had returned and had apparently been watching their entire spat.

"Are you here on official business, then?" the sprite said.

Theo started to say, "Not exactly" at the same time Kaz said yes. And then both turned to glare at each other.

This unsettled the sprite. He regarded them with a mix of distrust and distaste, and if he narrowed his eyes any further, he might as well just close them and save himself the effort.

"I am here on personal business," Theo said, hoping that might clear up any confusion.

The sprite pulled his head back in and slammed the door once again.

And once again, only a few moments went by before he was opening the door. He stepped fully out, resuming his initial and most likely official stance. Then, with all the charm and presentation of picnic leftovers kept out in the sun too long, the sprite cleared his throat and said, "Her Majesty, Queen

Blossom, ruler of the Dell Sprites, to grant an audience to Princess Amabel of the Oak Fairies, not in official capacity, here on personal time."

Theo didn't think the last part was necessary but schooled her face into a placid smile anyway, one she hoped looked at least somewhat regal while she waited for the queen to come out.

She didn't have to wait long. The suspicious sprite stepped aside, leaving the way clear for the queen to make her entrance, or exit, as it were.

The queen walked slowly out, pausing between steps like a bride down the aisle. Her ensemble was well suited for the march. She wore what appeared to be an upside-down rose, the bodice fitted around her top like a stem, the green edges stopping in a straight line right under her arms. The petals of the skirt spread out the farther down they went, until they created a train that swept out behind her, the interlocking pattern like fish scales. She was only slightly smaller than the other sprite, but her regalness made her seem much larger. That, and the crown that stood almost a foot high atop her head. It was made of twisted sticks like she had overturned a complicated basket. And at the very top, the branches spread back out again, giving them the illusion that they grew that way. Wound throughout weren't gemstones but shiny and smooth river pebbles the color of thunderclouds. It looked remarkably and uncomfortably heavy, and Theo couldn't tell if the sprite was wearing the crown or merely balancing it on her wineglass-stem neck.

Queen Blossom halted only a few feet in front of Theo and

the group. She exhaled a small, high-pitched sigh of annoyance that sounded like a melancholic piccolo as she took in the group. But she said nothing, instead expanding her wings and flying gently upward with the speed and smooth trajectory of a hot-air balloon. Theo turned to watch the queen fly past them to a tree opposite the maple. Theo hadn't noticed it when their focus was solely on the maple tree, but now that she saw it, she could tell why the queen would want to conduct the meeting there.. A limb had broken off midway up the tree trunk, leaving a spot like a platform that was slightly higher than Theo. On that was a throne the exact right size for a sprite, made from polished wood the color of honey, the back carved to look like leaves. And indeed, once she landed, Queen Blossom turned and sat down, adjusting her skirts around her.

Once settled, she looked at Theo.

Theo didn't know enough about sprites to determine whether their boredom and complete disregard of visitors to their court were specifically intentional to her or general cultural traits. She had seen more interest and excitability from a geriatric cart horse. Queen Blossom was staring at her with such apathy, Theo wondered if the heralding sprite told her the group had come to give a lecture followed by a demonstration on the speed at which grass grows.

For a moment, no one said anything. Then Theo curtsied, bowing her head as she did so, hoping that starting the discussion was the polite thing to do, or at least not terribly rude. "Queen Blossom, how lovely to meet you, and thank you for taking this audience with us. I—"

"You're Princess Amabel of the Oak Fairies? The missing princess?" The queen leveled the questions as accusations.

Kaz seemed to know Theo was about to deny it and elbowed her slightly.

Theo stifled a huff. "Strictly interpreting the situation, you could say that I am."

"What are you doing here? And who are you traveling with? These do not look like Oak Fairy court representatives." Her tone was so accusatory that Theo was convinced she'd next be suspected of stealing the queen's penny candy.

Well, someone got up on the wrong side of her bed of nails this morning.

Theo was trying to take the advice of Phineas, but currently, she didn't see the need to make Queen Blossom feel important. The queen was doing a satisfactory job of it on her own.

Right, then. If the queen wanted to cut to the chase, that was fine with Theo. Better than fine, actually. She did have a ticking clock above her head like the blade of a guillotine. The faster she could get this task for the puca done, the better.

She gestured to Kaz, Phineas, and Alby. "As for the people with me, they are my friends." Then she motioned to Arlys. "And associate." Theo figured he didn't want to be counted among her friends anyway, so maybe he appreciated the distinction. His face gave away nothing other than scorn, though, so Theo couldn't be sure.

"And as for what we are doing here, as your herald said, I am not on official court business, and overall, it is a long story not worthy of taking up any of your precious time."

The queen leaned just the slightest bit forward in her seat.

"What do you know of my 'precious time'?" Oddly, this question was phrased as a curiosity, not as some sort of indictment.

"Only that, as a queen, I'm assuming your responsibilities keep you plenty busy, and I appreciate you taking time away from those duties to meet with me."

This was clearly not what the queen wanted to hear. Queen Blossom's face fell back into its position of utter impassivity. "Get to your point, then, if you think my time is so valuable."

Fabulous. So much for buttering up the queen. Theo would have more success buttering up a wall and asking it to converse. With the queen's already chilly reception, Theo was afraid that if she brought up the reason for the visit now, the court would turn to ice.

"I'm actually here on behalf of the puca. He has requested that I come and speak with you to see if we could come to some sort of arrangement regarding his missing...something or other."

As suspected, this was also the wrong thing to say to the queen of the sprites, whose little fists suggested she had her reasons for dealing with the puca, and Theo was about to undermine them.

"Just as I suspected," Queen Blossom ground out. "I was hoping you came because your regent had received my letter and was coming to my aid. Common knowledge that you haven't been crowned yet, but still, I thought it was at least some display of respect for my court that Tace sent the princess in his stead. But no, I find out you are here on behalf of the puca, of all creatures. I can't tell if you're more human or fairy with you coming to my court for your own selfish reasons."

*Selfish reasons? How dare you.* Might they have been selfish reasons just a little while ago before Cecily and Lock were taken? Sure. But now Theo had to do this to save her friends from the mess she made.

Queen Blossom had her hands on the arms of the throne, readying to stand up, presumably to fly back to her tree and not come back out. This was a dismissal.

"Excuse me, Your Majesty. But I believe you are operating under the false assumption that I *want* to be here on puca business. I have met him, and trust me, I would rather be doing anything else, but I'm out of options and my time is going that way as well. You see, I'm in a bit of a quandary with very limited time to fix it.

"I had to enter into a bargain with him"—she pointed at Arlys—"because he was threatening my friend to get to me. Now I have two days left to try to figure out who killed the entire royal family and is still out for me. So with no more clues as to who the assassin could be, I made a bargain with the puca so he could hopefully tell me something useful and I could use the information to save my friends and myself."

Theo paused and took a breath.

"So you do understand the difficulties of time," Queen Blossom said.

Really? Out of the entire issue Theo laid out, that was what she was focused on?

"Yes, I suppose I do?"

Queen Blossom regarded Theo for a long moment. "I, too, am trying to protect the lives and livelihoods of the Dell Sprites. A job that has become particularly difficult as of late." She motioned to the forest around them.

So apparently it wasn't supposed to look this way.

"We Dell Sprites are responsible for the upkeep of these woods. We use our magic to sustain the trees. A symbiotic relationship, if you will. They rely on our magic, and we rely on them for our homes. However, at present, every hour, on the hour, the magic disappears, for various lengths of time. And I need it to stop. Not for lack of trying, but neither I nor my subjects have been able to do anything about it. Nor can I find anyone else to help me."

"That sounds terrible."

"Yes, it is a terrible sound." She did the slightest of solemn nods, seemingly not wanting to either topple the crown or snap her own neck with the shifting of weight. "But maybe you can help."

And now Theo was confused. Every hour on the hour magic disappeared for varying lengths of time? Involving an awful noise?

"Is it some sort of riddle?" Theo wasn't very good at those, having been notoriously confused by the metaphor in the Sphinx's riddle, which, unfortunately, also had to do with different times of day and also varying amounts of legs. Truth be told, she still thought it a bit of a stretch.

"What? A riddle? No, that's ridiculous. Why would I need help from a human with a riddle? It's the new bell in the church tower right up there. You passed it on your way in." Queen Blossom spoke as if this was the most obvious thing, that noticing bells in church towers was a feature in everyone's day. Again, maybe in Dell Sprite culture, it was.

"Wait, the bell is interfering with your magic?"

Queen Blossom looked at her as though Theo was a puzzle scant a few pieces. "Bells interfere with all magic."

Theo turned to Arlys. "Do bells interfere with fairy magic, too?"

He nodded once. "Yes."

Kaz elaborated. "When bells sound, magic completely disappears. For fairies, it can be quite painful." Even though it was a strange topic, Theo was hit once again with just how thankful and relieved she was that he was here. Even when they first met and he didn't like her, he never left her out to dry and wanted her to succeed, not just for his sake, either.

"But why just bells? Why not chimes or cymbals for that matter?"

Phineas shrugged. "Why do some mushrooms kill you while others are lovely in a wine reduction?"

*Huh.*

Theo also recalled when she was trapped in the fairy ring with Alby. He had quickly mentioned that bells can sometimes break a fairy ring.

Theo could have sworn she'd heard bells since coming to the fairy realm. But now that Theo actually thought about it, when was the last time? The clocks in Cecily's house used tiny mallets on tiny cymbals, when they even bothered to tell the time, anyway. Oh, the clock tower at Tace's party! But no... that played chimes. And she didn't keep a clock in her room since she had yet to find an occasion where she would need to know the correct time down to the minute.

The more she thought about it, the more she realized she'd really never heard a bell since being here. Maybe even longer, as the last time she could conclusively recall hearing bells was at Beatrice's wedding, when they went from the church back to the castle, bells banging and clanging the whole way.

Wait. Sneaky Bea. She really did think of everything when she was escaping Cecily.

And nary a bell since. In that subsequent time, she never had a reason to think about bells again.

"Yes," Queen Blossom finally answered. "When the bell rings the hour, our magic ceases to exist."

"Is it painful for you as well?" Theo asked.

"Not painful like it is for fairies. But we do lose our magic every single hour. For the forest, though, when the bell tolls, the magic is drained out of the trees and plants like blood. While they work hard to replenish it, the plants are losing strength, and it is taking its toll. We try our best, but with our own magic leaving every hour, we are also not as able to help them."

"How long has this been going on?" Theo asked.

"Years."

"And the puca had something to do with this?" Theo asked.

"The puca? No. He's terribly aggravating and for some reason a while ago he lived at the edge of our dell."

"So you took something from him?"

"Yes."

"Then would you be able to give me what you took and I will take my leave?"

This entire meeting was Theo saying the wrong thing, and that was exceptionally bad given how the queen reacted.

With a look of distaste that would have made Arlys proud,

she said, "So, not only has your regent ignored my request for aid, you show up *as a human familiar* not to help me, but to help the puca. And you want me to simply turn over that information and send you on your merry way while I continue to be disrespected?"

"Maybe I can help you and we can both walk away with something that benefits us," Theo said.

Queen Blossom watched her for a moment, her anger slowly being replaced by a devious smile. "Fine, then. Since a bargain with you could be beneficial to us both, I will offer you a deal. If you can remove that horrible noise, I will give you back what I took from the puca." Theo didn't miss the hint of a dare swimming in the queen's eyes.

Theo had seen that look before. The queen thought she could pull one over on Theo. And Theo wanted nothing more than to prove the queen's folly in that line of thinking.

Unfortunately, Theo had no clue as to how she could remove a bell even with her friends' help. How does one get a bell up a steeple in the first place? How does one take it down should it need to be repaired? Theo never would have thought her inadequate-bordering-on-nonexistent knowledge of bells would be what sabotaged her entire scheme. Bells, her undoing.

But thinking of repairing bells brought up a memory that was, up until this point, completely trivial and useless in her daily life. And because of it, Theo did know something about bells. Rudimentary, to be sure, but knowledge nonetheless, gleaned after one of the bells in town near Merrifall broke, the clapper falling off and damaging the stone floor. A banal controversy, but it gave the bored gentry conversation fodder for weeks (*What if there had been a child standing there?!*). And from that, Theo learned that bells had a few parts to them: namely the bell itself and the clapper inside—the metal stick that banged on the inside and made the noise. And the thought gave her an idea.

"I'll agree to your terms," Theo said. "In exchange for you providing me information on what you took from the puca, I will remove what is causing the horrible noise that is negating your magic and the magic of the forest."

Queen Blossom was nodding along, her smirk firmly in place. But then she added, "You will do that first before I share my information."

"Of course. Then it's a deal."

The queen gave her a satisfied look, as though she'd pulled one over on Theo. Fine.

"Wonderful," the queen drawled. "I would say see you in a few years, but it doesn't seem like that will be the case."

"Pardon? Why a few years?"

"Because it has taken the sprites months of planning for our attempts at removing the bell. You are human on a time limit. Not only that, but I know you're not a princess yet. You're still a familiar. So I'm not expecting much of anything from you. Give my regards to the puca." The queen brought out her devious smile again before standing up and flying back to her tree, disappearing through the door without so much as a backward glance.

Arlys, employing his favorite method of communication, turned to Theo and snorted. "What a ludicrous bargain to make. I hope you're not expecting my help, Princess Amabel. Even if I wanted to, I can't. Similarly to iron, I can't direct any magic toward a bell. If fairies could, don't you think we'd have destroyed every bell immediately? So what do you think you'll be able to do as a human? You might be able to knock it down without killing yourself or any bystanders, but then what? Are you going to insult the bell out of there? You're certainly not strong enough to drag it out. Neither am I or the rest of you." He gestured to Kaz and Phineas.

Theo gave him a patient smile that she knew would set him off. "I don't need your help, thank you."

And it did, as Arlys looked at her as if she'd served him a bowl of bells for breakfast. "Well then, what's your plan?"

"Don't you worry your angry little head about it." To which Kaz and Phineas snickered. One benefit of having Kaz and Phineas with her was that, while they might not have known the intricacies of her current plan, they knew in a general sense what she was doing; they, too, had made plenty of bargains. She answered them with a wink, but when she looked at Kaz directly, his smile faded. Hers did as well. This was going to be a long, uncomfortable day when one-fourth of her traveling companions could hardly stand the sight of her.

Theo turned and walked back up the path that would take them to the old church.

But when she reached the top, she didn't go straight inside. Instead, she went to the other side of the cemetery to the gardener's shack. When she opened the door, she was greeted with a plethora of tools, but she only had eyes for one: a hatchet.

With the others following behind her, she then went to the church.

The building was unlocked when they tried the door, and mercifully empty. She knew she'd have an awfully hard time trying to explain righteous vandalism to anyone who showed up. Just as Theo suspected, the inside was simple and small, only a handful of pews and a modest altar. But save for the area around the steeple ladder, a layer of dust coated everything, as though no one had been inside in quite some time.

Theo didn't wait before climbing the ladder to the top. The bell itself wasn't all that large compared to other bells Theo had seen and heard. If she stood next to it, the bell would only reach her knees. It was typically and simply made of bronze with very little adornment. She wondered why anyone would bother to keep repairing a bell in an old building no one had been using, but maybe it was for historical purposes.

The clapper inside the bell was also standard-issue bronze. And otherwise just as unremarkable as the bell—a metal pole about the size of her forearm with a metal bulb at the bottom. And fortuitously connecting it to the bell was a piece of wood with a stirrup-shaped metal hook through it, allowing the clapper to swing.

With her newly acquired hatchet, she started chopping. Everyone was silent, the *tack-tack-tack* of the blade echoing like the ticking of a clock, splinters falling to the floor as she worked. Soon enough, the metal noisemaker dropped straight to the floor when the last bit of wood finally gave up the fight.

"Nicely done," Kaz said as she climbed back down.

"Yes," Phineas said. "Can't say that I'm surprised, but once again you prove yourself to be very clever."

She scooped up the clapper and returned their expressions. "Thank you."

Arlys scoffed. "I don't know why you three are celebrating. You didn't remove the bell."

Kaz gave him a half smile, head cocked like he was just now considering Arlys. "Is this your first week as a fairy?"

"You'd think, right?" Theo agreed. Then turned to the fairy. "I would have otherwise expected better from a fairy."

"What's that supposed to mean?" Arlys asked.

"You're about to find out."

With that, she led them out of the building and back to the maple tree in the dell, Theo firmly gripping the clapper in her hand.

The same herald answered the door when she knocked.

"What?" he said with both the flatness and fortitude of a crepe.

"I'm here to claim Queen Blossom's end of the bargain."

He disappeared inside, returning shortly with the queen. Theo knew Queen Blossom wouldn't be thrilled to see her so soon after she thought she won, but it seemed to go beyond that, decorum going the way of magic at the stroke of midnight.

But she said nothing as she flew to her throne perch again.

Theo held up the clapper. "As promised, and thus concluding my end of our bargain."

The queen laughed humorlessly. "I do not accept. That is not the bell."

"Removing the bell was not in the terms of our agreement," Theo said with a smile.

"Yes, it was," the queen snapped.

"No. You said I was to remove what was causing that horrible noise. This delightful piece of metal is what bangs on the bell. Now that it is in my hand, you will find that when the next hour comes along and the bell tries to ring, no sound will be made. Horrible noise removed."

The queen's face was turning as red as her dress. "You know full well that is not what I meant!"

Theo shrugged. "I have learned that you must be very specific when making bargains, Your Majesty."

"I do not accept! I will not tell you anything about what I took from the puca!"

"That is your choice, Queen Blossom, but I would highly advise against it. I really have no desire to be taking on any royal familiars when I'm a fairy. Even if I am put into slumber, when I wake, you'll still be indebted to me."

"It might not be too bad, Theo," Kaz said from next to her. "I'm sure you could think of lots of fun errands to send her on."

"How true, Kaz!" Theo said, matching his mocking tone.

Queen Blossom was in danger of exploding out of her throne. "This is not a game!"

"Are you sure?" Theo asked. "You seemed plenty willing to try to best me just a little bit ago. What was that, if not a game?"

"My kingdom is dying! I have been ignored by your regent and now mocked by you when I am trying to restore magic to save both my people and our home."

Theo's smile and sense of victory faltered at the tears pooling in the corners of Queen Blossom's eyes.

The queen continued. "We have tried everything. And even when we are successful, our efforts have only provided us a week's reprieve before someone comes to fix it. We've tried destroying the bell, destroying the clapper, destroying the mechanism that rings the bell, and burning the ropes. Nothing has worked. You now stand here proud to have conned me."

Theo wanted to argue back and say that she had not conned her out of anything, and that next time Queen Blossom ought to be more careful when underestimating humans. But she didn't. Watching the queen wipe away angry tears had Theo feeling sorry for her.

Theo sighed. "Your Majesty, I am aware I have not provided a permanent solution. I simply do not have the time. However, if I make it through this, if I get what I need from the puca and save myself from either death or slumber, I will find a way to remove the bell entirely."

Queen Blossom glared. "I am making no further bargains with you."

"That wasn't a bargain. That was simply an offer. Consider it professional courtesy."

For a moment, Theo thought Queen Blossom would stick with her initial spite-filled threat and tell her nothing. But then, with her head held high, the queen said, "In addition, if you are not killed or put into slumber, I will have a formal invitation to your coronation and sit with the other monarchs and royals."

Theo almost laughed. Coronation? That was rich. Seemed like the queen couldn't figure out whether Theo was a lowly human familiar or a princess in training. But instead of telling Queen Blossom she had no intention of sitting on a throne, Theo said, "I will do that."

"Then I will tell you what I took from the puca." She leaned back in her throne, her tone once again bored. "I had placed upon him a simple truth charm. Easy magic, very successful. To break it, all you need to do is look into his eyes and tell him the real truth—not the one he's been charmed to believe."

"And the truth is..." Theo prodded.

If Queen Blossom's pause was any more dramatic, she could have performed it in a theater. "His favorite drink is hot chocolate."

Theo jerked back. "What? What does that have to do with anything?"

"That's what I took from him. I convinced him that he hates hot chocolate and he should never go near it. Remind him that he loves it."

"I... uh... that's it?"

"What were you expecting?"

"Honestly? Something with more consequence, I suppose."

"As I said, he is horribly annoying in general, and even more so about hot chocolate in particular. So I did something annoying in return. And may have saved some wildlife a headache or two. Truth charms can be a lot worse, you know. Very complicated. Layers upon layers until the receiver has no idea which way is up. This one was rather unimaginative in the grand scheme of things. Fitting consequences, I think."

Theo was nearly put into a drink-induced stupor from a drink she hadn't even consumed. The information to save her life had been hinging on a bell clapper and hot chocolate. What wildlife had to do with it she had no idea.

It was Phineas who finally cut Theo out of her daze by bowing to the queen and saying, "Thank you, Your Majesty. We shall take our leave."

Now she could finally get what she needed from the puca.

# Chapter 19

# Where Hot Chocolate Constitutes a Real Danger for the Wildlife of the Fen

The goat was easy enough to find. He was still in the small clearing, this time having an argument with the tree.

"Excuse me." It was only now that Theo realized she had no idea how to address him other than "the puca."

He turned to face the group and, unlike last time, was not surprised at all to find them back and in his clearing. He put his hooves on his hips and said with a chuckle while shaking his head, "If only the noise would quiet down, then I could hear the music. They're supposed to be quite good." But then he noticed the clapper in Theo's hands. "Is that what I forgot? It is bigger than a loaf of bread, isn't it?!"

"Oh, no. This is part of my bargain with Queen Blossom."

He used his front hoof to rub his chin while he studied it. "You know, I think you're right. Now that I'm looking at it, it doesn't ring any bells."

Theo wasn't sure if that was supposed to be a joke, as the puca didn't seem to think it was funny. Kaz and Phineas did, since she could hear them stifling laughs behind her. And if Arlys's groan was any indication, he was finding the puca about as funny as an ingrown toenail.

She was just about to remind him of what he forgot, but he seemed to have forgotten the very conversation they were having, as he became distracted by a snipe in the marshy water nearby. The little bird, for all Theo could see, was quietly minding its own business, searching for something to eat. Yet this offended the puca to no end. He ran at the bird, arms waving wildly while shouting, "Stop eating Mother's scones or you shan't fit into your party dress!" Then he added to himself, "No, no, that was too far back. Oh, but the new dress shimmers and shines." The poor bird, neither eating scones nor trying to put on an ill-fitting outfit, took to the skies like it was launched from a catapult. The puca paid no notice and instead stared at some cattails in consideration while he began humming again, the same song as before. It must have been very common, since Theo recognized it as one of the songs Beric really enjoyed playing.

*Uh-oh.*

So this was what everyone had been talking about. The puca seemed to be in some sort of spiral, gibberish spouting out of him like an ill-conceived fountain.

"Sir? Sir... Puca? We have some business to finish," Theo said, feeling like she was interrupting an important conversation.

But the puca stopped and turned to face Theo again. "Princess, princess, in distress. How is it you go? Fairy rings and noisy things and pretty friends all in a row!" He began cackling with some private jest.

This was looking more and more like a big mistake. Could she just walk away? Did any of this vacate the bargain she had made? What would the puca owe her if he didn't hold up his end of the bargain? Theo was ready to void the bargain entirely and call it square this instant. She certainly didn't want a puca attached to her. She'd go as mad as the puca if she had to spend any extended amount of time with him. And she really couldn't afford that right now.

No. She'd come too far to quit. So she plowed on, her sunken cost in this currently at the bottom of the ocean.

"If you are quite finished!" She was aiming for her best headmistress impression, and it seemed to do the trick. The puca halted and stared at her, the insects ceased their buzzing, and even the group she was with stood a bit straighter.

"Thank you," she continued. "Now, would you like me to remind you of what you forgot? I was successful at holding up my end of our bargain."

"Oh yes, yes!"

She walked closer. "I was told to look you in the eye and tell you the truth. Once it is revealed, you will remember it. All right?"

He nodded.

Theo wasn't sure how much gravitas she was supposed to

put into this. She felt like she should do something a bit more official to break the charm, but she honestly didn't know what that might be.

Nothing to do other than come out and say it, then.

She leaned down a little so she could look directly into the goat's yellow, unexpressive eyes.

"Your favorite drink is hot chocolate."

Those eyes went wide and he took a step back. Confusion started to slough off his face, as if removing it layer by layer to reveal surprise underneath. And with it, what appeared to be an oily sheen dripping down his body. Then, that surprise slowly morphed into understanding, his emotions moving at the speed of cold syrup.

"It is," he whispered. For a moment, he stood in quiet contemplation, presumably thinking about his favorite warm beverage. "She told me I hated it and that I never wanted it ever again.

"I think I'll have some now." His voice was small, almost childlike in its innocence. His ears drooped, his eyes went wide, his front hooves doing their best impression of being clasped together.

The puca conjured a steaming mug—most likely containing hot chocolate—and held the handle between his two toes, using his other front foot to hold underneath so as not to drop it. Based on how reverent he had sounded at the mere mention of the drink, Theo assumed he would sip it like wine, appreciating and savoring the flavor. Instead, he chugged it down to the chocolatey dregs, the heat not bothering him in the slightest. Once the mug was empty, he turned toward the water and, with no warning, chucked it as hard as he could.

In any other context, Theo might have been rather impressed at the throwing strength of this goat. The mug crested the fen like a majestic bird surveying its land, a twirling black shape transposed against the twilight sky. Theo couldn't see where it went, and she only knew it landed by the accompanying splash.

"I think I'll have another," the puca said sweetly, and then conjured a second steaming mug.

Theo, wide-eyed herself now and muddled at the interaction, said, "Could you please not throw—" which was quickly cut off when the puca downed the second in two big gulps and did exactly that.

Kaz, face scrunched in confusion, said to Theo, "The first one I thought might be a fluke, but now I am completely lost."

"I think we are witnessing the exact reason Queen Blossom took this away from him," Phineas said, noting how the queen had said he was "annoying" about hot chocolate. At the time, Theo couldn't possibly understand what would be obnoxious about an otherwise benign drink.

If he threw any more, the rest of the animals in the fen might start thinking mugs were a migratory species.

Following the second splash and a chorus of angry croaks from some displaced frogs, the puca finally seemed satisfied. The rest of the assembled group collectively managed to close their dropped jaws before bugs flew in.

Without warning, but with a snapping noise, a hare appeared in the goat's place. He was still the same color black, now with glossy eyes to match. The trousers were gone, and so was the ability to balance long enough on his back legs for him to walk. Instead, he hopped to the boulder and scurried to the top.

"I do so enjoy pants, but I do my best thinking without them," he said, by way of explanation, the hot chocolate now completely forgotten. Theo agreed with a jerky nod. "So, what is it you wanted to know?" the puca asked, his little whiskers twitching with each word. "Is it about you being a changeling?"

"Sort of? Not quite—"

"And about how you being a changeling was the source of a great many strifes in your life?"

"No, I don't think that it was. I only found out I was a changeling a few days ago—"

"And how everyone in your human life seemed to pick up that something was wrong with you and therefore were uncomfortable in your presence and maybe that had a lot to do with their behavior toward you?"

"Wait, what?"

"Makes sense though now, doesn't it? You aren't a human! You're just pretending to be!"

"No, I—pardon?"

"About the Saint-John's-wort?"

"No."

"About the iron?"

*"No."*

"So is our bargain concluded?"

"No! That isn't what I came for!"

"Oh. Then what do you want to know?"

"About someone trying to kill me!"

"Right! Right, right, right. I remember now. Give me a moment."

He then closed his eyes and began to hum that same song quietly to himself.

Alby approached Theo, cutting through the disorder with a tug on her hand. He smiled up at Theo and said just above a whisper, "I think he will give you great information. You'll see."

She nodded at him, unable to do much more. For the goblin's optimistic smile, she hoped he was right.

The puca opened his eyes. "I have the information you seek," he said with a solemnity of someone who didn't toss mugs, argue with reeds, or think best without trousers. And then he said no more. He just sat there, blinking his beady eyes at her.

"And?" Theo motioned, her patience having been siphoned away over the course of this entire mission by this bizarre creature.

"Oh, right. The information you seek."

"Is what?!"

He cleared his throat. Theo held her breath. Finally, some answers.

"Golden chicken."

When Theo watched him launch mugs like cannonballs with handles, she was confused. But this…this went far beyond confusing. All thought processes capable of working out any semblance of meaning had not just stopped, they quit in a hurry and took some silverware as plunder on the way out.

She knew what *golden* meant.

She knew what a *chicken* was.

And she knew their combined definitions did not equal meaningful information about a murder.

"I'm sorry. Did you say 'golden . . . chicken'?" Kaz asked, sounding just as confounded as she felt. And it sounded just as ludicrous coming out of his mouth as it did the hare's.

"Yes," the puca said. "I see in my mind's eye a golden chicken."

It seemed his information had done the same thing to the rest of the group. Phineas had his head in his hands, and if Arlys rolled his eyes any harder he would be able to see his own brain. Alby's eyes were shinier than usual, rimmed with tears that had not yet spilled over.

"One more time, just so I'm sure I am hearing you correctly," Theo said, a small part of her still hoping this was all a mistake and would work itself out in short order. "You are saying your answer to my question about who is trying to murder me is 'golden chicken'?"

"Yes!" He did not seem at all bothered by her insistence that he should repeat himself, and instead nodded and clapped like she had just concluded a tap dance, his furry paws making no sound at all. "And thus, our bargain is concluded!"

"What? No! I do not accept!" she shouted, sounding an awful lot like Queen Blossom. "That is not information. That is nonsense!"

"It must make sense because that is what I saw. Golden chicken. Our bargain is at an end."

And so was her optimism, the last shreds of hope stomped into the mud. The simmering pot that was her temper had now finally boiled over, and with it, rationality.

"That was nothing but inane blather!" Theo shouted at the nonplussed hare.

"No, it's not."

"I can do it, too, see? Chartreuse pickles! Fluffy sewing needle! Honeysuckle brandy bonnet!"

He shook his head sadly. "That was meaningless. You haven't the mind for prophecy, I'm afraid."

"Here's a prophecy for you: rabbit stew! Someone procure me a mug of hot chocolate! I'm going to wallop him with it!"

The puca was shocked, like he simply had no clue how her current mood could have manifested.

She had bargained away an entire day for this.

Theo started walking toward the boulder, realizing she already had in hand a weapon to exact her revenge. If the clapper was good enough for ringing a bell, it was good enough for ringing a hare. Kaz, thankfully or not, had managed to grab Theo's arm before she could.

"I think it is time for you to leave," the puca said. "Lovely to meet you!" Then he hopped off the boulder and down to the water, where he began discussing flower choices with a beetle.

"He's right," Kaz said, still holding on to Theo. "We should leave."

"I don't even know where we're supposed to go," Theo said, shrugging out of his grip.

"If you want a comfortable bed, I can find fifty in the Palace of the Fae," Arlys said flatly.

"So that idea is out," Kaz said while glaring at Arlys. "Does anyone without an ax to grind or a strong desire to be unhelpful have any suggestions?"

No one spoke up.

"This is what you get when you take suggestions from a goblin," Arlys growled.

With every heated word from Arlys, Alby seemed to shrink in on himself. His shoulders curved in and his head bent low like he was trying to disappear entirely.

"At least he had an idea and was trying to help," Theo snarled back. "I know that concept sits on very foreign shores for you."

She felt a little tug on her hand and looked down to see Alby. The moon reflecting off of his giant eyes made his pupils glow. But she could also see a line of silver at the base, tears not quite yet escaping.

"I'm sorry, Theo," he said, his voice just above a whisper. "I thought this would work. I've made a horrible mistake. I will go and leave you alone."

"What? No! No, Alby, listen. You didn't make a mistake. It was my decision to come here, not yours."

This seemed to reassure him, for which Theo was glad. However, she couldn't deny that the situation was going poorly. The clues she did have barely amounted to anything at all. The map brought them to nothing but an empty house and a grave. The coins were worthless and not used in fairy society anyway. *Golden chicken* was nothing at all. And unless Theo could develop psychic powers that extended beyond the grave in the next hour or so, any more clues the ogres could give her were gone.

Contrarily, with Theo's help there were now two arrests, an arson, and clock tower property damage. How was she going to be successful enough in this to get Cecily and Lock out of the Palace of the Fae? Maybe she should bow out early and cut and run.

And the aggravating cherry on top? The song the puca hummed was now firmly stuck in her head. Of all the songs to hum, why did he have to choose that one?

But then again, what if it was on purpose? She knew it was a stretch, but better than the unyielding nothing they were working with now. Maybe the song wasn't a complete coincidence.

"What if we went to Beric's house?" Theo asked.

Phineas nodded in consideration. Arlys, arms folded and vocalizing his displeasure by snorting like a bull with allergies, was upset she hadn't dissolved into a puddle of tears begging him to take her back to the palace.

"Settled, then," she said. But before she conjured any wind to transport them, she held up a hand. "Wait. Arlys, you need to swear to us that you won't tell anyone about where we're going to go, or that we're there, or that we are friends with the occupants." She had made this same bargain with him at the tree house, but that was about the tree house. In this new location, she wanted it reconfirmed he wasn't about to sell them out.

Arlys rolled his eyes. "Quit acting like I was the one who sent Ursula. If anyone else shows up to pick off the remaining members of Princess Amabel's incompetent entourage, it won't be me."

Theo wanted to smack the scowl off his face. But instead she said, "Well, you're in that entourage at present. Glad we're finally agreeing on your incompetence. So first, stop acting like we have no reason to be suspicious. Second, swear it. If you tell anyone the whereabouts of my friends and their homes, our bargain is void."

Arlys answered by looking at Theo like she'd packed up her common sense and mailed it to the other side of the world. As though trusting her friends was the highest of ridiculous notions. But to his credit, he said, "Fine. I swear I will not say a word of your friends' whereabouts to anyone lest I void the bargain between us. Happy?"

"With you? Of course not," Theo said. "But good enough. Let's go."

# Chapter 20
# Where Friends and Chickens Are Both Golden

The group landed at the edge of a wide field. The late hour and the silver light of the moon made Theo feel like she was on the shore of a calm sea, the swaying of the wildflowers and wheat in the wind reminding her of gentle waves. And in the center like an island was a large stone house.

In the months since Theo became a familiar and began spending time with her bandmates regularly, she'd also spent plenty of time at Beric's house. It was not any grand size like Cecily's, and often his version of a party was a small gathering in his drawing room, usually limited to musicians only. And because she was a frequent guest, she wasted no time before walking through the field to the front door.

The knocker had only just hit the plate before the door

burst open, arms yanked her inside, and she was wrapped into a tight embrace by Beric, Torian, and Lowen.

The rest of the group filed in after Theo, the door shutting behind them.

After a minute they let her out of the hug, but Beric still held her by the shoulders, looking her over. "Theo! You're here! I can't even begin to tell you how relieved I am to see you. What happened? Where were you? Where did you go? Why are you holding—is that a clapper to a bell?"

Theo looked down at her hand. Sure enough, the clapper was still there. Frankly, she had forgotten about it completely and only held it due to anger-induced muscle seizing that had her fingers gripped tightly around it.

"Oh yes. In fact, it is. As to your other questions . . . did you hear anything about me?"

"Well, that's cryptic. What about you? You completely vanished a few days ago. We went by your house, but no one was there. Then we heard you performed at the clock tower party—and rumor has it you were exceptional, by the way—but hadn't returned. Lock's house was also strangely empty. So we went to the palace to see if you were still at the party, but while the partygoers remembered the phenomenal harpist, no one had seen her since her performance. When we tried to ask anyone from the palace staff if you were still there, they wouldn't tell us anything."

Arlys, who up until this point had been unobtrusively channeling his inner plain brown rug, spoke up from the corner. "That is because it is none of your concern."

Beric, Torian, and Lowen looked at him as though only now just realizing he was here.

A flash of recognition passed over Beric's face. "Aren't you that strange, staring fairy who wanted to join the band? What on earth are you doing here?" he asked. Then he turned to Theo. "Did you let him into the band?"

"For the last time," Arlys snapped. "I am not looking to join your ridiculous band!"

They let his outburst go, but once they noticed him, her musician friends seemed to become aware of the rest of the group, too.

"Hello, Alby! Hello, Phineas!" Beric said merrily. Then he looked to Kaz. "And I don't believe I've met you before."

Theo stepped in to do introductions as Kaz waved a hello. "This is Cecily's former familiar, Kaz. I am the one who took his place." Theo saw Kaz flinch ever so slightly. "And, Kaz, these are my friends and bandmates, Beric, Torian, and Lowen."

"If you're a former familiar, what brings you back to the fairy realm?"

Again, Theo spoke instead. "We needed him to find the puca. I have a lot to tell you about the last few days."

"I'd say so," Beric said. "Why don't we take this to the drawing room? Seems like you have a bit of a story. And welcome to my home, Kaz. A friend of Theo's is a friend of ours." He then looked awkwardly at Arlys. "I didn't actually catch your name."

"Arlys," he said, leveling a contentious glare at Beric.

"Right." Beric nodded slowly. "Well, like I said, a friend of Theo's—"

"He's not a friend," Theo said with a dismissive wave. Beric raised his eyebrows but said nothing more about it when Arlys seemed to fully agree with her statement.

"Where are Cecily and Lock?" Torian asked.

Theo answered with a sigh as she sank down next to her on one of the sofas.

Beric had a penchant for luxury, just not the fancy kind. He was a creature of luxurious comfort. A fire in the massive gray stone fireplace kept the room at just the right temperature. The sofas and chairs, as well as the pillows on them, were all oversize and plush, in neutral colors that did not compete to overtake one another. Blankets abounded, scattered on the backs of every seat, as well as piled in a basket in the corner, just in case there weren't enough.

When everyone found a seat, or a corner to lurk in for Arlys, and had a drink near them, all attention focused on Theo, waiting for her to start talking.

The tiara-wearing elephant in the room was standing in front of her, batting her in the face. So, in the interest of eating that elephant one bite at a time, she started.

"Bit of news." Not her strongest opener, but she'd had a long day. She launched into the story starting with the garden party. When she got to the princess portion, her friends' faces went slack and they stared at her motionlessly.

"You're . . . you're Iara?" Torian managed to say.

"Oh, um, no," Theo said. "Turns out she's dead. I'm . . . the other one."

"Amabel?"

"Supposedly."

"You've got to be joking. You're having a laugh."

Theo shook her head. "That's why he's here," she said, pointing to Arlys. "Does he look like he's ever laughed in his life? He's with us because he wants me to go back into slumber, but since I'm still a familiar, he can't transport me there." Theo didn't think it was possible, but at that, Arlys's scowl deepened. If it went any further, they may have to find something to prop up his brow, as it was now in danger of falling off his face completely.

"So . . . where have you been the last few days? And why are you here and not in the palace?" Torian asked.

"Because someone either at the palace or who has access to the palace wants to kill me." While they sat silently, Theo continued to relay the last few days to them, what they found out, the ogre-led kidnapping attempt, the Perran-led attack in the yew forest, where Cecily and Lock were, and how they made it to the puca.

"The puca didn't exactly help," Theo explained. "After everything with the Dell Sprites, all he said was he saw in his mind's eye a 'golden chicken.' I don't know what that means, but he was constantly humming that song you like, Beric. The one we opened with at Cecily's party a month ago."

"Oh, I do like that song!" Beric said. "And the puca said 'golden chicken'?"

Theo nodded. "Yes, but he was saying a lot of other things, too, so that was just one more bit of nonsense."

But Beric frowned like he was seriously considering what she'd said.

"I don't think so," Beric said slowly. "Not 'golden chicken.' Gilded Hen."

"No, he definitely said 'golden chicken.' I even asked him to repeat himself. Ask them." She pointed to the others, who nodded their agreement.

"He saw the Gilded Hen," Beric said.

"Is that some sort of magical being I have yet to encounter?" Theo had never heard of a magical gilded hen, but given every other experience, she wouldn't be surprised.

"No. The Gilded Hen is a tavern."

"A tavern?"

"Yes," Beric said. "I used to play there a long time ago."

None of this made sense to Theo. "Why would the puca see a tavern?"

"Absolutely no idea," Beric said. "Do you think the puca meant there is something at the Gilded Hen?"

"At this point, I suppose anything is possible," Theo said. "But who knows? He was spouting gibberish the entire time. He did seem pretty confident in that, though." A little kernel of something hope-adjacent was growing in her chest. Like she was lost in the woods and saw a tree that looked slightly familiar.

"We should go!" Lowen said.

Beric smiled and nodded. "Good thing we have the perfect cover."

"What's that?" Theo asked.

Torian nudged her lightly. "How would you like to play at a venue where no one will be listening to the music while two drunk fairies have a fistfight in front of the stage? Our secret identity is just our actual identity—we'll go as the band!"

"That's actually perfect," Theo said. "We can get onstage, see what there is to see, hear what there is to hear."

Lowen nodded. "And then spend some time there afterward with no one giving us a second thought."

"Could we get there tonight?" Theo asked.

Beric frowned. "Tonight's no good if we want to get onstage. The night started a while ago, so it would be odd if musicians showed up this late looking to play. We need to go at the beginning of the night."

Kaz started shaking his head. "That won't do. We're on a time limit."

"You are under no obligation to come along, Kaz," Theo said, eliciting uncomfortable looks from everyone but Arlys.

"Ignore the lovers' spat," Phineas said to the group, to which Kaz and Theo both snorted. "But Kaz is correct that we are operating on a pretty snug schedule."

Her three fairy friends looked to Theo.

Theo realized then she hadn't really told them why Arlys was following them other than that he was from the palace. "If I don't figure this out in about two days, Arlys is going to put me back into slumber. Well, not quite. I entered a bargain with him. If I can't produce the assassin by then, I'll become his familiar, and thus he can do whatever he wants with me. And what he wants is to put me into slumber."

Her three fairy friends turned from her to Arlys, shocked.

"He can't do that!" Torian shouted, pointing an accusatory finger in his direction.

Arlys, meanwhile, didn't dignify her outburst with a response and instead continued to stare at them from the corner like he was haunting the place.

Theo sighed. "That was the bargain I made, unfortunately."

"Well then," Lowen said. "Let's eat, sleep, and then tomorrow night, we go to a tavern."

When the others all voiced their agreement, Arlys finally took a pause from lurking to put himself into the conversation. "Now, hold on just one moment. I do not consent to this plan."

"You have a problem with sleeping, eating, and music?" Lowen asked.

Phineas scoffed. "You would, wouldn't you?"

Arlys glared at them in return. "No. I mean going to the tavern. It isn't a good plan."

"We don't even really have a plan yet," Torian said.

"Exactly!" Arlys snapped. "We don't know what we're looking for or what we're walking into." He pointed a finger at Theo. "It is much too dangerous for you to go. What if someone recognizes you?"

Beric snapped his fingers, eyes lighting up with an idea. "He's got a point! What about this? Theo, we'll put a glamour on you. You've done it before, shouldn't be too hard. You too, Kaz and Phineas."

"No," Arlys said. "You're not spies! You're musicians!"

Kaz raised his eyebrows. "Exactly! Musicians playing music at a tavern are expected. Did you want us to go as politicians? Carnival barkers?"

"Besides, it isn't up to you," Theo said, once again sick of his snide attitude at everything and everyone close to her. "I think it is a perfectly reasonable plan." What's your idea? We can all put on the world's most boring clothes and all find corners to slink to like unfashionable, antisocial ghouls? Brilliant. Then we'll blend seamlessly and no average tavern patron will be suspicious in the least. Oh, no, sorry. Your idea is to not go at all and have me prance happily over to the palace to be put into slumber."

Theo was expecting another eye roll, scowl, or glare as the entire room went after him. But he only looked at Theo, pausing as his face fell blank, like his emotions had finally been pushed to the brink and he was left with nothing. "Really," he said to her. "Personal attacks again? I'm working to save your life, to protect you from *death*, and you take this opportunity to insult me? You miserable, ungrateful brat. I think it is pretty clear why people didn't like you in the human realm, and it isn't because you are a changeling."

"Oh, go frolic in a field of Saint-John's-wort," Theo snapped. "If you don't know where one is, let me know and I'll be happy to point you in the right direction."

Arlys scowled, a predictable response to what Theo was really insinuating.

He walked to the front door, stopping when his hand touched the handle. "I'll be back tomorrow. Beric, make sure your wards are secure." And with that, he walked out of the house, slamming the door shut behind him.

The rest of the drawing room was stunned into silence.

"Well, that was out of line," Torian said.

"I'd say," Lowen agreed. "What is he even talking about?"

They were looking at her like she was supposed to roll her eyes and laugh, tell them she had no idea what Arlys was going on about. But she couldn't. Theo didn't want to explain this to them, didn't want to tell them about the human realm and what kind of person she had been there.

Because Arlys wasn't out of line.

He was right.

She had never told her friends about her past. Not really. The closest she ever came was telling them she did not like it. Not that she had been a terrible person. Not that her misery and contempt were contagious, infecting everything and everyone around her. But Arlys had just given them a glimpse of who she really was as a person in front of the people who mattered most, and who she had carefully hidden the truth from.

"I think I will turn in as well," she said, looking at no one in particular and dashing out of the drawing room. She had spent many a night here before, so knew which guest room she could use. As soon as she made it up the stairs, she bolted inside and shut the door.

# Chapter 21

# Where Kaz and Theo Hash It Out

Theo managed to take off her ratty clothes, dirty from being in both a fen and a dell, and take a bath to further remove the remnants of the day. She found a robe in the closet and wrapped that around herself, figuring it would do in a pinch for pajamas.

But just when she was crawling into bed, there was a knock at her door. She went to open it and standing there, tray of food in hand, was Kaz.

She was surprised, but stood back, ushering him into the room and closing the door behind him.

"I thought you might be hungry," he said, lifting the tray just a little for emphasis. "I'm glad you're awake. Everyone else turned in for the night. Or early morning, at this point."

"I was about to." She was shocked her stomach wasn't grumbling louder considering she hadn't eaten anything all day.

He nodded and put the tray on the bed. "Then I won't stay long."

He was standing awkwardly in the middle of the room as she sat on her bed. Indecision flashed across his face as his attention kept waffling from her to the door, not sure where he was supposed to go. Theo was just about to let him off the hook and send him on his way when he turned to her. "So... how are you?" he asked, and then grimaced slightly.

"Fine, thank you," came out of her mouth like a reflex. Not that she had ever been one to discuss how she was feeling with any ease. Lady Martha Balfour had drilled this lesson into Theo's head since she could talk. In preparation for any conversation, the answer to the question of *How are you?* was always *Fine, thank you.* If she stubbed her toe while running from a house fire, when the authorities showed up and asked her how she was doing, she was expected to respond with *Fine, thank you* lest anyone think she was impolite, or worse—ill-bred.

But what was she supposed to say to Kaz instead?

She wanted him to miss her as much as she missed him, but had no idea how to tell him.

The truth of the matter was he didn't seem to miss her. Or want to be near her.

So why was he still here?

Oh, right. Because he couldn't transport himself anywhere. Maybe he was here to ask her for a transport back to his life. Everyone else was sleeping and she was the only one able to do it. He was desperate to leave.

"I can bring you home at any time. Or if you're not

comfortable with that, Phineas would do it." She tried to sound pleasant, giving him a dignified out. She was sick of fighting with him.

"Go home?"

"You agreed to help us find the puca and you did. So you can go back to your life now."

Kaz shook his head. "But... you only have two days left? I want to help."

"We don't need to find another puca." All right, that response wasn't so dignified.

He sighed. "You want me to go?"

She didn't answer that one. Which he took in the affirmative.

He nodded to himself, frowning, fiddling with the corner of his suit jacket. "I understand and won't make you do it. I'll go ask Phineas."

He walked to the door, pausing right before his hand touched the doorknob. She braced herself as she prepared to have the last thing she saw of him be his back.

But before he walked out of her life a second time, he turned to face her. "I know you hate me. And I'll leave you alone. But... I'm glad I got to see you."

It took a moment for his words to register.

*Excuse me?*

Theo wasn't sure what it was about Kaz that made her temper spark to life, but with that, he used dynamite. "Now, wait just one moment. You think *I* hate *you*? You've got that backward, mortal man!"

Kaz looked appalled. He dropped his hand from the doorknob and strode to the bed. "You believe I hate you?"

"Well, how could you possibly think I hate you?" Theo lobbed back, voice rising.

Matching her volume, Kaz said, "Because you're now a fairy's familiar on account of me. I was trying so hard to get out of being a familiar, and you paid the price—literally. I messed up your entire life! You're stuck as a familiar and I'm back in the human world. So I understand why you'd want nothing to do with me!"

Theo got off the bed to stand in front of him. Maybe she should have stood on the bed to give herself a bit of height, because now she was craning her neck to yell at him. Too late now. "That makes no sense, Kaz! I was spying on you all the time!"

"Well, I didn't know that until this morning, did I?"

"For your information, I spent a lot of time in a hole in a tree across from your house watching all your comings and goings. I even memorized your ludicrously boring human schedule. Why would I do that if I hated you?"

"Now, that goes toward my argument because that sounds an awful lot like step one in plotting my death."

"No!" Theo's voice was now shrill. "Just a hedgehog with an unrequited obsession and nothing better to do! But after today, I wish I had found a much more productive hobby because that one was incredibly pathetic. Granted, I knew that at the time, too, but it feels like that much more of a blow to my ego now that you know about it."

"Oh, *please*. You want to talk about pathetic?" Kaz nearly growled the words. "You've got nothing on me! You knew my schedule because every single day was exactly the same. I went through the motions like an automaton. For some flavor, I decided to get a haircut, thinking maybe that would do something for me. But it didn't! Now I'm still pathetic, just with shorter hair. And if you saw me so much, why didn't you ever talk to me?"

"And say *what*? You weren't supposed to have remembered me. You're saying I should have simply walked up and said, *Hello, I am a complete stranger to you, but before you left the service of a fairy, we were planning our lives together; no, wait, please don't call for the authorities.* But now I'm wishing I did, since I would have found out much earlier how you really feel."

This was a wholly new feeling, having an argument where the only person she insulted was herself, and it made her that much more incensed.

Apparently the same was true for Kaz. "Knock that off!" he shouted. "Again, *why would you think that*?"

"*Because you remembered me.* You never actually forgot me but still never came for me. Never wanted to see me."

"I wanted to see you every day!"

"Then why didn't you?"

"Because why would you want to see the person who ruined your life? And you proved me right! This whole day you have done your best to not even look at me. I figured you'd never want to see my face again!"

"Well, you're wrong because I always want to see your face!"

Theo and Kaz both froze, chests heaving like they had literally sprinted through their fight.

And in that next second, as Kaz reached for her, she reached for him, mouths crashing together. There was no time for gentle, tentative kissing. They went directly to fierce and passionate. Theo's hands went to the back of Kaz's neck, holding him to her, while Kaz put his arms around her. She had built this kiss up in her head every time she went to watch Kaz, dreaming about what it would be like to hold him again, to kiss him again, knowing that nothing would probably live up to it. But she was wrong. This was more than she imagined. It was every fantasy she'd had wrapped into one. Someone who saw everything—the good and the bad—within her and loved her because of it, never in spite of it. That sense of home she'd always wanted, here with her right now.

She ran her hands through his hair, shorter now, but still familiar under her fingers. She opened her eyes, asking for him to do the same so she could once again stare into his beautiful honey-molasses eyes, as he stared into hers.

He pulled her tight to his chest, walking them back to the bed.

Somewhere in the back of her mind, hidden behind the happiness and relief of having Kaz near her once again, was the reminder that this was fleeting. In a few days, she would be leaving.

*He is not mine to keep.*

But for now, for tonight, she'd let herself have him.

---

It was well into late afternoon when Theo finally woke. Kaz was still next to her, head on the pillow, snuggled deep into the blankets.

He stirred and blinked his eyes, first looking around the room like he was trying to figure out how he got here. Recognition crossed his face and he turned to look at her, smiling when he saw her. He reached over and pulled her close, planting a kiss on her cheek. "I thought I was dreaming there for a second. Glad you're really here."

"*Me too,*" she whispered.

They watched each other for a bit before Kaz spoke.

"You know," he started. "In the mess of last night's argument, we never talked about you being a fairy princess."

Theo snorted. "I don't know that there's much to talk about."

"Sure, there is. For one, why you seem to snap at everyone who calls you *princess.*"

"A few reasons. First, it is ridiculous, and second, I don't want the job."

"You didn't grow up wanting to be a fairy princess?"

"Of course I did. Six-year-old Theo would have loved this turn of events. But then, like you said, I grew up. I know it for what it is now."

"And what is that?"

"A life that is not my own." Theo paused, trying to decide how to explain. "When Bea and I were exceptionally bored, we used to play a game called If I'm in Charge and it was exactly what it sounds like. Musings of two little girls without a shred of power to their names. Of course we were just children then, so I once declared that ice cream would be served for breakfast. Bea proclaimed making children do lessons was a fireable offense and would not be tolerated. One of my favorites was that if you *didn't* come into the house with muddy shoes you'd be punished."

Kaz grinned at her.

"And even when I wasn't a child anymore, I still thought of that game. All the more so when I believed I was going to be a duchess. *When I'm duchess, I'll remove anyone who is mean to me, I'll plan parties so amazing that everyone in the kingdom would be begging for an invitation, and I'll do what I want, when I want to.* But well before I met Cecily, I learned that that is not how it works. Even if everyone liked me at the duke's estate, I'd still owe myself to them and to the duke. I was still going to be told what to wear, who to speak with, what I could and could not do, what I could and could not eat. I'd have responsibilities as a duchess that were nonsensical but compulsory.

"I thought I was free of that up until a few days ago. I purposely gave that up. And I know I'm not exactly free as a fairy's familiar, but at least I'm really only beholden to myself now. But now here it comes, roaring back with a vengeance—royal whether you like it or not, do exactly what we say because we're right and your opinion doesn't matter. Even worse, if I accept the role of fairy princess, it comes with immortality—I'd truly never be free of it."

"How do you know you won't like being a princess until you try? Maybe you'll like it much better than being a familiar."

"I can't exactly test the waters. I doubt Tace would be interested in me following him around as a human until I make a decision. I'd have to be turned into a fairy first. Right now it is more of a 'devil you know' situation."

Kaz looked at her for a moment with a thoughtful smile.

"Play the game with me now," Kaz said.

"What?"

"Let's play. If you were a fairy princess..." he goaded.

"I don't know. I don't want to play."

"Humor me."

She sighed. Fine. She would humor him since it really didn't matter anyway. But after a moment, she surprised herself by coming up with an actual answer. "If I were a fairy princess...I would make it so no fairy familiars were hurt or mistreated, or even disrespected. I don't think I could ever stop anyone from making a deal to become a familiar, but I think I would want to make some rules around it. And I would stop using humans at Palace of the Fae parties."

"See? That's a great idea."

Theo huffed and gave him a weak smile. "Too bad it will never happen. Though, you have to admit, this is all very standard for Theodosia Balfour."

"How so?"

"Because I'm never the one with the good luck, even if it seems that way. I get told I'm a fairy princess. But not the one everyone thinks is alive. No, I'm the other one. The one people thought was dead and mourned already. If I survive this, people are going to be disappointed they put flowers on the wrong grave. Though, maybe they'll be even more annoyed because they'll have to buy two bouquets, since the assassin is still out there. For comparison, when Bea tripped into her role as a princess, she flitted around the castle, planted a garden, and had tea parties. She didn't lead her own murder investigation."

Kaz smiled. "So, when you do survive this and turn into a fairy princess, are you going to start a garden, too?"

"Of course," she said. "Right after I collect a gaggle of ladies to follow me around like overgrown ducklings while they quack about how great I am, but before I open a sanctuary for orphaned potted plants with musical aspirations. Don't worry, I'll dedicate the music room to myself."

He burst out laughing and she couldn't help her grin in return.

They both got up shortly thereafter, Theo not really having the time to linger, as much as she might want to. Since neither of them currently had a fairy at their disposal to dress them, they put on their clothes from last night. Theo double-checked that her sliver of yew was still in her pocket before they went downstairs to find her friends.

# Chapter 22

# Where Theo Is a Great Musician but a Less-Than-Great Spy

Theo and Kaz went to the dining room, situated at the back of the house. The westward-facing windows were showing off the brilliant late-afternoon sky, the richest of blue at the top, fading to an orange like glowing embers. Long, wispy, pink-tinged cirrus clouds stretched across the horizon like a giant hand, as though reaching up to pull the afternoon down.

Beric, Torian, Lowen, Phineas, and Alby were sitting around a large, rustic pinewood table, Beric never having bothered to fix the dings and scrapes that revealed just how old the furniture was, the top like the face of a grizzled old man. He could fix it with a snap of his fingers, but Theo knew he liked how the imperfection added to the charm. A fire was roaring in the fireplace, but Theo could tell by the cozy atmosphere that magic was also involved in the temperature.

They either knew her well, didn't like confrontation, or a mix of both, but regardless, none of them questioned Theo on her hasty exit the previous night or her walk down to them with Kaz. Except for Phineas, who wiggled his eyebrows at them both before Theo shot him a warning glare.

Torian patted the empty seat next to her and conjured a quick meal of light fare and a cup of tea. Theo also took up her friend's offer to dress her, and yesterday's outfit was quickly swapped out with a simple green frock. She was also kind enough to do the same for Kaz, giving him a fresh shirt and pants.

Inconspicuously missing from the table was Arlys, no one mentioning his nonattendance at the meal or the house in general. Fine by Theo, and by the looks of everyone else, fine by them, too. But, as though summoned by the lack of interest in his absence, Arlys picked this moment to march through the door.

They all turned to watch him come in, Beric, Torian, and Lowen greeting him with polite smiles, Phineas and Kaz each watching him with a bored expression, and Alby and Theo looking anywhere else once they realized who it was.

Beric took a huge swig of his tea and then cleared his throat. "Just in time, Arlys. I was about to discuss our plans for our evening at the Gilded Hen. As I've said, I've been there before. A while ago, yes, but I know the ins and outs, and I should be able to get us a spot to play. Again, the crowd doesn't much care for music, which is why I've only played there less than a handful of times. But we're not going there to fundraise for tips. We'll stick to the boring classics, hope no one pays attention to us, and keep our eyes out. Once we're done, we'll wander around a bit and see what we can find."

"I still think this is a terrible idea," Arlys said, his snarly voice matching the rest of him.

"Noted. So will you be staying here, then?" Beric asked.

"Of course not. I'm coming."

Alby grumbled quietly next to Theo and she in turn gave him a half grin, letting him know she agreed with his sentiment completely.

"Then I've got great news, Arlys. Your wish came true. You're now in the band!"

Arlys rolled his eyes, crossed his arms, and mumbled something under his breath. "For the final time, I do not want to be in your band."

"Fine, then," Beric said, his mood not soured in the slightest. "You can be broody in the corner, I guess. Though, you could have shined on the tambourine. Phineas and Kaz, you can also wander around and see if you can find anything. There. Now that that's settled, let's talk glamours."

Theo hadn't had any need or want of a glamour since she plied Endlin with alcohol that fateful night. And why would she? There was no reason for her to hide who she was until now. But as the night fell on them, Theo found herself once again in disguise.

Beric didn't glamour anything other than her head, Torian creating a different dress beforehand, rightly assuming that Theo would need an unobtrusive glamour if she were to also play music while being incognito. Her dress was made of dark blue silk the color of a twilight halo over a black forest. The neckline hit just below her collarbones, and the cap sleeves allowed her arms to move freely so she could easily play her instrument. Likewise, the length was shorter than her typical dresses, this one skimming her calves instead of the floor, so as to prevent any mishaps from patrons accidentally stepping on the bottom. All in all, simple by fairy standards, but perfect for a performance in a tavern.

And Theo did look like a fairy. Her new red hair was neatly styled in a low braid to show off her pointed ears. Her frosty blue eyes appeared that much brighter contrasting against the dress, as though they were two bright stars shining overhead. The glamour was indeed lightweight, feeling almost identical sitting on her skin as her dress did.

Phineas and Kaz were also given lightweight fairy disguises, which was mostly just turning their ears pointy since no one knew who they were anyway. They were dressed in appropriate-for-a-tavern fairy frocks of dark pants and embroidered dark green tunics.

When everyone else deemed their ensembles impeccable, the group made for the tavern.

---

Like many magical establishments, and especially places of gathering, no one could transport themselves directly into the Gilded Hen. The tavern also did not allow anyone to transport themselves out. This mostly cut down on thieves and violence. No one could rob the place and transport themselves out before anyone was the wiser, and no one could punch someone in the face during a fight and beat the hastiest of retreats to avoid justice. This worked, for the most part, fights now having to take place outside, and should someone steal something, they'd better hope their feet were fast enough to carry them to the exits.

Unlike the taverns that Theo had seen in the human realm, the Gilded Hen was not in a city, squashed between two buildings as though it had tried to slip past them and gotten stuck. Nor was it in a small town acting as a waystation for weary travelers, with hitching posts outside and some drunks sleeping it off in the hay next to the horses. The Gilded Hen sat in the middle of a pine forest among the trees as though it had actually grown there, the logs from which it was crafted just as wide and tall as the trees surrounding it. Its roof was thatched with pine boughs that seemed more decoration than function, but more than likely had the benefit of magic to keep the weather out. The size and scale reminded Theo of a giant barn complete with sliding doors open to the night air, laughter and raised voices spilling outside in an indecipherable flood of sound.

And sure enough, perched on the top of a post next to the entrance was the golden statue of a chicken. Like many statues that came before it, this chicken was not average in size compared to its live counterpart. While anatomically correct, the statue would have come up to Theo's waist had it been on the ground. Theo wasn't sure if it was her imagination or if the artist had crafted this foul fowl monstrosity with a smugness that would put a rooster to shame. And who had even commissioned this piece anyway? Did they do it before or after naming the tavern? Which left Theo to wonder which came first, the chicken or the name? No matter. The group walked right past it and into the tavern.

Beric, Torian, and Lowen walked straight to the bar, leaning over the mahogany counter to flag down the barmaid. Theo, Alby, Kaz, and Phineas waited nearby, not wanting to crowd the patrons sitting on the stools so as not to draw attention to themselves. Whether he meant to take Beric's instructions to heart or not, Arlys set his cranky self down at a table in the far corner and was pretending he did not know them.

Theo used this time to discreetly look over the tavern. While she'd seen taverns, she hadn't been inside any. But this one seemed as unexceptional as they came. As she surmised outside, the inside did indeed resemble a barn. At the far end was a section of boards pretending to be a stage, raised up slightly on rocks. In front of that was a large space reserved for dancing. There was no one playing on the stage now, so the fairies, gnomes, pixies, elves, and other magical creatures were mostly milling around. The second level wrapped around the sides of the tavern, letting the people up there look down at not just the stage but the entire ground floor. Booths and tables were tucked into the sides, the patrons hunched over them in the dark like pill bugs under logs.

Soon enough, Beric was smiling and nodding at whatever the barmaid was saying, and after a moment, the three fairies came over with drinks and news that the band would be playing sometime during the night when the barmaid said they could, or remembered they were there. Newly acquired libations in hand, the group made for an empty table on the edge of the dance floor near the stage to wait. It was a good spot, as there were plenty of people walking by, so Theo was able to listen in to snippets of conversations or just watch anyone who looked a bit suspicious. Beric, Torian, and Lowen took turns visiting the bar every once in a while to see if the barmaid would let them play already.

Theo didn't know what she was expecting to happen when they were finally able to take the stage. But there was no formal introduction, no fanfare of any kind. Just the barmaid rapping her knuckles on their table and telling them they could play now. Kaz and Phineas held the table while the band went to the stage. Beric conjured Theo a harp, but instead of having her play front and center like she usually did, they put her off to the side with the hope it would make her blend in that much more. Alby stood next to her, triangle at the ready.

They opened with a song that would normally spark the dancers to life. Here in the Gilded Hen, it did not. Just as the band was only a step above the dance floor, so, too, was the audience only that much above apathy.

If her music had produced this result at any other party, she would have been dismayed. But now it was rather fortuitous. She was still able to play her songs while having a chance to search the tavern for clues, a lead, *something*.

But as the band played song after song, she was finding nothing. Likely because she still didn't know what she was supposed to be looking for. The entire clue was the tavern itself. What about this unremarkable place would help her at all? Their set ambled on, and finally after an hour of playing, Beric turned to the group and shrugged.

"See anything?" he asked Theo. She shook her head. Torian and Lowen did, too. Great.

Beric sighed. "All right. How about we call it on the music and split up. Walk around a bit, sit at the bar, see if there's anything we can find out."

She had no better idea, and nowhere to start, so she nodded. Beric vanished their instruments and, with drinks in hand, took Torian and Lowen toward a dark corner of the tavern, pretending to be chatting. Walking slightly apart from one another, Theo, Kaz, Phineas, and Alby went to the bar for another round of drinks. Not because they were thirsty, but because four patrons roaming around a drinking establishment without them seemed like it would call more attention to themselves than was necessary.

Theo sidled up to the bar, taking an empty seat and waiting her turn for the barmaid to come over. By this point, the hour was creeping up on midnight. She was close to reaching her last day and no closer to discovering anything. The people next to her, an elf on one side and a gnome on the other, also seemed to be in the same low mood as she. They had already ordered a second round since they were near the dregs of the drinks they were currently drowning their sorrows with.

The barmaid came back to the elf with his new drink, then looked at him expectantly. "Oh, right," the elf grunted. He reached into his pocket and came back out with a fistful of coins, slamming them down on the counter and saying, "Do any of these work?"

The barmaid sighed but riffled through them with her index finger, pulling some toward her and pushing others back to him. And while she did, Theo looked on, entranced. The elf had put down a variety of coins of all different sizes. Some were metal, some wooden, some made of seashells. She'd seen a mix very similar to this one not too long ago.

"There," the barmaid said, sliding her pile off the counter into her hand. "All settled." Then she turned to Theo. "What can I get for you?"

But Theo wasn't paying attention, and she jumped when the barmaid repeated herself louder.

Theo looked up at her and did a double take at the post behind the barmaid. Hanging on a post near the bar was a small painting, really only visible to someone sitting where Theo was, or who happened to be working behind it. Theo gasped at the subject of the painting: a troll. She hadn't met a great number of trolls in her life, yet she was positive she'd seen this one before. Only last time, this woman had been sitting with someone else. Here, Skella was painted alone.

"Why is there a portrait of her here?" Theo asked the barmaid instead of ordering a drink.

The barmaid tracked Theo's line of sight. "Oh, her? I think she's the owner's wife. At least that's what I heard."

"The owner? The owner of the Gilded Hen is Hodd?"

The barmaid raised her eyebrows in surprise. "Yes. Do you know him?"

"Is he here? Now?" Theo was honestly not sure what she wanted the answer to be. If the answer was no, she'd have come to the end of her current clues. If the answer was yes, she very well may be in heaps of danger.

The barmaid shook her head. "No. He doesn't come here

all that often. He has an overseer who looks after it in his stead—he's here now, though. Want me to get him for you? He's meeting with someone, but I can see if he's available."

Theo sucked in a breath, turning her head rapidly to search for her friends while simultaneously saying, "No. No, thank you. That's all right."

But the barmaid wasn't listening and instead was pointing at Theo. And Theo's heart froze in her chest when the barmaid put her other hand up to her mouth, tipped her face up to the balcony, and shouted, "Perran! There's someone here who wants to speak with you! Says she knows Hodd!"

If Theo was better at this, she may have acted a bit more calm, cool, and collected. Maybe kept her face at more of a controlled neutral. As she was not a professional actor, or even an amateur for that matter, her face twisted to full horror before she had the sense to stop it. Perran was among the last people she wanted to see, and her face, unfortunately, reflected that.

Theo whipped around to look up to the balcony where the barmaid was shouting. At the name *Perran*, Kaz, Phineas, and Alby turned around on their barstools, too. And sure enough, responding to the sound of his name being called, looking down at Theo, was Ursula's right-hand man.

Beric, Torian, and Lowen were pushing through the crowd toward her. Torian grabbed her arm. "We have to go *right now*! Ursula is here!"

But Theo hadn't looked away from the balcony. Nor did she have to. As Torian said it, rising from the same table as Perran was Cecily and Lock's aunt.

For a brief moment, Perran looked at the scene with confusion, as anyone would when a stranger was staring at them with abject terror for reasons unknown. And sadly for their incognito efforts, Theo's friends weren't actors, either. Perran shifted his gaze first from Theo to Beric, who had gone still as a statue, and then to Torian, whose head was whipping back and forth between Theo, Beric, and the others like she was watching an out-of-control billiards game. Regrettably, this caused Perran to track her line of sight, and thus he spotted Phineas, Lowen, and Alby. And though Perran had never met Kaz, it was easy enough to determine he was with them. Like everyone else in their group, he, too, had stopped and stared.

Perran then started to look wildly around the entire tavern, as though he would find even more familiar faces. Which he did. And while Theo didn't turn to look, she knew exactly whom he had spotted as he was speed-reading the crowd, since his eyes froze on the back corner of the bar right where Arlys was.

With every person in their group Perran clocked, a bit of confusion was pushed off his face, anger replacing it like someone was molding his expression out of clay in real time. And when he finally got back to Theo, he was furious. She was still in her disguise, but it didn't take much for him to piece this mystery together that the only person Arlys was tasked with following was missing from the group and subsequently replaced by a different woman who seemed to know exactly who he was.

What felt like hours of staring was realistically only mere seconds. But even that precious time would have been put to good use had she managed to do anything other than stand stock-still in the dead center of the tavern.

Perran used his time to point down at her and, in a voice that rattled the beams, shouted, "Princess Amabel!"

Unlike when the band was playing, this got everyone's attention. Conversations halted, but the tavern itself didn't fall silent. Every patron turned toward the source of the voice, the noise of scuffing feet sounding like a herd of sheep had been let in. Everyone could then see Perran with his arm outstretched in Theo's direction like an emperor in a colosseum lording over the entertainment.

"The redhead in the blue dress. Seize her!" Perran shouted.

He didn't specify who should seize her, but that didn't matter. The people who were set about the task apparently knew who they were. Five grim-faced ogres were now barreling through the crowd like bulls in a town square. The people who weren't being shoved were moving voluntarily out of the way.

Theo thought the two ogres who tried to kidnap her in the palace were large, but they were on the smaller side compared to the ones who were after her now.

Theo didn't know which way to go. She was rooted to her spot, her legs deciding that instead of being composed of muscle and bones capable of moving her out of harm's way, they were two sacks of jelly presently estranged from her brain.

Alby, for all his talk about not being seen, now took the opposite approach. He jumped up on the bar, grabbed a jug of alcohol nearly as large as him, and smashed it to the floor, shouting, "Run for your lives!"

And it was exactly what that moment needed. Theo didn't know what the jug had contained, but it was now evaporating in a cloud of blue smoke billowing over the bar. Pandemonium reigned as the tavern patrons, unsure before, now launched into full-scale panic for the exits. In the chaos, Theo ducked down, letting go of her glamour to get rid of her distinctive red hair, and moved with the crowd. She looked back at the bar just in time to see Phineas yanking Alby off the bar and joining the stream of fleeing patrons.

In the mix of shouts and shoves, she heard her name. Kaz was fighting against the tide to reach her. When he finally made it through, he grabbed her hand and they both ran for the exit.

Beric, Torian, and Lowen were also right behind her as they joined the escape attempt. But two ogres, finally figuring out the delicate art of weaving between people, were flanking them, like highway robbers trying to cut them off at the pass.

"We'll stall him while you get out of here," Torian shouted.

"But, no—" Theo started. However, Torian shoved her toward the exit.

"Go! We'll catch up!" Then Torian, along with Beric and Lowen, spread out, creating a wall between Theo and the oncoming ogres. The people were like a raging river, and her bandmates were the dam, blocking the flow of people and clogging up the ogres' path. It worked like a charm, and with enough space between them and the ogres, her three bandmates finally turned around and rejoined the escape.

They were all almost to the threshold. If they could make it just a little bit farther outside and past the wards, they could all vanish.

Out of the tavern. Open air.

Phineas and Alby were still in front, Kaz right behind them pulling Theo. And just a bit behind her were Torian, Beric, and Lowen.

Theo just crossed the wards as Torian screamed. Theo turned to see that the ogres had reached her friends, and they were now on the ground being wrapped in iron chains.

"We have to go back!" Theo shouted. But Kaz held tightly to her, not letting her try to get to her friends.

Phineas was already conjuring a swirl of wind just as Perran pushed his way out of the tavern. There was a frenzied look in his eyes, and for a moment it seemed like he was about to make a run for them. But he knew, just as they did, he wouldn't make it before Phineas vanished them.

"Run!" Beric shouted.

Ursula also finally shoved her way out of the tavern, taking in the three bandmates wrapped in iron, Perran snarling with anger, and Theo about to make her escape.

"Princess Amabel!" Ursula shouted. "If you want your friends to remain unharmed, you will turn yourself in now!"

"Don't do it!" Lowen screamed.

"Midnight tomorrow night! At the Palace of the Fae!" Theo called back. "I want my friends, Cecily, and Lock. If they are unharmed, I will turn myself in. If they are not, you will never see me again!"

Theo didn't wait for Ursula's response. She and Kaz stepped into the swirl of wind with Phineas and Alby, and in a blink, they were gone.

# Chapter 23

# Where Theo Gets the Unwritten Version of a History Lesson

Phineas landed Theo, Kaz, and Alby right next to the field at Beric's house. They waited for just a moment before bolting for the door, not halting until they had reached the drawing room. But once there, Theo traded racing for pacing. She was still out of breath, her lungs and heart not noticing she wasn't actively running for her life anymore.

Phineas had gotten rid of his small glamour and was mirroring her head-holding, but was cradling his while sitting in a chair, staring blankly at the floor. Alby was slowly walking circles around the room, his jewelry clacking gently.

Theo stopped her pacing to look at Kaz. He was seated, ears also back to normal, and gripping the wooden armrests of the chair so tightly they were in danger of splintering. "What was that about, Theo?" he snapped. "What do you mean by midnight at the palace?"

"Exactly what I said. I'm going to the palace to get my friends," Theo said.

"No. You can't just give yourself up." Kaz's speech was rising in both pitch and speed. "We can still figure out something. We can—"

"Kaz, *it's over.* The investigation has failed. My bargain runs out in one day."

"So? We have new clues! Hodd must be the killer, right?"

Theo threw her hands out. "Probably! But even if we are absolutely positive he is, my bargain with Arlys states that I must *find* the killer—not just name him. How are we going to track down Hodd in a day? Ask Perran nicely if he can give us the address to his boss? That is, if Perran hasn't already gone to ground now that we know who he works for. And why is a fairy working for a troll? Regardless, he'd have to be foolish or desperate or both to go back to the Palace of the Fae now. Even if we managed to tell everyone in the kingdom to be on the lookout, he will not be found tomorrow."

"That doesn't mean you should sacrifice yourself!" Kaz said.

"Perran has my friends, which means Hodd has my friends. If he is the killer, he wants me. But you're wrong about me giving myself up. I have no intention of doing that. Ursula and Perran don't know I made a bargain with Arlys, and certainly don't know that the bargain runs out tomorrow night. By the time they hand over my friends, I'll belong to Arlys—I won't be able to turn myself over to them."

"All well and good," Phineas said, finally looking up. "But what if Ursula and Perran don't release them? You know, on account of that little habit of hers—lying?"

Theo sighed. "Well, we have one full day remaining to figure something out. Regardless, at midnight tonight, I'm going to be at the palace."

"*Over my dead body*," came Arlys's voice from the entrance to the drawing room.

The four friends whipped around. From the looks of him, his fight at the tavern had lasted quite a while, making his "dead body" threat seem not too far out of the realm of possibilities. His nose had been broken again, this time much more severely, and appeared as though it only just healed, the blood that dripped down his face giving him the look of a very gruesome mustache and beard, the front of his shirt still wet and bright red. Combined with his crazed eyes and tangled hair, he didn't look like he descended into madness so much as tripped and hit every stair on the way down.

But Theo stood her ground. Which not only served the purpose of letting him know she wouldn't be intimidated, but also allowed Alby to slip out of the room without the fairy noticing.

"There is no way you're going to the palace," Arlys said, his threat sounding a lot less harsh with the slightly nasal inflection from his bloody nose.

But his belittling finger pointed in her face set her off.

"You do not get to tell me what to do—especially in that tone," she said, her own finger now pointing back at him. "You are ineffective at your self-confessed one job of protecting me and have only succeeded in impeding me in trying to save myself. I might as well just hold your hand as we walk in circles shouting, *Here I am! It's me! Princess Amabel! Feel free to kill me now!* for all the protective duty you've provided."

"Well, you are reckless and impulsive, and every decision you have made has been to spite me. How am I supposed to protect someone actively working to defy me?"

"If it helps, I did some planning this time," she said with a tilt of her head, goading him further. "And why does this even matter so much to you? You despise me. Probably as much as the assassin. Consider this an opportunity to wipe your hands clean of me." Anyone else would have thrown in the towel at this point and declared defeat. Not Arlys, though. He was fighting tooth and nail for someone he hated and it didn't add up.

"Why does it matter to me?" he snarled incredulously. "Because I was there!"

Theo stared at him, then finally asked the question she should have from the beginning.

"Who are you?" Theo asked, her voice reflecting only cold curiosity.

"I told you. I am one of your secret keepers and one of your protectors."

"Those words mean absolutely nothing to me. Why *you*?"

Arlys stared at her, the vein on his forehead resembling a snake that was about to slither into his brain.

"Answer me!" Theo shouted.

"I am working for the good of this kingdom. For King Redren and Queen Lilliana. For you to carry on their legacy of a prosperous kingdom. That, princess, is what I'm fighting for. Even though you are actively working against me, I will continue to fight for the king and queen's vision of the future."

"Their legacy? A few more years and it could be considered legend! A myth! You're doing all this to bring back a reign that ended one thousand years ago? It doesn't make any sense! Why did you know me as a child? Why are you so obsessed with the king and queen? Why are you so fixated on who you imagine me to be?!"

His next words exploded out of him like a faulty pressure cooker, coating the room in a spray of sizzling, molten anger. "It's not you! It was *never* for you! It was for my mother who died to save you!"

Theo jerked back. "Your mother? Who was your mother?"

Arlys let out a choppy breath. "Emmalina of the Maple Fairies. She was your nanny. The one who took you out of the palace the night of the assassination to save you."

"My nanny?"

She had seen him angry before, but not like this. Not with a fury so deep she could feel it rumbling from underground. But just as she thought he was going to erupt again, he paused, and his face fell blank, like his emotions had finally been pushed to the brink and he was left with nothing. "You know, you never once asked how you survived. Throughout all this, you weren't even the slightest bit curious about the people who sacrificed for you." His voice was quiet, but the stillness was all the more unnerving. Without the anger to keep it warm, his words were cold, bleak, and hopeless as he continued. "My mother talked about you all the time. Do you want to know what sort of person you were? Because you weren't like this." He motioned at her. "The Princess Amabel she knew was one of the kindest people she had ever met. Even at such a young age, you cared about everyone around you—especially your sister. You loved her. And Iara would look at you like you could do no wrong.

"That night, you and your sister were playing in the nursery with both of your nannies. Iara became upset because she couldn't find her favorite toy. None of the adults could find it, but you said you knew where it was. The other nanny had suggested she pick another toy for now, but you begged my mother to take you to where you had last seen it. And when you two were on your way back, my mother noticed something was wrong. She smelled smoke and, though she hadn't seen anything, knew enough to run." Arlys took a breath, pushing his hair back away from his face before continuing.

"She took you home to protect you. I was there when she arrived. You had both inhaled a bit of the yew smoke, but since you were so small it started to affect you quicker. She didn't know what to do. My mother was *dying* in front of me, but only worried about you.

"We managed to keep you alive through the night, but you weren't doing well. She called for Tace, knowing it was risky, but he made a secrecy promise with her for your safety. He could never tell anyone your whereabouts until you were back in the fairy realm—if he did, he would die. If he betrayed it, the moment he uttered your location, he would drop dead. And Tace stayed true to his secrecy vow. He didn't know who you were until he met you a few days ago. Since my mother was getting worse, she made me a secret keeper, too. Until you were brought back, no one except for my mother, Tace, and I would know where you were. And the three of us put you into slumber to prevent your death. Tace returned, telling everyone that it was Iara who was missing, in the hopes of throwing off whomever was still searching for you.

"My mother made me promise her then and there that I would protect you. That I would carry on the work that meant so much to her. For the princess who meant so much to her." Arlys closed his eyes. "My mother died shortly after. The yew she had inhaled was too much for her to overcome." When he opened them, they were once again focused on Theo. "And now you are throwing your life away while spitting on her grave. Everything I have done for the past one thousand years is being torn apart. You are throwing your life away as if it has no value!"

"Funny that the fairy desperate to get me to the palace all of a sudden doesn't want me to go. And stop acting as if I wanted things to turn out this way. I don't remember Iara. Or Redren and Lilliana. I wish I did. I wish, for many reasons, this whole thing had never happened and I had gotten the chance to grow up with the people you remember. But I didn't. I don't know them. I didn't even know what family was until I came here. The people who love me whether I'm at my highest or lowest. And now the only people I have ever felt were my real family are at the palace in terrible danger. I am sorry it has come to this. I hope you know that her sacrifice for me is not wasted, because I'm using the chance she bought me to save people. And for that, I am eternally grateful. I know this isn't how you envisioned me, or what you think a princess is supposed to do. But, Arlys, look at me. Really look at me. I am not, nor will I ever be, that princess you think I should be. Do not try to stop me. Do not get in my way."

He took a breath and held up his finger as though gearing up for another lecture. But before he could get a word out, a clock sounded from somewhere in the house, a jaunty tune played on chimes, then tolling twelve more notes. It was midnight.

Arlys blew out the breath through his teeth and put his hand down as his shoulders sagged in relief. "I tried to be reasonable. I tried to explain why you should care. This ends now. Princess Amabel, you're coming with me and we're putting an end to this foolishness. You are going into slumber immediately. You will be safe, I will see to it that your friends are released, and we can try again when the assailant is caught. Had you been mature about this whole thing, you would have had more of a chance to say your goodbyes. As it is, we must leave."

She raised her eyebrows. "And how, pray tell, are you going to take me away right now?"

He didn't answer and instead struck out like a viper, wrapping his hand around her arm. But, as she knew it would, his anger turned into shock when she wasn't vanishing.

"How are you doing that?" he growled when he couldn't transport her. "You bargained away today and it is now after midnight!"

Since Cecily wasn't here and someone had to do it, Theo

put on her best demure smirk and, with a flirty lilt in her voice, asked, "I did? What did I bargain for?"

Arlys opened his mouth to speak and then closed it as realization dawned. And then swiftly sunsetted right back into anger.

"That's right, Arlys," Theo said, the smirk growing into a knowing smile. "You didn't actually complete that bargain. Kaz was never missing his memories, and therefore, you did not restore them."

Arlys let out a feral roar. Phineas and Kaz, who had come to stand next to Theo, were blasted back to the couches with a flick of Arlys's hand. Ropes wound around them both, completely immobilizing them.

Arlys finally let go of Theo, but only so he could magically shove her onto a different couch and bind her in ropes as well. He paced for a moment, his hands running through his hair as he mumbled to himself.

He halted and turned to face Theo, and she could see that in his eyes, underneath the mania, was a little burst of smugness. "I might not be able to take any of you, but there is nothing in our bargain that said I couldn't impede you or run out the clock. And you'll notice, I'm not using your friends against you since you're tied up, too, nor am I taking them anywhere, so this is well within the bounds of our deal.

"You think I'm so cruel, but what you failed to realize when you made your bargain was that I could have done this at any time. And I should have the moment Cecily was taken. But I was kind. I was protecting you for just a bit longer so you could accept what was going to happen and say goodbye to your friends. But now I am done. There are no fairies to protect you anymore, and no one coming to help. We are going to sit here until midnight tonight. If you try to transport yourself out of here, I'll just hold on to you, so I wouldn't bother."

Due to being distracted by his own outburst, he didn't hear the soft *clack-clack-clack* coming from behind him as he stared at his tied-up humans. And thus, caught wholly unawares when Alby snuck up behind him, bell clapper in hand, and swung for the back of his legs, knocking him forward onto his hands and knees. Arlys would have been further taken by surprise if he had remained conscious, but at the same time his knees hit the floor, Alby used his makeshift weapon to club him in the head.

Arlys's head didn't ring like a bell with the contact and instead made a dull thud, his body creating an even bigger thud when it hit the ground.

Phineas gasped. "Is he dead?!"

Alby poked him with his foot and Arlys groaned. "Doesn't look like it. Why? Did you want me to hit him again? I'm not sure I want to, but I will give you the clapper after you're untied and you can do what you want, I suppose." Then the goblin walked over, pulled a small pocketknife from some recess of his jacket, and began cutting the ropes off Theo. Once she was free, she untied Kaz while Alby cut the ropes off Phineas. True to his word, Alby did try to pass off the clapper to Phineas, who shook his head.

Unfortunately, given that Alby had about as much strength behind his swing as a cup of tea with the bag left in too long and Arlys was fast-healing by nature, the fairy wasn't going to stay down for long. He was already blinking and starting to move a bit.

"Come on, we have to go," Theo said as Arlys groaned again, working to get his legs underneath him.

She didn't know how long Arlys would stay on the ground and she wasn't about to risk transporting right in front of him. Instead, she took Alby by the hand, his other still clutching the clapper, and the four friends ran out the door, aiming for the edge of the field. There they could at least find some cover in the trees in order to make their escape.

The sky was black, the moon offering only enough light to see the line between the field and the wilderness beyond.

They were halfway when Arlys stumbled out of the house. He managed to get down the stairs and she could just barely make out his form as he wobbled and flailed with disjointed movements, like a scarecrow brought to life.

But he was gaining ground, his movements getting slightly more precise with each step.

As she neared the tree line, she started to conjure a wind, willing her feet to go faster.

Arlys was only a few feet behind her now, and she wasn't going to make it. She was desperate for a weapon, something that could stop him. But then she remembered she had one. From her pocket, she pulled the small sliver of yew. He grabbed her by the shoulder, spinning her around. But she held out the shard toward him like it was a mighty sword.

"I took this from the yew forest," she snarled. "Lay one more finger on me and I stab you with it."

He stopped and retracted his hands, shock and anger competing on his face. Both he and Theo knew this was not a threat to be taken lightly. All it would take was a tiny scratch and he would be down for the count. He took a step back, watching the wind swirl at her feet as Kaz, Phineas, and Alby stood close behind her.

"There is nowhere you can hide," he growled as the wind whipped around higher over her. But he couldn't have been more wrong. She knew exactly where to hide. She'd known this whole time.

Theo knew how to make a fairy bargain.

And thanks to Beatrice, she also knew how to break one.

"You'll never find me!" Theo shouted back. "And when our bargain ends, you'll get everything you deserve"—the last word coming out only a blink before they vanished.

# Chapter 24

# Where Theo Reveals Her Plan

When the wind cleared, they found themselves up to their knees in an expansive field of yellow flowers. Or in Alby's case, up to the top of his head. The night still wrapped itself around them, making it look like they were standing on an island in a sea of black. For a few minutes, no one said anything, all of them working on catching their breath and lowering their heart rates.

"Where are we?" Kaz asked, once he was able to speak again.

But before Theo could answer, Phineas, who had also been looking around, barked out a laugh. "I knew it! *I knew it!*"

"What?" Kaz asked, eyes wide at his friend's outburst.

But Phineas just kept laughing.

Theo shrugged.

"Will someone please explain!" Kaz snapped.

Phineas pointed at Theo. "You had this planned the whole time, didn't you? This was where you were going to go at midnight! I *knew* something was off about that bargain!"

Kaz gave an aggravated groan. "*What are you talking about?*"

"Look around you, Kaz!" Phineas laughed. "You've seen this ploy before!"

And Kaz did for a moment, still with an angrily confused expression. But as he scanned their surroundings, his eyes widened. Then he burst out laughing, too.

Theo couldn't help her wry smile as they finally realized the endgame of her deal with Arlys. "I gave him fair warning he would regret crossing me. Though, it is quite freeing knowing I was going to punish a fairy who has earned it."

What Arlys didn't know when he made a deal with Theo was that she had no intention of going with him willingly when her four days were up. No, she was using her stepsister's blueprint for fairy bargains: get what she wanted and hightail it out of there. At the end of her time limit, when Theo inevitably failed to find the assassin, she was going straight to one of the fields of Saint-John's-wort that Beatrice's followers had planted around the kingdom. Even if he found her, he'd have no way of getting to her. Because this field of Saint-John's-wort also happened to have a barn with just enough cast-iron door handles, hinges, and tools to make a handy little barrier in the highly unlikely event he could get through the flowers.

"If Arlys was going to play dirty, then so was I. He decided to hold my friend hostage, so, for a lovely bit of revenge, I decided I would take a chunk of his magic hostage in return—and that would happen the moment I didn't pay back the bargain."

"I'm still sorry I got captured, Theo," Alby said from behind some flowers.

"Don't be," Theo said. "I'll admit the timeline I agreed to wasn't exactly ideal. But I knew that, no matter what, he and the others were going to keep coming after me, leaving my options extremely limited. So I made the deal. I was just never going to pay it back."

Phineas was still laughing, shaking his head. "Did Cecily know?"

"Cecily figured it out from the get-go. I'm sorry I didn't tell you; I just didn't know how to do it with absolute confidence Arlys wouldn't overhear. If he suspected anything, I'd lose the element of surprise."

Phineas raised his hands in surrender. "I completely understand. I'm mostly shocked at myself that I didn't see this coming."

There was a brief moment of silence before Kaz spoke. "Right, so are we going to camp out in this field?"

Theo motioned to where the barn was. "Follow me."

Thankfully, there were no animals inside, the barn most likely the last remnants of a farm before the land was turned into a giant garden. The four of them went inside, shutting the door behind them. Kaz found a lantern hanging in the corner and lit it, as the others found various buckets and stools to sit on.

"What now?" Kaz asked.

"Well, it is after midnight on the last day, meaning we have the rest of today to decide on a plan," Theo said.

"I, for one, think we should at least try to sleep a bit," Phineas said, stifling a yawn.

"After we decide on a plan," Kaz said, leaning forward to rest his elbows on his knees.

"It has only been four days—the clock tower party is still happening," Theo said. "So I say we meet them in the garden. It is wide open and impossible to guard every inch—we wouldn't be trapped anywhere."

"Theo, what if you don't go at all? You can stay here, and Phineas and I will get them out," Kaz said.

Theo snorted. "Nothing against you and your determination, but your plan is to go into the Palace of the Fae—a human and a familiar—and escape with five fairies? Sorry to say, that will never work. They're looking for me and will only give up my friends if I turn myself in, so I have to be there. But I told them I would only turn myself in if my friends were unharmed, so I will demand to see them. Ursula will be forced to bring out Cecily, Lock, and my friends in front of the whole party. I can be the bait, keep everyone's eyes on me, and when I do, you will get them out."

Kaz shook his head vehemently. "But then how are you going to get out? We can't just leave you in the garden. Arlys also knows we're going to the palace, so he'll be after you, too. I will not participate in this plan if it means leaving you behind with Arlys and Ursula. And, nothing against your recklessness and general disregard for your own well-being, but how will the addition of one more familiar's magic tip the scales in our favor?"

"I have no intention of staying. I'll run fast and far. We'll just need a distraction. Something long enough to allow me the time to transport myself out."

"*Put on a song and dance* kind of distraction, or *blow something up like Cecily* kind of distraction?" Phineas asked.

"I like the song-and-dance idea!" Alby supplied.

"Do you sing or dance?" Phineas asked the goblin.

"I do not."

But the suggestion of music combined with Kaz's fair point about the insignificant amount of magic they possessed gave Theo an idea. "What we don't have is magic, and that's why the fairies think we're helpless. But what if we took away their magic."

Kaz shook his head. "With what, iron? That won't work. We can't transport iron and I doubt they'll just have some lying around in a convenient location somewhere in the palace."

"No, not iron," Theo said flatly.

Kaz continued. "Saint-John's-wort is out, too. It would certainly be a distraction, but it would also make the fairies we're trying to rescue sick."

"Of course not Saint-John's-wort. No yew, either—I have no intention of killing anyone."

"Well then, quit leading us on and come out with it. What is your grand plan?" he snapped.

"I'm trying to tell you, you're just not letting me finish! Bells! We'll use bells!"

"Interesting idea, Theo," Phineas said. "But we already established that we have no way of lifting or moving a bell big enough to do anything significant. I don't know how much of a distraction handbells will cause."

"We don't need to move one," Theo rebutted. "After all, what makes a bell?"

"Is this a philosophical question?" Phineas asked.

"Now you're really leading us on," Kaz said.

Theo waved her hand dismissively. "All right, that time I was. Anyway, what if we turn the clock tower into a giant bell? At the stroke of midnight, pandemonium. When their magic is rendered useless, we all get out."

She was met with faces varying in levels of disbelief. Kaz was looking at her like she suggested they add costumes and a full choral ensemble to Alby's song-and-dance idea. Phineas looked like he was trying to figure out a nice way to shoot down the idea. And Alby just looked confused.

"How are we going to turn the clock tower into a bell?" Phineas asked. Theo didn't miss the little curl of skepticism that floated around the question.

"The clapper!" Theo said, still not persuading anyone. She turned to Alby. "I would need your help with that, my sneaky friend. Do you think you'd be able to put the clapper in the clock tower before midnight?"

"With what clapper, Theo?" Kaz asked, making a dramatic show of looking around them. "It is still at Beric's house."

Instead of answering, Alby ran out of the barn.

"So, was that a no from Alby?" Phineas asked while Kaz said, "The clock tower idea is out, then."

But before they could say anything else, Alby came running back into the barn, carrying the clapper on his shoulder like a pike. He stood in front of Theo and gave her a resolute, stoic nod. "Yes, I can do it!"

"Wonderful," Theo said, with a smile and quirked eyebrow for Kaz. "We'll go to the palace close to midnight and get them to bring out our friends. When the clock strikes twelve, we take advantage of the chaos and make a run for it. Immediately after the bells stop tolling, I'll transport myself back here and wait for you."

Kaz huffed. "Fine. Bells. Even if that works, we're still missing arguably the most important part of this plan. How do we get inside the palace? They know you're coming. They'll be watching every entrance and exit, and any other way you could sneak in."

"They know you're a hedgehog, too," Phineas added.

"Oh, I wasn't planning on sneaking in or slipping by them unnoticed," Theo said with a sly grin.

"You're doing it again," Kaz groaned.

"Fine! We'll walk right in," Theo said.

"What? And how are we going to manage that?" Phineas asked.

"No matter what," Theo said, "Arlys thinks I'm going to think like what he thinks a human should think."

"Same answer to the new statement: What?" Phineas asked again.

Kaz snorted. "She's trying to say that Arlys will expect her to sneak in, either as herself or as a hedgehog, because that's what he assumes a human would do."

"Exactly!" Theo said, pointing to Kaz. "He—and I would put money on every other fairy he or Ursula has on the lookout for us—will be expecting us to try to not only sneak in, but do it poorly. What they won't be expecting is the exact opposite. We're going to walk right through the front door. Another trick I learned from my stepsister." Granted, it wasn't at a fairy palace, but still, Beatrice marched right on into the castle without any questions from the guards.

"Interesting idea, Theo. Kaz and I might be dressed well enough to get into the palace, but without a fairy dress—sorry, your current outfit doesn't qualify—we have no way of getting in. They'll spot you immediately."

"Another thing I learned from my time as a royal. It doesn't matter what I'm wearing. You'd be surprised by how little confidence it takes to get into places."

She paused, trying to gauge their reactions. "So, all those in favor?" she asked, raising her hand.

Alby's hand shot up immediately.

Theo watched Kaz and Phineas.

Finally, Kaz sighed. "I just want to be on record right now saying I am not thrilled with this plan."

"Noted," Theo said.

"But I'll do it," he said as he raised his hand, too.

"I'm certainly not staying here," Phineas said as his hand went up.

Theo smiled.

"However," Phineas said with a loud yawn. "For right now, I'm in favor of this *sleeping* idea."

Probably for the best. Theo figured it wouldn't be a great start to their plan if they were falling asleep at the door to the palace.

With no beds, the four of them climbed up into the dusty hayloft to get a few hours of sleep.

Theo found a cozy spot next to Kaz, while Phineas and Alby made their own little hay nests in the corners.

Theo waited until she could hear the slow, steady breathing from the other two before talking to Kaz.

"Kaz, can I ask you something?" she said, her voice close to a whisper.

"Of course."

"You don't have to give me an answer right now, or you can tell me straightaway if your answer is no, but I was thinking... After tonight, would you want to stay here with me? Now, hear me out first. I know I won't be aging and you will be, but that still gives us plenty of time to be together. Also, I fully appreciate this is a barn and we'd have to do some redecorating at the very minimum, but we could make it work."

Kaz was quiet, and Theo was not brave enough to look at him. "But if you don't want to, I understand."

"I want to. I absolutely want to."

She sat up so she could look at him. "You'd be giving up your very lovely house."

He smiled. "I'd take being with you in a hovel over without you in a house anytime."

And when they kissed, it felt very much like a new beginning.

---

By the time they woke, the sun was high in the sky. The sounds of birds chirping, and the view of dust motes dancing by in the shafts of sunlight coming in from the roof greeted Theo when she opened her eyes.

Phineas and Kaz both woke soon after, Kaz with an unfortunate drool spot on his shoulder from where Theo had been sleeping, tucked in close, but if he minded, he didn't mention it. Alby was the last to wake, having found a comfy corner to curl up in, hugging the clapper.

After a few big stretches from everyone, they came down from the hayloft.

Theo turned to the goblin. "Still think you can get that clapper to the palace?"

"The plan is still on?"

"The plan is still on."

He gave her a resolute nod. "I won't let you down."

"Then we'll see you there tonight. Good luck."

"You too, Theo!" And with that, the goblin ran out of the barn and disappeared.

For the next few hours, Theo, Phineas, and Kaz went over the plan a few more times but otherwise didn't do much of anything except count down the hours until midnight.

At first the hours felt endless, but as the clock neared midnight, they seemed to fly by, and before she knew it, she was walking out of the barn back to the field with Kaz and Phineas.

She managed to rebraid her hair and pick the bits of hay out of it, but that was all she could do. Her dress was dingy from the tavern and wrinkly from the hayloft. Even without a mirror to confirm, she was confident she'd never looked worse for a party. But she was beyond caring.

"Ready?" she asked Phineas and Kaz.

"No," Kaz said. "But let's go."

In a swirl of wind, they went to the Palace of the Fae.

# Chapter 25
# Where Theo Goes to the Palace

The trio landed a short distance away from the palace entrance. As Cecily was a fairy of high social standing, Theo had never actually used the front entrance before, status allowing Cecily to arrive directly inside the palace.

The two wooden doors, nearly three stories high, were inlaid with swirling patterns of colored glass and gemstones to form giant oak tree motifs. They stood open, revealing the foyer behind. And Theo knew beyond that was the atrium, and then through there, the garden.

Almost a completely straight line to her target.

"Just like old times, isn't it?" Phineas said as they stood facing the palace.

Theo took a breath and then stepped forward.

Only to be held back by a hand around her arm.

"Wait, Theo," Kaz said. "You know I do not like this plan.

There are so many places where it could fail."

Theo leveled a look at him. "You could have rehearsed a slightly more uplifting speech. We had the time."

"No . . . I just want to say . . ."

Theo was about to interrupt and point out their very strict timetable, but he spoke again.

"If the plan fails, if things go wrong, promise me you'll get out. Get out and save yourself."

"Kaz, it won't go wrong."

"Then it's an easy promise."

"All right," she said slowly. "I promise."

He sighed and was about to say more. This time, Theo did stop him. "We have to get inside. Let's go."

The fairies expected her to sneak in. So instead, she walked in the dead center of the path, up the stairs, and into the foyer, Kaz and Phineas on either side of her a few steps behind. People did stop to stare, mouths dropping open as she walked calmly through the fray. As they made their way through the atrium, fairies moved out of her way, whispers of *Who is she?* following her as she strode past.

With any luck, the perplexed onlookers would think the worse-for-wear trio were dressed that way due to some new fashion statement being made by their fairy, as opposed to looking like the familiars who came to the palace after their farm chores.

But Theo was selling it. She channeled every uptight titled lady she'd ever met as she lifted her chin and glided across the atrium. Her eyes were on the garden but her face serene, as if she didn't have even the smallest care to turn her head and see who else was around her. And in this case, she didn't.

Just before the atrium, Kaz and Phineas broke off, slipping into the garden unnoticed.

Had she walked in with them, she would have gone unnoticed as well. But that did not make for a very convincing distraction. She needed all eyes on her. And she was going to get it.

From where she stood, she could see into the garden. Tace and Aimon were sitting on the dais beneath the clock tower in their usual spots. Though it felt like a lifetime had passed in the previous few days, everything still looked as it had before. This party was still as extravagant, and attendance was high. But where Tace would have normally looked rather jovial, today he was sitting upon the throne with his head resting on one hand, pouting like a sullen child who'd dropped his ice cream cone.

Aimon wasn't quite as depressed but did seem fidgety, as though Tace's sour mood was a lumpy pillow beneath him.

The clock said ten minutes to midnight.

Now all Theo could do was hope Alby had done what he needed to.

Instead of walking through where Kaz and Phineas did, she went to the two heralds near the entrance.

"Excuse me, I need to be heralded into the ball," Theo said to the duo, who until that very moment had paid her no mind. But now their faces went from impassivity to confusion. Heralding a human familiar to a party at the palace was simply not done. In fact, it was laughable. Which was their reaction after they looked her up and down, noting her clothes and hair.

She chuckled politely along with them.

"Go on, human," one of them said, dismissing her with a wave of his hand toward the party.

"Listen, I don't have a lot of time to cut you down to size right now, as I am on a strict schedule. Just know it would involve your unfoundedly smug faces and unearned sense of self-importance. Trust me, it would have been devastating. So, herald me into the ball. They're expecting me."

The heralds couldn't decide whether to keep laughing or shove her out of the palace. "Expecting you? Who are you that they'd be expecting a human? Get out of my sight before I bring you down to the dungeons."

Giving out the title she didn't want and would be just as happy to never hear again, Theo said, "Princess Amabel of the Oak Fairies."

Then they finally did take a good long look at her, their faces going slack. Whatever they saw had them startled. They stood stock-still until one of them nodded. Theo wondered if they had been told to keep their eye out for her but simply assumed they wouldn't have to bother too much with it since the princess wouldn't be walking in the front door.

One of the heralds nervously cleared his throat, turned to the garden, and, with his voice amplified by magic, shouted out the name.

It worked like a charm.

The music halted almost immediately, the notes ringing out in sharps and flats as the musicians forgot what they were doing, the sound hanging in the air like smoke. Conversations died as comprehension dawned and the crowd spun to face her.

Tace stood, mouth hanging open in surprise and awe. The few remaining fairies who were either dubious or confused had their suspicions and mysteries cleared up just by looking at the regent. His expression all but confirmed what the herald had said.

Eight minutes to midnight. Time to move.

With all eyes on her, she walked toward the dais, the crowd parting like curtains on a stage, leaving nothing between her and the clock tower.

She stopped before she reached the dais, giving herself enough room for when she would need to run. She did not curtsy, or bow, or even dip her chin. And as Tace took a step toward her, she held up her hand, halting him.

The crowd seemed to be collectively holding their breath, waiting for something to happen.

Theo was also not about to waste any time on small talk or pleasantries. "Ursula of the Birch Fairies and Perran of the Hornbeam Fairies have unlawfully detained my friends in the palace under your authority. I demand you release them."

By Tace's furrowed brow, Theo could tell that was not what he expected her to say. "What?"

She raised her voice, hoping the acoustics of the clock tower would send her words to the crowd behind her, too. "Cecily of the Ash Fairies, Locklan of the Ash Fairies, Beric of the Chestnut Fairies, Torian of the Beech Fairies, and Lowen of the Walnut Fairies. I want them back. Now."

The regent was having difficulty finishing any sentence he started, the language so jumbled he might as well have been picking words at random. Aimon was wavering between looking at Theo and his partner, not sure what to make of the situation.

It appeared to Theo that Tace had no idea her friends were here. Though, that wasn't all too surprising considering she strongly doubted Ursula would fess up to being in league with another fairy who was subsequently working for a troll assassin.

The plan was working just as intended when Ursula herself walked into the garden and toward the dais, the crowd parting for her as well. As expected, she was wearing her hair combs like a crown, a dress that rivaled a sunset for beauty, and the necklace that made her impervious to iron. She climbed the stairs and stood between the thrones of Tace and Aimon.

For a moment, Theo and Ursula stared at each other, Ursula vying for the attention of the crowd, and Theo not relinquishing it. Theo had seen this game play out before. Ursula wanted Theo to repeat herself, to make it sound like she was pleading instead of demanding. So Theo kept her head high and her mouth shut.

Six minutes to midnight.

Theo was about to ask her to get on with it. Ursula's subsequent dramatic pause for effect was really cutting into Theo's time.

"Mother," Aimon said quietly, breaking the uncomfortable silence before Theo or Ursula could. "What are you doing?"

Ursula ignored her son and instead held up her hands. The crowd began to murmur, and Theo turned to steal a glance at what was causing it. A large fairy ring was popping up, mushrooms sprouting from directly behind her feet to just before the entrance to the atrium, cutting a large hole in front of the clock tower.

Ursula finally spoke, but only to Theo. "You will put yourself in that fairy ring behind you. Once you are contained, your friends will be released."

Another ploy. Ursula could have easily grown the fairy circle around Theo but didn't. Her hands stayed that much cleaner if she could get Theo to trap herself.

"Now wait a moment—" Tace began, anger beginning to bubble into his astonishment.

But Ursula cut him off. "You wanted me to find the princess; I found the princess. So she doesn't weasel her way out of this again—"

"Hedgehog out," Theo said.

"What?"

Theo smiled.

Ursula clicked her tongue and carried on. "So you don't get away again, you'll stand in that fairy ring. Then we will release your friends."

Tace balked. "You really kidnapped her friends?"

Ursula ignored the regent, staring hard at Theo.

Theo gave a small shake of her head. "You will bring them here first. Once I see them, I will step into the ring."

Ursula narrowed her eyes at her but then relented. "Fine. Guards! Go get the prisoners."

"Prisoners?!" Tace shouted while Aimon was at war with his panic as he stared at his mother.

Four minutes to midnight. Theo needed the guards to hurry.

Thankfully, they did. A moment later, Cecily, Lock, Beric, Torian, and Lowen were led out, and while not handcuffed, each had iron bracelets around their wrists. They were escorted to the front of the dais where they stood in a row facing her. Good. Now they, too, had a clear shot out of the garden when this party was forcefully ended.

But the group was followed by Perran, his icy-white hair glowing in the low light. And when she looked at him among the fairies, she got that feeling again—there was something uncanny, unfamiliar about him.

He was watching her in return with that same intensity as in the tavern. His fingers twitched at his sides, legs tensed and coiled, like a tiger who had chosen his prey out of the herd of antelope and was just waiting for the opportune moment to strike.

Her friends all looked at her with surprise—except Cecily.

With a pensive expression, she looked Theo up and down. "Interesting choice of ensembles, my homespun Theo. Not the direction I would have gone in had I dressed you for this party."

"Oh, *will* you shut up!" Ursula snapped.

While she had Cecily's attention, Theo subtly tipped her head. Cecily followed the hint to see a familiar face. Kaz was meandering nonchalantly toward the front of the crowd. Cecily smirked, but it grew into a full smile when she next spotted Phineas moving into position as well.

Theo glanced up to the clock tower. And there, peeking out from behind one of the branches of the stone tree, was Alby. She raised her brows in a silent question and he nodded back.

"Now it is your turn, princess."

Less than one minute.

Without taking her eyes off of Ursula, Theo took two steps back, placing herself within the fairy ring.

Then the clock struck midnight.

# Chapter 26

# Where There Are Twelve Bells Between Life and Death

**The first bell.**

With the first clang of the clapper, what once were chimes now rang out with notes that reverberated in Theo's bones, as though in competition with a cathedral.

And with the cacophony came the pandemonium. Mostly confused screaming as the entire crowd was rendered magic-less with one blast of sound.

**The second bell.**

Fairies, operating on instinct alone, were sprinting in every direction, some back into the palace, some fleeing through the gardens.

Tace and Aimon, being the closest to the clock tower, were covering their ears, faces squeezed shut in pain as they tried to run. Tace stumbled down the stairs, reaching back for Aimon. But Aimon was trying to help Ursula from up off her knees. She was also covering her ears and screaming as her son tried to pick her up.

Theo looked to where her friends had been. Phineas and Kaz were leading them through the gardens and heading straight for the woods, Phineas in front and Kaz behind.

That was her cue.

With the fairy ring's magic rendered null by the bells, she easily stepped out and started running after her friends.

**The third bell.**

As she ran, she could see the group in the distance, until the path turned and they were out of sight.

**The fourth bell.**

But right after Kaz made the turn, Perran bolted out from behind a tree, blocking that direction.

The garden was consumed in chaos, fairies sprinting every which way like a herd of oversize, startled feral cats running with neither rhyme, reason, nor a sense of direction.

She was far enough away from Perran to choose another way out before he could catch her—fulfilling her promise to Kaz would be easy.

But she stopped short halfway between the fairy ring and Perran at the far end of the garden.

Because she realized he was not fleeing with the other fairies, even with the bells still tolling. His face was rigid with hate and anguish, and for some reason her brain couldn't make sense of, his whole body was blurry.

But Theo didn't move.

**The fifth bell.**

Perran wasn't crying out in pain; he wasn't holding his ears. But something was wrong with him.

Theo watched in horror as his form warped and stretched unnaturally away from his body, Perran twisting in agony as it did.

The face of someone else was showing through in pieces.

Try as he might to hold on to the glamour, the bells were stronger. His disguise was slipping, disintegrating. How fully it had covered him meant he had been wearing a glamour so heavy and complex it must have taken all his strength to hold on to it and not crumble under the weight.

Every bit of unease she had felt when she looked at him, his uncanny nature, his ungainly walk, the way he braved the yew forest without a second thought—all came crashing down on her as Perran's disguise vanished completely.

He wasn't a fairy at all.

**The sixth bell.**

She was right—it did take someone very strong to have held on to that glamour.

Facing her now was a troll. Proportionally, he wasn't all that different from the disguise that was Perran. But where Perran's skin was nearly white, the troll's skin was a patchwork of varying shades of gray, bumpy and uneven like he was made of stone. His eyes were also gray, but just barely, like snow on a cloudy day. A stream of black hair flowed over his shoulders and nearly to his waist, dull, absorbing light rather than reflecting it.

She'd seen this troll before—on a portrait in a cave.

Perran didn't work for Hodd.

Perran *was* Hodd.

**The seventh bell.**

In some distant part of her mind, she realized she had actually managed to complete the bargain she made with Arlys. She had agreed to find the assassin by the stroke of midnight. And *ta-da*! There was the murderous fellow now.

Too bad Arlys, or anyone for that matter, wasn't here to witness it. Or protect her from him. The garden was empty.

Exits were everywhere; all she had to do was start running.

But Hodd began shouting, and she was rooted to the ground.

**The eighth bell.**

His voice rang out, reverberating off the clock tower. "Cecily, Locklan, Phineas, Beric, Torian, Lowen, Alby, and Kasra! I know who they are. I know where they live. And if you leave this garden, *I will kill them all* before coming for you."

**The ninth bell.**

And yet, if she stayed, she assured her death. Not only that, Hodd would kill her with no witnesses.

He would get away with it again.

No. Not this time.

She knew if she made a run for it right now, he'd follow.

For her friends and for the family she never knew, she turned and ran.

**The tenth bell.**

She wasn't leaving the garden. Instead, she ran for the fairy ring, Hodd's shouts of anger chasing her.

If she could get there fast enough, she could run straight through, trapping him behind her.

**The eleventh bell.**

Somewhere far behind her, she could hear her name being called. But she wouldn't turn around.

She passed the barrier of mushrooms. Now she just had to make it to the other side.

**The twelfth bell.**

The last note echoed across the garden as she ran for the barrier, arms outstretched.

And as it faded, she slammed into a solid, invisible wall.

Theo spun around, pressing her back to the cold, invisible barrier, watching Hodd run toward her, his teeth bared. In his hand was a knife, slender and sharp like an icicle.

She knew then: This was how she would die.

She was going to die alone to protect her friends, to show the world who murdered her family.

Dying in place of those she loved always sounded romantic in storybooks. But in this moment, she didn't feel romantic. She didn't feel noble. She felt adrift in a sea of terror.

And yet, she wasn't regretful. She'd make this choice a million times over for the people who had become her family.

He was so close now, knife raised high.

She didn't weep, or scream, or plead. She just squeezed her eyes shut.

Someone was still shouting her name.

First, an explosion of pain, and then strong, solid arms wrapped around her and threw her to the ground.

# Chapter 27

# Where There Are a Few Fairies Between Life and Death

Death wasn't as serene as she thought it would be. It was loud. Very loud, and extremely painful.

Voices, mingled with screaming and crying, were swarming around her like angry bees. And yet, she couldn't make out a single one. She wanted to open her eyes and tell everyone that her body really hurt and maybe they could do something about it. But her eyes weren't answering to her, and neither was her mouth.

Was she not dead?

"Theo. Theo!" a particular voice said from very close.

She knew that voice. Kaz was next to her.

"Do something!" he shouted, and she hoped he wasn't shouting at her.

"Theo, just hold on," he said, this time much gentler, though his voice was shaky. "You'll be fine. Please hold on."

Theo wished it was only Kaz talking to her, because the voices were getting louder, but she could still only understand snippets.

". . . dying!"

". . . She's not going to die . . ."

". . . familiar . . ."

"change . . . fairy . . ."

". . . heal faster . . ."

". . . not fast enough!"

". . . I'll do it!"

*". . . then do it!"*

". . . get these damn bracelets off . . ."

". . . quickly . . . mortal . . ."

Beyond her pain, she could feel hands on her body. And as soon as that registered, she felt her magic draining from her like it was a waterfall, fast and raging. Followed closely by an awful, immediate uptick in the pain.

She wanted Kaz to talk to her again, to tell her what was happening. Because to not know was terrifying.

Suddenly, she felt as though she was cut loose from the fabric of space and time. Nothing above her, below her, or on either side. The pain, that a moment ago was all-consuming, was gone in an instant. She felt nothing at all.

But the relief was short-lived. An itchy sensation like brambles being scraped down her skin took over. Not exactly painful, but certainly uncomfortable. She wanted to scratch at it, but while she could feel her arms again, they were still not taking directions, thus rendering her hands completely useless in this instance as well. Unfortunately, all she could do now was withstand it. If this was dying, it was most unpleasant.

And then, something new. Magic—coursing through her, from the top of her head to the tips of her toes. She could recognize it as fairy magic, seeing as she had spent the last months imbued with a bit of it, but this was different. Where her magic as a familiar had been a little stream, this was a lake.

Just as she felt filled to the brim with magic, it stopped. And she felt . . . *wonderful.*

"Why isn't she waking up?" Theo recognized this voice as Lock's.

"Give her a moment," Cecily said.

"Theo? Can you hear me?" It was Kaz again, his hands on her face. "Can you open your eyes?"

Could she? She didn't know. She'd stopped trying to see if her body functioned during the scratchy bit, and hadn't retried in the meantime.

This time, her body followed her simple directions, and her eyes opened. Color swirled back into her vision like ink in water. And out of that, the world around her started to take shape again. She was looking at the night sky, the stars sparkling like sequins. Faces appeared, popping into her peripheral vision and composing a frame around it, everyone's eyes wide in expectation.

She searched the faces until she found the one she wanted to see most. Kaz's honey-molasses eyes were staring straight into hers, but they were wet and terrified still.

"Am I dead?" Theo asked.

Kaz's brows went up in surprise. "No, you're not dead."

"What happened?"

Kaz didn't answer and instead asked, "Do you think you can sit up?"

"I think so."

He gently helped her sit up and, after successfully completing that challenge, got to his feet, slowly pulling her to standing. In addition to Cecily and Kaz, Phineas, Alby, and Lock were also there.

But she didn't see Beric, Torian, or Lowen. Theo quickly looked to Phineas.

"They escaped, Theo," Phineas said, understanding who she was looking for.

She breathed a sigh of relief. They'd done it. Her plan might have gone so far off the rails it was on fire in a ravine, but somehow, it worked.

And yet, everyone was watching her with trepidation and concern.

"Why is everyone looking at me like something is wrong?"

Cecily cocked her hip. "Listen, my sparkly new Theo, who isn't really mine anymore, we needed to make a decision and didn't exactly have hours to deliberate before you'd reach the point of no return. Truly a life-and-death situation. So, by panicked voting and a bit of crying, we made the choice for you." She shrugged. "I would say sorry, but I'm not so I won't."

"What choice?" Theo asked.

Cecily smiled. "Changeling no more. You're a fairy, darling."

Theo looked down at herself, at the backs of her hands,

her arms, not seeing much difference. "What do I look like?" she asked, reaching up to touch the tips of her ears, now both ending in points.

"You look like you," Phineas said. "Just with pointy ears and a bit brighter of a complexion."

Theo looked to Kaz, who smiled. "Still you," he said. "How do you feel?"

She thought about it, holding up her hands. "Like me, but with more magic."

Cecily clapped her hands together, getting everyone's attention. "Right, I would say it might be nice for our royal Theo to test out her magic a bit. But first, I think we should really consider a problem closer at hand. Namely, the troll standing right there."

# Chapter 28

# Where Evil Plots and Cemetery Plots Converge

She turned her head frantically to where Cecily was pointing to look for the troll and saw him standing only a foot away from her. Adrenaline kicked in before rational thought, shooting her backward into her friends.

But he was no longer coming after her, the mushrooms at his feet intact. He was still trapped in the fairy ring, pressed up against the barrier, banging on it with fists and feet, the knife now on the ground.

Now that the bells had finished chiming, fairies were coming back into the garden. Guards, followed closely by Tace, Aimon, and Arlys, were running toward Theo and Hodd.

Theo threw out a hand, motioning them to stay back. And surprisingly, they did.

She took a small, cautious step forward as Hodd kicked the barrier again, screaming to be let out.

He stared at her, eyes wild. When she was close, Hodd pointed an accusatory finger at her face and started shouting. "You took her! Give her back! You stole her! You're keeping her! Tell me where! I'll get her back when you're dead! I want her back!" He started to sob. "Just give me my wife back."

*What?*

He was accusing her of stealing his wife? When? He was saying it with so much certainty, though, that she even did a search of her memory just to double-check. The only other time she could have committed the crime would have been when she was a toddler one thousand years ago. She was well-liked among the fairies and, by all accounts, adorable, but nowhere had anyone said she was also a criminal prodigy with physical strength beyond her years. If anyone would have told her, it would have been Arlys, and he was mum about that side of her.

"I do not have Skella," she said.

"Liar!" He pounded on the barrier right in front of her face, primal rage and immense sadness reflecting back at her. "You and your family took her! And when you are dead, she will come back to me."

"It would be impossible. Skella is dead." Theo had seen her grave with her own eyes, and it had been reconfirmed by the barmaid at the Gilded Hen.

"I know she is dead! I know that! You took her body!" he screamed loud enough to rattle the leaves of the clock tower. "I made a deal, evil child, that when the family who is keeping her and preventing her from coming back to me is dead, she will be free to return. Fairy magic will bring her back when *you* die!"

When Theo was sulking and Phineas told her the story of Dante, Phineas relayed that there was no magic that could reverse death. And yet, Hodd was convinced that she was responsible for preventing that from happening. Of all the things to be accused of, preventing the return of the dead was unexpected.

But then another memory came to her. In the yew forest when she had inadvertently gotten near Skella's grave site. When Hodd came after her, he all of a sudden turned back, as though something prevented him from getting too close. As though something didn't want him to see the truth.

*The truth.*

Was this a truth charm?

She returned his glare, staring deep into his hateful eyes. "Fairy magic can't bring back anyone from the dead," she said. "Skella is gone."

He stopped screaming and his face went slack. A sheen started coming off of him, like a layer of oil dripping down his body until it dissipated. Even though she had suspected, she gasped at what she had just done.

Hodd staggered, eyes wide with shock. Then he fell to his knees, hand on his heart like a knight wounded in battle. With his next breath, the screaming started again, different this time—an excruciating lament of a heart shattering.

As he crumbled, Ursula sprinted back into the garden. "Guards!" she shouted, snapping fingers at anyone in a uniform. "Take Hodd away immediately! Do not listen to anything he has to say!"

Whether from breaking their trances or annoying them

into movement, the snapping in the guards' faces spurred them to action and they began moving toward the fairy ring.

Aimon was switching between watching his mother and watching Tace. The regent stood a distance away, like he was another statue in the garden, confused and horrified. Meanwhile, Ursula was still trying to rally the guards, gesturing with broad, sweeping movements, as though interpretive-dancing her frustration. "Remove him immediately! He is responsible for murdering the royal family and a danger to Princess Amabel!"

"Now, Mother," Aimon started in his soft, soothing tone. "Let's give Tace a chance to—"

"*Be quiet* and let me handle this! This isn't the time to be weak or fragile!" she shrieked at her son. Aimon, used to being able to calm his mother, jerked back like he'd been slapped.

Hodd, meanwhile, was indifferent to anything happening around him. Anything other than Theo. On his hands and knees, slowly, like it was hurting him to do it, Hodd crawled back to the barrier in front of Theo. As he screamed and sobbed, she felt like she was watching someone die. A pain so thick it was almost tactile pouring out of him.

"She told me," Hodd said to her, choking on a sob before he could finish. "She told me Skella's spirit was being held hostage. By King Redren. If I ended his reign, and his family's reign, she would be brought back. If I killed the royal family, you could no longer hold her and she would be raised from the dead." He let out another anguished cry. "I didn't want to. But I did it because she said she would bring Skella back when you were dead."

And then his voice turned pleading. "But I was merciful for you, your family. It was painless. I made sure it was painless. But you didn't die, and so Skella couldn't come back to me." He started shaking his head. "Lies. It was all lies. What have I done?" He collapsed to the ground. "*What have I done?*"

"Who told you this?"

"Skella is dead. She died in my arms. I buried her. But no magic can bring someone back from the dead. I thought I knew that. Why did she make me believe differently?"

"Who, Hodd?" Theo pleaded.

Ursula was still attempting to rally more guards and had taken to screaming in their faces as they listened to Hodd, shouting directions to *shut him up* and *get him out of here.*

"Please, Hodd. Who put the truth charm on you?" But Hodd just shook his head and cried.

When it looked like he would say no more, Arlys came from behind Theo and stepped into the fairy ring. "I'm going to take him to the dungeons." He looked to Tace first, who was still swaying on his feet, then to Aimon, who gave him a nod. But as Arlys tried to pull Hodd up to standing, confusion scrunched his brow. He whipped his head to Theo and said, "I can't transport him."

Theo's eyes went wide with the new realization. "Hodd, are you a familiar?"

His head hung low, but he nodded. Then he looked up, staring into her eyes.

"Ursula of the Birch Fairies."

The moment the words were out of his mouth, he dropped to the ground, dead.

# Chapter 29

# Where Theo's Mother Had Been Desperate, but Never This Desperate

The collective intake of breath from everyone in the garden sucked all the air out of the atmosphere. At least that's what Theo felt when she tried to breathe and found herself near fainting.

Hodd had just broken a secrecy vow—and paid with his life.

There was a moment after the great gasp where everyone was stunned into silence. Aimon's mouth was open, no longer able to produce any noises that came close to telling the guards what to do and was mostly just squeaks. Tace was staring wide-eyed at the dead troll.

And then everyone began talking at once, swiveling their heads to look at Ursula, who hadn't heard Hodd and was still desperately yelling at the guards. But with the new silence, she stopped, turning in confusion now that the entire garden was staring at her with varying levels of anger and disbelief.

Seeing no action being taken by Tace or Aimon, Arlys ran the few steps toward Ursula, first grabbing her arm, then ripping the necklace off over her head. "Guards, take her to the dungeon!" Two of the guards she had been berating only moments ago launched into action, ready to grab Ursula.

But before they could take her away she shouted, "Aimon, do something!"

Aimon, verbally knocked out of his stupor by his mother's frantic shrieking, walked over to where the guards were holding her. The placid side of Aimon came out, and he looked relieved to have something to do again. "Now, how about we all just take a moment to calm down," he said in his soothing tone.

The guards relaxed their grips just slightly. But like an actress playing to the back of the theater, Ursula dramatically dropped her arms, shoulders drooped, and then added an overdone sigh of relief. "There must have been some terrible mix-up. Arlys, you abuse your power." Then she turned to Aimon. "I would like to launch a formal complaint for the mishandling of this situation. I expect Arlys to be removed from his post forthwith. Now, let go of me this instant." She added a pointed look at Arlys, as though she'd already made this threat to him and was thrilled to call it to action.

Aimon shifted uncomfortably on his feet. In a much lower and now somewhat nervous voice, he said, "Mother, you know I do not have the authority to do that."

"Then get the regent over here right now and make him

release me," she snapped, the "poor, innocent mother" veneer starting to slide off.

Cowed into it, Aimon went to collect Tace, who was slowly coming to his senses.

Even though Ursula had just demanded Aimon speak to his partner, she started shouting at him anyway, not content to let her son handle it.

"Tace, do you see how Arlys is treating the mother of your partner?"

"You did it?" Tace asked, so dazed Theo was worried this might be his new permanent demeanor.

Ursula tried her routine on the regent. "Your Highness, I was just as surprised as anyone when Perran, whom I thought was a trusted confidant, turned into a troll. If I am guilty of anything, it is being too trusting and taking people at their word. I'm truly devastated that I was taken advantage of in that way." Ursula held out her hands, palms up as if putting herself and her pure spirit on display.

Tace ignored her and turned to the guards behind him. "Bring the iron."

Ursula's face changed from innocent-adjacent to a scowl that could launch a thousand complaints. "Aren't you going to stop them, Aimon?"

Like his life depended on making sure everyone was calm, Aimon put his hand out toward his partner. "Tace, I can't imagine my mother would be capable of something like this. Mother, if you just answer their questions, I'm sure we can get this sorted."

Theo knew that, in every volatile household, there was

always someone who felt they needed to be the dynamite defuser. Before this, it was quite clear Aimon had never met a situation he couldn't suspend with just a polite tone and some slow nodding, adding a reassuring smile when things had really gotten out of hand. But with his mother refusing to cooperate and Aimon's toolbox of conflict resolution upended and empty, he was folding in on himself. "Mother, if you didn't do it—"

"If you're not going to help me, then what good are you, you useless boy." Then she turned back to Tace. "Are you even sure he said my name? Who was there to hear it? Her?" Ursula pointed at Theo. "You'd take the word of a stranger over me?"

"We all heard it, Ursula," Arlys said.

"Then he was mistaken! I simply have no reason to plot against the royal family. I was cleared of any involvement one thousand years ago and have worked tirelessly for your regentship ever since. Even when my own daughter was being investigated, I remained a loyal member of this court. Now please, let's all be reasonable and release me, and we can get to the bottom of this."

Cecily sauntered over. "Then iron should be no problem for you, dear aunt."

Ursula gritted her teeth at her niece. "This is none of your concern or business. Aimon, remove her!"

Cecily returned the outburst with a smile. "I'm currently representing the best interests of Princess Theo Amabel. And her best interest currently is to know why you murdered her whole family." She turned to Theo. "Though, for formality's sake, Theo, would you agree with both of those statements?"

"Uh, sure."

"Wonderful. Seems I've been officially, royally promoted to advisor of Princess Theo Amabel. At least *someone* in our family has a position at court, right, Ursula? Not like this layabout." She pointed to Aimon. "Though, I fully appreciate now is not the time to decide on my official title, so I'm perfectly fine with tabling that discussion until a less fraught time."

Aimon hadn't reacted to Cecily and was staring at his mother in horror. But he made no further move to help his mother as iron chains were wrapped around her.

Kaz came up next to Theo and took her hand. She clung tightly to it.

With Ursula's magic muted, Tace was able to compel her to talk.

"Did you orchestrate the assassination of King Redren and his family?"

She wasn't in any sort of dreamy state, as though she'd been bespelled, and was instead glaring at Tace as she answered, "Yes."

"How?"

"With a truth charm, a bargain, and a secrecy vow."

"You'll have to do better than that," Cecily drawled, and while Theo caught the look of admonishment from Tace, Cecily either didn't catch it or didn't care.

Ursula then glared at Theo, as if this was all her fault. "I found someone weak and grieving. With a simple truth charm, I was able to suggest that the royal family was preventing his dead wife from being returned to him. And that if he killed them, his wife would be brought back. Then I made him an offer. He would become my familiar in exchange for killing the royal family. As my familiar, I could keep him quiet. And if he ever broke the truth charm, he'd be unable to kill me for revenge. He asked what was stopping me from killing him the moment it was done and thought himself quite clever when he asked for a secrecy vow. If either one of us implicated the other in the murder, we would die. Additionally, if I killed him, I would die, too. I agreed. After all, he wanted to see his wife again. He wasn't going to risk his life for that."

"Did you come up with the assassination plan?" Tace asked.

She scoffed. "No. All his idea. Though, I gave him a glamour and he put the yew in the woodpile. That was actually clever. But the murder weapon was unknowingly brought in by a fairy simply doing their job. To which everyone chalked up to a horribly unfortunate accident."

How devious of Ursula to further remove herself from any knowledge of the crime itself.

Where Aimon was shrinking, Tace was bolstered by his anger, his presence tripling in size. "I welcomed you into my home. The love of my life's mother. And advisor to my court. And you do this? *Why?*"

Theo was hoping for remorse and would have settled for even the smallest crumbs of penitence. And yet, the fairy responsible for so much destruction, for tearing apart Theo's family as well as her own, was only angry she hadn't succeeded.

As much as she could, Ursula was fighting the compulsion to talk. Her mouth was working like it wanted to form words, but then her eyes would go wide and she'd slam her jaw shut.

Maybe it was because Theo had grown up with the less intense version of Ursula for a mother, but she could see the reason like it was standing in front of her. Because it was. *He* was. Aimon. Her own mother, Lady Martha Balfour, spent her life plotting how to hurl her daughters into the upper echelon of society by catapult. And she did some terrible things in the name of that goal. Lady Balfour would have done anything short of murder to make it happen. Ursula was willing to go that extra step.

"You wanted your son to be royalty," Theo said, answering for her.

Everyone turned to look at her.

"I overheard you talking to Endlin. You said something to the effect of 'at least one of my children knew how to keep a royal partner' when berating her. Even I have heard the rumors that you were trying to have your daughter married to the king. But he married Lilliana, so the hope of her, and by proxy you, becoming royalty was dashed. Until Aimon began his love affair with Tace. Unfortunately, that wasn't a quick solution, either. Tace was fourth in line for the throne behind the king and his two daughters, and probably would never become first. Unless the line of succession was taken out entirely. Your motive was to put Tace on the throne and turn Aimon into royalty."

Theo kept going. "It must have nearly destroyed you when I got away. Because then your plan failed spectacularly. Tace ended up not even bothering to try to claim the throne. Which meant no title for your son. How angry were you when you realized your whole plan was for naught?"

"That little brat said he didn't care about a title anyway. He could have been king consort and helped his entire family. What a waste."

Aimon clutched his stomach like he'd been gutted.

Ursula narrowed her eyes at Theo. "You refused to die. Because of you, I was left with a furious troll I was unable to kill.

"We had been looking for Iara to no avail. When we found out that the princess had been brought back, who she was, and that she was a familiar to my own niece, I knew I had to do something. I do care about my family. I *do*. Hodd didn't know who you were until you met Tace. And once he learned that, he was not above killing Cecily to kill the princess. My niece might not care about her own life, but I was going to protect her."

"Why didn't you just kill me yourself?" Theo interjected. "You had plenty of opportunity."

"Because of the bargain. He had to kill you, or he wouldn't be fulfilling his bargain. If I did it, the bargain would be incomplete. If I were to kill you, I'd be preventing the completion of my own bargain and everything would be undone. Plus, I didn't want to get caught. The best I could do was trap you so he could finish it. I tried fairy rings, even iron on your wrists, but you would never stay put."

Just as fast as her ire had been launched at Theo, Ursula turned to her son. "I was giving you everything!"

For a moment, the husk of the fairy that was Aimon just watched her. But then anger crept across his features, twisting his mouth into a sneer. "Don't you dare claim to have done this in my name. By destroying Tace's life and the lives of the royal family, you have destroyed mine. I renounce my place in the royal court. There will never be royal titles for your children. And I renounce you. You are no longer my mother." Aimon turned his back on her and, without looking at anyone, walked back into the palace.

Ursula's eyes blazed, but before she could make any sort of rebuttal, Tace held up his hand.

"I don't need to hear any more. Take her to the dungeon," he said.

Theo had done it. She found the person who killed the family she never had a chance to know, who destroyed countless lives, and whose attempt on her own life turned her into a changeling.

She thought if the killer was caught, she'd be happy. And yet, as the guards led Ursula to the dungeon, her shouts of indignance billowing after her, Theo did not feel that way.

# Chapter 30

# Where a Friend in Need of Battle Armor Is a Friend Indeed

Ursula was gone from the garden, but guards and the crowd were still standing around, not sure what to do next. What Theo wanted more than anything now was to go home—her actual home with Cecily, where she could curl up in her own bed and cling to the man holding her hand while she still could. She turned to Cecily to say as much, but Tace got to her first.

He approached, his entourage of guards closing ranks around them. Theo wasn't ready to start a conversation, so she waited until he did. At first, she wasn't sure he was going to speak, either, and instead he simply stared at her while trying not to cry.

But after a few false starts, he said, "Princess Amabel, I

wanted to tell you this sooner. I owe you an apology. I say this not in the hopes that you will forgive me, but that maybe you'll have a better understanding of me. I do believe I could have handled everything differently. I was so overjoyed, not realizing that you might not be. It was quite a bit of information thrown at you all at once and was very unfair of me to do that to you. You were so brutally ripped away from me, and to save you, I had to make the hardest decision of my life. But I did it in the hopes you'd one day return to me. To us. Even though my memories of you are from such a short moment in time, they are some of my most cherished. When I finally got to meet you, I kept forgetting that you'd have no memory of me. Or that you were a completely different person than who I had known. I had spent the past thousand years picturing what our reunion would be, and I know now how terribly unfair that was for you. It must have been quite difficult to have been met with that.

"And I should never have unilaterally decided to put you back into slumber without speaking with you. It sent you running from the palace—from me—and it feels unforgivable. I am so very sorry for all of it. I know we can't start over, but I want you to know those kinds of decisions will never again be made without your input."

Theo didn't know how to respond to that, even though she appreciated it. So instead, she said, "And I apologize for vandalizing your clock tower. I hope it can be set to rights quickly."

Tace gave her a sad smile. "It was supposed to be my gift to you, to honor your family, but yes, I think it would be best if we took out the bells." His smile faded once more. "I'd like to make plans for a memorial service for Iara and an official welcome for you. That is, only if you decide you'd like to take up your role as princess, which I will leave up to you."

Theo watched his face fall further the longer she went without replying.

He dipped his head once and then turned to Cecily. "I am trusting you will keep her safe and keep your home open to her for as long as she wants?"

"Host a freeloading royal in my home until she feels like leaving? Well, I suppose I can, since I am her top advisor at present—royal title imminent."

Kaz snorted from next to Theo, to which Cecily replied with a wink. Tace responded with the smallest of eye rolls, and after one more apology and wishing them well, he walked back into the palace.

The guards around them were just starting to dissipate from around Theo when what sounded like a battle cry echoed out from behind them, and an instant later, three of the guards were knocked to the ground.

In their places stood Beric, Torian, and Lowen, dressed and ready for war, if that war was against bedroom furniture. Using his belt, Beric had managed to secure pillows to either side of his head, blocking his ears. Wherever they had just come from now had a bed with only three posts, as the fourth had been broken off and was being used as his club. Torian, hissing like a cornered cobra, was doing her best interpretation of a shield-maiden who got lost and ended up at a soiree. She had taken an end table and, similarly to Beric, had reduced its leg number by one, that missing leg now her battle-ready sword. But she had gone further, bringing the entire table with her and using it as a makeshift shield. Against what, Theo had no idea, but Torian was nothing if not prepared. But she hadn't bothered with headgear. Instead, she seemed to have ripped out the guts of a pillow, the cotton shoved in and tufting out of her ears. Lowen was the only one of the trio with anything close to actual weaponry as he wielded a fire poker. As all the soft, fluffy options for blocking ears were taken, Lowen had resorted to grabbing globs of candle wax to stick into his.

"Let Theo go!" Beric shouted, practically foaming at the mouth.

Since they couldn't hear anything, including one another, Lowen at the same time screamed out, "You will not put her into slumber!"

Torian, meanwhile, just let out another raging shriek, pointing her table-leg sword at a guard in a challenge.

The guards looked wholly confused, including the ones on the ground who were more stunned than injured. Unsure about what exactly they were supposed to be doing against the warrior equivalents of rabid hamsters, the standing guards simply backed up.

The weight of everything that had just happened, and the gratitude of what was happening now, suddenly reduced Theo to tears. Her friends, with obviously zero combat training, had come back for her and were ready to fight off royal guards to rescue her.

The enraged musicians, experiencing a pause in their offensive, finally realized that no other fairy was protecting their ears and seemed otherwise fine. Some guards, as well as Phineas and Lock, were doing their best *put the furniture down* gestures.

Torian finally found Theo in the mix, and Theo took the opportunity to nod and also motion with her hands that weapons could be lowered now. Torian dropped her sword and shield, then pulled the cotton from her ears.

"Theo? Are you all right?" she asked, while still stealing suspicious looks at the guards.

Theo wiped her eyes as she smiled. Kaz let Theo go as Torian sprinted for her, then wrapped her into a fierce hug.

Beric and Lowen also lowered their weapons and removed their respective ear protections. "Is it already over?" Beric asked, then turned to Lowen. "See? I told you we were taking way too long to come up with a battle strategy."

"You came back to rescue me?" Theo cried pulling Beric and Lowen into the hug and squeezing the three of them tight.

They let go of one another, but Beric put a hand on her shoulder. "You have to understand, it is near impossible to find a competent harp player. We weren't about to let you get away. Clever thinking with the bells." He turned to see Alby standing nearby. "I assume we have you to thank for that, then?" Beric asked with sincerity. To which Alby smiled in response, his chest puffed out with pride. Beric moved toward him and knelt down. "Well, job well done, my friend. Completely unexpected and brilliantly executed."

"Hold on a minute," Lowen said. "You're a fairy!"

"I was told it was this or die. Hodd nearly got me." Theo still hadn't had time to work out how she felt about it.

It was only then her bandmates looked around, spotting the

fairy ring and the guards who had thrown a sheet over Hodd's body.

"So you caught him, then," Beric said.

Cecily held up a finger. "Ah yes, thank you for reminding me, Beric." She turned to a guard. "Would you please find Arlys and tell him that the royal advisor to Princess Theo Amabel, Cecily of the Ash Fairies, is requesting—nay, demanding—his presence in the garden immediately?"

The guard nodded once and strode off.

Cecily then smirked at Theo. "Interesting turn of events that I'm now working for you, isn't it?"

"Are you, though?" Theo asked with a grin of her own.

Cecily put a hand on her hip. "Anyone's guess, really."

Arlys strode up behind them with a scowl. "I'm right here. I never left the garden."

"Super. Thank you for responding to my summons with such haste. Anyway, I believe you have some unfinished business with our princess. Something to do with the bargain and saying the words to let her out of it since, to the surprise of everyone—almost everyone. Not me, Theo. I believed in you the whole time—she managed to find the killer, plus an evil mastermind. Really just a formality, but important nonetheless."

With a face surprisingly free of scorn, he faced Theo. "Princess Amabel, you have paid your bargain in full."

While she was relieved to be free of her bargain with Arlys, she also felt a stab of pity for the fairy and what he must be feeling. He'd been working in close proximity to his mother's murderer for one thousand years. Theo had no memories of what had happened, but Arlys remembered every minute. And while she had no admiration for how he handled himself around her and their bargain, she could understand where he was coming from.

So, instead of a cutting remark lording her success over him, she simply nodded once.

"Now that that's settled," Cecily said, "I suggest we take this back to my place."

# Chapter 31

# Where Theo Says Hello to a New Familiar and Goodbye to an Old One

Everyone immediately made for the drawing room. Drinks and food appeared on every surface with the snap of Cecily's fingers. Theo sank down into one of the couches. Kaz sat next to her, drink in hand and arm around her. She didn't stop herself from leaning into him.

Even with all the joy, the mood was a delicate one. Smiles and laughs abounded, but whenever conversation would drift to the darker moments of their adventures, they would veer sharply back into safer territory. Theo knew they would talk about it eventually, but for right now, she was happy to just be with her friends.

When they talked about Theo becoming a fairy, they skipped over the part of why it had been necessary at the time, and instead focused on what the future might hold. Cecily promised to teach her how to conjure all manner of food and drink; she was a little bit more hesitant on the dresses, but only because she had such a fun time dressing Theo herself. Beric said he would teach her how to smite enemies by turning them into frogs. Lock only asked if she would still be playing music at parties, to which the entire band answered with a rousing "*Yes!*"

Truth be told, Theo still hadn't had a quiet moment to really think about it.

But while they were talking about fairy specifics, a question came to Theo. "If you turned me into a fairy, you must have found a replacement for me as your familiar. Who?"

She looked sharply at Kaz, the only unbonded human in the house. But he shook his head.

"Me," came the reply from the other side of the room, Alby's hand raised in the air like he had been called for attendance.

Theo didn't hide her shock. "Really? Alby, why?"

Alby shrugged. "You're my friend."

"I don't know what to say. Thank you doesn't seem big enough."

"You don't have to say more than that. You saved my life in the fairy ring. So, when you were dying, I saved yours. And now I can stay friends with you forever. It wasn't a hard decision."

"You saved my life a few times this evening, Alby."

Torian grabbed her glass and held it high. "A toast to Alby! Our dear friend and hero to the fairy realm." And while she said it with a smile, there was no joking or condescension. It was met with a chorus of clinking glasses and cheers from everyone. Alby puffed out his chest and smiled, and Theo wasn't sure she'd ever seen anyone so happy.

---

The friends laughed, talked, and drank until the morning sun was streaming in through the curtains. The party was winding down, everyone falling asleep where they happened to land. Torian was laid out on a sofa, gently snoring like an aggressively purring cat. Lowen fell asleep like a reclining Roman, a blanket draped over him like an accessory rather than a functional cloth. Of her musician friends, Beric was the last to go, leaning his head back and telling everyone for the first few minutes that he was simply "resting his eyes" before falling asleep for real. Alby had just declared he was going to bed and moseyed out of the room. To where, Theo didn't know, but she was confident he'd turn up. Phineas and Lock had been playing a round of cards but now were each nodding off, no one knowing where they were in the gameplay, or even what game they were playing at all.

The only one still remotely awake was Cecily, who was lounging on a sofa, smoking her pipe. But finally, she, too, gave in. "I think I'm ready to wrap up this party. Kaz?"

Theo was tucked tightly to Kaz on another sofa, wanting both to fall asleep in his arms and to stay awake so she wouldn't lose a moment.

He planted a kiss in her hair and whispered, "Are you awake?"

She nodded and sat up. Holding out his hand, he stood and led her to the foyer.

When they reached the foyer, out of sight of the drawing room, Kaz pulled her toward him. She melted into him as he kissed her. She kissed back, her fingers running through his hair.

When he pulled away, he led them both to one of the benches that dotted the foyer.

"I should ask how you're doing," he said. He hadn't let go of her hand and was now holding it between both of his.

"Overwhelmed. I think it will take a very long time before I have a grip on the situation."

"Are you upset with Cecily for making that choice for you?"

"I can't tell yet. I wish it was a decision I got to make myself. But I'll never regret the decisions I made that led to it. If I had known that making the choice would lead to my friends' safety, of course I'd choose it. I think somewhere deep down I always knew it would end this way. Bea lasted a year and a half on the run—not exactly forever." She gave a humorless chuckle. "I guess I did run from my problems—just in the wrong direction."

Kaz was quiet for a moment. Then he asked, "What does it feel like to be a fairy?"

"Not much different, to be honest. I don't know if it was because there was a fairy in here somewhere this whole time or if the familiar magic was most of the way there. However, while I certainly have more magic, I don't know how to use it. It feels like I asked to travel somewhere and was given the parts to assemble my own horse and carriage to get there."

"You have a very long time to figure it out."

"Cecily volunteered to teach me, but I think I'll have to find a secondary instructor. I don't think she's operating completely by the book."

He laughed. "Might be more fun that way." After a moment, and much more quietly, he asked, "Do you think you'll move to the palace eventually?"

"I have no idea. Tace would love that. Not sure about me yet. I think if I do, it wouldn't be because I was taking over as princess. I'd like to learn first. Learn how to be a fairy first and foremost, then what it means to be princess of the fairy realm."

"I know you didn't want this, but I hope you do become a princess, Theo. I think you'd be good at it. The kingdom won't know what hit them."

She huffed a laugh. "I don't know. The whole time I was with Arlys, he expected me to be Beatrice, basically. Docile, friendly. What if the rest of the kingdom feels the same way he does and is horribly disappointed?"

"You don't always believe this, but you are so much easier to love than you think. And plus, word of your daring capture of the most notorious criminal the fairy realm has ever seen while simultaneously rescuing your friends by turning a clock tower into a giant weapon will be spreading like wildfire by now. You're a hero. And when they say that to your face, don't you dare downplay it."

She grinned. "I'll try not to."

And once again, a silence took over. She knew what was coming and she hated it.

Theo took his hand. "I'm sorry I broke my promise to you. I might have saved everything else, but I wrecked our plans." She tried a small laugh, but it didn't come out with as much sincerity as she'd hoped. "Living in a field of Saint-John's-wort is not very plausible anymore."

Nothing about them was plausible anymore.

But she wasn't ready to say goodbye for a second time.

She would never be ready.

And yet she knew he was not hers to keep.

She couldn't hold him with her, keeping him like he was a breakable toy until he grew old, resenting her for stealing whatever chance he could have had at a normal life.

"Tell me to stay, Theo," he said, the desperation that he tried to hide spilling out around the edges. "And I will."

She wanted to tell him so many things. That she loved him more than she thought she could love anyone. That he was the first person who saw exactly who she was and never balked. But she was afraid that if she did, she wouldn't be able to let him go.

She couldn't tell him to stay.

So she said nothing.

He watched her for a moment longer before nodding to himself. He stood and pressed a kiss to her forehead. "No matter what, I will never stop loving you, Theo. And I'm glad I got to see you one more time."

With that, he walked down the hall, back toward Cecily. Theo didn't follow, having no desire to see him leave her. She heard Kaz quietly say his goodbyes to Phineas, Lock, Alby, and her bandmates, then heard Cecily tell them she'd be back soon.

Theo was still on the bench when Cecily returned a bit later. Pipe in hand, Cecily sauntered into the foyer and took a seat next to Theo.

"So," Cecily said, watching a plume of smoke waft through the chandelier. "Are you going to resume your hobby of spying on Kaz? You could still turn into a hedgehog, if you wanted to. Happy to teach you. Or you could design your own glamour. That could be fun! The possibilities are endless."

Theo narrowed her eyes at her. "You knew I was doing that?"

"You can't possibly think I wasn't watching you go into the woods and not come back out for a few hours. I didn't think you were making the most of your new life as a familiar by picking up a bird-watching hobby. I only had to follow you once."

She looked at Cecily. "You didn't tell me where he was for *closure*, did you?"

Cecily took a big drag on her pipe. "I don't know what you're talking about, my skeptical Theo. Why would I ever expect you to go find him, hmm? I simply have no motivation to promote the happiness of two of my darling familiars who can't stand to be apart from each other."

"But there's no way to be together anymore. I can't be the one to steal his life from him. And I can't have him only to watch him die."

Cecily shrugged. "If you insist." She stood up and walked back to the drawing room, puffs of smoke following her as she went.

Theo left the bench to walk up to her room. And it was only when she shut and locked the door behind her that she let herself cry herself to sleep.

# Chapter 32
# Where Theo Is on the Other Side of a Familiar Bargain

She woke up sometime later to a strange feeling in her stomach. When she had gone to bed, it was early morning, and looking at the night sky told her she'd slept for the entire day. Not surprising given the little amount of sleep she had in the past few days.

At first, she wanted to blame the small pulling feeling in her stomach on the food and drink she'd had earlier. Except, accompanying the feeling was a clear image in her mind of a small pond in a park that looked an awful lot like the one across from Kaz's house. And the strange sensation wouldn't let up.

Curiosity getting the better of her, she decided to go.

It would be a while before she could conjure herself a

magical outfit without worrying it would turn into an embarrassing situation. So in the meantime, she went to the closet to get dressed, selecting a plain and slender gray silk dress and putting her hair in a simple braid.

Transporting herself as a fairy wasn't that much different than when she was a familiar. It was just faster. She thought about the park, and instead of calling forth the wind that would have taken her, she just appeared there.

She'd never been to this park at night, mostly because she couldn't see into Kaz's house during that time. She'd also never been close to the pond before. Not because she didn't want to, but because, similar to her lack of nighttime visits, the pond did not have the appropriate vantage point for peering through a certain unsuspecting man's windows. But it was just as lovely now as it was when the sun was shining, the stars overhead reflecting in the pond like it was lit from below. The ducks had taken to their nests, and the water was silent and still.

Movement from beside the pond had her turning, her eyes widening in surprise.

Kaz was standing up from where he sat at the water's edge. He had changed out of the fairy clothes he'd been sent home in and was now in his uniform of smart wool pants and a crisp white shirt. His hair wasn't slicked back, and instead, his waves were loose around his face, shorter than they were when she met him, but her heart still fluttered at the sight.

"Kaz? What are you doing?"

He said nothing, wiping his hands on his pants before bending to pick up a small bouquet of yellow flowers and a wineglass filled to the brim with a light-colored liquid. Then he held out both for her expectantly. Remaining at his feet was the bottle itself, the corkscrew in the grass next to it.

She played along, taking the flowers from him. Ten small yellow flowers, open to the night. Evening primrose.

"Cecily gave me those," Kaz said while Theo inspected them. But she halted when she suddenly remembered the significance of this small bouquet.

"Did you *summon* me here?" she asked. He nodded and gestured to the wineglass still outstretched. She cut him a bewildered look but accepted it and took a sip. It wasn't the deep tartness of plum wine, though. With the bright, summery flavor dancing across her palate, she guessed it was peach instead.

"Can you tell me what is going on now?" she asked. But he just shushed her.

He cleared his throat. "I welcome you, fairy, and am honored and humbled by your presence and acceptance of my invitation. I have requested an audience with you to beseech you for your assistance."

Her first instinct was to laugh at his words, but there was not a hint of humor in any part of his face. In fact, given his set jaw and rigid posture, she'd say he was nervous.

"All right," she said slowly, still not quite sure of what was going on. "What do you need help with?"

"There is a woman I am deeply, madly in love with. The great love of my life. I've been around for over three hundred years, so that is really saying something. She's fiery, courageous, determined, one of the best friends anyone could ever hope to have. And she is so, so beautiful—the person I love looking at the most. The problem is we belong to two different worlds, and she is an immortal fairy princess. I know she loves me, too, but she thought she had to give me up so I could live my life. I need her to know that it is not a life I can live without her. Because without her, I am dying slowly and painfully. I belong with her."

Theo wiped away a tear. "And how do you want me to do that, when I'm terrified of watching you grow old, of one day having death steal you away from me?"

He answered with a question of his own. "Do you want to be with me, Theo?"

"More than anything."

His posture, which up until now was tight enough to affect circulation, relaxed, the harsh planes of his face smoothing back out.

"Then I want to make a bargain with you," he said. "To love you every day for as long as you'll have me—for eternity, if you want."

As much as she believed his words, she was still confused by what he was asking of her. "Oh? And what are you going to give me in payment for this impossible bargain."

He smiled at her then, the slightest hint of mischief hiding in the corners. "The only thing I have to bargain with is myself."

She sucked in a breath with the realization. "You want to be my familiar?"

He nodded. "To be yours forever, if you'll let me. I love you, Theo, more than I ever knew I could love. And we don't have to let anything stop us from being together anymore. Say yes."

She couldn't tell if the noise that came out of her was a laugh or a sob. She didn't have to say goodbye to him. He could truly stay with her forever. Then she really was laughing. With surprise, relief, and utter joy.

She straightened up and, in the most regal voice she could muster, her own smile growing with every word, said, "I, Princess Theodosia Amabel of the Oak Fairies, will love you, and be loved by you in return for all eternity, the payment of this bargain being yourself, bound to me forever."

Kaz closed the few steps between them, taking her face in his hands. Then he kissed her, not like it was their end, but as fierce and wild as their beginning.

He pulled back but didn't let her go.

"*Then say the magic words*," Theo whispered.

He smiled, broad and brighter than she'd ever seen. She looked into his honey-molasses eyes while he stared deeply into hers as he said, "It's a deal."

---

And with Kaz by her side, Theodosia did what princesses in fairy tales tend to do. She lived happily ever after.

# ACKNOWLEDGMENTS

First and always, thank you to my husband, Will. I don't even know how to convey how much your love and support means to me—if I tried it would take up this entire section. So I will simply say the best things in my life happened because of you. Thank you for being by my side through it all.

My two beautiful children, Isla and Malcolm. Thank you for being the wonderful people you are. Thank you for being on this wacky journey with me. For your patience and forgiveness, even when I didn't earn it. For your pride in me. I am so honored to be a part of your lives.

Thank you to Stephanie Clark. I'm forever grateful to you. This has been my dream my whole life, and it wouldn't have happened without you. Thank you for championing Theo and me.

Thank you to Bethany Weaver for your belief in me. And thank you to the entire Weaver Literary Agency family. You are some of the most supportive, encouraging people I've ever met.

Thank you to Bryn A. McDonald, Lauren Panepinto, Brit Hvide, Maggie Curley, Alex Lenciki, Tim Holman, and everyone at Orbit US for being so great to work with. It has been so much fun.

Thank you to Alexia E. Pereira and Zoë van Dijk for your incredible work.

Thank you to my extended family: Linda and Mike Mayo (who raised one of the best people I've ever met), Eileen and Paul Frangione, Elizabeth and Jeremy DuClos, Kristin and Matt Ruggiero, Lindsey and Mike Mayo, Aimee Mayo, and every other family member and friend who has cheered me on.

Thank you to the ball pythons, Smoky and Yara, and the leopard gecko, Drake, who kept me company while writing and are overall amazing beings. I wish everyone could see how gentle, funny, and curious you are.

And to Birch. We weren't supposed to lose you this soon. The days are lonelier without you here, and I miss you checking up on me and saying hi when I'm writing. Thank you for being the best dog we could have ever asked for. I hope we lived up to being the family you deserved. I hope you always felt loved, wanted, and important. We love you and miss you, sweet girl.

It is scary putting my work out into the world. And I am so grateful for the people who reached out to tell me how much Theo meant to them, and how they saw themselves in her. It is such an honor to know she has made an impact on your lives.

And my eternal thanks and gratitude to anyone who has read this book. It truly means more than I can say.

# MEET THE AUTHOR

*Anna Solo Photography*

LAURA J. MAYO is a fantasy writer who lives in New Hampshire with her husband, their two children, and two ball pythons named Smoky and Yara. Unsurprisingly, many of Laura's other interests are solitary, including reading, sewing, cooking, baking, admiring her air plants, and getting figuratively lost in deep, dark woods.

Find out more about Laura and other Orbit authors by registering for the free monthly newsletter at orbitbooks.net.

# RAISING READERS

## Books Build Bright Futures

Thank you for reading this book and for being a reader of books in general. We are so grateful to share being part of a community of readers with you, and we hope you will join us in passing our love of books on to the next generation of readers.

**Did you know that reading for enjoyment is the single biggest predictor of a child's future happiness and success?**

More than family circumstances, parents' educational background, or income, reading impacts a child's future academic performance, emotional well-being, communication skills, economic security, ambition, and happiness.

Studies show that kids reading for enjoyment in the US is in rapid decline:

- In 2012, 53% of 9-year-olds read almost every day. Just 10 years later, in 2022, the number had fallen to 39%.
- In 2012, 27% of 13-year-olds read for fun daily. By 2023, that number was just 14%.

Together, we can commit to **Raising Readers** and change this trend. How?

- Read to children in your life daily.
- Model reading as a fun activity.
- Reduce screen time.
- Start a family, school, or community book club.
- Visit bookstores and libraries regularly.
- Listen to audiobooks.
- Read the book before you see the movie.
- Encourage your child to read aloud to a pet or stuffed animal.
- Give books as gifts.
- Donate books to families and communities in need.

BOB1217

**Books build bright futures**, and **Raising Readers** is our shared responsibility.

For more information, visit **JoinRaisingReaders.com**

Sources: National Endowment for the Arts, National Assessment of Educational Progress, WorldBookDay.com, Nielsen BookData's 2023 "Understanding the Children's Book Consumer"

Made in the USA
Middletown, DE
28 September 2025

18388572R00210

About the MAYA

ANSWERED!

Annabel Savery

W
FRANKLIN WATTS
LONDON • SYDNEY

First published in Great Britain in 2024 by Franklin Watts


Author and editor: Annabel Savery
Series designer: Rocket Design (East Anglia) Ltd
Consultant: Ian Mursell, Mexicolore (www.mexicolore.co.uk)

HB ISBN: 978 1 4451 8697 9
PB ISBN: 978 1 4451 8696 2

Franklin Watts
An imprint of
Hachette Children's Group
Part of Hodder & Stoughton
Carmelite House
50 Victoria Embankment
London EC4Y 0DZ

An Hachette UK Company
www.hachette.co.uk
www.hachettechildrens.co.uk
Printed in Dubai

Note to parents and teachers: every effort has been made by the Publishers to ensure websites are suitable for children, that they are of the highest educational value, and that they contain no inappropriate or offensive material. However, because of the nature of the Internet, it is impossible to guarantee that the contents of these sites will not be altered. We strongly advise that Internet access is supervised by a responsible adult.

Picture acknowledgements (bg = background, b = bottom, t = top, c = centre, r = right, l = left): Alamy: Jeffrey Thompson 22. Shutterstock: Adichrisworo 24, Aksol 6, 33t, 71, Nata_Alhontess 36, Aluna1 84, Arty Design 50br, Daniela Barreto 41t, Bioraven 33b, Bittercactus 18, Cat arch_angel 78, Complot 86, Anastasia Crowley 58t, Cube29 29, 69, Dn Br 48, Dr Black 43b, Epine 25, 46cl, E-salamander 60, Essi 17, ex_artist 57, Malysh Falko 54b, Fargon 87, First vector trend 38, Flipser 53, Fona 74, Benton Frizer 72t, Peter Hermes Furian 5, 62, Giraffe_art 35, Gnurf 4, Govindamadhava 108 73, Great19 16t, Grop 49b, Gwens Graphic Studio 88, Iconim 20, Iocote 72b, In Art 81, IrDesign90 61, Irkin 23, Irmaira 31, Isaeva_Art 76, Istry Istry 34t, 34c, Receh Lancar Jaya 89, Juliann 90b, r.kathesi 9, Kong Vector 3, 11, Leremy 30, Kate Macate 66, Malenkka 10, Antonov Maxim 45, 83b, Miceking 13, 54t, Mind Pixell 82, Modisketch 90t, MoreMass 46cr, MoreVector 55, 95, Morphart Creation 14, 19, 32, MP2021 27, NazArt 15, NotionPic 8, Katia Om 75, Onot 56, Owatta 12, 42, Alexander_P 50bl, Oleksandr Panasovskyi 68, pikepicture 41tb, Prokhorovich 28, ProximaCentauri1 51, Pumbria 43tbg, Receh Stock 59, Rudvi 70, Sabelskaya 65, Semanche 91, Victoria Sergeeva 37, Sidhe 77, Md Sifat 67 inset, StockSmartStart 26, 92, Studiostoks 63, Tanaya 52, Tartila 83t, Kantor Tegalsari 39, Anastasia Teriohina 44, Terpsychore 16c, Bodor Tivadar 47, Vector Tradition 21, Yaraslau Veramei 58b, Kelsey M Weber 40, Roman Ya 85, Yaichatchai 72c,
Cover illustration & p64: Alan Brown
All additional design elements from Shutterstock or drawn by designer.



All facts and statistics were up to date at the time of press.

# THE MAYA

Central America is peppered with sites of the ancient Maya. You might know that they built gigantic pyramids and ate lots of chocolate, but there's lots more to discover about the Maya and archaeologists are learning more every day!

WHAT WAS POK-TA-POK? LEARN THE ANSWER IN QUESTION 21.

COULD THE MAYA WRITE? THE ANSWER IS IN QUESTION 83.

DID THE MAYA GO TO WAR? FIND OUT IN QUESTION 89.

EVER WONDERED WHERE CHOCOLATE CAME FROM? FIND OUT IN QUESTION 31.

The letters **BCE** and **CE** appear in LOTS of history books, but what do they mean?

**BCE** stands for **BEFORE COMMON ERA** – these dates are before the year 0. The higher the number, the older the date is; for example, 735 BCE comes before 734 BCE.

**CE** stands for **COMMON ERA** – these dates are after year 0. The numbers rise higher as they become more recent.

QUESTION 1

# WHO WERE THE MAYA?

The Maya people built a great civilisation in southern Mexico and Central America, beginning around 900 BCE.

At the height of their civilisation the Maya numbered in the millions. They built incredible stone buildings, studied maths and astronomy, invented calendar systems, farmed the land and – perhaps most excitingly – produced chocolate! Thanks, Maya!

**fact** Don't get your Maya mixed up with your Aztecs! They were different civilisations who lived in different parts of Mesoamerica.

QUESTION 2

# WHAT IS MESOAMERICA?

Mesoamerica is a term used by historians and archaeologists to describe the region of southern Mexico and Central America when the first civilisations lived there, before it was divided into the countries we know today. The Central American countries include Belize, Guatemala, Honduras and El Salvador. Evidence of civilisations such as the Maya, Olmec, Zapotec and Aztecs has been found in the Mesoamerican region.

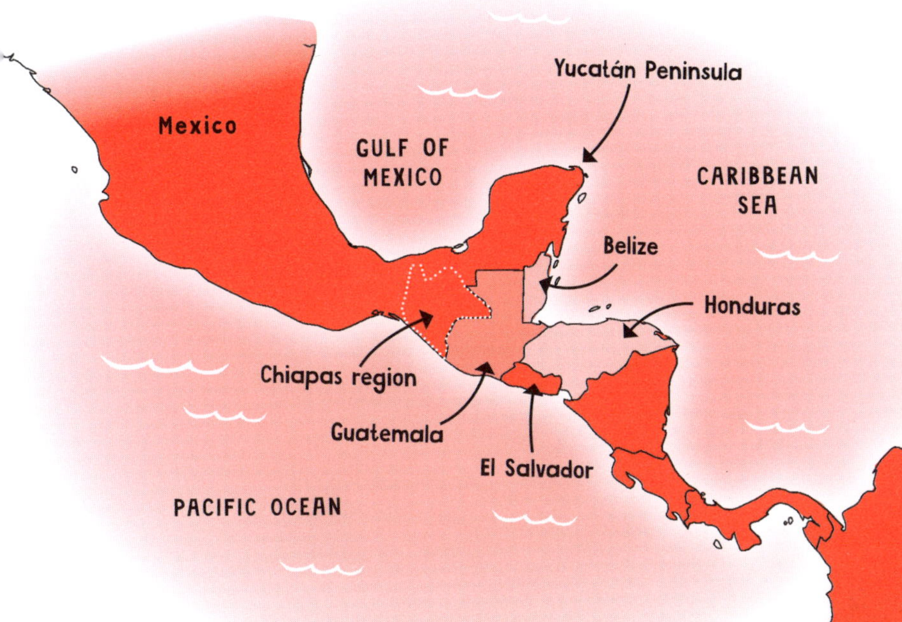

# WHEN DID THE MAYA LIVE?

Ancient civilisations have lived in Mesoamerica since around 2000 BCE. The Maya began in around 900 BCE. They were at their strongest from 200 CE to 900 CE, a time known as the Classic Maya period. They declined around 900 CE (see Q96), and their time after this is known as the post-Classic period. In 1520 CE Spanish invaders arrived in Mexico and tried to take over. The Maya fought back, had to change their lives, and their descendants continue living in their lands today.

**fact** What else was happening in 200 CE?

- ★ The Roman Empire was expanding.
- ★ The Han Dynasty ruled China, but was in decline.
- ★ The Moche people controlled northern Peru.
- ★ The Kushan and Parthian empires ruled the Middle East and northern India.
- ★ Christianity was spreading through the Middle East and Europe.
- ★ Paper had been invented and was spreading into the west by trade routes known as the silk roads.

# WHERE DID THE MAYA LIVE?

Historians divide Maya lands into three regions within the area known as Mesoamerica (see Q2): the northern lowlands (modern Yucátan, Mexico); the southern lowlands (Belize and northern Guatemala) and the southern highlands (Chiapas, Mexico and southern Guatemala).

QUESTION 5

# WHERE DOES THE NAME MAYA COME FROM?

The name 'Maya' comes from the ancient city of Mayapan, which was their main city at the time of the Spanish invasion. The Maya didn't call themselves 'Maya' though. People identified themselves with the city they came from, such as Palenque or Tikal.

Also – if you describe something from Maya times, you say 'Maya' not 'Mayan', for example, '*That's a great Maya headdress!*' Except if you are talking about languages. Then you say Mayan languages.

QUESTION 6

# DID THE MAYA LIVE IN THE JUNGLE?

The area the Maya lived in included rainforest, yes, but also plains, volcanic mountains and areas of coastline. In the Classic Maya period (see Q3) many of the big settlements were in the southern lowlands region, bordered by mountains to the south and west. There was a rainy season and a dry season, so the Maya had to be careful about using and storing water. The climate was hot and humid, which means they had to learn when was best to grow crops and how to build houses that would stay cool. Over time, the Maya developed ways of farming (see Q32) that helped them to make the most of their environment.

**fact** Today, the tops of some Maya buildings can still be seen peeping out of the rainforest canopy.

QUESTION 7

# HOW BIG WAS THE MAYA CIVILISATION?

It is hard for us to know exactly – they didn't record all their people as modern countries do. However, at the height of their civilisation historians talk about millions of people living in thousands of cities in hundreds of kingdoms. The busiest cities supported more than 50,000 people and these were surrounded by rural populations too.

The land mass that the Maya occupied is thought to have been around 400,000 square kilometres – about the same size as the US state of California today.

QUESTION 8

# HOW MANY MAYA CITIES WERE THERE?

Maya lands were not united as one kingdom, but divided into many cities that controlled the area of land around them. Each city was ruled by a powerful leader. Through time, there were as many as 50 cities that rose and fell in importance.

QUESTION 9

# WHAT WERE THE MAYA'S IMPORTANT CITIES?

During the Classic Maya period cities such as Palenque, Tikal, Calakmul and Copán were important centres for trade and power. Later, in post-Classic times, cities such as Uxmal, Chichén Itzá and Mayapan grew in power.

QUESTION 10

# WHAT WERE MAYA CITIES LIKE?

Maya cities were built up over centuries, beginning as small villages. Each city was different, but they all had a palace for the ruler (see Q20), step pyramids, temples, ball courts and a central plaza.

The Maya planned their cities carefully. Often the buildings lined up with key compass points or were positioned to catch the Sun's or Moon's light at certain times of year. Structures were built to suit their landscape, for example, important buildings might be set on higher ground to avoid damp or soft areas.

**fact** At its height, the city of Tikal had a population of around 90,000 people.

Hmm, let's not build in this swamp!

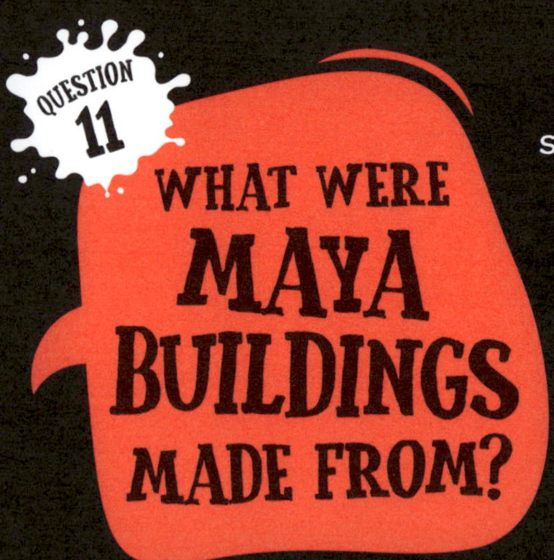


# WHAT WERE MAYA BUILDINGS MADE FROM?

Stone was the main building material for big structures, such as pyramids and palaces. The Maya used limestone, sandstone and a volcanic rock called tuff. Archaeologists have found stone quarries throughout the Maya region. The Maya had no big machinery so all quarrying and moving of stone was done with stone tools (see Q34) and human-power!

Wood was another key building material for the Maya. Archaeologists think that high pyramids may have had wooden temples on top of them. Ordinary homes were made from wood and mud (see Q41). Most biodegradable materials have disappeared over time so it is hard to find evidence of them.

QUESTION 12

# HOW DID THE MAYA BUILD SUCH BIG CITIES?

The Maya had a good understanding of geometry and used their own number system to work out how to build massive structures. Often, new pyramids were built over existing ones to make them bigger. Excavating them is like peeling an onion, as there are more layers hidden underneath.

How the Maya moved the stones from the quarries, archaeologists just don't know! They could have used log rollers, ropes and a whole lot of human-power. We do know that they used a type of mortar to stick stones together and a type of plaster, called stucco today, to cover buildings when they were finished.

fact The remains of Maya buildings are grey today, but in Maya times they were painted bright colours, red in particular.
Heave the stones!

# WHAT ARE STELAE?

Stelae are upright, tall stones found in many ancient Maya cities. They were carved with images of rulers and were put up to show their power. They also have dates and inscriptions that record great deeds or battle victories. We can learn a lot about Maya rulers from them.

At the site of the city of Copán, over 60 stelae have been found. They are carved with pictures of gods and rulers and, in Maya times, were painted bright colours to show off their beautiful clothing, jewellery and headdresses.

A stela at Copán

**fact** The tallest stela discovered is at Quiriguá, in south-east Guatemala, and it is 10 metres high!

QUESTION 14

# WHO RULED OVER ALL THE MAYA?

The Maya never united as one kingdom or empire. They are treated as one civilisation today because the many groups across the region held similar beliefs and cultural traditions.

Each Maya city was ruled by a king, or occasionally a queen (see Q15). Rulers were thought to be divine, which means to be part god. The role of king was passed down the male line, only passing to a woman when there was no male alternative. Maya rulers are usually called kings, but the Maya word for high ruler is *ahau* or *ajaw* – for both say 'ah-how'.

**fact** Passing the rule of a city to an heir created ruling families within the Maya, called dynasties.

# WERE THERE MAYA QUEENS AS WELL AS KINGS?

Yes, queens are pictured alongside kings in Maya art, but they didn't often rule alone. Historians think there were around 25 to 30 female rulers compared to the hundreds of kings! Marriages were made between rulers of different cities to make alliances, so noble women often moved to a new place when they were married.

Lady K'abel was the most powerful queen that we know of. She ruled alongside her husband K'inich Bahlam II between 672 and 692 CE but was just as or even more important than him! Her title *kaloomte* meant 'supreme warrior'. Together they ruled the territory of El Perú-Waká in modern-day Guatemala.

**fact** Lady K'abel's tomb was found in 2012 in the main temple in Waká – it contained jade jewellery and ornaments. One of the most interesting objects is a white jar carved in the shape of a conch shell with the figure of an old woman emerging from it.

QUESTION 16

# WHAT WAS LIFE LIKE FOR A MAYA RULER?

As the job of ruler was passed down through the family, future kings were trained from birth to be the next ruler. It was a life of luxury, with the best food and clothing, but there was also a lot to learn. Rulers were expected to perform many religious and traditional rites, including bloodletting (see Q61). They were trained to fight and to lead warriors, and they also played an important role in the ball game *pok-ta-pok* (see Q21).

Kings and warriors are often shown wearing jaguar skins as a sign of power. A grand ceremony was held when a new king came to power.

fact Maya kings were allowed to have more than one wife!

QUESTION 17

# WHO WAS PAKAL THE GREAT?

King Pakal – full name K'inich Janaab Pakal – is one of the most famous Maya rulers. He ruled the city of Palenque for around 68 years from 615 to 683 CE. He commanded the building of a grand temple – the Temple of Inscriptions (see Q63) – inside which he was later buried.

Pakal came from a royal family: his great-grandmother and grandfather were rulers. Pakal was just a boy when he inherited the throne, so his mother ruled alongside him. Palenque was in a bad way when Pakal came to power, but it was restored and prospered during his reign, making it a strong city again.

King Pakal's name glyph (see question 83)

**fact** Pakal's full name K'inich Janaab Pakal means 'sun face shield'!

QUESTION 18

# WHAT WAS FOUND INSIDE KING PAKAL'S TOMB?

King Pakal's burial chamber was decorated with paintings of nine warriors. Inside it was a stone coffin (sarcophagus) with Pakal's body inside. The lid was carved to show Pakal being reborn. Inside, Pakal was found wearing a beautiful jade funeral mask and with valuable jade jewellery around him. This is one of the most important finds from Classic Maya times because the carvings give us so much information.

A tomb near Pakal's is thought to be that of his wife. Her remains were covered in a red powder known as cinnabar, so she is known as the Red Queen!

Carvings of warriors and rulers decorated the Maya temples.

**fact** Palenque is a word used by the Spanish to describe Pakal's city. Historians think the original Maya may have called it *Lakamha* meaning 'big water'.

QUESTION 19

# WHO WAS JASAW CHAN K'AWIIL I?

Jasaw Chan K'awiil I was the 26th ruler of the city of Tikal. He reigned between 682 and 734 CE.

The city of Tikal was in decline when Jasaw Chan K'awiil I began his reign. It had been beaten in war by a rival city, thought to be Calakmul. In 695, Jasaw Chan K'awiil was able to defeat Calakmul in turn, and his victory began a new era for Tikal. He built great monuments, including two famous pyramids. Today they are known as the Temple of the Great Jaguar, where his tomb lies, and the Temple of the Masks.

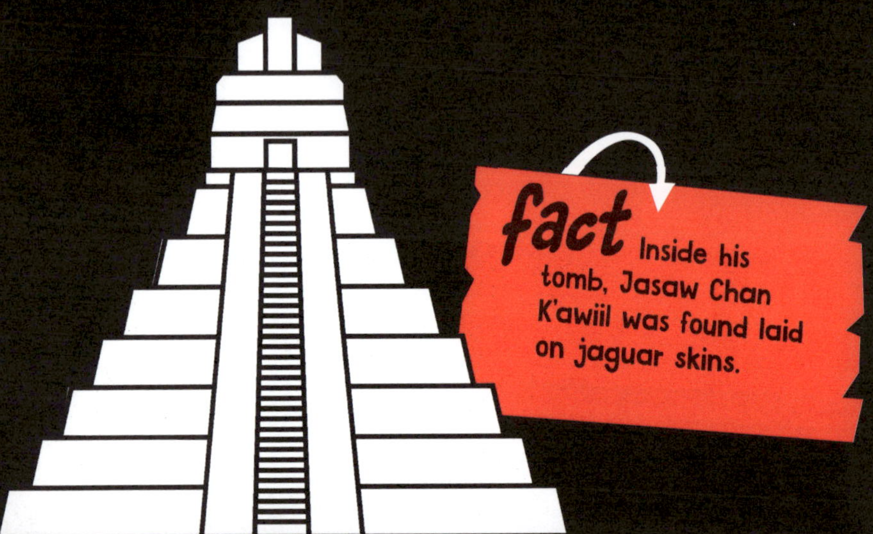

fact Inside his tomb, Jasaw Chan K'awiil was found laid on jaguar skins.

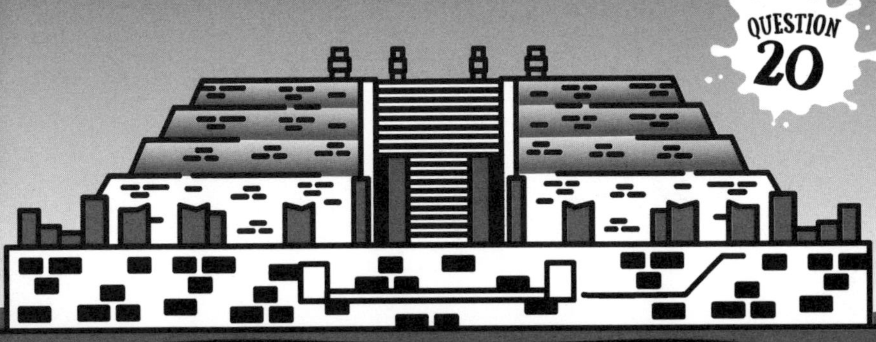

QUESTION 20

# WHAT WERE MAYA PALACES LIKE?

Maya rulers were the wealthiest people in Maya society. They ordered the building of palaces and monuments to themselves, their ancestors and the gods. The king and the royal family lived in or close to the palace.

Palaces were big, with many rooms and often had multiple storeys. Some had towers that were used as look-outs or as observatories. The walls were decorated with paintings and doorways may have been been elaborately carved.

**fact** The palace at Palenque had lavatories and a steam room as well as halls and bedrooms, cooking rooms and workshops!

QUESTION 21

# DID THE MAYA PLAY SPORTS?

Yes, and one game was more important than any other: pok-ta-pok. Versions of this game were played throughout Mesoamerica by many different cultures. This game was far more than just a sport – it had religious and political significance. For example, sometimes a ball game might be played instead of cities fighting each other in battle (much better!).

Players hit the ball with their hips, elbows or knees. Pok-ta-pok was played on a court shaped like a capital I that had sloping sides. The aim was to get the ball into the opposite team's end or through a hoop set high on the wall.

**fact** Pok-ta-pok players wore lots of protective clothing, including padded belts and leg protectors!

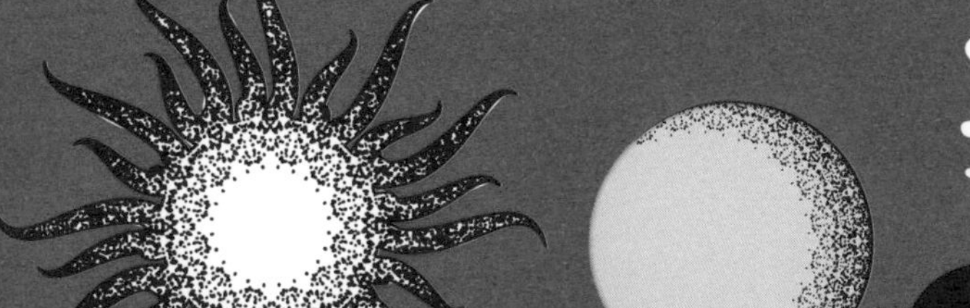

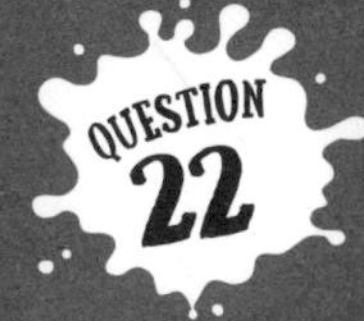


Hey, I wanted to be the Sun!

# WHAT IS THE MAYA LEGEND OF THE BALL GAME?

Pok-ta-pok even finds its way into Maya religious stories. Hero Twins, Xbalanque and Hunahpu, were born from the goddess Xquic. Their father, Hun H'unahpu (also called Yum Kaax) was the god of maize (but we'll get to him later – see Q55).

The Hero Twins are faced with many challenges. In one story, the twins play pok-ta-pok against the lords of Xibalba, the underworld. When the twins win, their father is released from captivity in the underworld and the twins then rise into the sky to become the Sun and Moon.

**fact** The Maya believed that the ball had its own spirit!

QUESTION 23

# SO WHAT DID THE MAYA USE FOR A BALL?

You might be surprised to hear that the Maya used a rubber ball, just as we do for some sports today. It weighed around 1.5 kg and was about the size of a human head. Some people believed that the Maya used a skull as a ball, but this was just a myth!

Look out!

Before the Maya, the Olmec people – whose name even means 'people of rubber' – had discovered rubber's bouncy properties. Early rubber was made by mixing sticky white fluid from rubber trees with the juice of morning glory vines. The Spanish conquistadors who came to the region in the 1500s were amazed at the bouncing balls!

**fact** The process that made rubber balls bouncy is called vulcanisation. The Maya discovered this long before it reached Europe.

It's alive!

QUESTION 24

# WHAT DID THE MAYA DO FOR FUN?

One popular Maya pastime was *patolli*, a type of board game played with dice. Patolli boards were carved into surfaces, such as floors or benches, rather than being carried around. Many boards have been found in temples and palaces, so it is thought that the game was played mostly by the higher levels of society and may have had religious meaning.

I've got my lucky beans!

A patolli board was the shape of a cross, divided into many small squares. Archaeologists can only guess how it was played, but they think that players threw beans and moved along a number of squares depending on how the beans landed.

QUESTION 25

# WHAT LANGUAGE DID THE MAYA SPEAK?

The Maya civilisation was made up of many different groups, most of which had their own language. The languages of people who lived near to each other had similarities and they grew more different the further apart people lived. There are thought to have been over 30 Mayan languages.

QUESTION 26

# DO PEOPLE STILL SPEAK MAYAN TODAY?

Yes, there are around 28 Mayan languages still spoken today. These have changed over time, but have their roots in the Classic Mayan languages of ancient times. Some Maya words passed into Spanish and other European languages when the Spanish conquistadors arrived (see Q94).

Saqär k'a? – Good morning/ How are you?

QUESTION 27

# WHAT WAS IT LIKE GROWING UP IN MAYA TIMES?

A lot of our knowledge of the Maya comes from carvings on grand monuments, which means we know little about daily life, such as washing, sleeping or childhood games.

We do know that among Mesoamerican cultures generally, parents were loving and their priority was to raise helpful members of the community. Most children were taught to do the same job as their mother or father. At around the age of four, children were no longer thought to be infants; at around eight years old they would take on more adult tasks; and by 13 they were considered to be entering adulthood.

**fact** Children probably remained naked until the age of about four when they started wearing clothes!

QUESTION 28

# WHAT WAS IT LIKE TO BE RICH IN MAYA TIMES?

Pretty good! At the top of Maya society were nobles and priests. The nobles were made up of the ruling family – the king, his queen and their children, and their extended family too. Just below the royals were the people who supported them – scribes, priests and military leaders – who also had high status in society. They lived in bigger, grander houses near the centre of the city.

The rich made up just 5 to 10 per cent of the population. They had the best food and the finest clothing. While they ordered elaborate monuments to be built, the ordinary people in the lower levels of society would have done the hard work.

Bring me all the best food!

QUESTION 29

# WHAT WAS IT LIKE TO BE POOR IN MAYA TIMES?

I make clothes.

Around 90 per cent of the population in Maya times might be classed as 'ordinary' or 'poor'. These were the non-noble people and were made up of traders, load-carriers, craft workers, farmers and enslaved people who served the nobility.

I'm a farmer.

Most people lived in simple houses with families of three to five people. Homes were arranged around a communal courtyard where people worked together to make crafts and produce food. Their diet was simple, based on the foods they could grow or collect from the land around them.

I make pots.

I make tools.

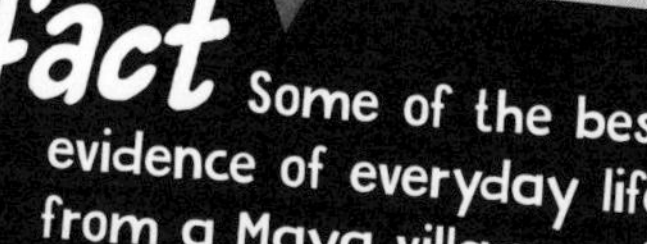

**fact** Some of the best evidence of everyday life comes from a Maya village, called Cerén, in modern-day El Salvador. It was buried by a volcanic eruption in around 600 CE and only re-discovered in 1978.

These monuments are hard work!

QUESTION 30

# WHAT SORT OF JOBS DID THE MAYA DO?

Lots of ordinary people were farmers and each household often had a specialist craft, too, such as making tools or vessels to carry water in. Women produced thread and wove it into cloth. Many men became warriors and there were professional ball-players too!

Noble people might become priests, performing public and private ceremonies such as marriages. They could also be scribes who recorded Maya history.

The Maya created huge monuments that needed the labour of many ordinary workers, but also required an architect to design them, and specialist craft workers to inscribe stones and to decorate the plaster work.

**fact** Women worked mainly in the home but could also be market sellers, marriage arrangers or shamans (a type of spiritual healer).

# WHERE DID MAYA FOOD COME FROM?

The Maya lived off the land they worked on – there were no supermarket deliveries in Maya times!

Farmers grew staple foods, such as maize, beans and squash, but families could grow other foods in their own gardens, such as tomatoes, avocados and chillies. Cacao trees were used to produce cacao for drinking and some families had their own trees.

Hunters caught animals for meat, and fishermen brought fish and seafood to local markets. The Maya ate turkey, rabbit and deer, along with other meats such as monkey, tapir and armadillo!

!
I've always found those armadillos a bit crunchy!

QUESTION 32

# WERE THE MAYA GOOD FARMERS?

Maize

To feed their large population, the Maya needed to be GREAT farmers. They worked out inventive ways to get the most out of their land. On hillsides, farmers created terraces of level ground they could grow crops on. In swamp areas, they built raised areas to farm on.

Crops could also be grown together to make the best use of space. Squash plants held the soil in place and grew along the ground, while maize grew tall. Beans, which are climbing plants, could then be grown up the maize stalks.

**fact** In Maya legend the first people were thought to have been made from maize (see question 52).

QUESTION 33

# WHY DID THE MAYA BURN THEIR LAND?

To gain new farmland, Maya farmers would clear ground by cutting and burning areas of forest. The ash from the burnt vegetation made the soil richer. The forest land became less fertile after about two years and would be left for around five years to recover. Today, this practice is known as slash-and-burn.

# DID THE MAYA HAVE TOOLS?

Yes, but nothing like the mechanical ones we have today! Maya tools were made from wood and stone. Volcanic rocks such as obsidian and flint could be shaped to have sharp cutting edges and were used to make tools for digging and chopping, and weapons.

QUESTION 35

# WHAT DID THE MAYA EAT?

A whole lot of corn! Maize is the name for the crop that corn comes from, and it was grown everywhere. Corn was eaten by everyone: it was made into round discs called tortillas, into dumplings called tamales and also into a nourishing drink. (Unlucky if you didn't like corn!)

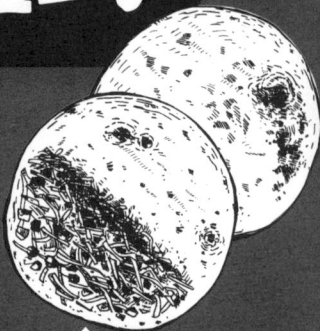

Tortillas

Other staples were beans and squash, which were cooked into stews. Flavour was added with chillies, other spices and tomatoes. Meat and fish were cooked into stews but eaten mainly by the wealthy and on feast days.

The Maya also ate fruits that grew locally, such as guava and papaya, custard apples and sweetsop.

Tamales

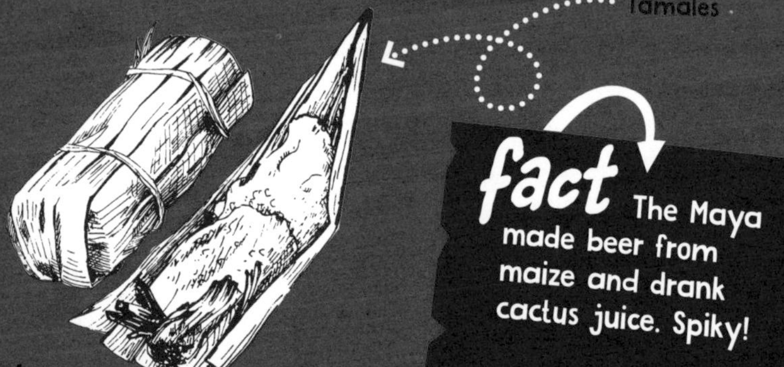

**fact** The Maya made beer from maize and drank cactus juice. Spiky!

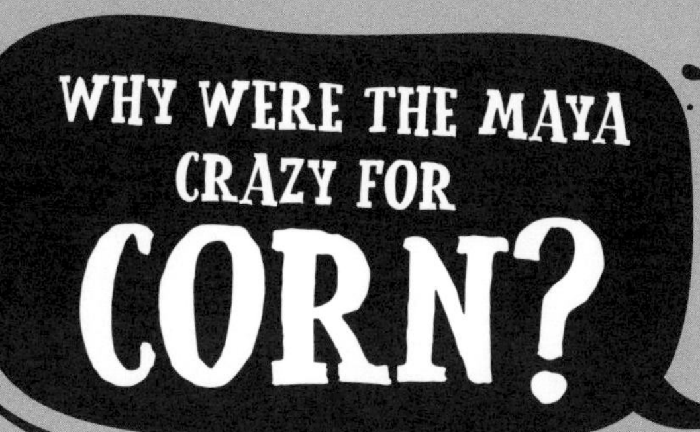

QUESTION 36

# WHY WERE THE MAYA CRAZY FOR CORN?

Corn was essential to life in Maya times. It was a reliable crop that grew in lots of different places and it was a good source of energy. The sap from the plant could be made into a drink, and the leaves could be used in cooking, too.

As maize was so important for life, the maize god was important in Maya beliefs. He is shown with an ear of corn for his crown with the leaves falling down as his hair.

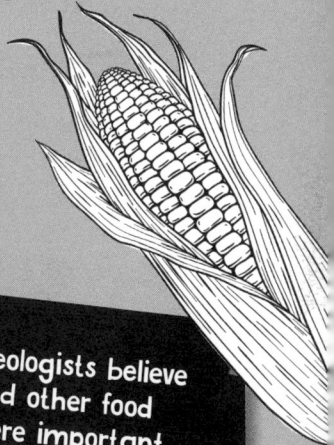

**fact** Archaeologists believe that maize and other food plants that were important to the Maya were probably brought into the region by hunter-gatherer peoples around 5,000 years before!

# DID THE MAYA DISCOVER CHOCOLATE?

The answer is that we can't be completely sure. The cacao tree and its fruit may have been discovered by the Olmec people (see Q2), but the Maya were the earliest people for whom we have written evidence of using chocolate.

The Maya word for cacao was *kakawa* (pronounced *ca-cow*). The fruit of the cacao tree is a pod full of small beans. The beans must be fermented, dried, roasted and shelled before being ground into cocoa powder that can be made into drinks. We know about the Maya's love of chocolate from images on ceramics and murals, from carvings and writing in codices (see Q86).

**fact** There are 20 different types of cacao tree!

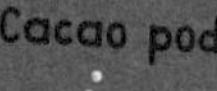


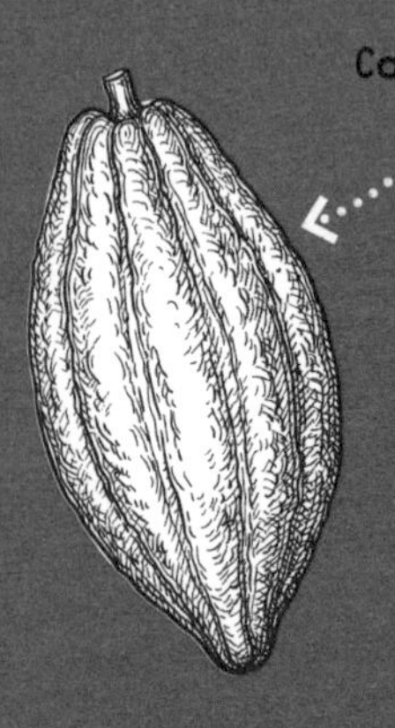

Cacao beans

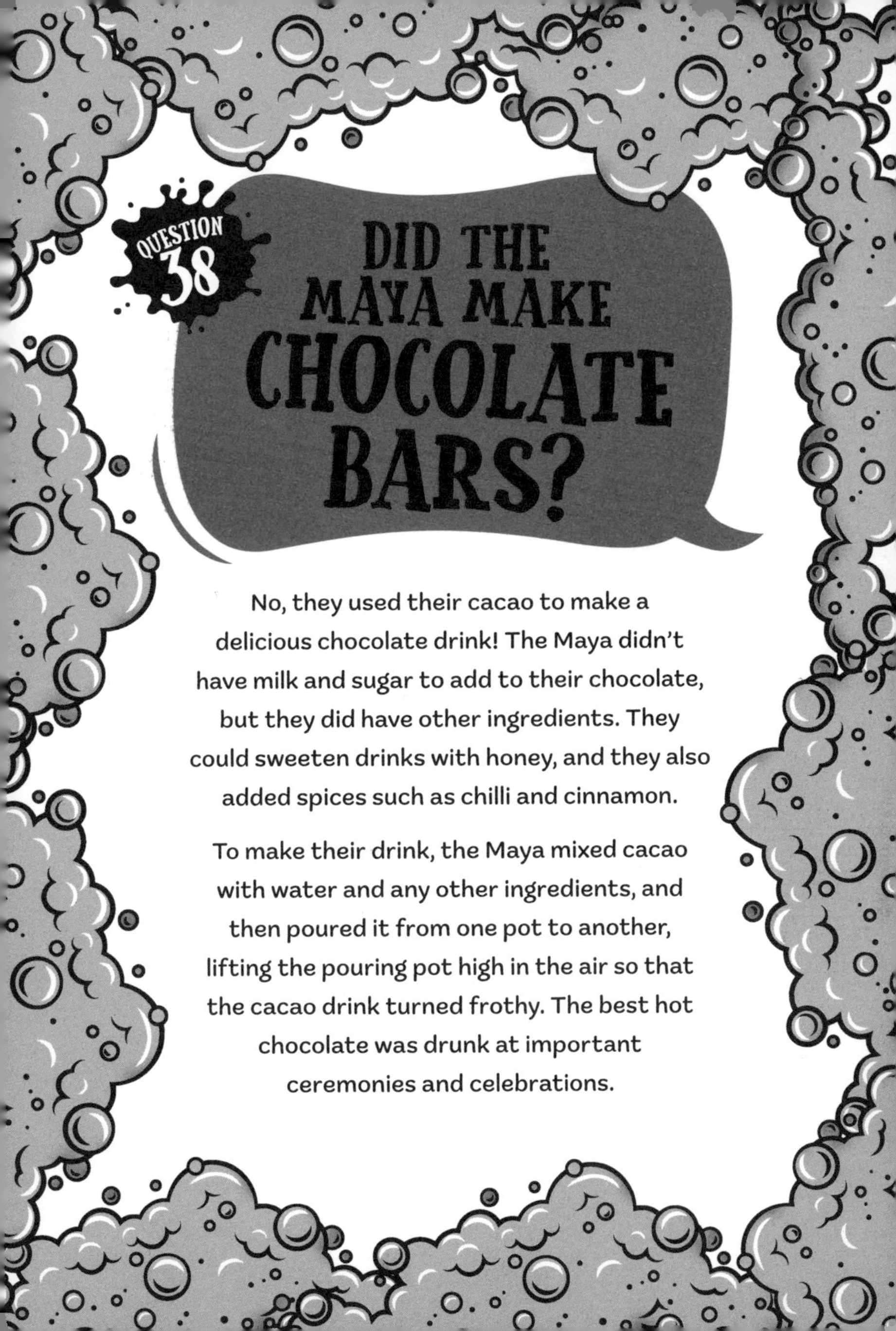

QUESTION 38

# DID THE MAYA MAKE CHOCOLATE BARS?

No, they used their cacao to make a delicious chocolate drink! The Maya didn't have milk and sugar to add to their chocolate, but they did have other ingredients. They could sweeten drinks with honey, and they also added spices such as chilli and cinnamon.

To make their drink, the Maya mixed cacao with water and any other ingredients, and then poured it from one pot to another, lifting the pouring pot high in the air so that the cacao drink turned frothy. The best hot chocolate was drunk at important ceremonies and celebrations.

QUESTION 39

# WHY WAS CACAO SO IMPORTANT TO THE MAYA?

Maya books show that cacao was a sacred food for the Maya, rather than just a treat. It was thought to have been the food of the gods and so it was used in many religious rituals, such as the one held when a child was born, and weddings. In the Maya legend where seeds for corn are discovered, cacao is found at the same time.

Cacao beans were paid in tribute from one city to another (see Q89) and were even thought to have been used as a form of money. Archaeologists have found clay beans too, which may mean that people tried to make fake cacao beans!

Hang on, this bean is fake!

**fact** The Maya used cacao as medicine – to treat chest conditions and burns and to clean wounds.

QUESTION 40

# DID THE MAYA REALLY BREED NON-STINGING BEES?

Hey, where's my stinger?

Yes, the Maya are thought to be the earliest recorded beekeepers in the Americas. They bred a species of bee native to the Americas that don't sting. The Maya kept hives of these bees and used their honey and wax. Honey was used to sweeten food and drink, and wax was used in religious rituals – both were also important trading goods.

Bees were kept in sections of hollow trees called *jobons*. These were plugged at each end and the honey taken out a couple of times a year. There was a bee-sized hole in the plug to let the insects in and out.

**fact** Today, most honey in Mexico is made with stinging European bees, which were introduced in the 19th century because they produce more honey.

QUESTION 41

# WHAT SORT OF HOUSES DID THE MAYA LIVE IN?

Ordinary homes were often made up of three parts – a room for sleeping, a storehouse and a kitchen. They were made from a mud-and-straw mix called adobe that was plastered over woven sticks and vines, with a leaf-thatch roof. They didn't have windows and the door was an open space. Maya homes were designed to be cool in the hot climate.

The Maya spent little time inside the home – it was used mainly for sleeping. The roofs of buildings stretched out away from the sides of the house, creating a shaded area that could also be used for cooking, eating, working and socialising.

What's that rumbling noise?
fact Central America is vulnerable to earthquakes but it is thought that houses built with woven walls were flexible enough to withstand them!

QUESTION 42

# WHERE DID THE MAYA COOK?

Maya homes were centred around the hearth, where all the cooking was done. The hearth was made up of three stones with a fire in the centre. The three hearthstones represented three stars in the sky that the Maya believed were set in the sky by the gods at the start of creation. Even today, when the Maya build a house, they place the three sacred hearthstones on the ground first and only THEN build the walls and the rest of the house! Women cooked on a wide flat stone that was set over the fire.

**fact** Archaeologists have found as many as 70 pots in a Maya home. They were probably used for water and food storage.

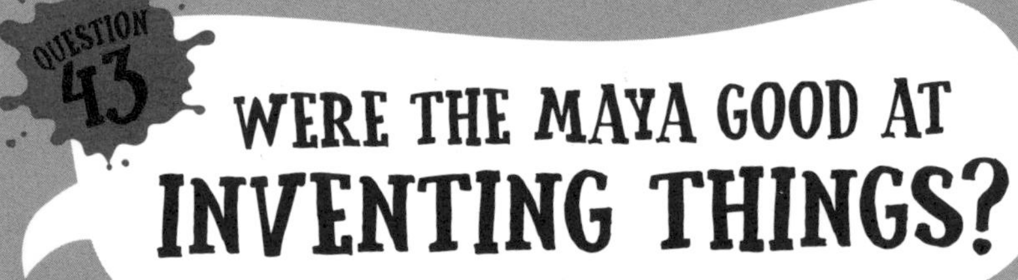


# WERE THE MAYA GOOD AT INVENTING THINGS?

Definitely! The Maya were advanced in astronomy, maths, writing and calendar systems. This was incredible for a time when there were no scientific instruments or digital devices to help them out.

One of the largest Maya cities, Tikal, was not near a natural water source. Archaeologists have found great reservoirs there created by the Maya to support the city's huge population. The Maya also created some of the earliest water filtering systems.

The Maya came up with a way of making cement in around 300 BCE, which they used when building their palaces and other structures – many of which are still standing!

**fact** One Maya city, Yaxchilan, was surrounded by a river that was too full to cross in the rainy season so Maya engineers built a suspension bridge over it. Great work!

QUESTION 44

# IS IT TRUE THAT THE MAYA BUILT ROADS THROUGH THE JUNGLE?

It is! Roads were hugely important for travel and communication in Maya times. During the wet season, it was difficult to travel through muddy jungle and swamp lands. The Maya built *sacbeob* (roads) that stretched through the rainforest, connecting different settlements. The roads were raised about a metre above the jungle floor and could be 9 metres wide. They were even paved with flat stones.

# DID THE MAYA USE CARTS TO MOVE GOODS?

QUESTION 45

No, they didn't have any big animals to pull them. Instead, they used a backpack system to move goods and building materials. Goods were loaded into the backpack frame, called a *mecapal*, and supported by a strap around the forehead.

# DID THE MAYA HAVE MARKETS?

They did! An old idea that the Maya didn't have markets has been proved wrong with more recent discoveries. The reason for the mistake is that few permanent market sites and little written evidence had been found.

Today, we know that the Maya loved to shop – just like any other civilisation! Some cities had permanent marketplaces. Others hosted market stalls for a day and stall holders travelled around to different sites. Many of the goods sold in markets were organic (plant-based), such as food and fabric, and have rotted away over time, leaving no evidence.

**fact** Diego de Landa was a Spanish bishop who wrote about the Maya. He said: The occupation to which they had the greatest inclination was trade.

QUESTION 47

# WHAT GOODS DID THE MAYA TRADE IN?

Many items were for everyday living: fruit and vegetables, tools, salt and pottery. There were luxury items too, such as jade, decorative pottery, gold, feathers and obsidian.

The luxury goods at any Maya market depended on the natural resources of that region. The Maya territory covered such a vast area that what was plentiful in one place might be rare further away. Jade is a precious stone that was found naturally in one particular riverbed, today in Guatemala. Obsidian is a volcanic rock that came from the highlands – it was used for everything, from mirrors and jewellery to weapons and tools.

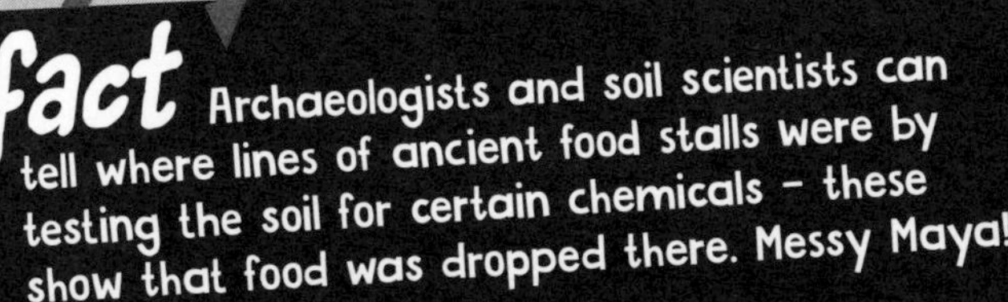

**fact** Archaeologists and soil scientists can tell where lines of ancient food stalls were by testing the soil for certain chemicals – these show that food was dropped there. Messy Maya!

QUESTION 48

# DID THE MAYA USE MONEY?

Not in the way we do today. In Maya times, products were exchanged using a barter system, where goods of equal value were swapped for each other.

To work as money, items had to be of the same size and material. Copper axe heads, cloth and cacao beans could all be used in this way, although copper was not used by the Maya until around 1300 CE. There is a mural (wall painting) in Guatemala that dates from the 7th century and shows a woman swapping cacao beans for corn dough.

I'll trade this squash for your chillis.
Deal!

**fact** In the 16th century, the Spanish reported that workers were paid in cacao beans!

QUESTION 49

# IS IT TRUE THE MAYA LOVED FEATHERS?

Yes, it is! Feathers were valued for their splendid appearance. They were used to create headdresses and to decorate all sorts of accessories, from fans to shields. Wall paintings and carvings show gods and people wearing feather costumes. Craft workers made spectacular costumes for people to wear at religious ceremonies.

Feathers came from quetzals and other brightly coloured birds, such as scarlet macaws and parrots or parakeets. The Maya also used feathers from ravens, orioles and turkeys. Together, they gave clothes a great variety of colours and shapes.

**fact** Feathers were hard to get and easily damaged, which kept their value high!

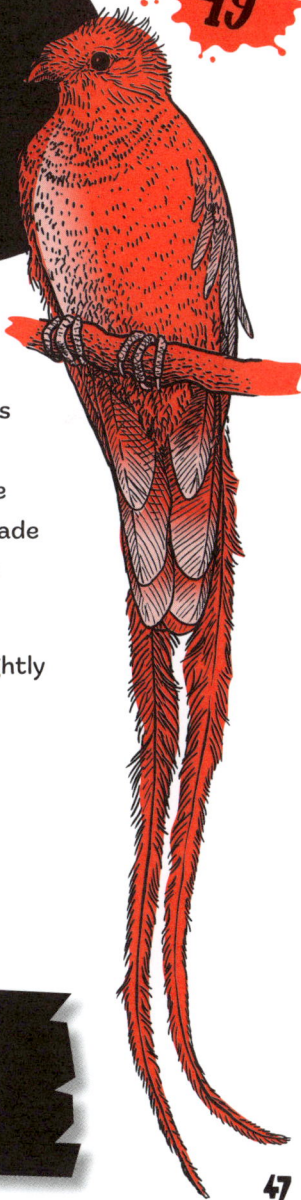

# CAN ARTIFACTS TELL US ABOUT MAYA TRADE ROUTES?

They can. By studying the land today, we know which natural resources appear in different places. So, when a jade mask, for example, is discovered in a region where there isn't any jade naturally, we know it has come there by trade.

A great way to follow Maya trade routes is by looking at discoveries of obsidian. This volcanic rock was used just about everywhere in the Maya world. However, obsidian changes slightly in colour and in its chemical makeup depending on where it is from. This means objects can be traced back to their source, even thousands of years later.

An obsidian spearhead

**fact** Some Maya traders worked locally, others travelled great distances across Maya lands. Still others were sea traders along the coast.

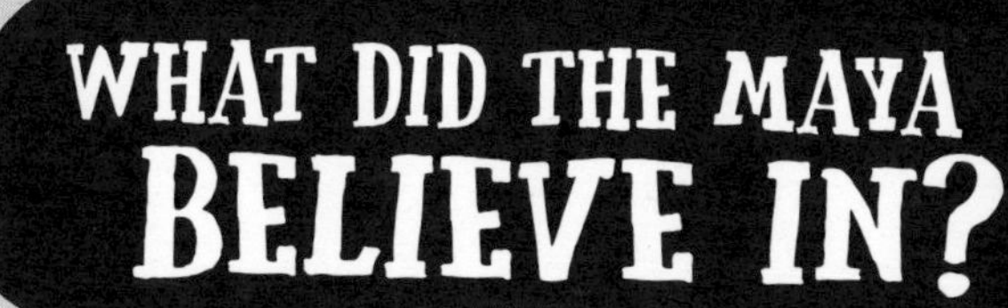

# WHAT DID THE MAYA BELIEVE IN?

QUESTION 51

The Maya believed there were many gods and goddesses (deities), each of whom was linked to an element of the natural world or human life. They believed that the gods created humans and that their kings could talk with the gods. To lead happy lives, the Maya needed to keep the gods happy with rituals and gifts.

Maya beliefs ran through every part of their lives. For example, when they planted crops, they gave thanks to Chac (or Chaak), the rain god, who had helped the first humans to discover corn.

**fact** The Maya believed that at sunset the Sun travelled through the underworld as a jaguar and rose again as a bird.

QUESTION 52

# HOW DID THE MAYA BELIEVE THE WORLD BEGAN?

The Maya believed the world began with a great sea, and in the sea were six gods. They created the Earth from the sea and planted a tree that grew to separate the sky, land and underworld.

The gods created animals first and then decided to make humans. They tried to make humans with mud and then with wood, but these humans could not worship the gods, and so they were destroyed.

Lastly, they tried to make humans from corn. Men were made from white corn and women from yellow corn. These people could worship the gods and began to live on Earth.

**fact** In one version of the creation story, some early humans made from wood escaped and became the monkeys in the trees.

QUESTION 53

# WHAT DID THE MAYA UNIVERSE LOOK LIKE?

The Maya believed that there was the sky, the Earth and the underworld. Between them grew a great Ceiba tree (see Q52). The Maya underworld was called Xibalba (say *she-bal-ba)* and had nine levels. The sky had 13 levels and, at the top, was a paradise called *Tamoanchan*, which means 'place of misty sky'. Mountains were believed to be the home of the gods, and Maya pyramids were built to represent them.

Different Maya stories tell that the Earth is an alligator or turtle, or that the Earth is flat with four corners, and that gods support the corners.

**fact** Each of the compass directions was linked to a specific colour: red for east, white for north, black for west and yellow for south.

Ceiba tree

# WHAT HAPPENED WHEN A MAYA PERSON DIED?

The Maya believed that after death, the soul went to Xibalba, the underworld. From there, it needed to make its way through the levels of the under and upper worlds, to reach paradise. A jade bead was placed in the dead person's mouth as money to use in the afterlife. People were also buried surrounded by gifts, food and objects, such as weapons, tools or cooking utensils, that might be useful in the afterlife.

Ordinary people were buried under their home as their spirits were thought to help the living. Noble people were buried in special tombs and rulers in fine temples.

**fact** Archaeologists think that some great rulers were cremated and their ashes mixed with rubber to become rubber balls!

QUESTION 55

# WERE THERE LOTS OF MAYA GODS AND GODDESSES?

There were around a dozen key gods and goddesses, but some sources list over a hundred! This is because one deity could appear in different ways, and take different forms and names. Here are some of the main ones:

- ★ Itzamná, the creator god. He was lord of the heavens, day and night, and he created writing and books.
- ★ K'inich Ajaw, the Sun god. He is often linked with great rulers.
- ★ Chac (also Chaak), the rain god. He was important for a people who relied on their crops doing well.
- ★ Yum Kaax (also called Hun H'unahpu), the maize god. He was often shown as a young man with an ear of corn as a headdress.

**fact** There were also gods of the underworld, sky, war, merchants and even cacao!

QUESTION 56

## WHO WAS LADY RAINBOW GODDESS?

Ix Chel was also known as the Lady Rainbow goddess. She was the goddess of childbirth, healing and weaving. In Maya art, she is shown as an old woman with snakes and spindles in her hair.

Another female deity was the moon goddess. She is shown as a young woman holding a rabbit because the Maya identified a rabbit shape in the shadows on the Moon.

QUESTION 57

## DID ALL MAYA PEOPLE HAVE SPIRIT COMPANIONS?

Yes, spirit companions are thought to have been a type of joined spirit that each person had. Spirits are linked to the 20 calendar day signs (see Q66) and were worked out from the date that a person was born. Each spirit was linked to a natural element, such as the sky, rain and night, or an animal, for example an eagle, jaguar and deer. Spirit companions stayed with a person for their whole life – except at night when they would go wandering!

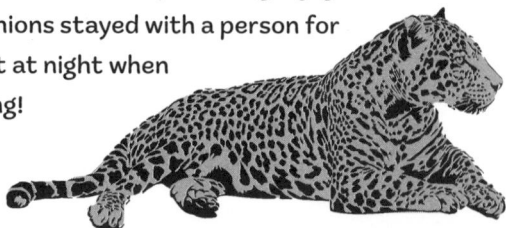

QUESTION 58

# WHAT IS THE POPOL VUH?

The *Popol Vuh* is a book written in the 1500s by the K'iche Maya people. It was written at the time of the Spanish conquest, around 1520 CE, to record and preserve Maya heritage.

*Popol Vuh* means 'book of community' and the book records the Maya creation story (see Q52), the story of the Hero Twins (see Q22) and information about the ruling K'iche family and their lands. It reads like a poem and so historians think it would have been read aloud.

Unlike other Maya books, the *Popol Vuh* escaped being burnt by the Spanish invaders.

**fact** The *Popol Vuh* has been translated from Mayan many times. Each translation brings different meanings and interpretations of the original book.

# QUESTION 59 WHERE DID THE MAYA WORSHIP?

As Maya religion ran through all aspects of their lives, the Maya celebrated and performed religious rites at temples but also in their communities and at home.

Pyramids were built with flat tops and temples were built on top of them. Religious ceremonies took place at these temples, making them visible from a long way away. People gathered in the open space around the pyramid, to celebrate.

Some religious ceremonies were held in caves or underground water sources called *cenotes* (see Q80). These were thought to be gateways to the underworld.

# DID THE MAYA REALLY SACRIFICE PEOPLE?

QUESTION 60

We don't know for sure. Human sacrifice was considered to be a gift to the gods by many ancient cultures. They believed that the gods created Earth and people, and that they needed to be kept happy with gifts. Some historians believed that the Maya did practise human sacrifice and that the victims were most likely to be prisoners taken in war. Others say there is not enough evidence to know for certain.

# WHAT WAS BLOODLETTING?

QUESTION 61

More common than human sacrifice (see Q60) was bloodletting. This meant cutting or piercing a soft part of the body, such as the earlobe, so that blood would flow out. Often the blood was collected in a bowl containing paper and the paper burnt, sending the smoke up to the heavens. Like human sacrifice, the blood was a gift for the gods.

The Maya used stingrays, cactus spines, sharp knives or other objects to perform bloodletting.

QUESTION 62

# WHAT IS INCENSE AND WHAT WAS IT USED FOR?

Incense is a type of resin, a thick sticky liquid that comes from some trees. Resin collected from copal trees was burned to make a sweet-smelling smoke. It was believed that the smoke carried prayers upwards to reach the gods and the spirits of those who had died.

Burning incense was part of rituals and religious ceremonies such as marriages. Some families may have made their own incense burners from clay. Often these burners showed an animal and were designed so that the smoke wafted from the animal's mouth!

**fact** Other religions, such as Islam, Buddhism, Christianity and Hinduism all use incense in their worship and ceremonies.

QUESTION 63

# WHAT WERE MAYA TEMPLES LIKE?

Temples were built on top of high step pyramids. Some had a carved stone piece on top known as a comb. Inside temples, the walls were covered with inscriptions and paintings that told of Maya kings, their families, the nobles, great battles and other aspects of Maya life.

The Temple of Inscriptions at the ancient city of Palenque was built between 600 and 700 CE by the ruler K'inich Janaab Pakal I and his son. Inside, the walls are decorated with Maya symbol writing, called glyphs (see Q83), and the doorways are carved with gods and the figures of Pakal's mother and son. Below the temple was Pakal's tomb.

**fact** The writings in the Temple of Inscriptions are the longest set of readable Maya glyphs that have been found.

Temple of Inscriptions

QUESTION 64

# WHAT DID MAYA SHAMANS DO?

Maya shamans were an important part of the life of the community. They were believed to be able to communicate with the spirit world and to divine (work out) signs from the gods. One way that they did this was by throwing natural substances, such as stones or minerals, on the ground, and reading a pattern in the shapes. Shamans were also asked for help with illness and could provide plant remedies or perform chants and rituals to help people.

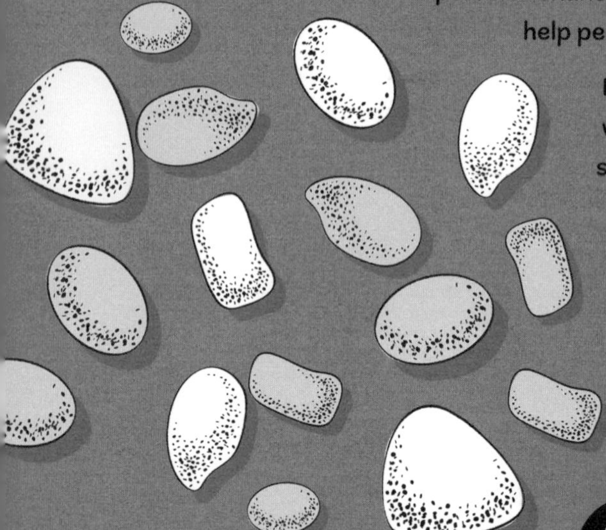

Both men and women could be shamans and they still practise in Maya communities today. In different areas, they are known by different names.

Oh that's bad luck!

# WHY WERE THE MAYA SO INTERESTED IN STARGAZING?

QUESTION 65

Many Maya monuments rose high above the jungle canopy and they also built dedicated observatories. The Maya used them to watch the paths and patterns of the stars, the Sun, Moon and Venus. Recording their movements meant that the Maya could measure long time periods and create an accurate calendar.

The Maya also believed that the movements in the sky were the movements of the gods. They watched them closely and made sure any important events, such as a war, happened when the gods were at the right place in the sky.

**fact** The Maya accurately recorded the length of a year on Venus as 584 days – modern science records it at 583.92 days. Not bad!

QUESTION 66

# HOW DID MAYA CALENDARS WORK?

The Maya had two calendars that they worked out by studying the movements of the Sun and Moon (see Q65). These built on those of earlier Mesoamerican peoples.

One calendar, the Haab, used a solar year of 365 days – just as we do today. It had 18 months, each with 20 days, and a five-day 'month' at the end. The other calendar was a ritual or sacred calendar known as the Tzolkin. It had 260 days, divided into 20 names and 13 numbers. Each day was given a number, name, day and month.

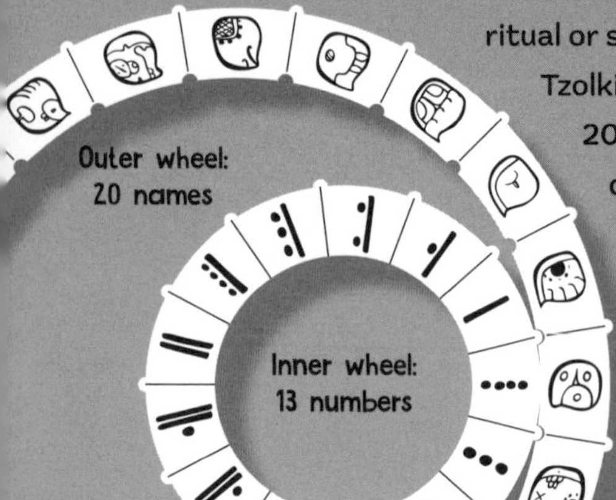

Outer wheel: 20 names

Inner wheel: 13 numbers

The Tzolkin calendar

**fact** The two calendars worked together, like wheels turning at the same time. They would align – reach the point they started at – only every 52 years.

QUESTION 67

# WHAT WAS THE LONG COUNT?

This was a Maya system that recorded HUGE amounts of time. It worked in multiples: 20 days made a month, 18 months made a year (*tun*). Then 20 years made a *katun* and 20 katuns made a time period called a *baktun*. The Maya believed the Long Count lasted 13 baktuns which is 5,128 years. They dated the start of the world to 13 August 3114 BCE.

QUESTION 68

# DID THE MAYA PREDICT THE END OF THE WORLD?

No! This was a VERY popular misconception that people got into a muddle with. On 21 December 2012 the Long Count (see Q67) was set to end. Some believed this was the Maya predicting the end of the world, but actually, their Long Count began a new cycle. Archaeologists have found Maya inscriptions describing the Long Count and its everlasting cycles.

It's the end of the world!
That's not what we said!

# WHAT CLOTHES DID THE MAYA WEAR?

The climate in Maya lands was warm and humid, so the Maya didn't need to wrap up warm.

Most women wore a type of tunic called a *huipil* or long skirt with a simple top. Most men wore a piece of cloth wrapped around the hips and between their legs, called a loincloth. Wealthier people had brighter, highly decorated clothes. Everyone wore accessories to brighten up their outfits. They also had bands of cloth, or sashes, that were decorated with feathers or colourful fabrics.

**fact** Maya artworks show capes and cloaks being worn, but most often by men and as part of religious ceremonies.

QUESTION 70

# WHAT WERE MAYA CLOTHES MADE OF?

Most clothes were made from agave or cotton fibres. Both plants grew naturally in Mesoamerica. Fluffy cotton bolls were picked and cleaned. Agave leaves were soaked, and the fibres pulled out and dried. The fibres were spun into thread and woven into cloth. Weaving was usually women's work and done at home.

Some cloth was richly decorated with feathers, beads and patterns. For grand occasions or special costumes, the Maya might use leaves and flowers, precious stones and jaguar skins to decorate their clothes.



**fact** Thread for cloth could be dyed using plants such as indigo to make blue; cochineal insects to make red; or marine mollusc shells to make purple.

# DID THE MAYA WEAR JEWELLERY?

Yes, just about everyone wore jewellery such as earrings, necklaces, rings and bracelets, but the wealthier you were the more precious items you had. Murals and other artworks also often show people wearing ear spools. These are circular earpieces that stretched the earlobe. Ouch!

Many pieces of jewellery were made from jade and obsidian (see Q47). Seashells were also used to make jewellery and later in Maya times, around 1000 CE, metals such as gold were used to make rings and other jewellery.

**fact** War captives had their earrings changed for paper ones to show they had been beaten!

QUESTION 72

# WHAT WERE MAYA HAIRSTYLES LIKE?

Just like today, there were lots of different hairstyles. Historians look at images on pottery or other artworks to work out what the fashions were!

Both men and women wore their hair long and tied up – usually high on the back of the head. The ponytail might be left loose, but was often braided and tied with bands. People might also wear decorations of flowers or feathers in their hair.

Cloth could be wrapped around the head too, like a scarf. There were also different types of hat, often with wide brims to provide shade from the Sun.

QUESTION 73

# DID THE MAYA WEAR SHOES?

I usually go barefoot at the weekend!

Sometimes! Maya art shows shoes being worn during ceremonies and dances. They were brightly coloured, made from feathers or jaguar skin or paws. They might also have had rattles or bells attached so that the performer made a noise when moving. Some shoes are thought to have had wooden soles or to have been made like stilts.

It's hard to know what ordinary people wore on their feet. Historians think that the Maya wore sandals when travelling a long way, but whether people wore them every day or went barefoot is not known.

**fact** Records from Spanish conquistadors (see question 94) say that the Maya wore sandals made from rubber, but no evidence of these has been found ... yet!

QUESTION 74

# DID MAYA RULERS WEAR SPECIAL CLOTHES?

Rulers wore the finest clothes and jewellery the Maya world had to offer. The king wore a headband with a jade stone or ornament set into it. For special occasions and ceremonies, royals had elaborate costumes decorated with ornaments made by specialist craft workers. The aim of royal costumes was to impress the ordinary people with their power and glory!

Maya art gives us clues about what noble people wore. As rulers, their wives and other members of the court often had glyphs (see Q83) drawn above their heads, so historians can work out who was who.

My hat is better than yours!
Mine is so heavy!

QUESTION 75

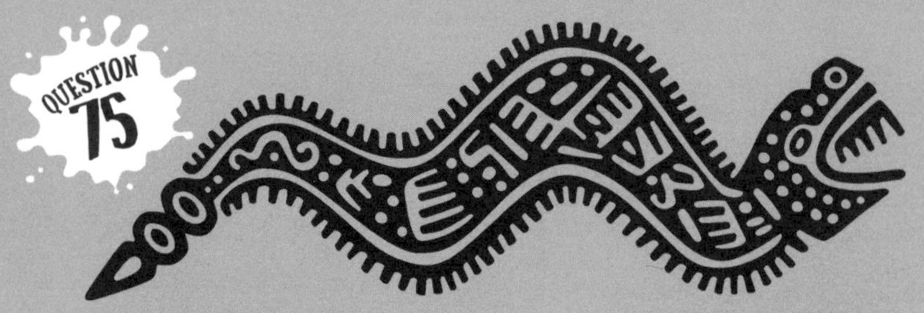

# DID THE MAYA HAVE TATTOOS?

Perhaps ... Maya murals and paintings often show people with patterns or shapes on their skin. However, it is hard to know whether these were painted on for ceremonies or made into permanent tattoos.

Body art often used the colours black, red and white, and sometimes blue and brown. Black was most often used for ball players, warriors or those involved in bloodletting (see Q61). Red shapes on one vase mark the ruler out from the rest of the figures. His queen also has red markings on her face, which may have been used to show her youth and beauty.

**fact** It's thought that tattoos were a sign of rank but could also be a sign of punishment as thieves might have their cheeks marked!

QUESTION 76

# WHY DID THE MAYA WEAR FANCY HEADDRESSES?

The Maya believed that the head was the centre of the being. In Maya art the headdress worn by a person often shows who they are. Splendid headdresses were worn to show the importance of individuals such as kings, queens, ball players and warriors.

Many headdresses contained long, brightly coloured feathers. These were expensive because they were difficult to get and could easily be damaged. Other headdresses were made from jaguar skins and the heads of other animals, such as eagles, vultures and deer. They could be decorated with shells and jade ornaments.

**fact** Defeated war captives are often shown in art without headdresses or armour.

## QUESTION 77 DID THE MAYA MAKE MUSIC?

Yes! Music was an important part of Maya rituals, celebrations and warfare. They had instruments similar to ours today: things to shake, hit and blow into! Gourds, a fruit that can be hollowed out and dried, were made into rattles and shakers. Whistles, flutes and ocarinas were made from clay, turtle shells were made into drums with drumsticks made from bone or antler.

## QUESTION 78 DID THE MAYA REALLY DANCE ON STILTS?

Yes, a person standing on stilts appears in one of the Maya books, or codices (see Q86). Historians aren't exactly sure why the stilt dance was performed. It may have been part of a ceremony to ask for a good growing season and harvest. Some Maya communities still perform stilt dances today.

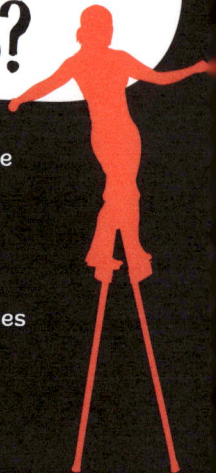

QUESTION 79

# DID THE MAYA HAVE BATHS?

Yes, but they were not the kind of bath tubs that we splash about in today! The Maya used sweat baths that were similar to modern saunas. The walls were heated by a fire outside. People entered through a small hole and sat inside. Water was poured on the hot coals to create steam.

Sweat baths were used by the whole community. We know that they were used in healthcare, but we don't know whether people used them regularly to sweat out dirt and germs or only when ill. For regular washing, the Maya probably used natural water sources: lakes, streams, rivers and the sea.

**fact** It is thought that a dozen people could fit into the sweat bath at Cerén – cosy!

QUESTION 80

# WHAT ARE CENOTES AND HOW DID THE MAYA USE THEM?

Cenotes are sinkholes or natural wells that form in the ground. Cenotes can be metres or hundreds of metres deep and wide. The water inside them is clean because it comes up from deep underground. These were important sources of fresh water for the Maya, who built ladders down into them.

Cenotes were seen as sacred. Their openings were often misty and they were thought to be entrances to the underworld. The Maya threw offerings into cenotes and held ceremonies inside them.

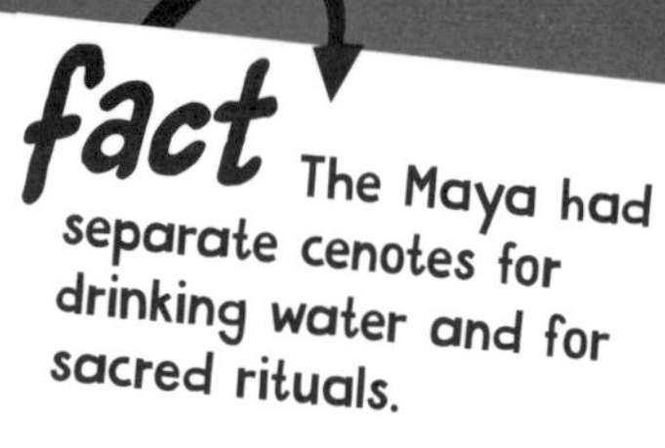

fact
The Maya had separate cenotes for drinking water and for sacred rituals.

QUESTION 81

# WHAT WAS MAYA ART LIKE?

The Maya produced fine artwork, including sculpture, carving and ornaments made from jade, flint and, later, metals such as gold. Maya art reflects their lives: many pieces show gods or rulers, the natural elements or scenes from Maya life.

Along with carving tall stone stelae (see Q13) the Maya also recorded history in pictures called murals. The Bonampak murals are some of the most famous. At this site, the inside surfaces of one building are covered with painted pictures. These artworks give an insight into Maya life: their ceremonies, costumes, musical instruments, weapons and more.

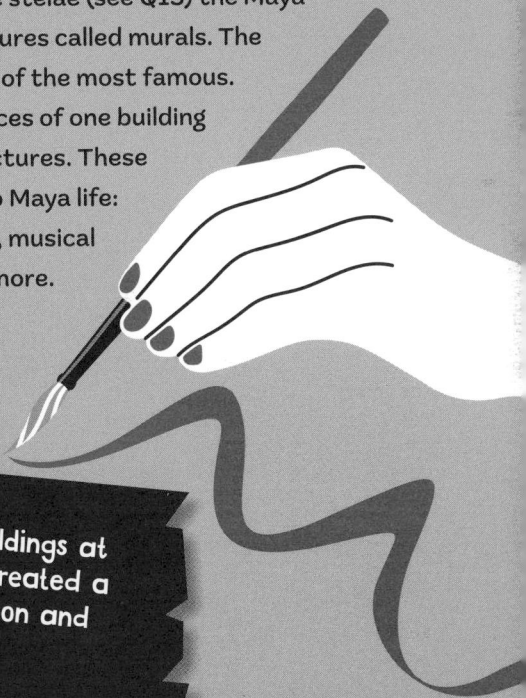

**fact** Inside the buildings at Bonampak the Maya created a bench for people to sit on and admire the paintings!

# WERE THE MAYA GRAFFITI ARTISTS?

Yes! Graffiti is a great source of information on the Maya. It was usually made by ordinary people, and so helps us learn more about their everyday life. Maya graffiti was made by carving, rather than drawing or painting. Most marks were made by using flint tools to cut into the plaster on walls.

Maya graffiti includes human figures and patolli boards (see Q24). Historians think graffiti may have been created for many different reasons: some was just like doodling in someone's spare time, some might mark a spiritual presence in a building, other graffiti might be used to teach children.

**fact** One piece of graffiti shows a person gazing into a mirror made from obsidian.

QUESTION 83

# COULD THE MAYA WRITE?

Armadillo

Yes, but not with letters. The Maya developed a system of picture symbols known as glyphs. Each glyph represented either a full word – such as alligator or mountain – or a sound. Historians study Maya artifacts and carvings to work out what the different glyphs mean. There are a huge number of glyphs and they changed through Maya times.

Alligator

Glyphs were set out in two-block columns. You read each two-block line to the bottom of the column, and then moved to the next column – a little like reading the columns in a newspaper.

Dog

Monkey
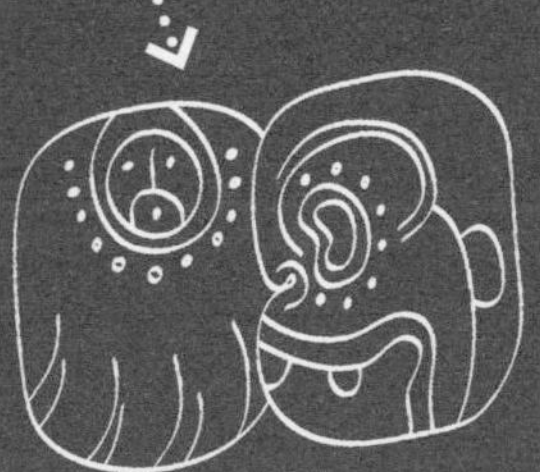

**fact** The Maya had number symbols too. They used dots and dashes, with a shell for zero.

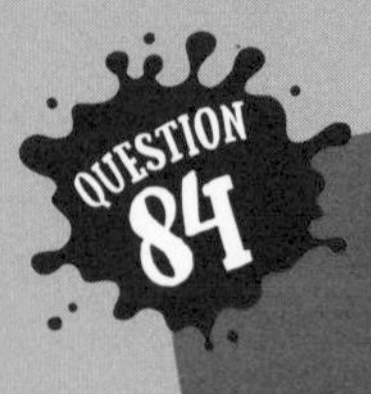


# DID THE MAYA HAVE PAPER?

Yes, they made it from plant fibres, such as those from the bark of the wild fig tree. Once processed, the paper was covered with fine white plaster, or gesso, before being written on. They used brush pens, feather quills, and sharpened reeds to write with.

QUESTION 84

# COULD ALL MAYA PEOPLE WRITE?

We don't think so – it's likely that only the nobility were taught to write. Books were written by scribes and were read by priests and rulers. As there was so much writing on monuments and other public places, it may have been that most people could understand the most common glyphs

# WHAT DID THE MAYA WRITE BOOKS ABOUT?

Maya books are known as codices. They were written about all parts of Maya life: their religion and history, their studies of astronomy and everyday activities too, such as hunting. Along with the glyphs there are pictures that show activities such as people planting corn, making cloth or giving gifts to their gods. The Maya used books to record the movements of the Sun, Moon and planets, and to record events in their calendar.

Maya books didn't have pages, as ours do today. They were written on long continuous papers that were folded back and forth in a zigzag shape known as a screenfold.

MAYA BEDTIME STORIES

**fact** Just four ancient Maya codices survive today. Huge amounts of Maya writing were burned by the Spanish as they tried to convert Maya people to Christianity.

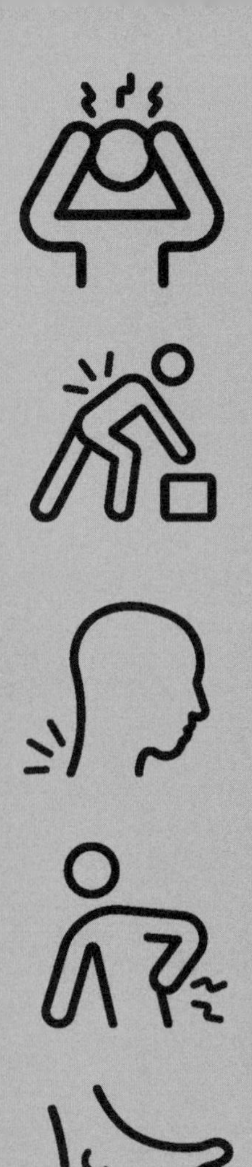

# WHAT ILLNESSES DID THE MAYA GET?

The Maya had to cope with many of the same illnesses and injuries that we do today. For example, historians believe they suffered from tropical diseases, such as a skin disease called pinta, as well as eye and dental problems, and conditions such as epilepsy. Warriors were wounded on the battlefield and people had injuries from physical work too. Childbirth was more dangerous in Maya times than it is today.

Some illnesses were thought to be caused by going against one of the Maya laws and upsetting a spirit or deity.

QUESTION 88

# DID THE MAYA HAVE MEDICINES?

Yes! The rainforest was the perfect place to find plant medicines. The Maya treated pain, stomach upsets and all sorts of other illnesses with natural remedies. Scientists today believe many Maya remedies were very effective.

Maya people were treated by shamans (see Q64). They made remedies from plants or minerals and there were also treatments such as sweat baths or massage. Remedies could be drunk, smoked, rubbed on the skin, or given as an enema (up the bottom). The Maya also practised some surgery, set bones and stitched wounds using human hair.

**fact** The Maya practised dentistry – they were able to create prosthetics, or replacement teeth. They also filed teeth into shapes such as points and decorated them with precious stones such as jade and turquoise!

That sure is a dramatic smile!

QUESTION 89

# WHO DID THE MAYA GO TO WAR AGAINST?

Rivalries between cities raged throughout Maya times. For example, the great city of Tikal fought the city of Calakmul; Calakmul also fought the city of Palenque. Cities and their rulers challenged each other for power, influence and wealth. It was important for Maya rulers to be seen to defeat other cities and to take other rulers or their family as prisoners.

Big cities, such as Tikal and Palenque, had 'vassal cities'. These were less powerful cities that paid tribute to the larger city to keep peace with them. Tributes were paid in goods, such as cloth, and made cities wealthy.

fact Key to a Maya defeat was to take the rival city's ruler captive!

QUESTION 90

# WERE THERE BATTLES IN MAYA TIMES?

Yes! In 562 CE Tikal was defeated by Calakmul, possibly with the help of a smaller city called Caracol. Later, in around 695 CE, Tikal took revenge and defeated Calakmul. Battles could change a city's fortunes. The victors took wealth and tribute from defeated cities, making them rich and powerful. Later, the Maya strove to fight off the Spanish invaders (see Q94).

VS

QUESTION 91

# WHAT SORT OF WEAPONS DID THE MAYA HAVE?

Maya warriors had weapons made from sharpened flint or obsidian and wood. These included spears, arrows and darts which could be hurled at the enemy. They had broadswords and clubs too, and long-range weapons like the *atlatl* or javelin-thrower. For protection, warriors had shields and also wore layers of padded cotton clothing.

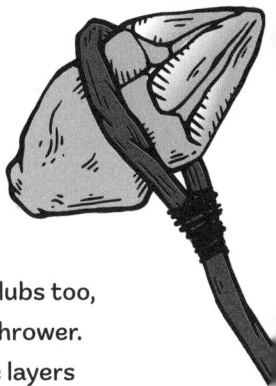

# WHAT HAPPENED TO THE MAYA?

The Maya civilisation grew in strength until around 800–900 CE. Around this time, the powerful Maya cities such as Palenque and Tikal declined and were eventually abandoned. This may have been because of wars between the cities or drought leading to food shortages, but no one knows for sure.

What we do know is that by around 1000 CE, the Maya populations had shifted and the most powerful cities, such as Chichén Itzá and Mayapan, were based on the Yucatán Peninsula (see Q2). In around 1500, Spanish conquistadors arrived on the Yucatán coast, bringing disaster (see Q95).

QUESTION 93

# WHAT'S LEFT OF CHICHÉN ITZÁ?

Many of this city's spectacular buildings can still be seen today. More than 20 buildings, including an observatory, a palace, ball courts and temples, have been found, with over 70 roadways connecting them.

One of the biggest structures is a step pyramid called the Temple of Kukulkan. Twice a year, the setting Sun casts a shadow across the temple's 365 steps that looks like a snake!

Chichén Itzá is thought to have been abandoned around 1400 CE, but still had great spiritual importance for people in the area.

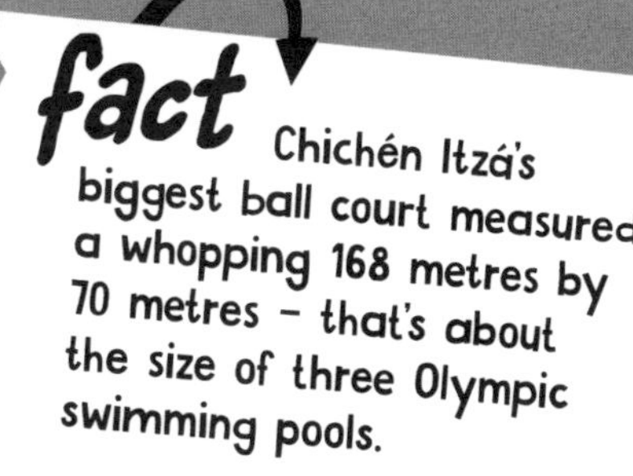

**fact** Chichén Itzá's biggest ball court measured a whopping 168 metres by 70 metres – that's about the size of three Olympic swimming pools.

# WHO WERE THE SPANISH CONQUISTADORS?

By the 15th century, European ship technology had advanced enough for explorers to set sail on long voyages. After the expeditions of Spanish adventurer Christopher Columbus found riches in the Americas, many others set sail to find wealth too.

Conquistador is a Spanish word meaning 'he who conquers'. The conquistadors were trained and armed as soldiers, and came from all over Europe, but mainly from Spain and Portugal. Their expeditions were paid for by the Spanish rulers who received treasure in return. Conquistadors wanted to become rich by conquering native people and their lands.

# HOW DID THE SPANISH BEAT THE MAYA?

QUESTION 95

Well, some historians don't believe they ever really did.

When Spanish conquistadors arrived in Yucatán in about 1517, there were around 16 Maya cities. Fighting between the Maya meant that it was harder for them to fend off the Spanish invasion. Some Maya rulers allied with the Spanish to defeat rival cities. Other Maya rulers tried to live with the Spanish, with some accepting Christianity in order to be able to rule themselves, but continuing to practise their own religion at the same time. However, much of the land was taken over and many Maya were enslaved by the Spanish.

We're here to make trouble!
Yes, yes, we know, you've already told us!
fact The Spanish had horses and dogs that they used in battle. The Maya had never seen such animals before!

QUESTION 96

# WHEN DID THE MAYA CIVILISATION END?

Although some date the end of Maya times to a battle between the K'iche Maya and the Spanish in 1524, there were many other fierce battles. Throughout the next 300 years, fighting often broke out between the Maya and the Spanish and other Europeans that came to Central America.

In 1821, an elite group governing Guatemala and Mexico gained independence from the Spanish. However, the new rulers took rights and land from many Maya groups. Rebellion and war continued through the 19th and 20th centuries.

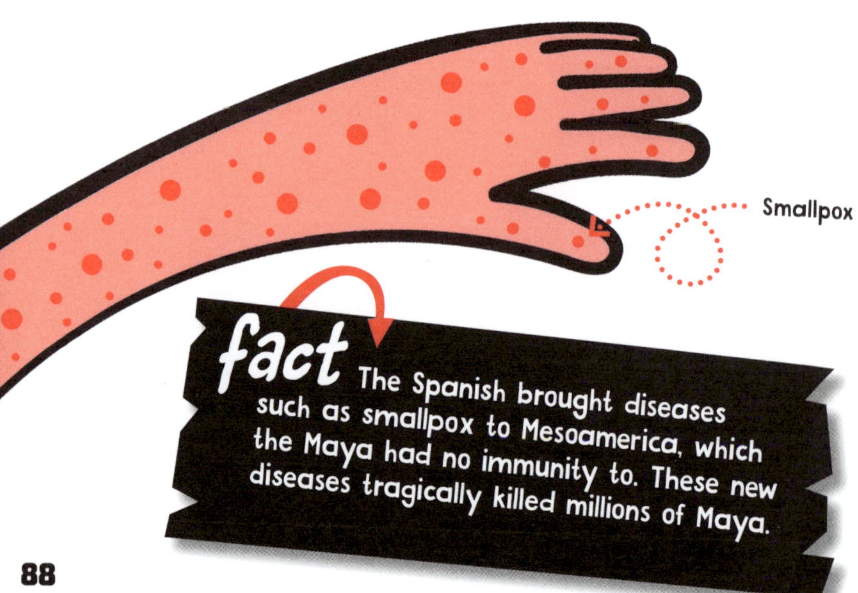


**fact** The Spanish brought diseases such as smallpox to Mesoamerica, which the Maya had no immunity to. These new diseases tragically killed millions of Maya.

QUESTION 97

# ARE THERE MAYA PEOPLE LIVING TODAY?

Yes, there are many Maya communities living in parts of Guatemala, Belize and Mexico today and over 30 Maya languages are still spoken, alongside Spanish. Although modern Maya do not build the massive pyramids that their ancestors did, they practise many other aspects of Maya culture, including using the Maya calendar, wearing traditional clothes, making the same crafts and growing and eating similar foods.

While we know more about Maya history today, people still face discrimination and unfair treatment. Many people have campaigned for greater rights for the Maya and for their heritage to be better recognised.

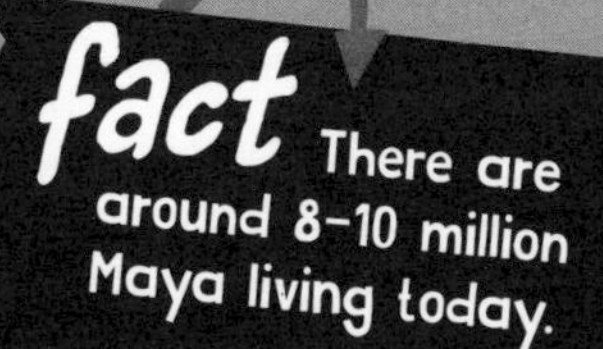

fact There are around 8–10 million Maya living today.

QUESTION 98

# HOW DO ARCHAEOLOGISTS STUDY THE MAYA?

Archaeologists first discovered Maya sites in the 1800s. Since then, they have been a source of fascination and wonder. Today, archaeologists can use clever techniques to work out the age of the objects that they find.

LiDAR is an exciting technology that uses planes and lasers. It shows archaeologists what the ground is like without disturbing the valuable rainforest habitat that has grown over Maya ruins. Space archaeology is another way of studying the land, this time using satellite imagery. If scientists can see that the plants in one area have certain characteristics, it might mean that Maya ruins lie there – as their building materials have changed the soil.

**fact** LiDAR has helped archaeologists to discover 3,000-year-old ruins in the Guatemalan rainforest – a large Maya pyramid with causeways leading up to it.

QUESTION 99

# WHAT CAN WE LEARN FROM THE MAYA?

The Maya relied on their environment and knew how each plant could be used. Today, scientists looking at traditional Maya crops, such as corn, chocolate and chia, have shown that they contain many valuable nutrients.

Scientists are also looking into the way that the Maya used resources, particularly wood. Forests were essential to the Maya for food, fuel and medicines. They protected and managed them, but there may also have been times that overuse caused problems for their environment. The Maya likely learned from these times, just as we can today.

Hmm, I guess this means I can eat more chocolate!

# MAYA TIMELINE

| | |
|---|---|
| 2000 BCE | Early civilisations live in Mesoamerica |
| 900 BCE | Beginning of Maya civilisation |
| 200 BCE – 900 CE | Classic Maya period |
| 600 CE | Volcanic eruption covers the village of Cerén |
| 615 – 683 CE | Reign of King K'inich Janaab Pakal, in the city of Palenque |
| 682– 900 CE | Reign of Jasaw Chan K'awiil, in the city of Tikal |
| 900 CE | Post-Classic Maya period |
| 1517 | Spanish forces (conquistadors) arrive in Yucatán |
| 1524 | Battle between the K'iche Maya and the Spanish forces |

The dates here give approximate time periods for each historical period. Historians generally agree on these dates, but new information is being found all the time!

## SERIES TIMELINE

**STONE AGE BRITAIN**
2.5 million to 2,500 years ago

**ANCIENT EGYPTIANS**
3000 BCE – 30 BCE

**ANCIENT GREEKS**
1200 BCE – 323 BCE

**BRONZE AGE BRITAIN**
2,500 BCE – 800 BCE

**SHANG DYNASTY**
1600 – 1046 BCE

**IRON AGE BRITAIN**
800 BCE – 43 CE

**ROMANS**
753 BCE – 500 CE

**ANCIENT MAYA**
200 – 1519

**VIKINGS**
750 – 1066

**SONG DYNASTY**
960 – 1279

**KINGDOM OF BENIN**
1180 – 1897

**AZTECS**
1325 – 1521

# GLOSSARY

**alliance** an agreement between two or more groups to work together

**astronomy** the study of stars, planets and other natural objects in space

**biodegradable** able to break down into the ground naturally

**ceramics** objects made from clay

**cinnabar** a red mineral found naturally that ancient cultures used to make bright red-orange colouring

**creation** the beginning of the world, or the making of the Universe, Earth, plants and creatures; many cultures have their own myths to explain how the world began

**epilepsy** a medical condition that affects the brain; it can cause people to have seizures or collapse

**ferment** when the sugars or other chemicals in a food change; cocoa beans are left to ferment to change and improve their flavour

**geometry** a type of maths that looks at shapes, lines and angles

**inscribe** to carve words or images into an object's surface

**limestone** a soft, pale-coloured stone used for building and making cement

**mortar** a paste made from a mixture of ground rock, sand, water or other substances that is used to hold bricks together

**mural** a wall painting

**observatory** a building designed to give a view of the night sky, allowing astronomers to study it

**ocarina** a wind instrument, often shaped like an egg, with a mouthpiece and fingerholes

**oriole** a type of bird with black, yellow or orange feathers

**peninsula** a long, narrow piece of land that is almost completely surrounded by water

**reservoir** a man-made lake used for storing water

**sandstone** a type of rock that contains sand, often used in building

**sarcophagus** a rectangular container, usually made from stone, that coffins or dead bodies are placed in; they are often highly decorated

**species** a type of animal; animals of the same species have the same characteristics and habits, and can reproduce together

**stucco** a type of fine paste, called plaster, that is used to cover walls and ceilings

**tribute** a payment made from one state to a more powerful one, to prevent the powerful one from attacking

**tuff** a rock formed by volcanic activity

**utensil** a small tool, usually one used in cooking, eating or other household tasks

**vulcanisation** a process of changing natural rubber to give it different properties, such as making it stretchier or harder

# MAYA WORD BANK

**AHAU OR AJAW** king or ruler, say *ah-how* for both

**ATLATL** a javelin-throwing device

**HAAB** the Maya calendar that recorded the solar year

**HUIPIL** tunic dress worn by the Maya

**JOBON** a section of hollow tree branch used for keeping bees

**KAKAWA** the Maya word for cacao

**KALOOMTE** a title meaning supreme warrior

**MECAPAL** a frame for carrying loads that is worn on the back and supported by a forehead strap

**PATOLLI** a Maya board game

**POK-TA-POK** a popular ball game

**POPOL VUH** a Maya book

**SACBE** a road

**STELA** a tall stone carved with figures or information, set in an upright position

**TAMOANCHAN** a paradise or upper level of the sky, meaning 'place of misty sky'

**TZOLKIN** the Maya ritual calendar

# FURTHER INFORMATION

## BOOKS

**The Genius of the Maya**
*Izzi Howell, Franklin Watts, 2020*

**History in Infographics: The Maya**
*Jon Richards, Wayland, 2018*

**A Question of History: Why Were Maya Games So Deadly? And other questions about the Maya**
*Tim Cooke, Wayland, 2021*

## WEBSITES

**There's loads of information on the Mexicolore website and many Maya questions are answered by experts:**
www.mexicolore.co.uk/maya/

**The website of archaeologist Dr Diane Davies has great information and activities:**
www.mayaarchaeologist.co.uk/school-resources/

**This website from the Smithsonian is packed with Maya information and has an animation of the Maya creation story:**
maya.nmai.si.edu/the-maya/creation-story-maya

# INDEX

# OTHER TITLES IN THE 99 QUESTIONS SERIES

978 1 4451 8686 3

978 1 4451 8690 0

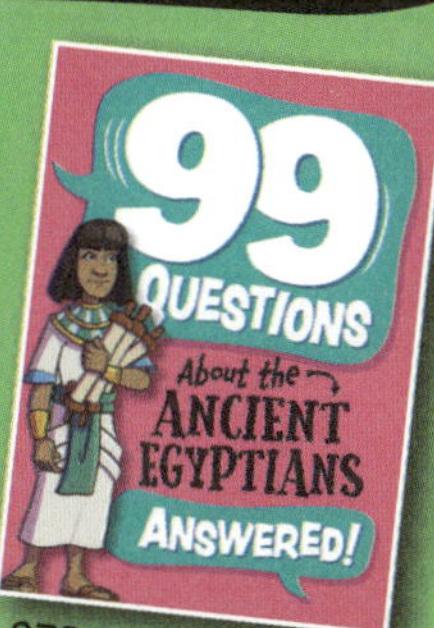

978 1 4451 8692 4

978 1 4451 8694 8

978 1 4451 8697 9

978 1 4451 8698 6

978 1 4451 8701 3

978 1 4451 8702 0

978 1 4451 8705 1

978 1 4451 8706 8